X-MEN

CURSE OF THE MUTANTS

WRITER
VICTOR GISCHLER

PENCILER
PACO MEDINA

INKER
JUAN VLASCO

COLORIST
MARTE GRACIA

LETTERERS
VC'S JOE CARAMAGNA & CLAYTON COWLES

COVER ART
ADI GRANOV

ASSISTANT EDITOR
JAKE THOMAS

ASSOCIATE EDITOR
DANIEL KETCHUM

EXECUTIVE EDITOR
AXEL ALONSO

COLLECTION EDITOR: JENNIFER GRÜNWALD • EDITORIAL ASSISTANTS: JAMES EMMETT & JOE HOCHSTEIN • ASSISTANT EDITORS: ALEX STARBUCK & NELSON RIBEIRO
EDITOR, SPECIAL PROJECTS: MARK D. BEAZLEY • SENIOR EDITOR, SPECIAL PROJECTS: JEFF YOUNGQUIST • SENIOR VICE PRESIDENT OF SALES: DAVID GABRIEL
BOOK DESIGN: JEFF POWELL • EDITOR IN CHIEF: JOE QUESADA • PUBLISHER: DAN BUCKLEY • EXECUTIVE PRODUCER: ALAN FINE

MEN: CURSE OF THE MUTANTS. Contains material originally published in magazine form as X-MEN #1-6, X-MEN: CURSE OF THE MUTANTS SAGA and X-MEN: CURSE OF THE MUTANTS SPOTLIGHT. First printing 2011. dcover ISBN# 978-0-7851-4846-3. Softcover ISBN# 978-0-7851-4847-0. Published by MARVEL WORLDWIDE, INC., a subsidiary of MARVEL ENTERTAINMENT, LLC. OFFICE OF PUBLICATION: 135 West 50th Street, New k, NY 10020. Hardcover: $24.99 per copy in the U.S. and $27.99 in Canada (GST #R127032852). Softcover: $19.99 per copy in the U.S. and $22.50 anada (GST #R127032852). Canadian Agreement #40668537. **nted in the U.S.A.** ALAN FINE, EVP - Office of the President, Marvel Worldwide, Inc. and EVP & CMO Marvel Characters B.V.; DAN BUCKLEY, Chief Executive Officer and Publisher - Print, Animation & Digital Media; JIM KOLOWSKI, Chief Operating Officer; DAVID GABRIEL, SVP of Publishing Sales & Circulation; DAVID BOGART, SVP of Business Affairs & Talent Management; MICHAEL PASCIULLO, VP Merchandising & Communications; JIM EEFE, VP of Operations & Logistics; DAN CARR, Executive Director of Publishing Technology; JUSTIN F. GABRIE, Director of Publishing & Editorial Operations; SUSAN CRESPI, Editorial Operations Manager; ALEX MORALES, lishing Operations Manager; STAN LEE, Chairman Emeritus. For information regarding advertising in Marvel Comics or on Marvel.com, please contact Ron Stern, VP of Business Development, at rstern@marvel.com. Marvel subscription inquiries, please call 800-217-9158. **Manufactured between 1/3/2011 and 1/31/2011 (hardcover), and 1/3/2011 and 8/1/2011 (softcover), by R.R. DONNELLEY, INC., SALEM, VA, USA.**

9 8 7 6 5 4 3 2 1

Things have been rough on the X-Men. They lived through Norman Osborn's Dark Reign, a near-genocide at the hands of Bastion and many other catastrophes ever since they moved out to San Francisco. But after a few of their worst months ever, things are finally looking up. They have strategic safety on their Island home (called "Utopia") and the strong leadership of Cyclops. They've now been welcomed back to the City on the Bay and have seen the dawn of a new Heroic Age. It looks like the X-Men may finally find peace.

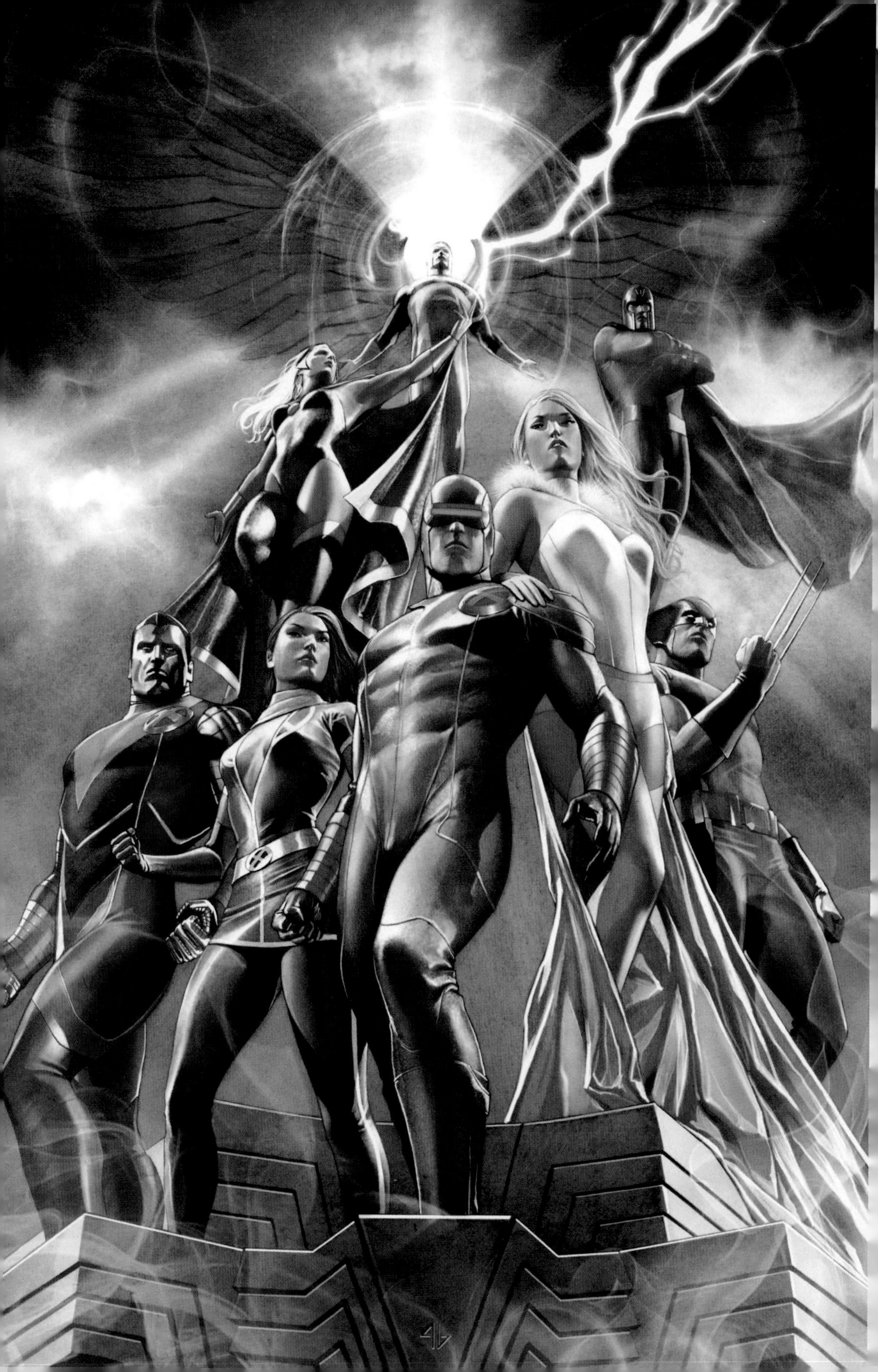

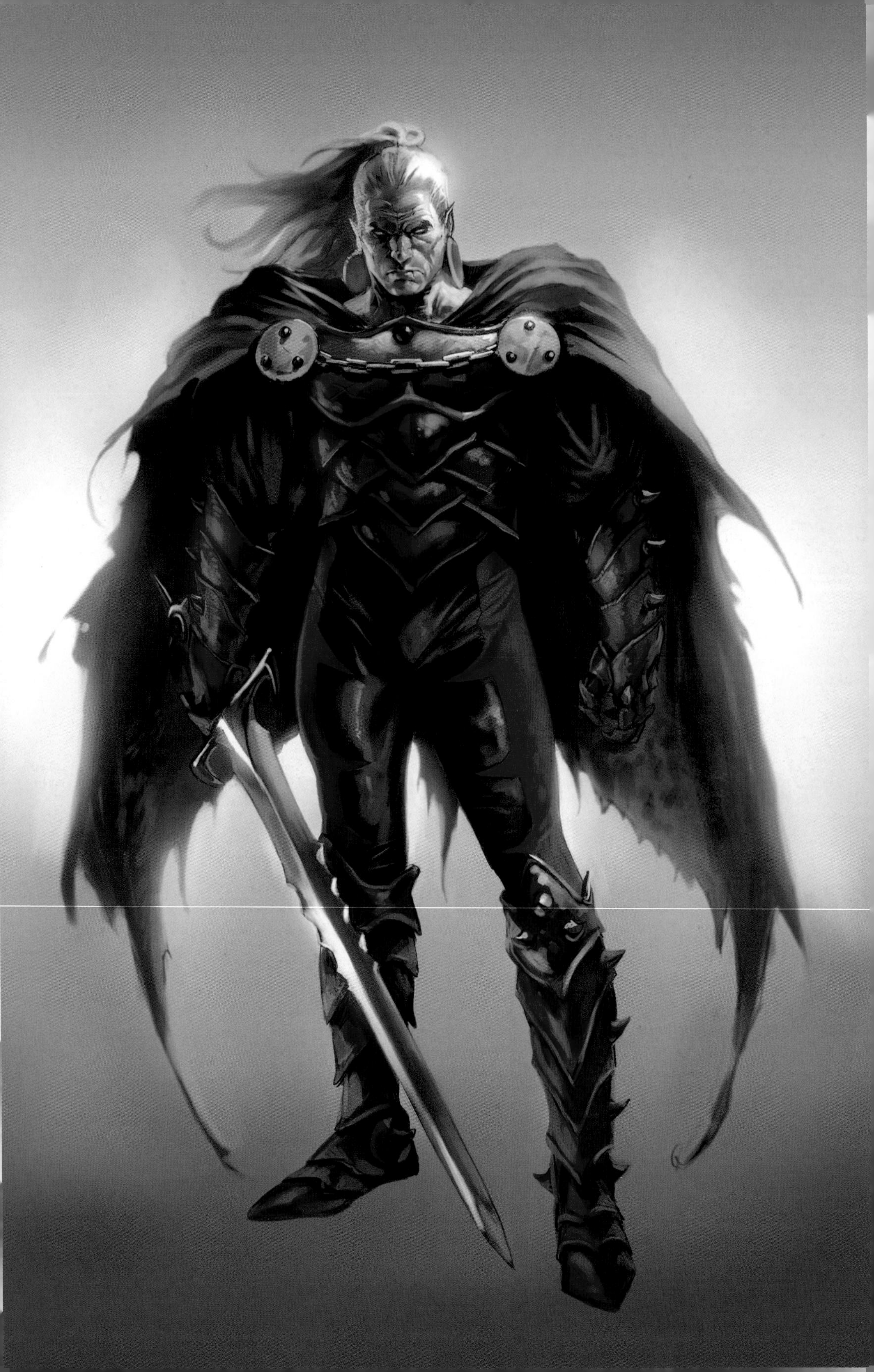

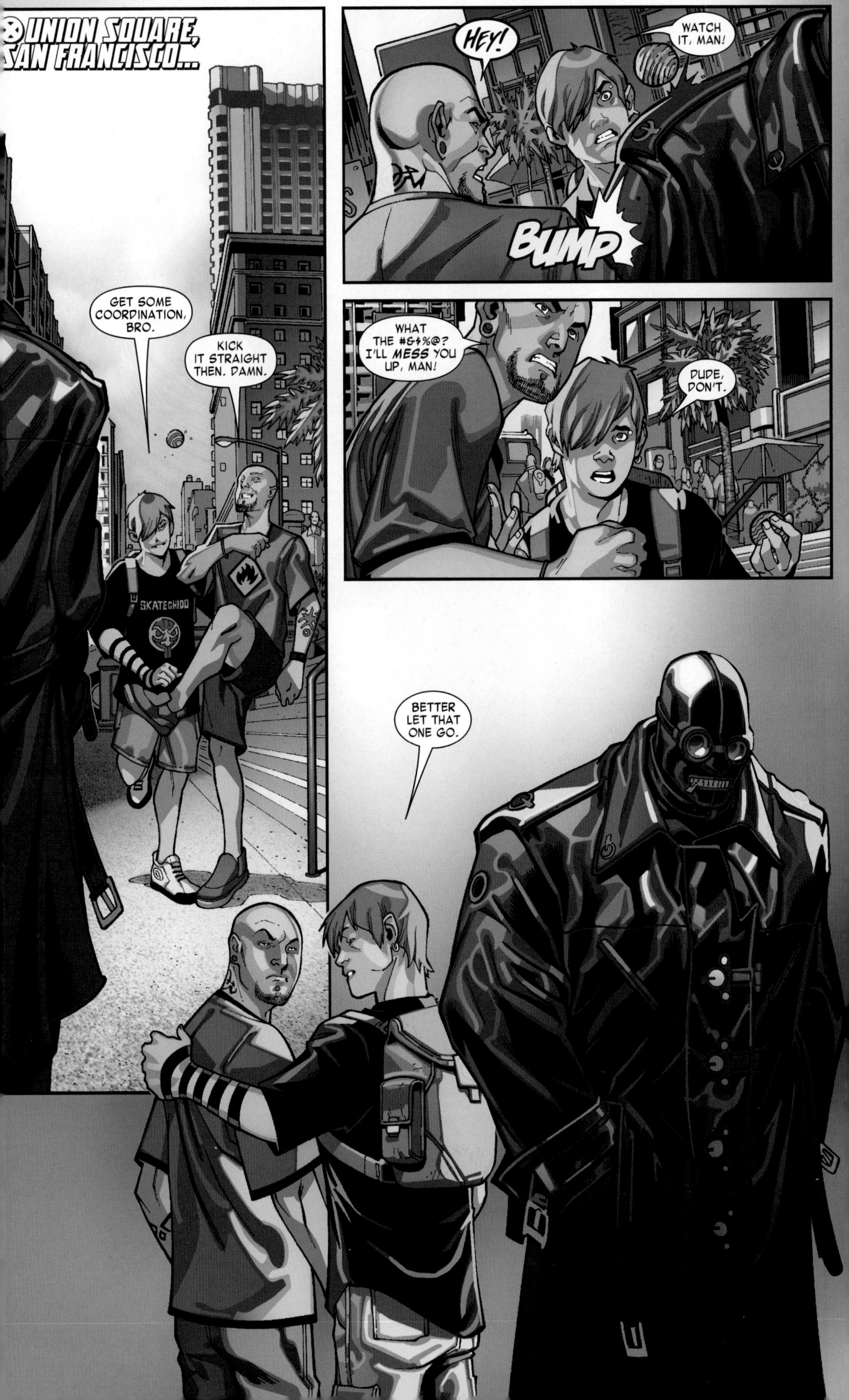
UNION SQUARE, SAN FRANCISCO...
GET SOME COORDINATION, BRO.
KICK IT STRAIGHT THEN. DAMN.
HEY!
WATCH IT, MAN!
BUMP
WHAT THE #&$%@? I'LL MESS YOU UP, MAN!
DUDE, DON'T.
BETTER LET THAT ONE GO.

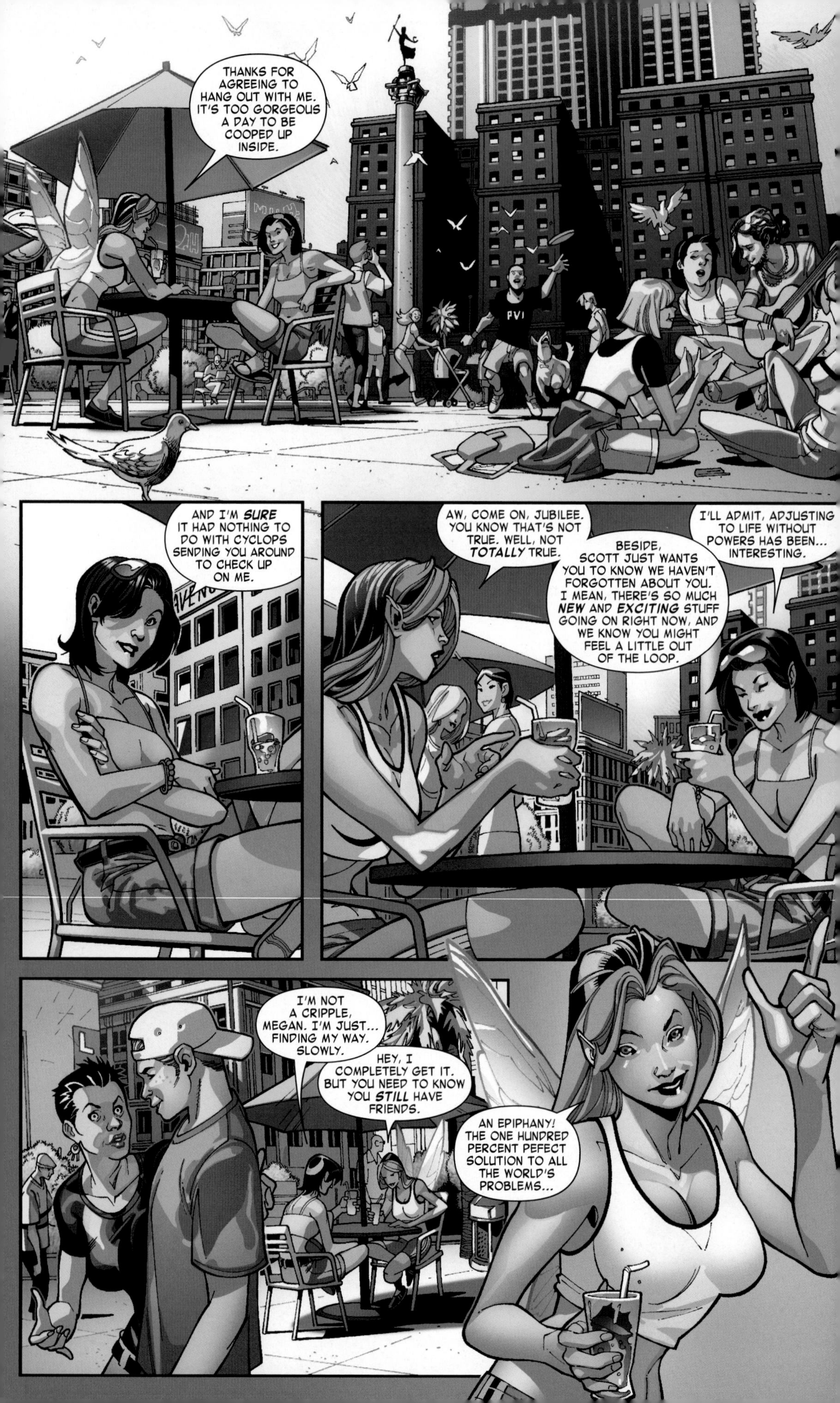
THANKS FOR AGREEING TO HANG OUT WITH ME. IT'S TOO GORGEOUS A DAY TO BE COOPED UP INSIDE.
AND I'M SURE IT HAD NOTHING TO DO WITH CYCLOPS SENDING YOU AROUND TO CHECK UP ON ME.
AW, COME ON, JUBILEE. YOU KNOW THAT'S NOT TRUE. WELL, NOT TOTALLY TRUE.
BESIDE, SCOTT JUST WANTS YOU TO KNOW WE HAVEN'T FORGOTTEN ABOUT YOU. I MEAN, THERE'S SO MUCH NEW AND EXCITING STUFF GOING ON RIGHT NOW, AND WE KNOW YOU MIGHT FEEL A LITTLE OUT OF THE LOOP.
I'LL ADMIT, ADJUSTING TO LIFE WITHOUT POWERS HAS BEEN... INTERESTING.
I'M NOT A CRIPPLE, MEGAN. I'M JUST... FINDING MY WAY. SLOWLY.
HEY, I COMPLETELY GET IT. BUT YOU NEED TO KNOW YOU STILL HAVE FRIENDS.
AN EPIPHANY! THE ONE HUNDRED PERCENT PEFECT SOLUTION TO ALL THE WORLD'S PROBLEMS...

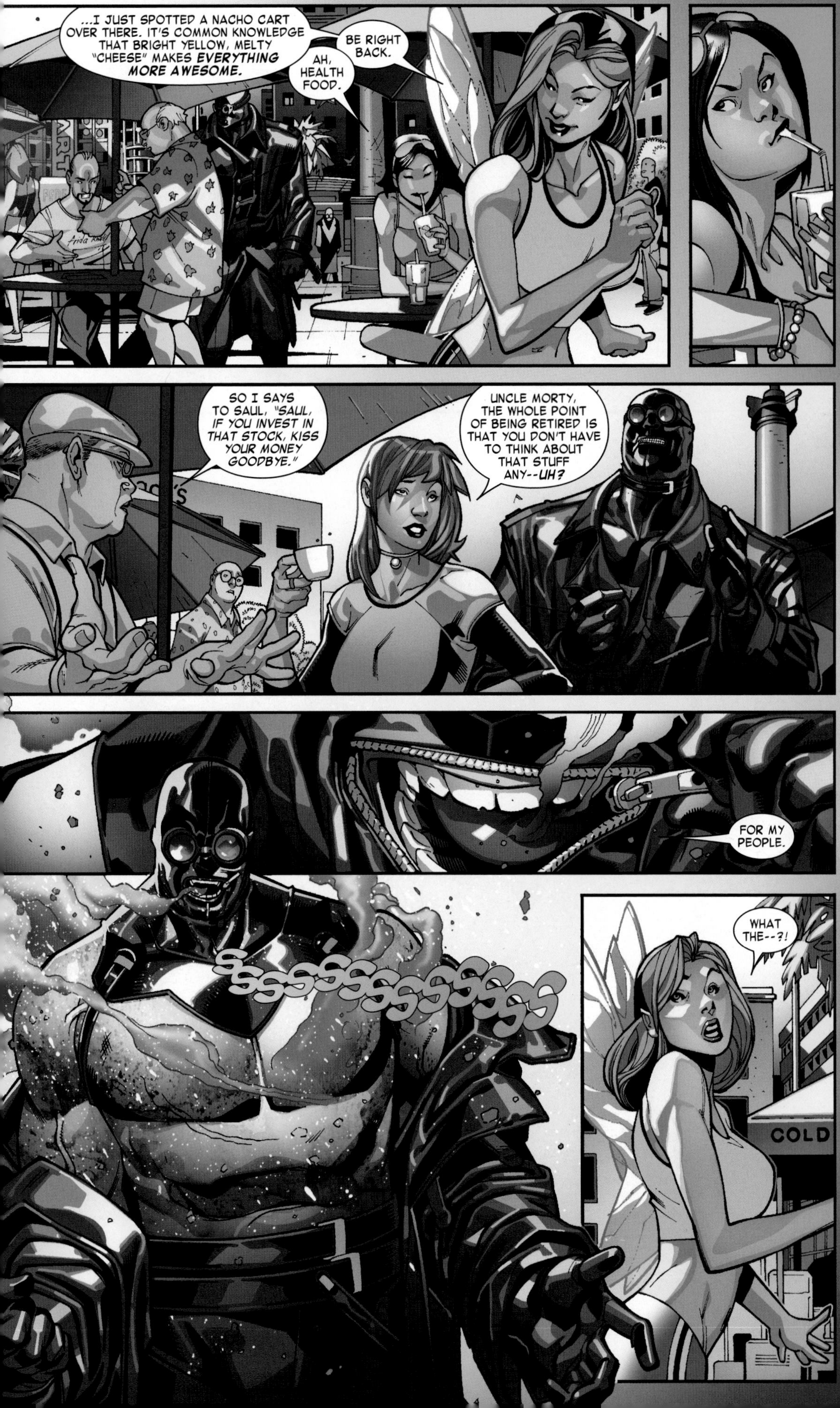
...I JUST SPOTTED A NACHO CART OVER THERE. IT'S COMMON KNOWLEDGE THAT BRIGHT YELLOW, MELTY "CHEESE" MAKES *EVERYTHING MORE AWESOME.*
AH, HEALTH FOOD.
BE RIGHT BACK.
SO I SAYS TO SAUL, "SAUL, IF YOU INVEST IN THAT STOCK, KISS YOUR MONEY GOODBYE."
UNCLE MORTY, THE WHOLE POINT OF BEING RETIRED IS THAT YOU DON'T HAVE TO THINK ABOUT THAT STUFF ANY--*UH?*
FOR MY PEOPLE.
SSSSSSSSSSSSSS
WHAT THE--?!
COLD

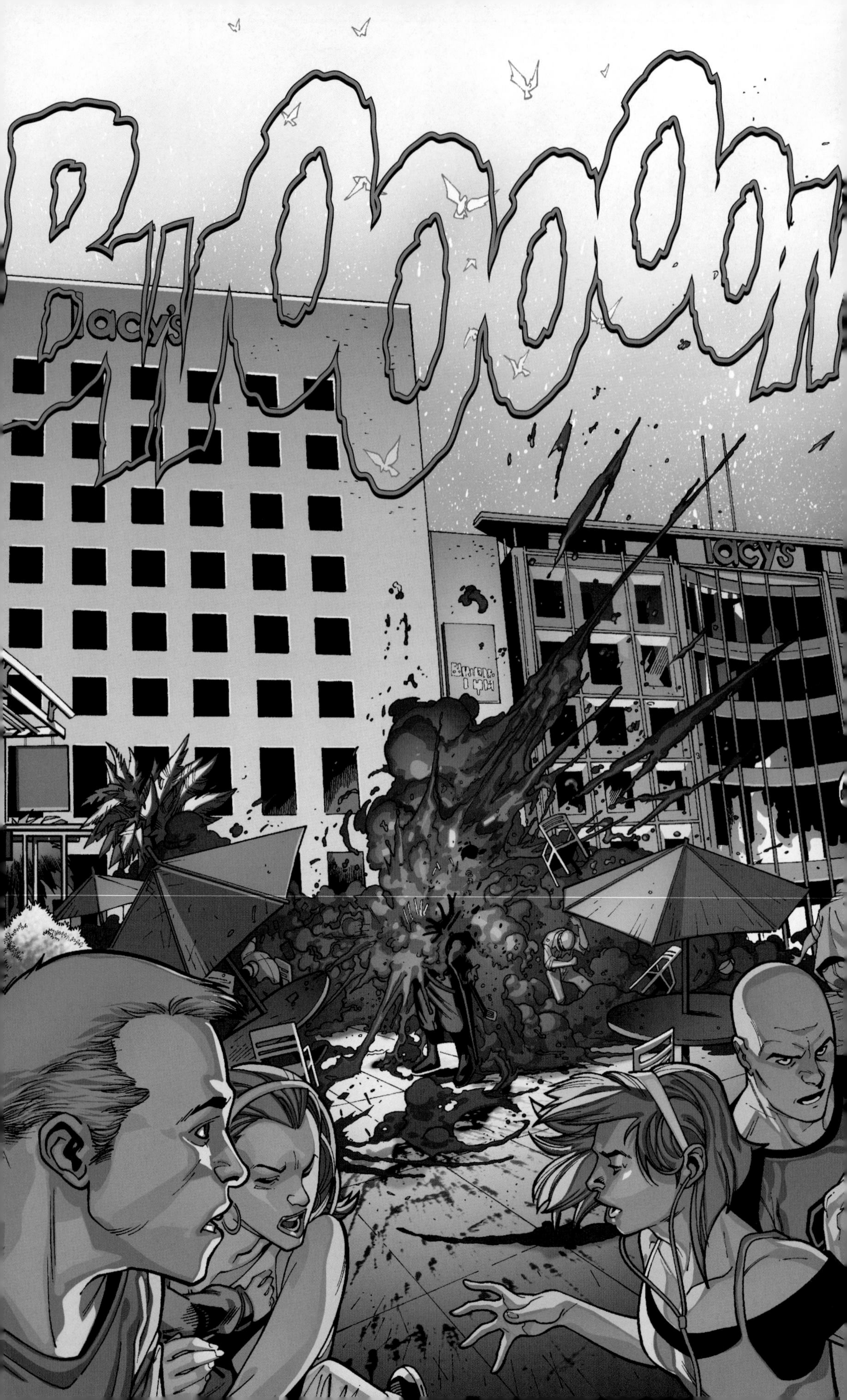
BLOOOOOM

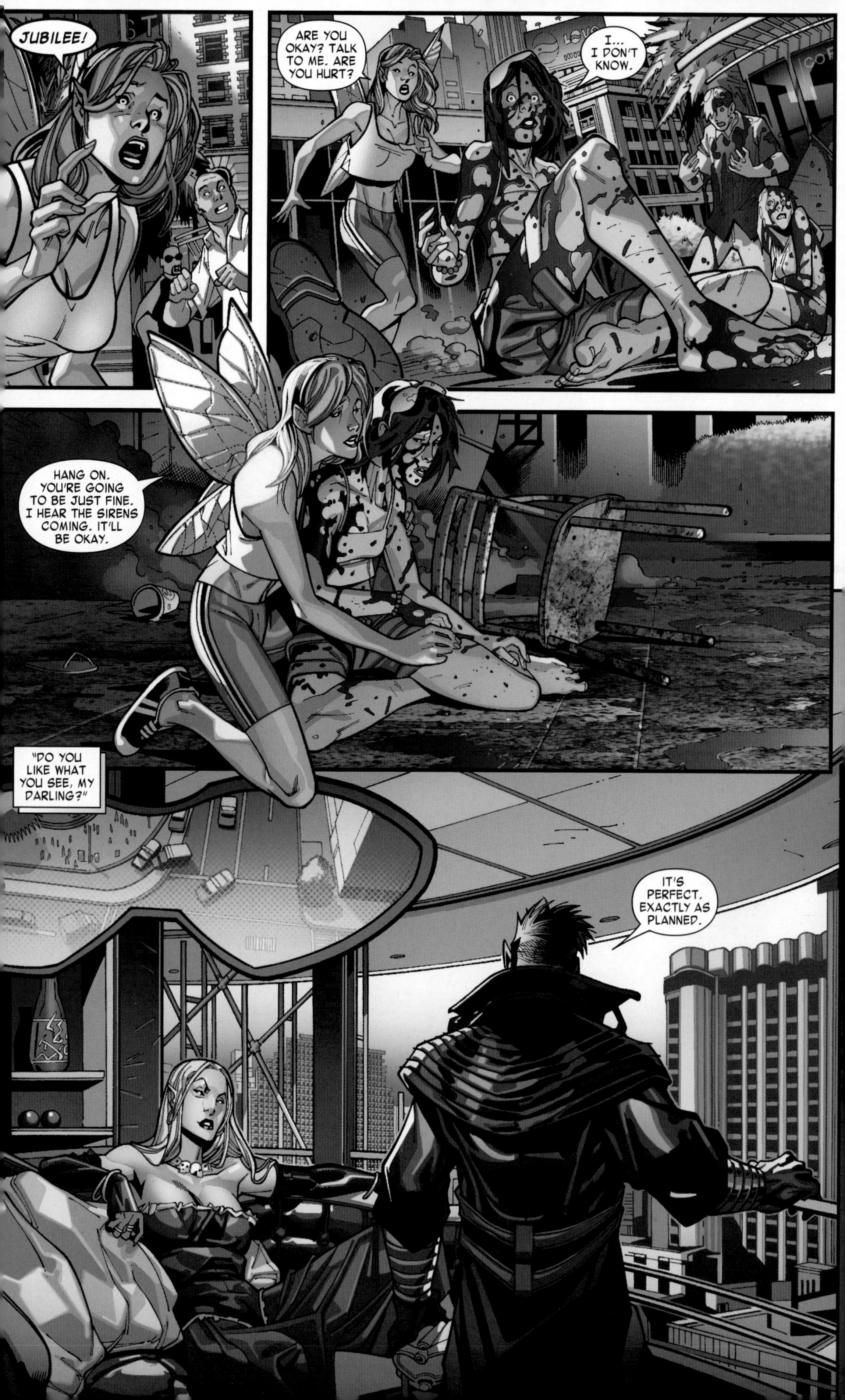
JUBILEE!
ARE YOU OKAY? TALK TO ME. ARE YOU HURT?
I... I DON'T KNOW.
HANG ON. YOU'RE GOING TO BE JUST FINE. I HEAR THE SIRENS COMING. IT'LL BE OKAY.
"DO YOU LIKE WHAT YOU SEE, MY DARLING?"
IT'S PERFECT. EXACTLY AS PLANNED.

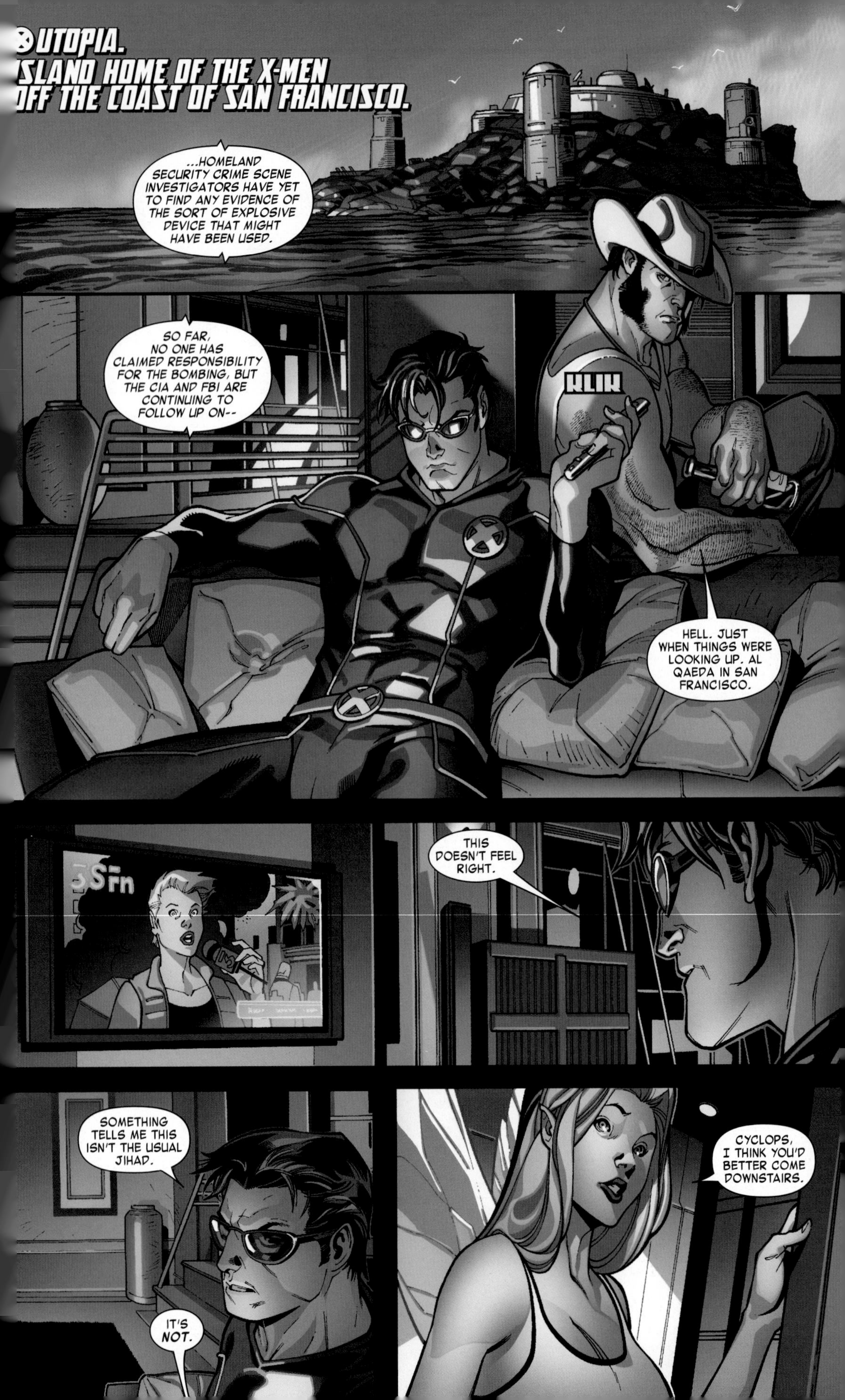
UTOPIA.
ISLAND HOME OF THE X-MEN
OFF THE COAST OF SAN FRANCISCO.
...HOMELAND SECURITY CRIME SCENE INVESTIGATORS HAVE YET TO FIND ANY EVIDENCE OF THE SORT OF EXPLOSIVE DEVICE THAT MIGHT HAVE BEEN USED.
SO FAR, NO ONE HAS CLAIMED RESPONSIBILITY FOR THE BOMBING, BUT THE CIA AND FBI ARE CONTINUING TO FOLLOW UP ON--
KLIK
HELL. JUST WHEN THINGS WERE LOOKING UP. AL QAEDA IN SAN FRANCISCO.
THIS DOESN'T FEEL RIGHT.
SOMETHING TELLS ME THIS ISN'T THE USUAL JIHAD.
IT'S NOT.
CYCLOPS, I THINK YOU'D BETTER COME DOWNSTAIRS.

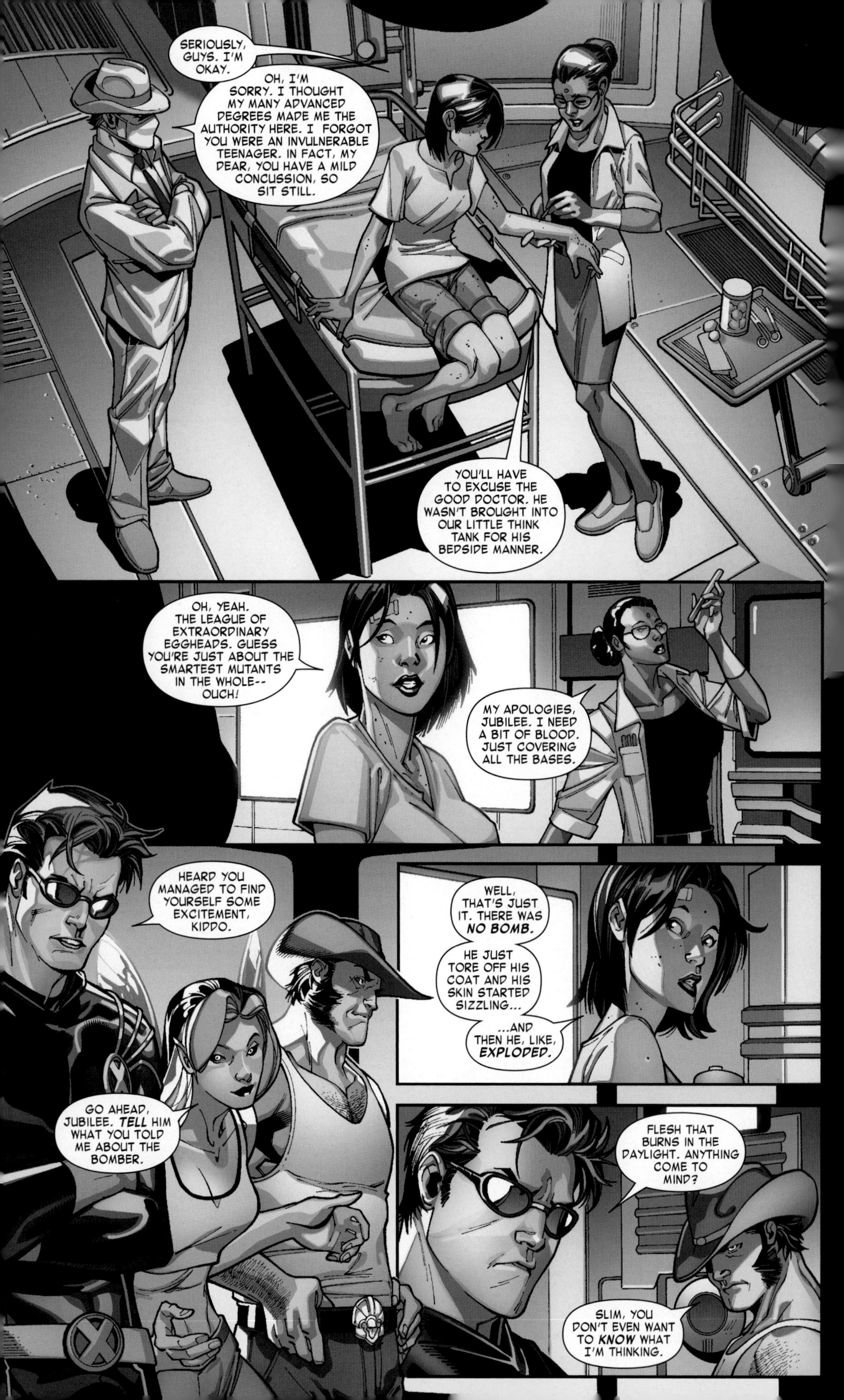
SERIOUSLY, GUYS. I'M OKAY.
OH, I'M SORRY. I THOUGHT MY MANY ADVANCED DEGREES MADE ME THE AUTHORITY HERE. I FORGOT YOU WERE AN INVULNERABLE TEENAGER. IN FACT, MY DEAR, YOU HAVE A MILD CONCUSSION, SO SIT STILL.
YOU'LL HAVE TO EXCUSE THE GOOD DOCTOR. HE WASN'T BROUGHT INTO OUR LITTLE THINK TANK FOR HIS BEDSIDE MANNER.
OH, YEAH. THE LEAGUE OF EXTRAORDINARY EGGHEADS. GUESS YOU'RE JUST ABOUT THE SMARTEST MUTANTS IN THE WHOLE-- OUCH!
MY APOLOGIES, JUBILEE. I NEED A BIT OF BLOOD. JUST COVERING ALL THE BASES.
HEARD YOU MANAGED TO FIND YOURSELF SOME EXCITEMENT, KIDDO.
GO AHEAD, JUBILEE. TELL HIM WHAT YOU TOLD ME ABOUT THE BOMBER.
WELL, THAT'S JUST IT. THERE WAS NO BOMB.
HE JUST TORE OFF HIS COAT AND HIS SKIN STARTED SIZZLING...
...AND THEN HE, LIKE, EXPLODED.
FLESH THAT BURNS IN THE DAYLIGHT. ANYTHING COME TO MIND?
SLIM, YOU DON'T EVEN WANT TO KNOW WHAT I'M THINKING.

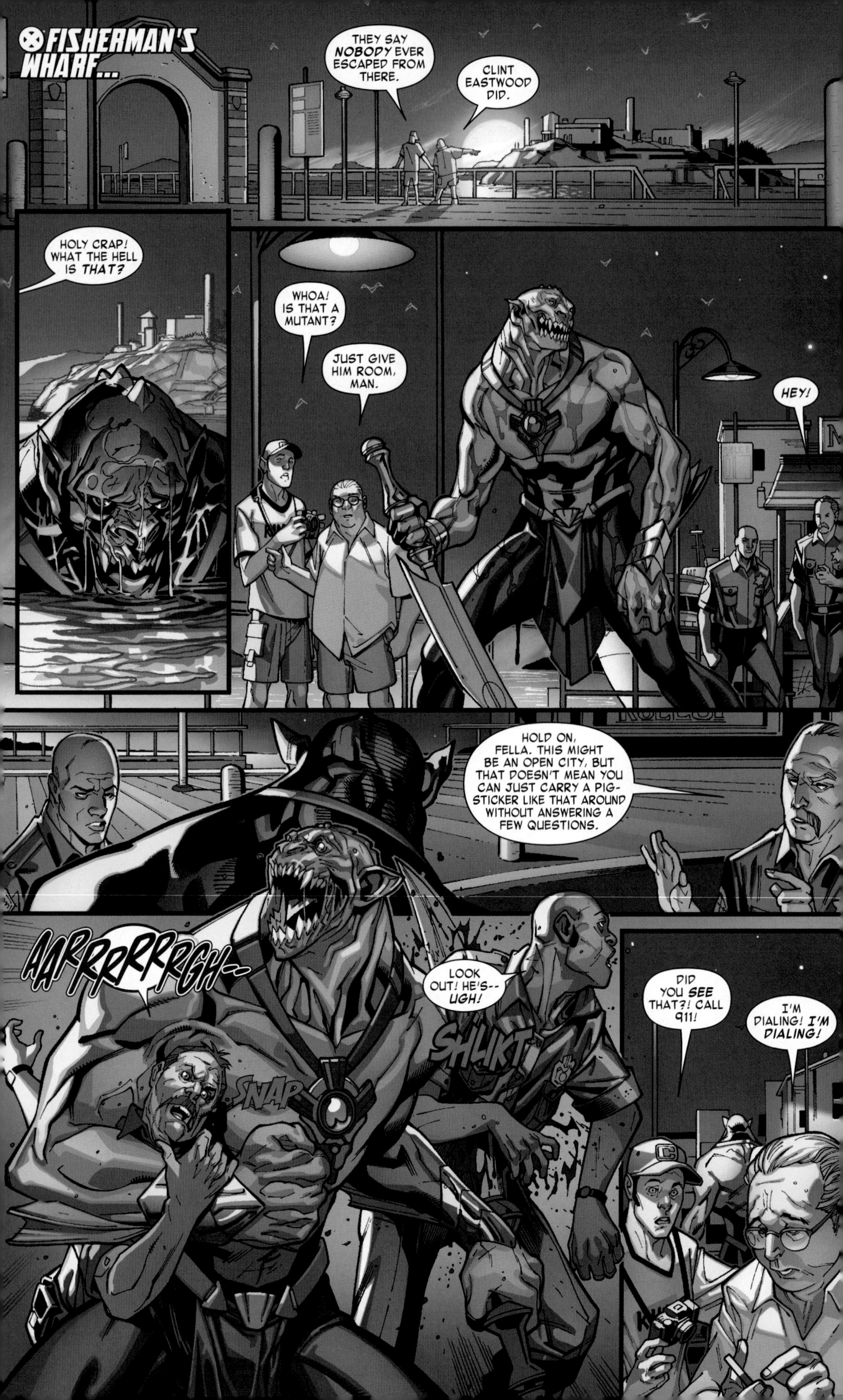
FISHERMAN'S WHARF...
THEY SAY NOBODY EVER ESCAPED FROM THERE.
CLINT EASTWOOD DID.
HOLY CRAP! WHAT THE HELL IS THAT?
WHOA! IS THAT A MUTANT?
JUST GIVE HIM ROOM, MAN.
HEY!
HOLD ON, FELLA. THIS MIGHT BE AN OPEN CITY, BUT THAT DOESN'T MEAN YOU CAN JUST CARRY A PIG-STICKER LIKE THAT AROUND WITHOUT ANSWERING A FEW QUESTIONS.
AARRRRRRGH--
LOOK OUT! HE'S-- UGH!
SHUKT
SNAP
DID YOU SEE THAT?! CALL 911!
I'M DIALING! I'M DIALING!

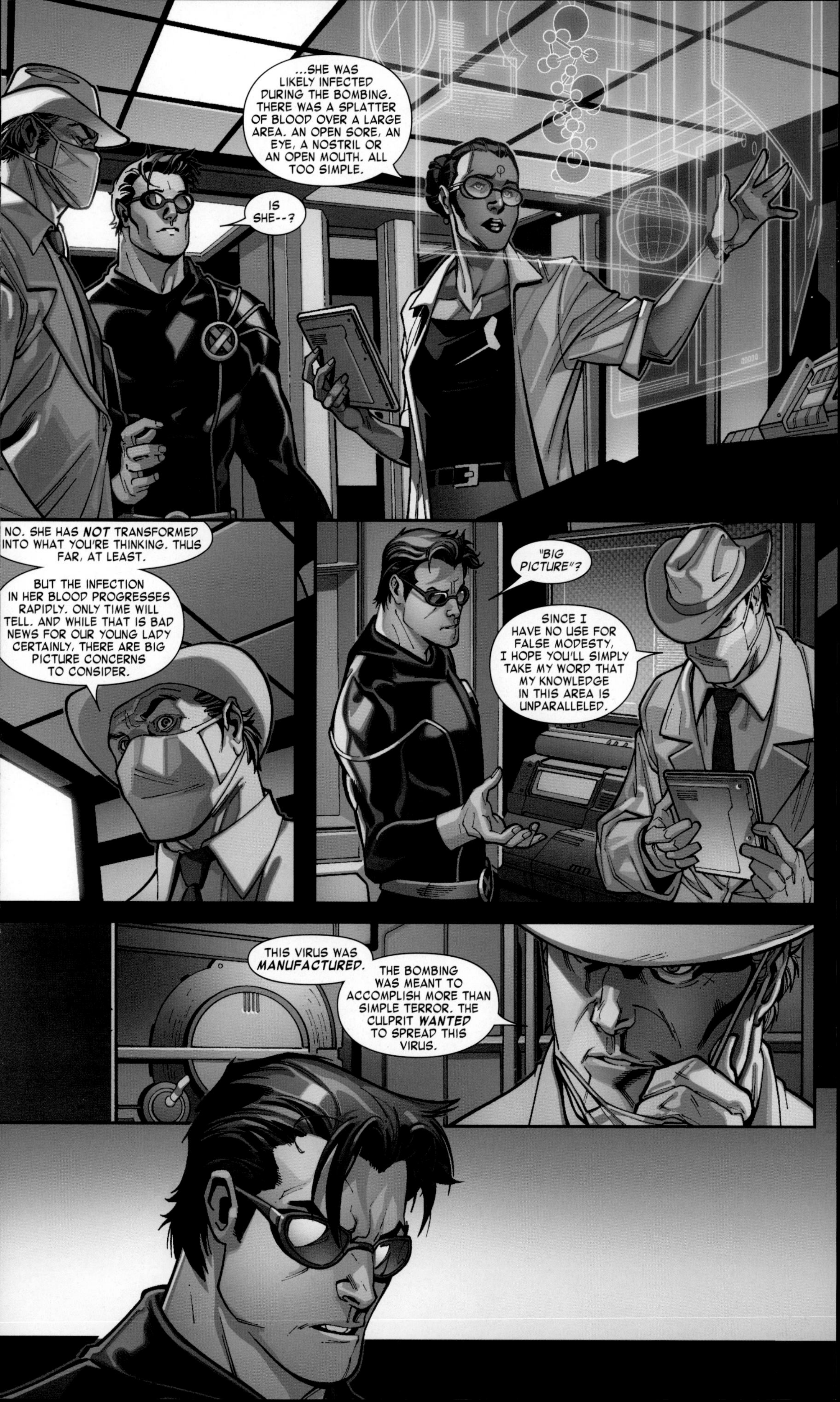
...SHE WAS LIKELY INFECTED DURING THE BOMBING. THERE WAS A SPLATTER OF BLOOD OVER A LARGE AREA. AN OPEN SORE, AN EYE, A NOSTRIL OR AN OPEN MOUTH. ALL TOO SIMPLE.
IS SHE--?
NO. SHE HAS NOT TRANSFORMED INTO WHAT YOU'RE THINKING. THUS FAR, AT LEAST.
BUT THE INFECTION IN HER BLOOD PROGRESSES RAPIDLY. ONLY TIME WILL TELL. AND WHILE THAT IS BAD NEWS FOR OUR YOUNG LADY CERTAINLY, THERE ARE BIG PICTURE CONCERNS TO CONSIDER.
"BIG PICTURE"?
SINCE I HAVE NO USE FOR FALSE MODESTY, I HOPE YOU'LL SIMPLY TAKE MY WORD THAT MY KNOWLEDGE IN THIS AREA IS UNPARALLELED.
THIS VIRUS WAS MANUFACTURED.
THE BOMBING WAS MEANT TO ACCOMPLISH MORE THAN SIMPLE TERROR. THE CULPRIT WANTED TO SPREAD THIS VIRUS.

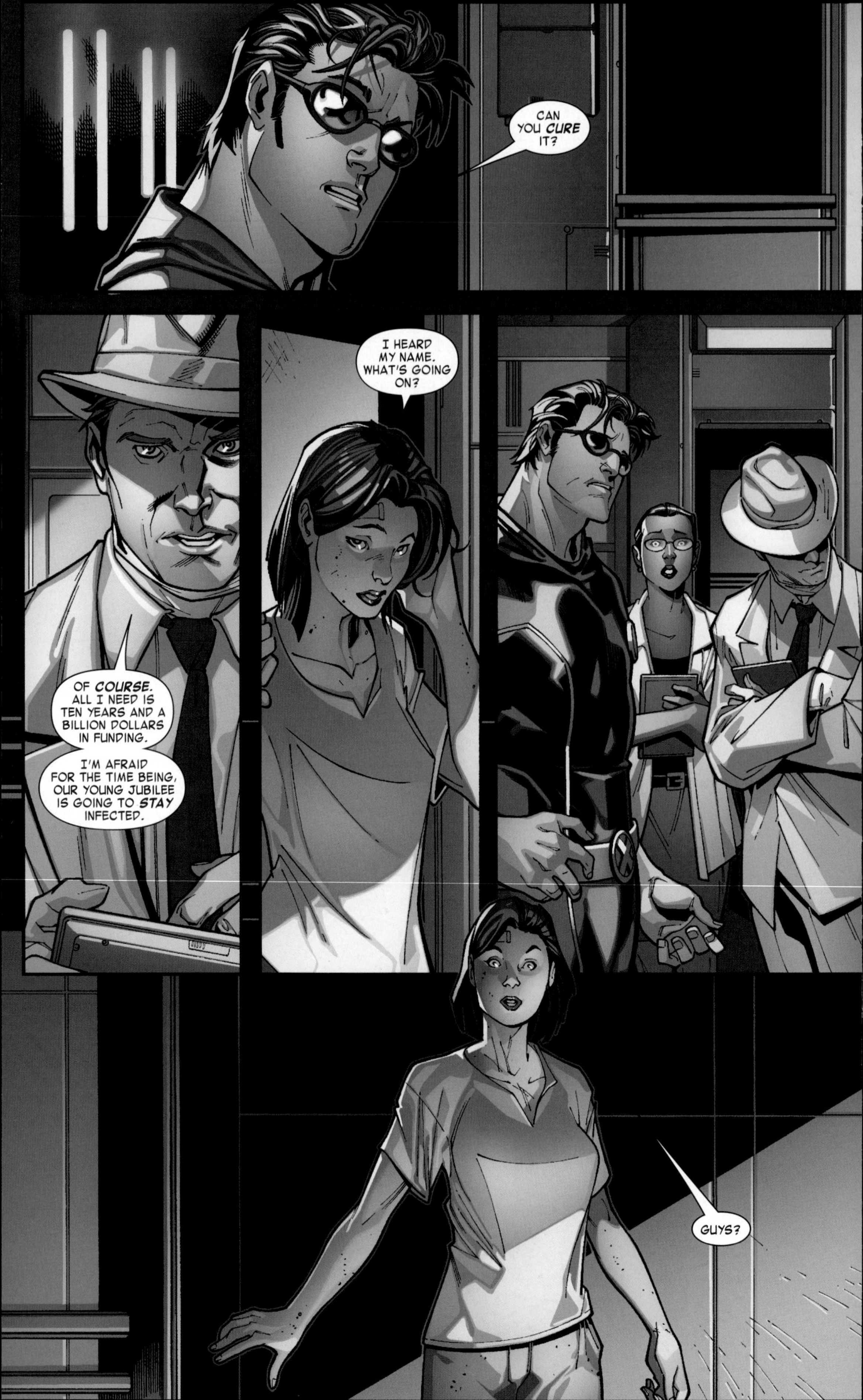
CAN YOU CURE IT?
OF COURSE. ALL I NEED IS TEN YEARS AND A BILLION DOLLARS IN FUNDING.
I'M AFRAID FOR THE TIME BEING, OUR YOUNG JUBILEE IS GOING TO STAY INFECTED.
I HEARD MY NAME. WHAT'S GOING ON?
GUYS?

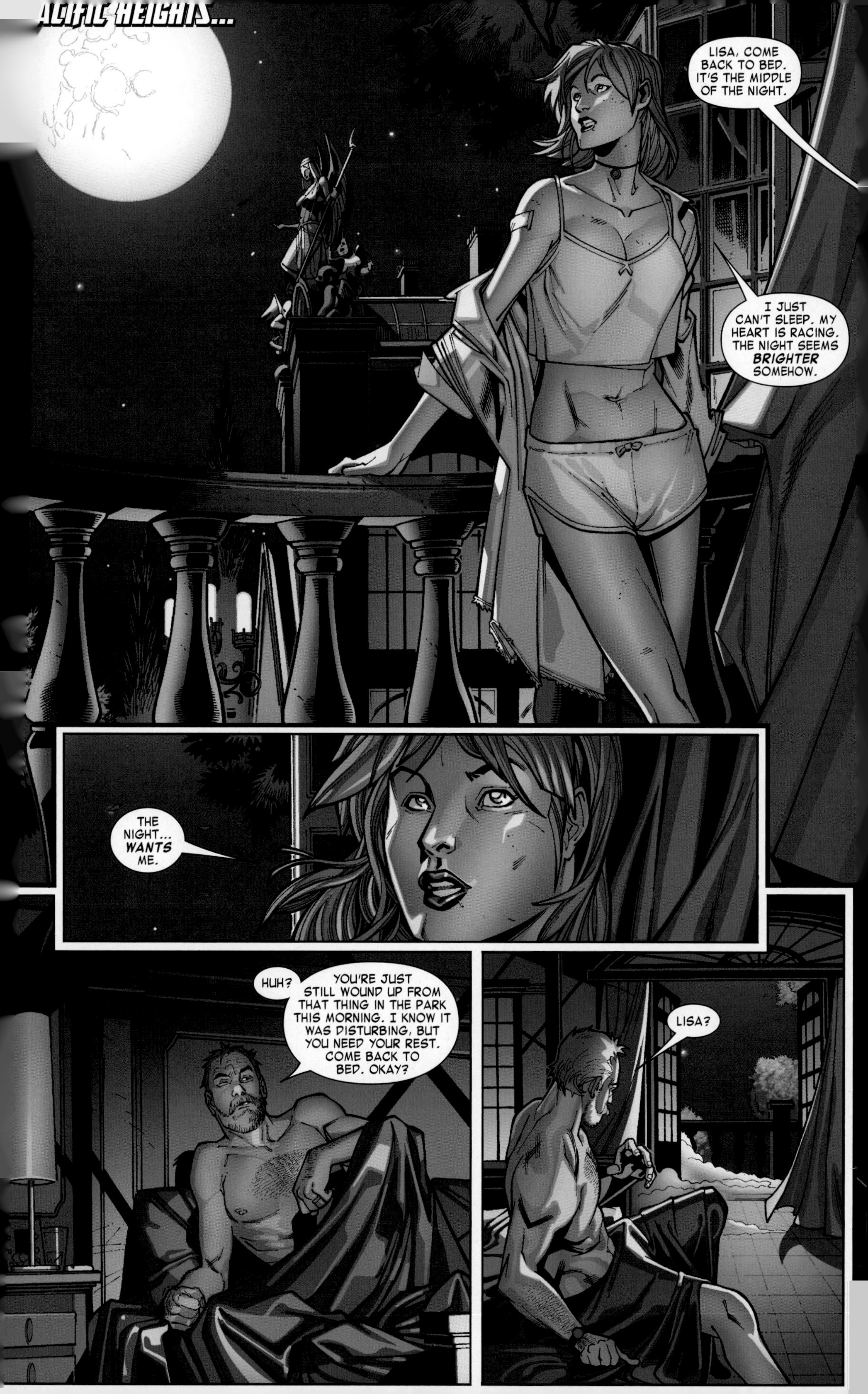
...ACIFIC HEIGHTS...
LISA, COME BACK TO BED. IT'S THE MIDDLE OF THE NIGHT.
I JUST CAN'T SLEEP. MY HEART IS RACING. THE NIGHT SEEMS BRIGHTER SOMEHOW.
THE NIGHT... WANTS ME.
HUH?
YOU'RE JUST STILL WOUND UP FROM THAT THING IN THE PARK THIS MORNING. I KNOW IT WAS DISTURBING, BUT YOU NEED YOUR REST. COME BACK TO BED. OKAY?
LISA?

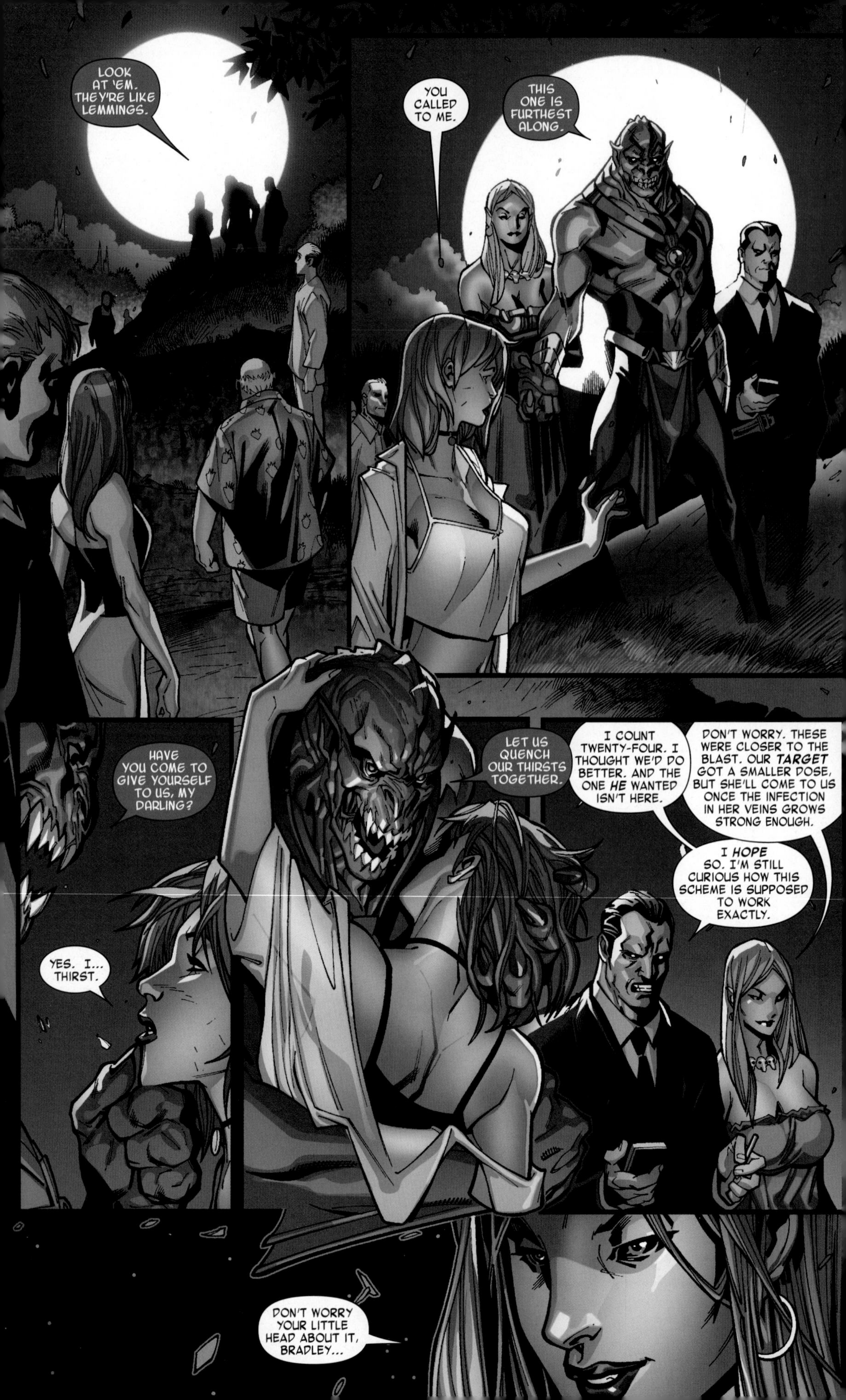
LOOK AT 'EM. THEY'RE LIKE LEMMINGS.
YOU CALLED TO ME.
THIS ONE IS FURTHEST ALONG.
HAVE YOU COME TO GIVE YOURSELF TO US, MY DARLING?
YES. I... THIRST.
LET US QUENCH OUR THIRSTS TOGETHER.
I COUNT TWENTY-FOUR. I THOUGHT WE'D DO BETTER. AND THE ONE HE WANTED ISN'T HERE.
DON'T WORRY. THESE WERE CLOSER TO THE BLAST. OUR TARGET GOT A SMALLER DOSE, BUT SHE'LL COME TO US ONCE THE INFECTION IN HER VEINS GROWS STRONG ENOUGH.
I HOPE SO. I'M STILL CURIOUS HOW THIS SCHEME IS SUPPOSED TO WORK EXACTLY.
DON'T WORRY YOUR LITTLE HEAD ABOUT IT, BRADLEY...

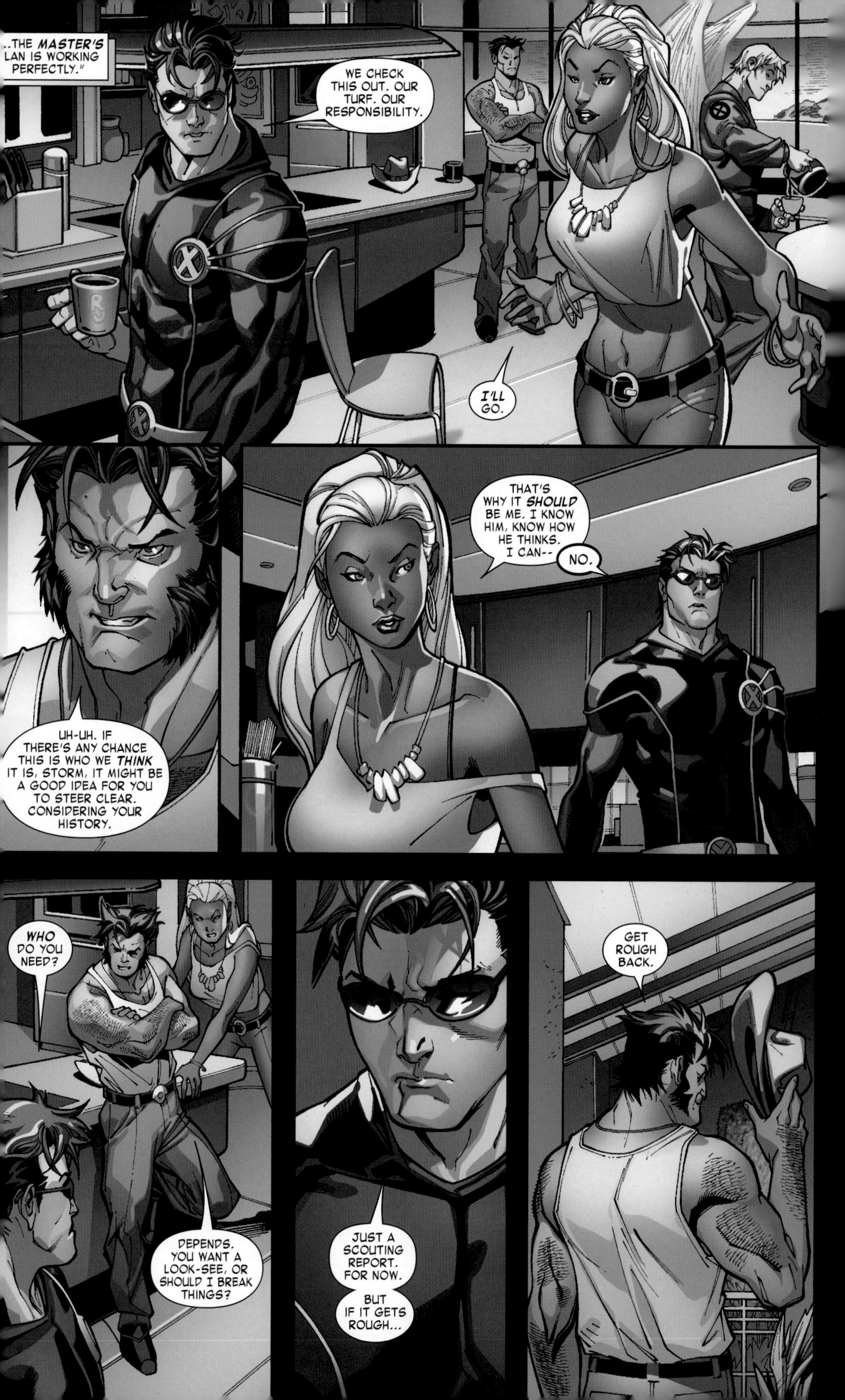
..THE MASTER'S
LAN IS WORKING PERFECTLY."
WE CHECK THIS OUT. OUR TURF. OUR RESPONSIBILITY.
I'LL GO.
UH-UH. IF THERE'S ANY CHANCE THIS IS WHO WE THINK IT IS, STORM, IT MIGHT BE A GOOD IDEA FOR YOU TO STEER CLEAR. CONSIDERING YOUR HISTORY.
THAT'S WHY IT SHOULD BE ME. I KNOW HIM, KNOW HOW HE THINKS. I CAN--
NO.
WHO DO YOU NEED?
DEPENDS. YOU WANT A LOOK-SEE, OR SHOULD I BREAK THINGS?
JUST A SCOUTING REPORT. FOR NOW.
BUT IF IT GETS ROUGH...
GET ROUGH BACK.

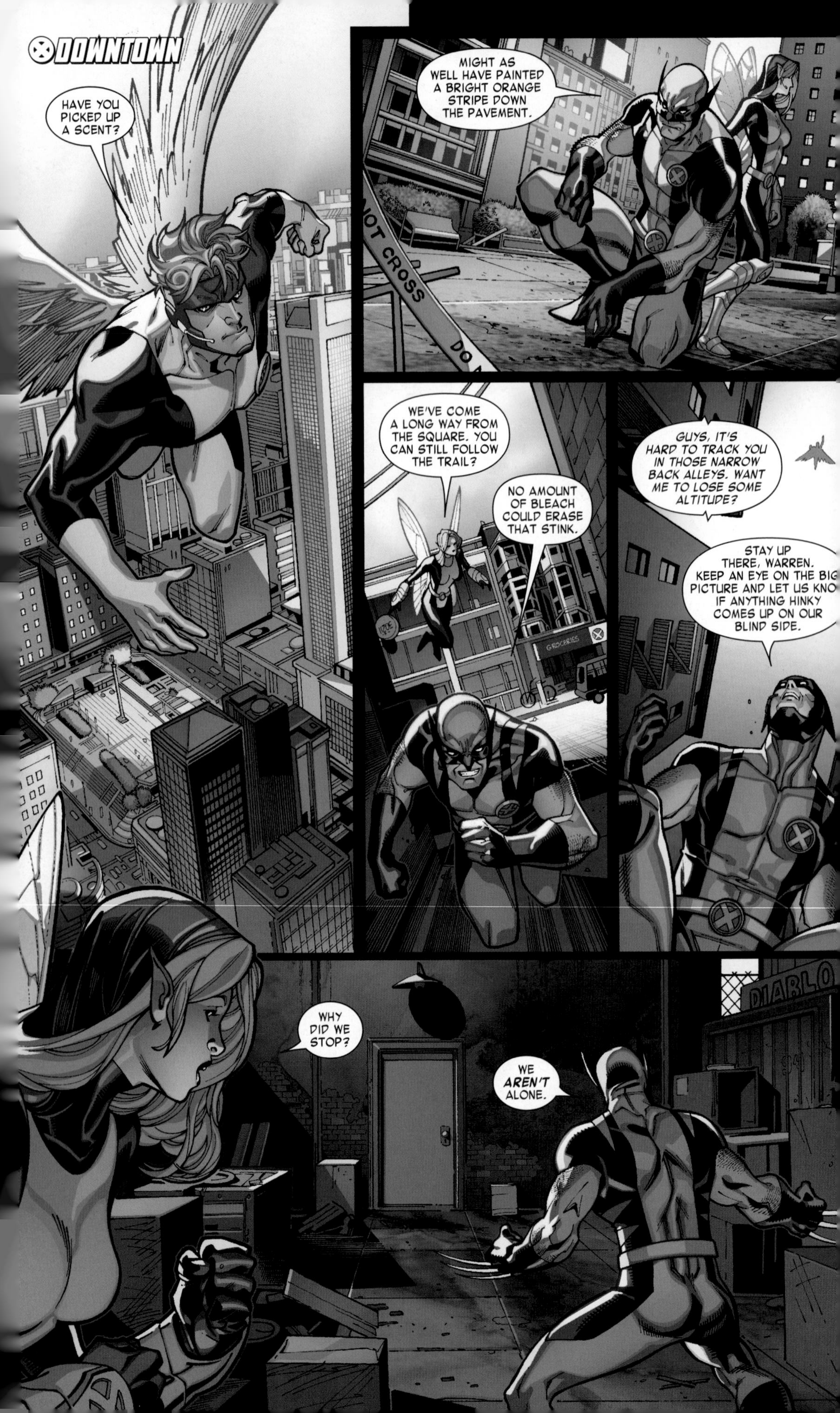
DOWNTOWN
HAVE YOU PICKED UP A SCENT?
MIGHT AS WELL HAVE PAINTED A BRIGHT ORANGE STRIPE DOWN THE PAVEMENT.
WE'VE COME A LONG WAY FROM THE SQUARE. YOU CAN STILL FOLLOW THE TRAIL?
NO AMOUNT OF BLEACH COULD ERASE THAT STINK.
GUYS, IT'S HARD TO TRACK YOU IN THOSE NARROW BACK ALLEYS. WANT ME TO LOSE SOME ALTITUDE?
STAY UP THERE, WARREN. KEEP AN EYE ON THE BIG PICTURE AND LET US KNOW IF ANYTHING HINKY COMES UP ON OUR BLIND SIDE.
WHY DID WE STOP?
WE *AREN'T* ALONE.

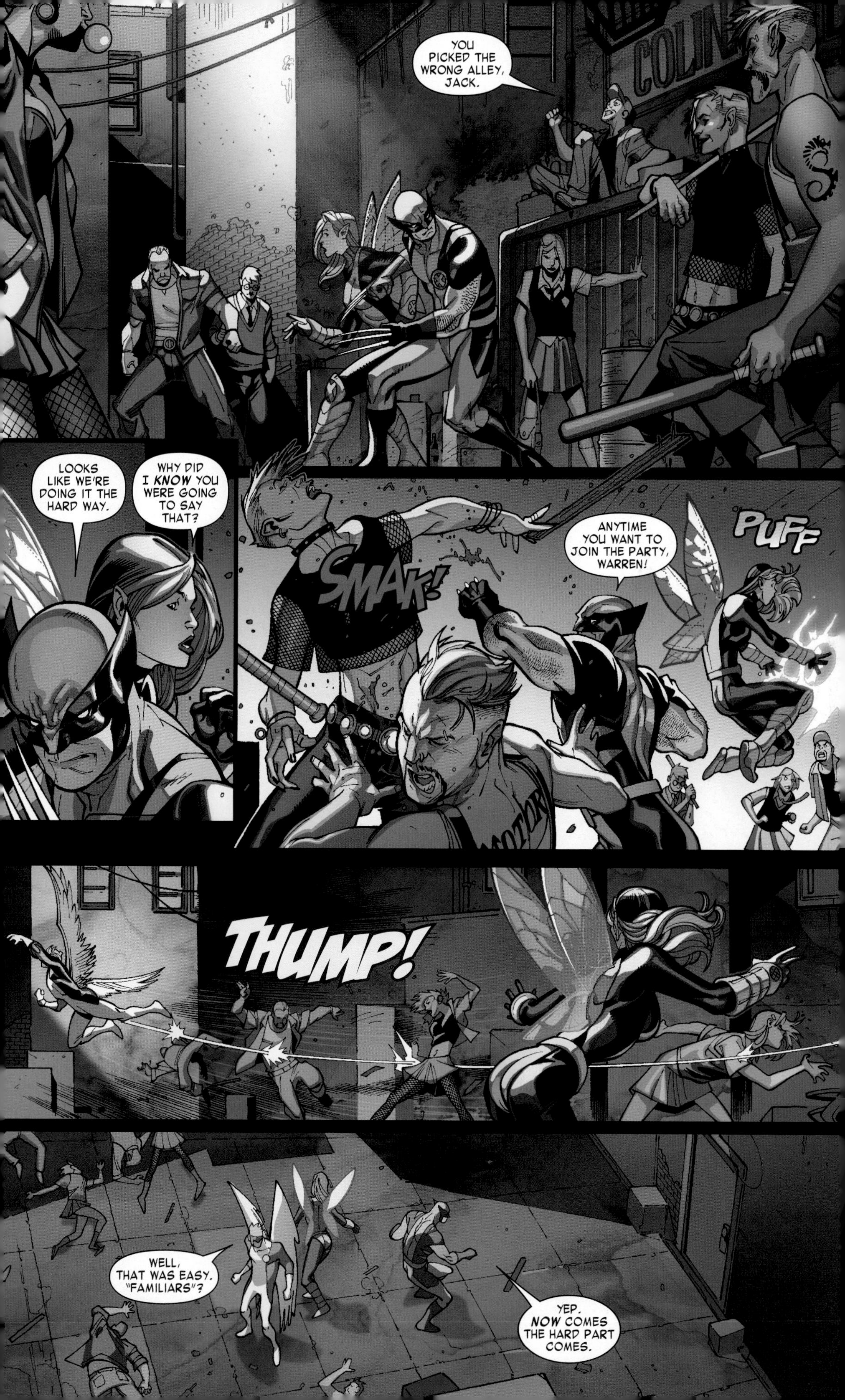

COLIN
YOU PICKED THE WRONG ALLEY, JACK.
LOOKS LIKE WE'RE DOING IT THE HARD WAY.
WHY DID I *KNOW* YOU WERE GOING TO SAY THAT?
SMAK!
ANYTIME YOU WANT TO JOIN THE PARTY, WARREN!
PUFF
THUMP!
WELL, THAT WAS EASY. "FAMILIARS"?
YEP. *NOW* COMES THE HARD PART COMES.

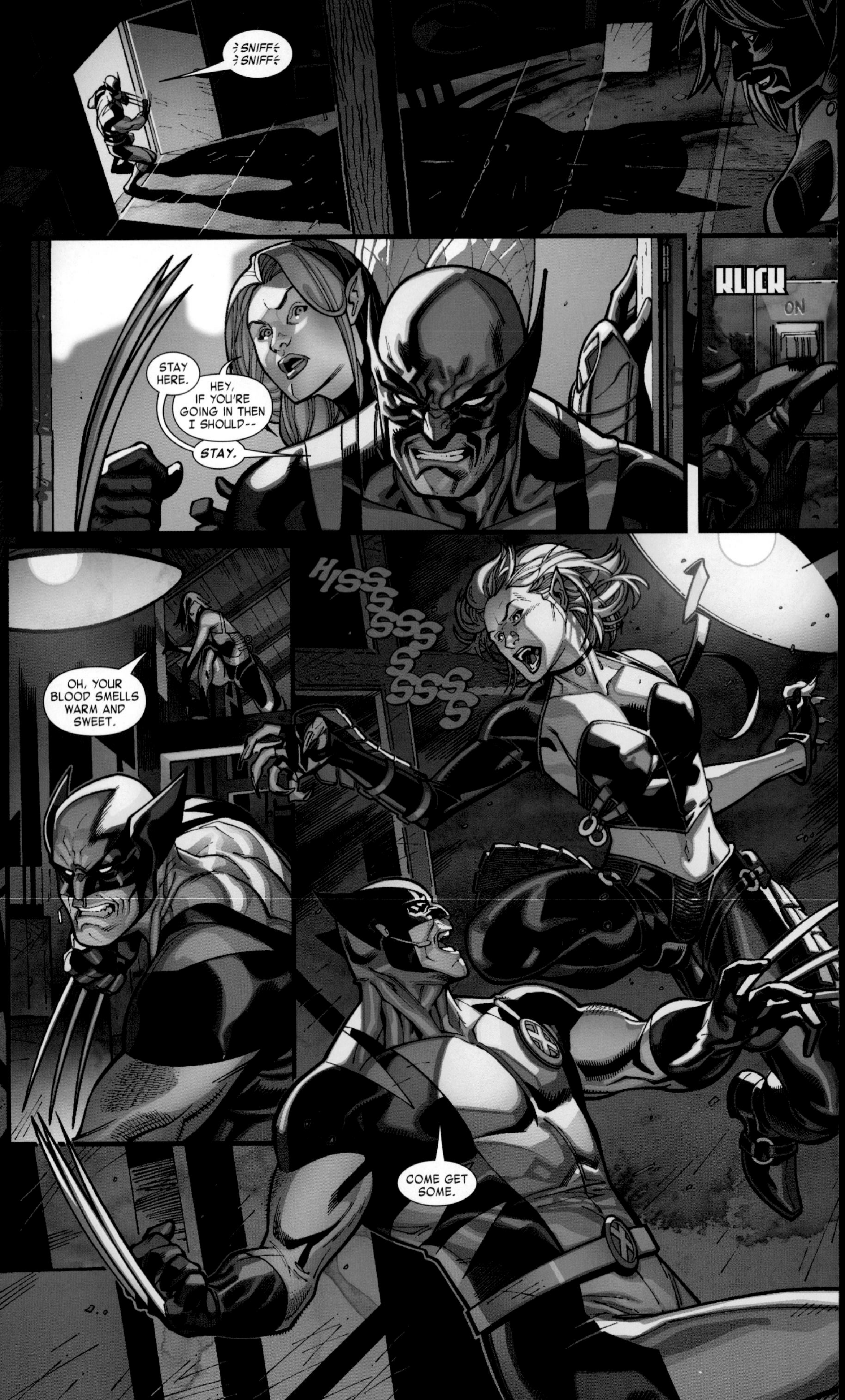
SNIFF SNIFF
KLICK
ON
STAY HERE.
HEY, IF YOU'RE GOING IN THEN I SHOULD--
STAY.
HISSSSSSSSSSSS
OH, YOUR BLOOD SMELLS WARM AND SWEET.
COME GET SOME.

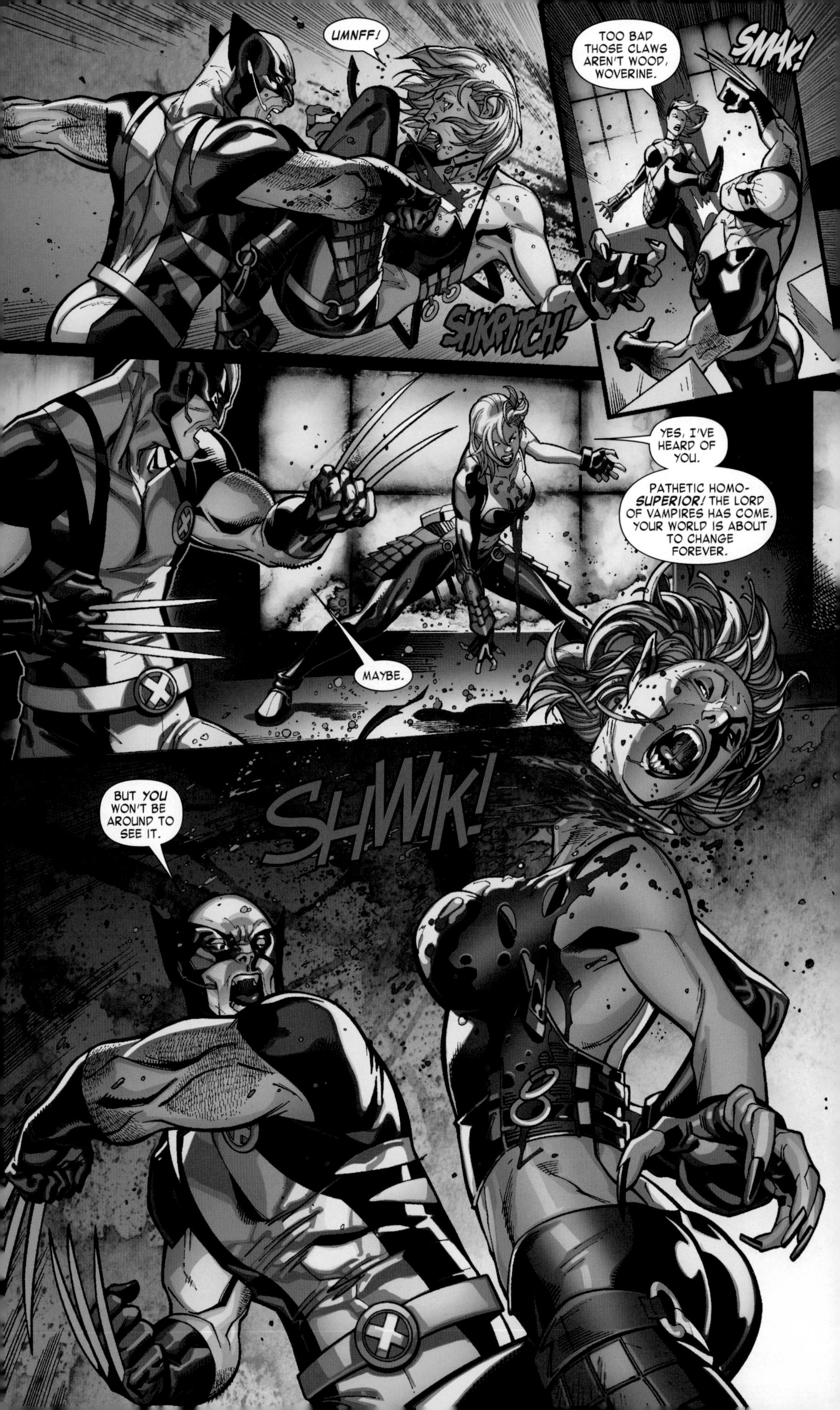
UMNFF!
SHKRTTCH!
TOO BAD THOSE CLAWS AREN'T WOOD, WOVERINE.
SMAK!
YES, I'VE HEARD OF YOU.
PATHETIC HOMO-SUPERIOR! THE LORD OF VAMPIRES HAS COME. YOUR WORLD IS ABOUT TO CHANGE FOREVER.
MAYBE.
BUT YOU WON'T BE AROUND TO SEE IT.
SHWK!

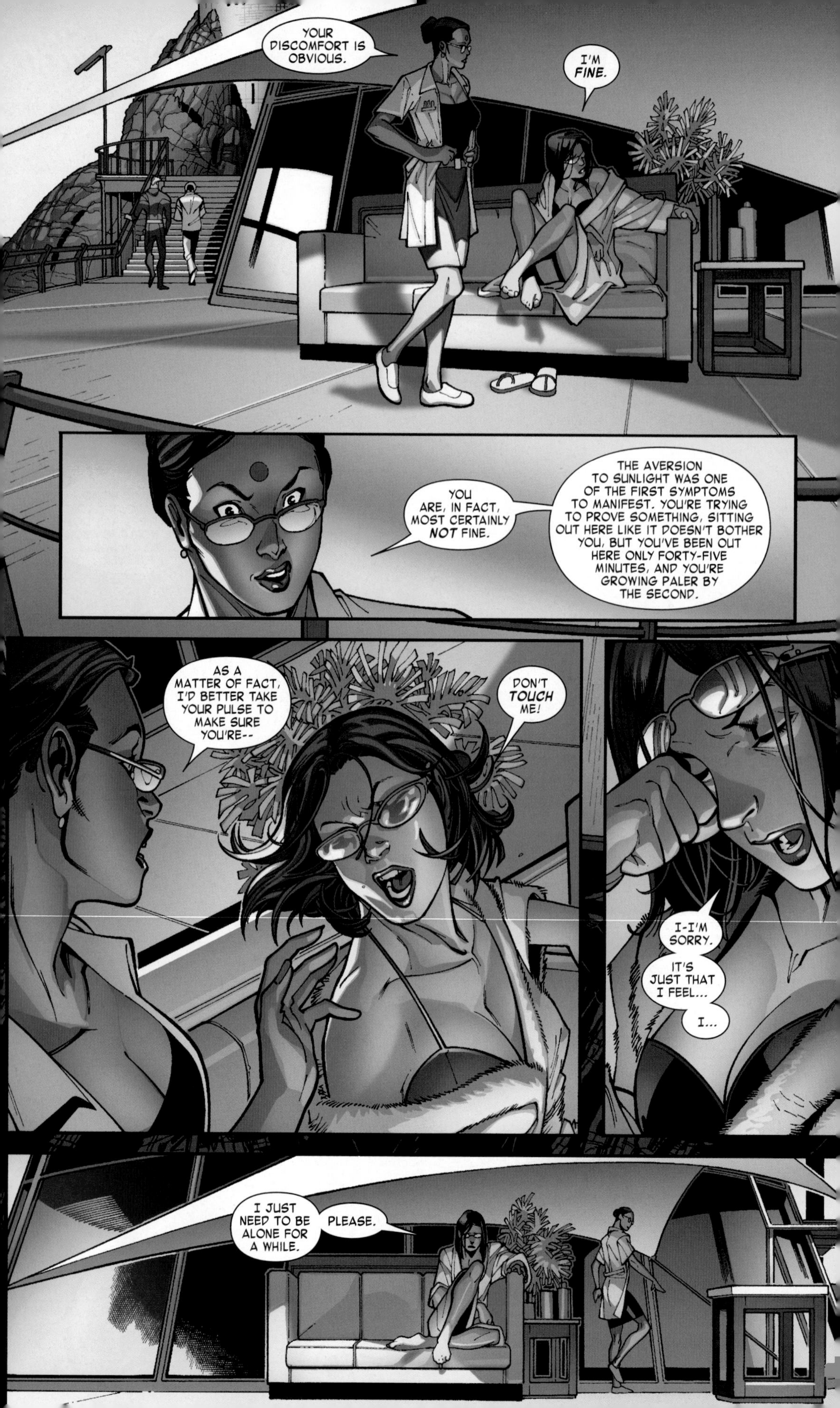
YOUR DISCOMFORT IS OBVIOUS.
I'M *FINE.*
YOU ARE, IN FACT, MOST CERTAINLY *NOT* FINE.
THE AVERSION TO SUNLIGHT WAS ONE OF THE FIRST SYMPTOMS TO MANIFEST. YOU'RE TRYING TO PROVE SOMETHING, SITTING OUT HERE LIKE IT DOESN'T BOTHER YOU, BUT YOU'VE BEEN OUT HERE ONLY FORTY-FIVE MINUTES, AND YOU'RE GROWING PALER BY THE SECOND.
AS A MATTER OF FACT, I'D BETTER TAKE YOUR PULSE TO MAKE SURE YOU'RE--
DON'T *TOUCH* ME!
I-I'M SORRY.
IT'S JUST THAT I FEEL...
I...
I JUST NEED TO BE ALONE FOR A WHILE.
PLEASE.

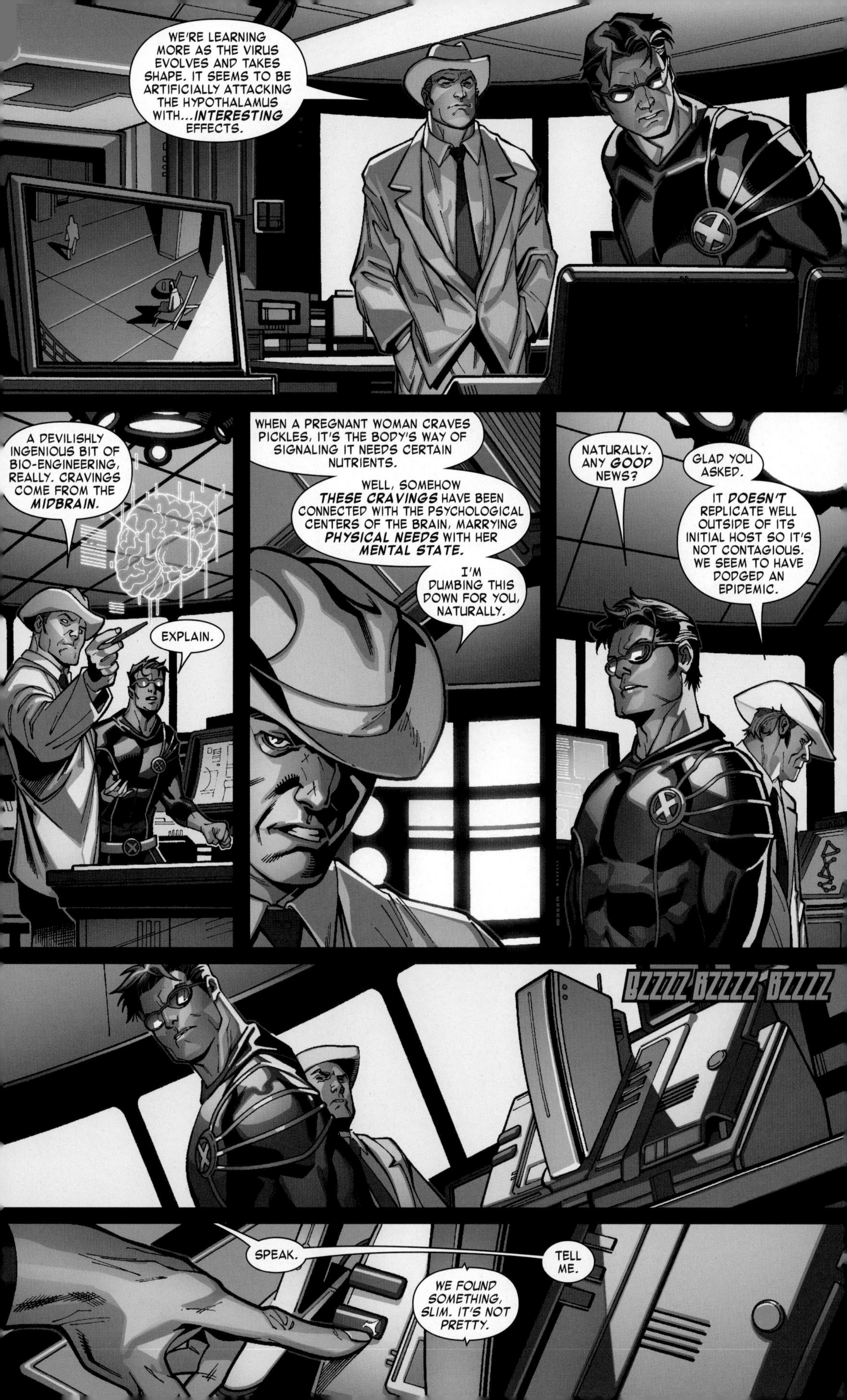
WE'RE LEARNING MORE AS THE VIRUS EVOLVES AND TAKES SHAPE. IT SEEMS TO BE ARTIFICIALLY ATTACKING THE HYPOTHALAMUS WITH...INTERESTING EFFECTS.
A DEVILISHLY INGENIOUS BIT OF BIO-ENGINEERING, REALLY. CRAVINGS COME FROM THE MIDBRAIN.
EXPLAIN.
WHEN A PREGNANT WOMAN CRAVES PICKLES, IT'S THE BODY'S WAY OF SIGNALING IT NEEDS CERTAIN NUTRIENTS.
WELL, SOMEHOW THESE CRAVINGS HAVE BEEN CONNECTED WITH THE PSYCHOLOGICAL CENTERS OF THE BRAIN, MARRYING PHYSICAL NEEDS WITH HER MENTAL STATE.
I'M DUMBING THIS DOWN FOR YOU, NATURALLY.
NATURALLY. ANY GOOD NEWS?
GLAD YOU ASKED.
IT DOESN'T REPLICATE WELL OUTSIDE OF ITS INITIAL HOST SO IT'S NOT CONTAGIOUS. WE SEEM TO HAVE DODGED AN EPIDEMIC.
BZZZZ BZZZZ BZZZZ
SPEAK.
TELL ME.
WE FOUND SOMETHING, SLIM. IT'S NOT PRETTY.

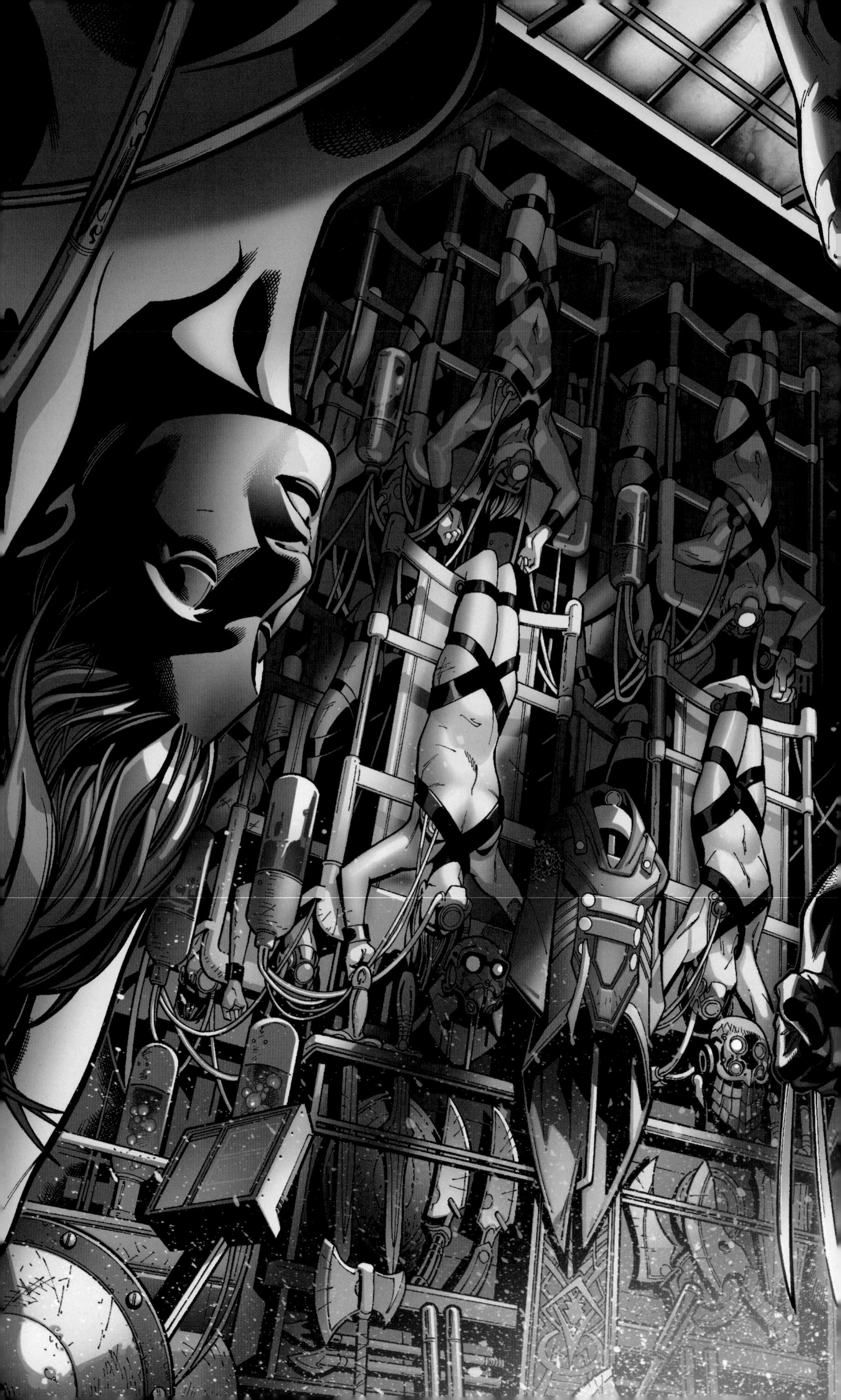

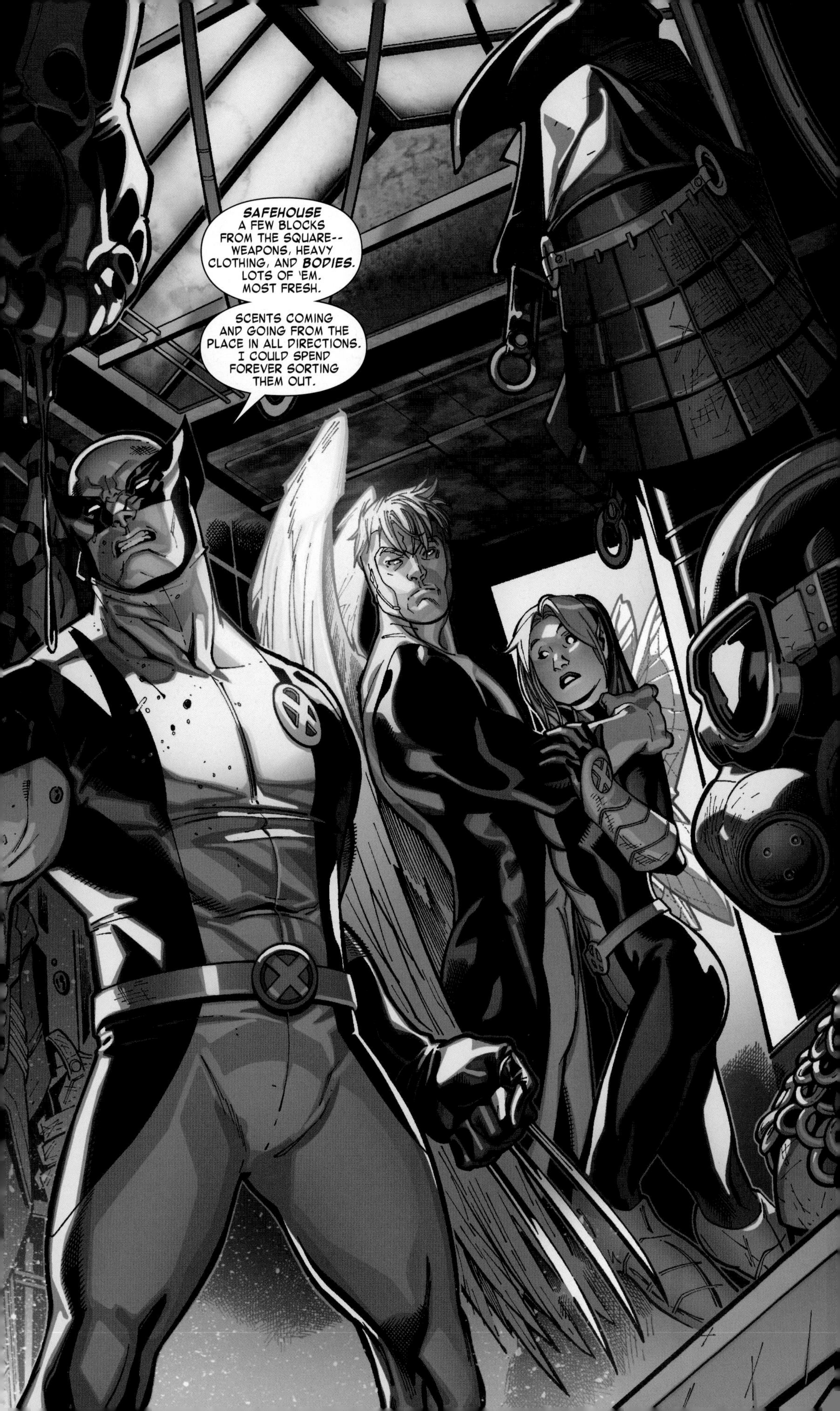
SAFEHOUSE A FEW BLOCKS FROM THE SQUARE-- WEAPONS, HEAVY CLOTHING, AND BODIES. LOTS OF 'EM. MOST FRESH.
SCENTS COMING AND GOING FROM THE PLACE IN ALL DIRECTIONS. I COULD SPEND FOREVER SORTING THEM OUT.

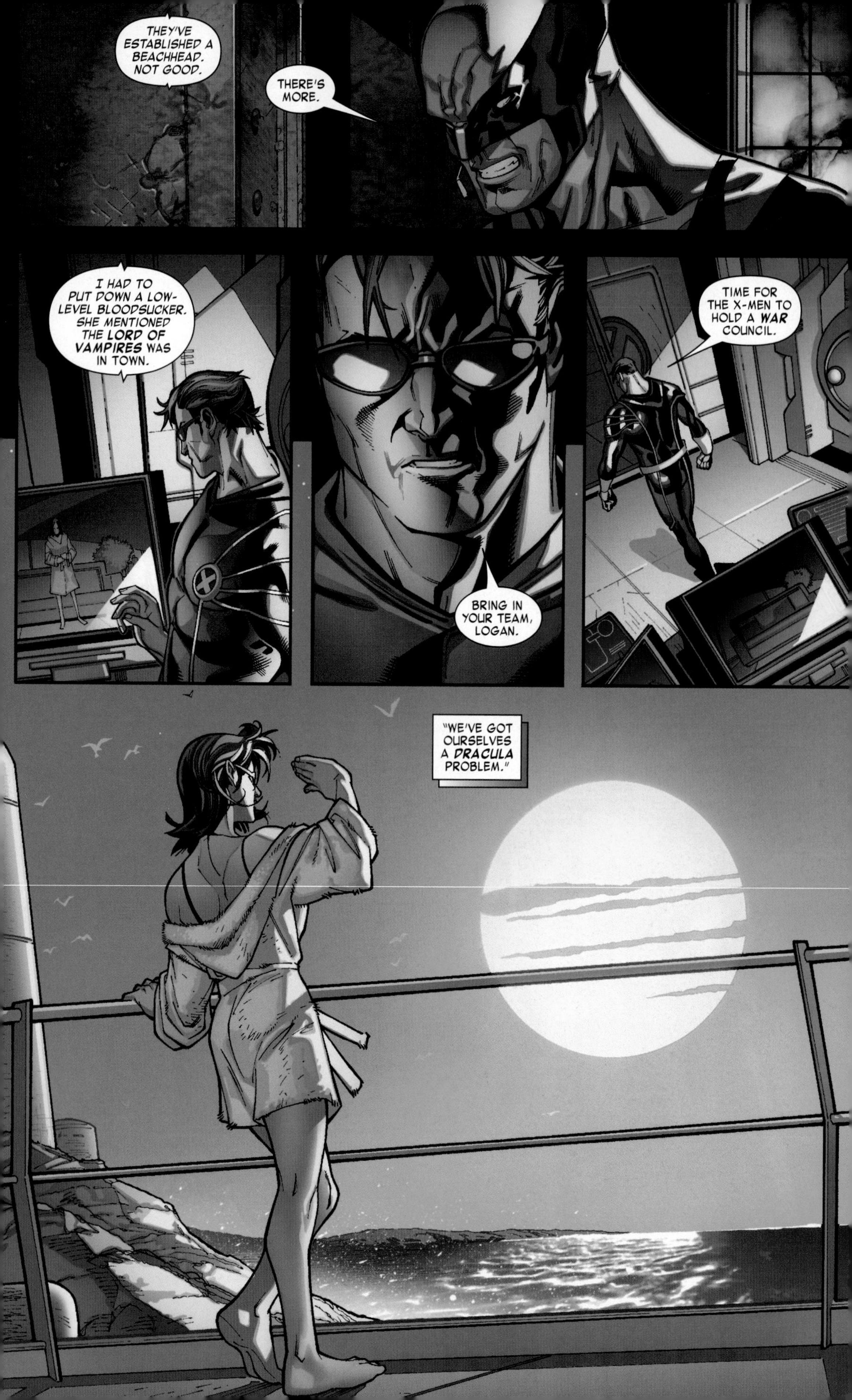
THEY'VE ESTABLISHED A BEACHHEAD. NOT GOOD.
THERE'S MORE.
I HAD TO PUT DOWN A LOW-LEVEL BLOODSUCKER. SHE MENTIONED THE LORD OF VAMPIRES WAS IN TOWN.
BRING IN YOUR TEAM, LOGAN.
TIME FOR THE X-MEN TO HOLD A WAR COUNCIL.
"WE'VE GOT OURSELVES A DRACULA PROBLEM."

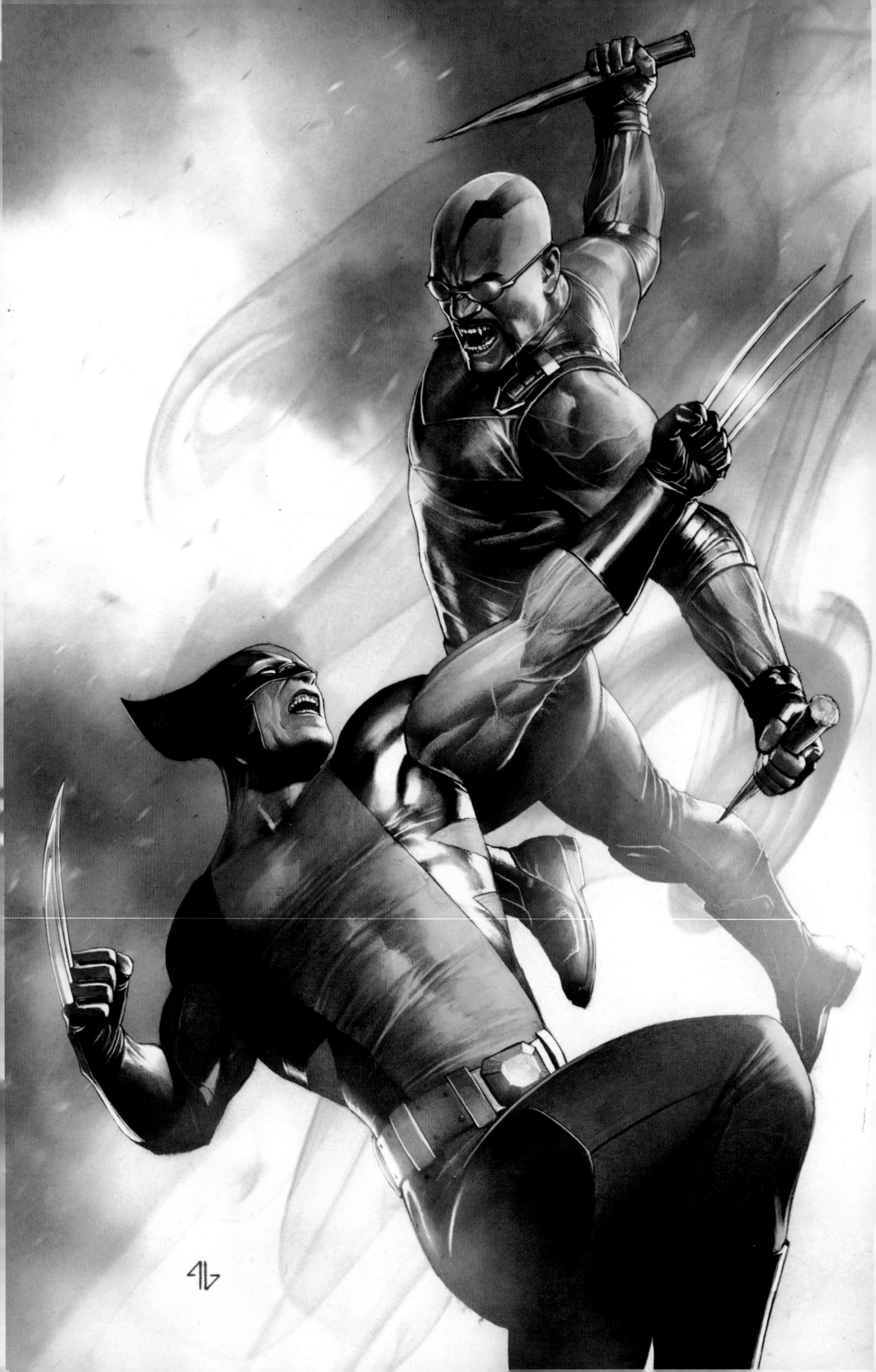

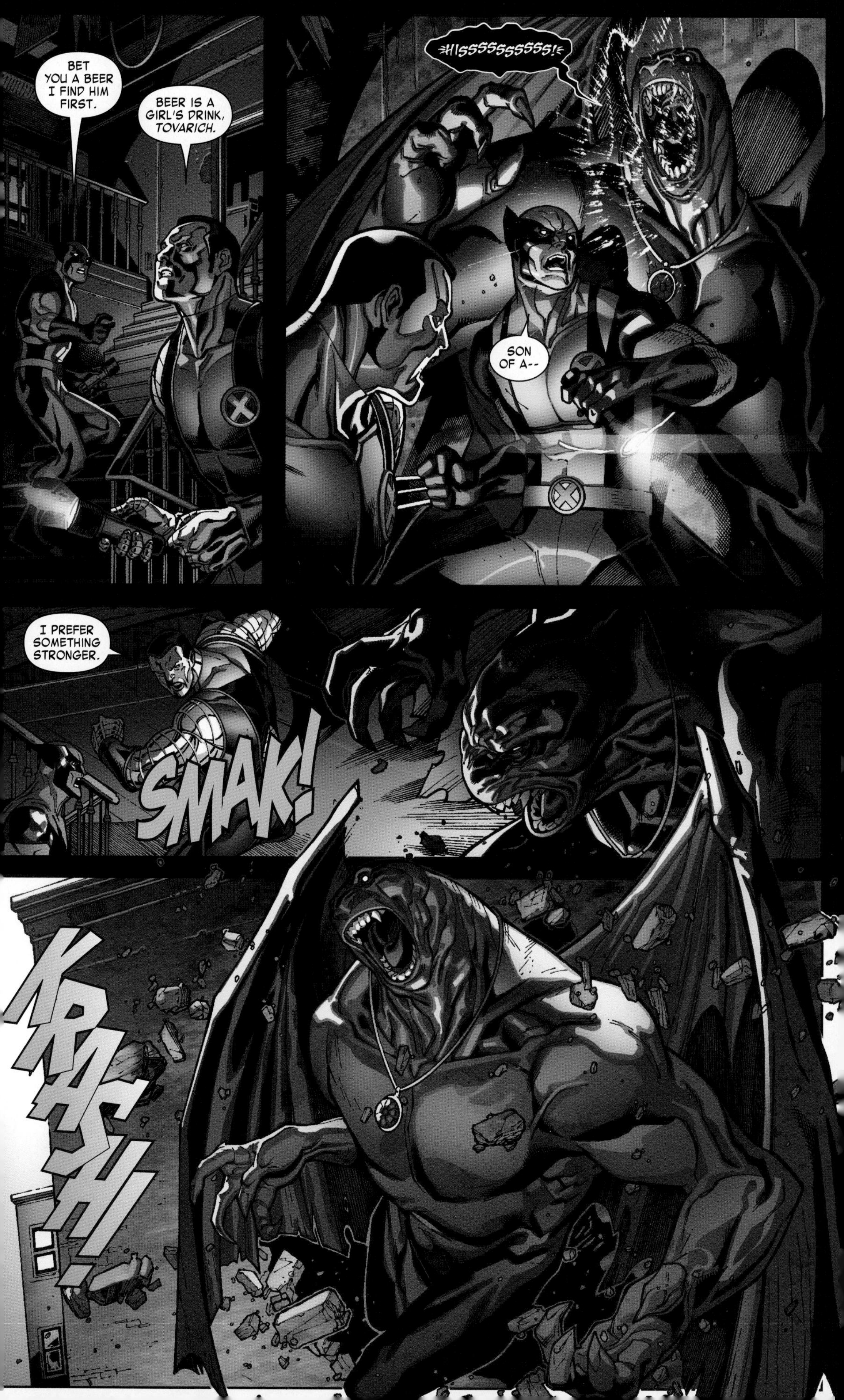
BET YOU A BEER I FIND HIM FIRST.
BEER IS A GIRL'S DRINK, TOVARICH.
HISSSSSSSSSS!
SON OF A--
I PREFER SOMETHING STRONGER.
SMAK!
KRASSH!

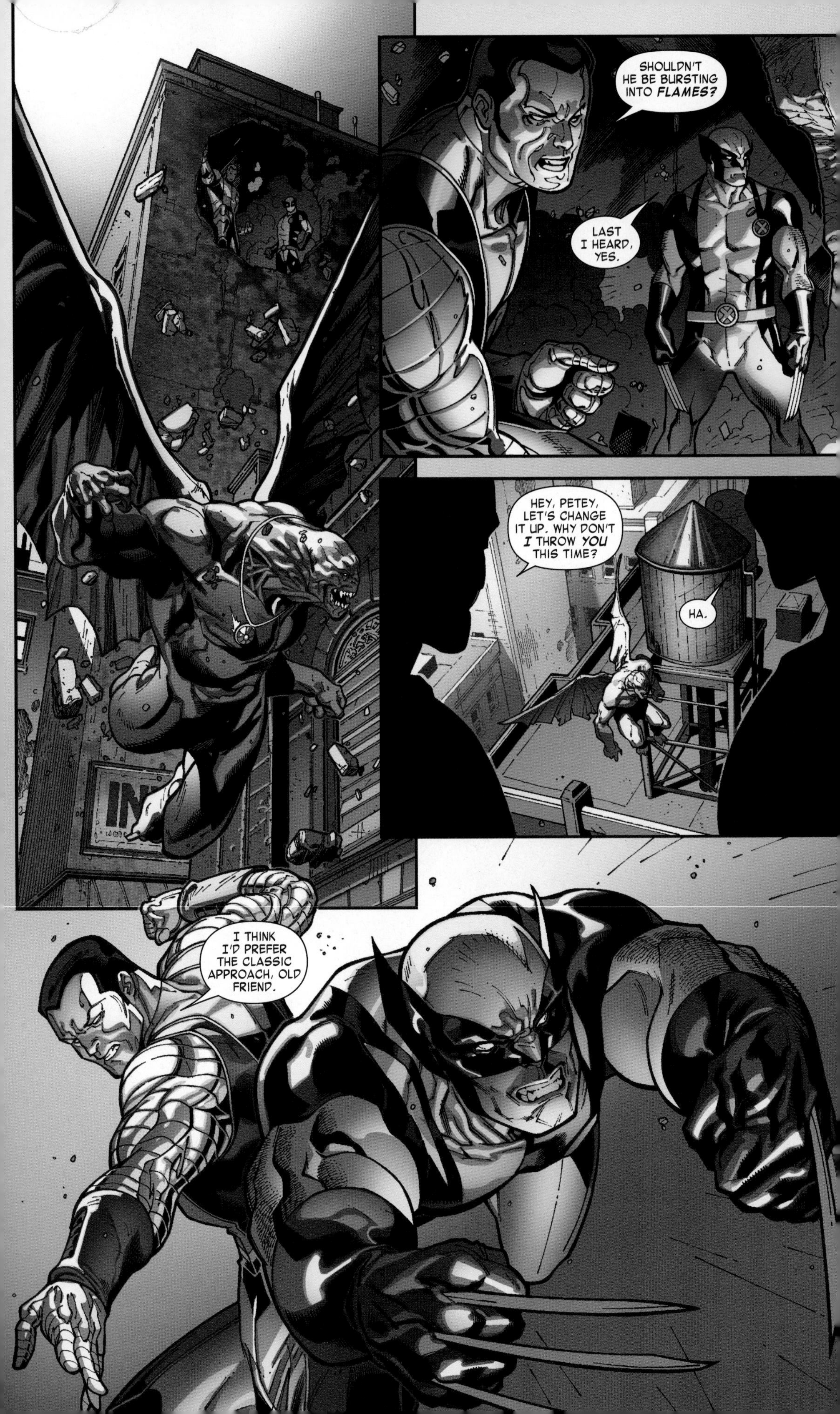
SHOULDN'T HE BE BURSTING INTO FLAMES?
LAST I HEARD, YES.
HEY, PETEY, LET'S CHANGE IT UP. WHY DON'T I THROW YOU THIS TIME?
HA.
I THINK I'D PREFER THE CLASSIC APPROACH, OLD FRIEND.

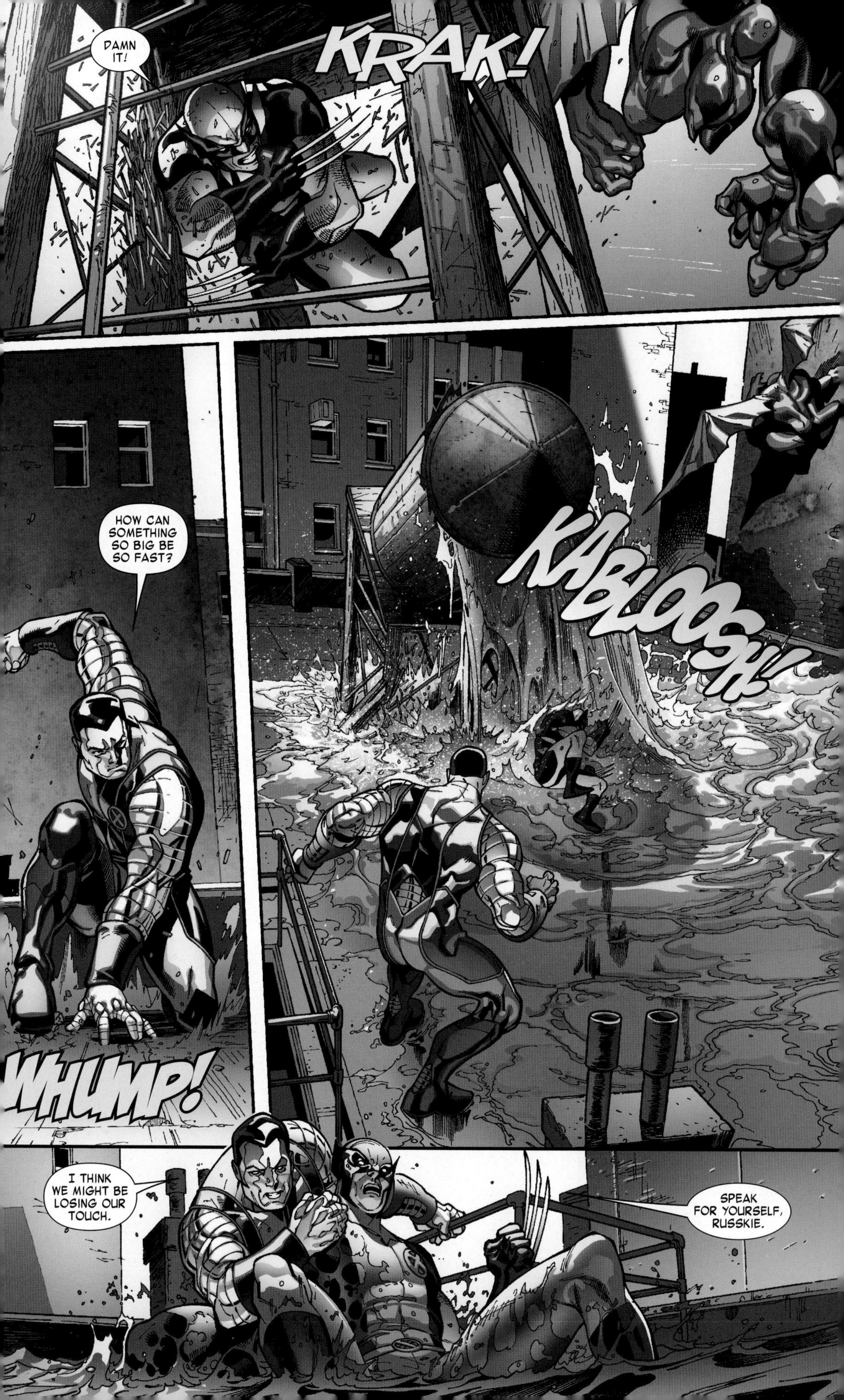
DAMN IT!
KRAK!
HOW CAN SOMETHING SO BIG BE SO FAST?
WHUMP!
KABLOOSH!
I THINK WE MIGHT BE LOSING OUR TOUCH.
SPEAK FOR YOURSELF, RUSSKIE.

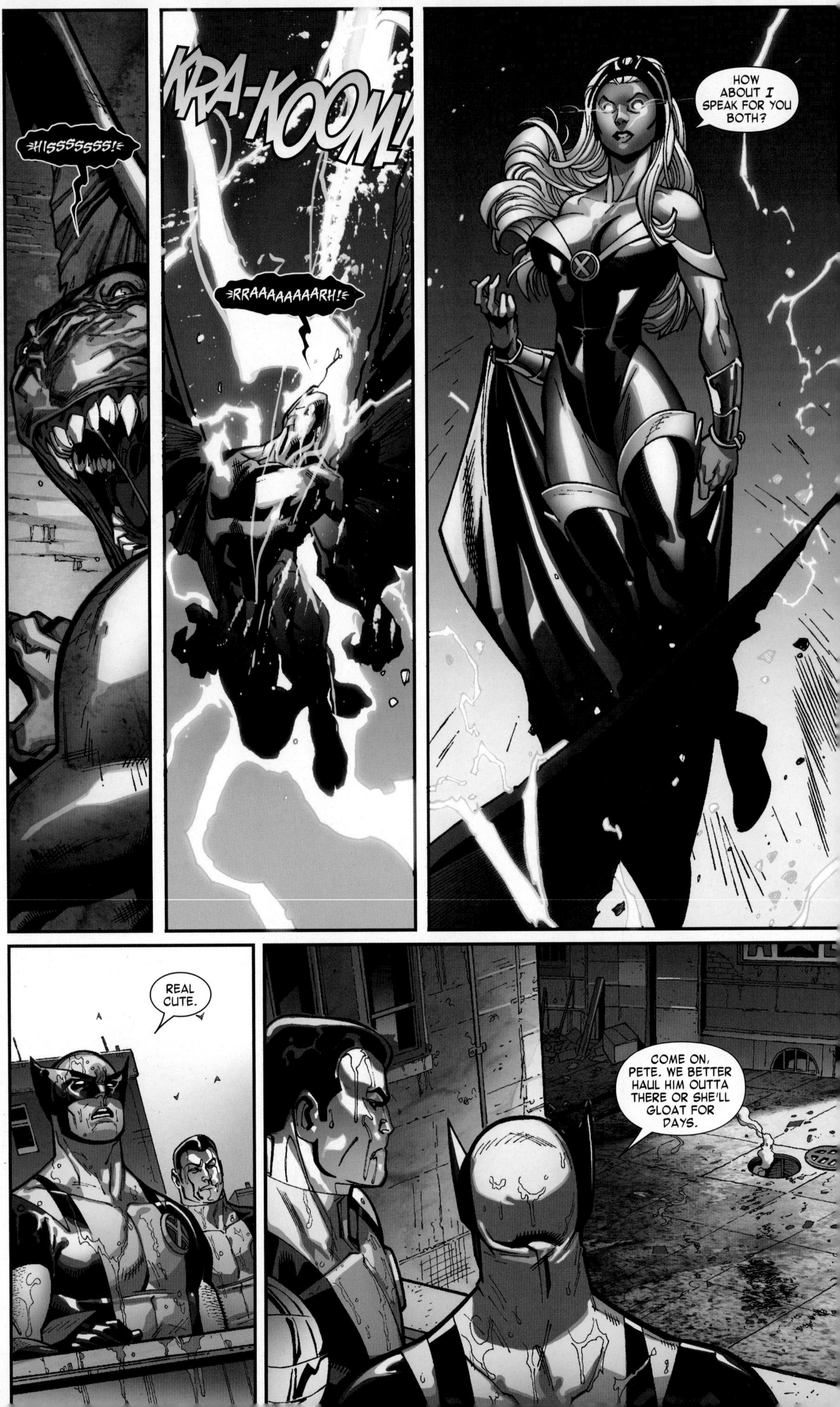
HISSSSSSS!
KRA-KOOM!!
RRAAAAAAAARH!
HOW ABOUT I SPEAK FOR YOU BOTH?
REAL CUTE.
COME ON, PETE. WE BETTER HAUL HIM OUTTA THERE OR SHE'LL GLOAT FOR DAYS.

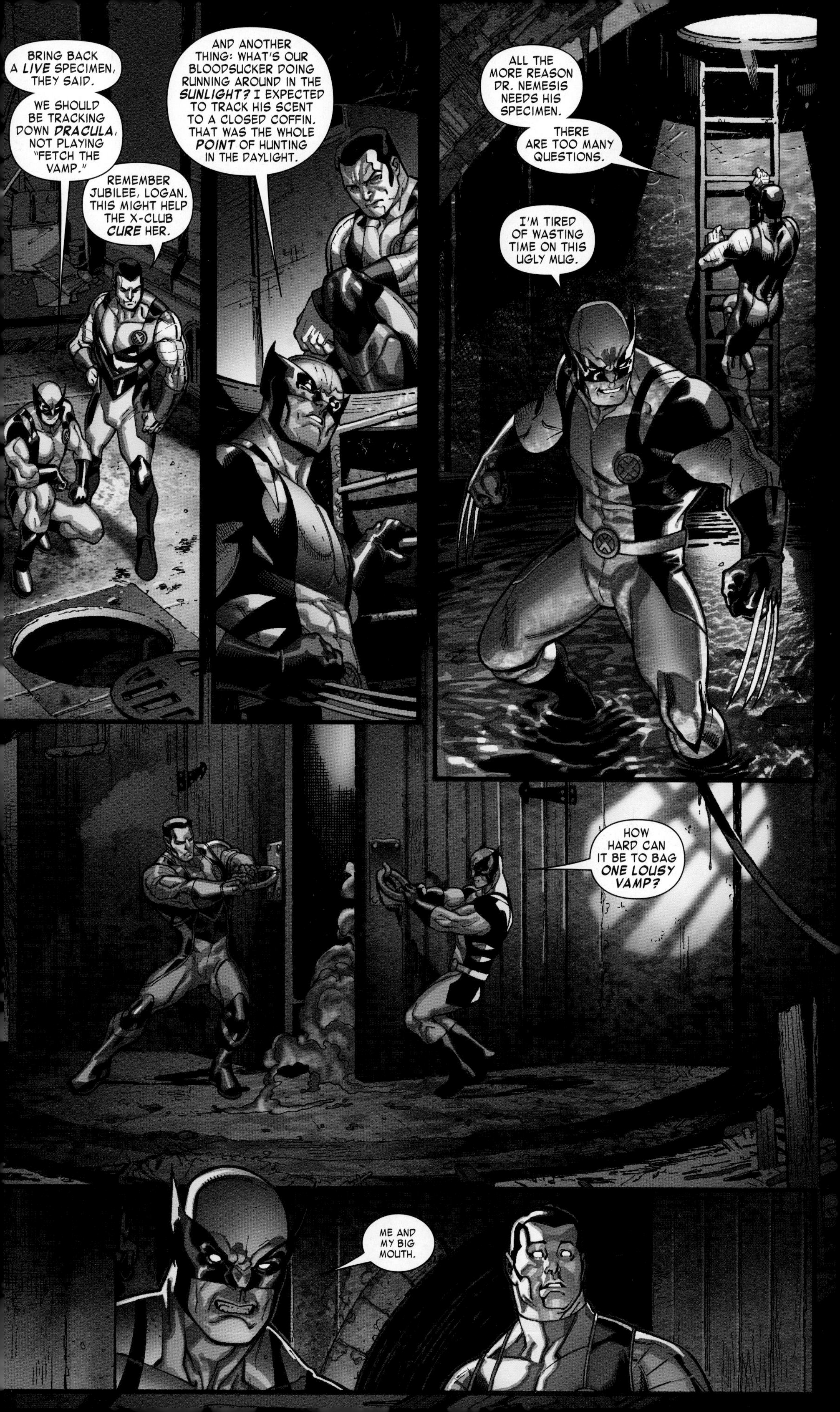
BRING BACK A *LIVE* SPECIMEN, THEY SAID.
WE SHOULD BE TRACKING DOWN *DRACULA*, NOT PLAYING "FETCH THE VAMP."
REMEMBER JUBILEE, LOGAN. THIS MIGHT HELP THE X-CLUB *CURE* HER.
AND ANOTHER THING: WHAT'S OUR BLOODSUCKER DOING RUNNING AROUND IN THE *SUNLIGHT?* I EXPECTED TO TRACK HIS SCENT TO A CLOSED COFFIN. THAT WAS THE WHOLE *POINT* OF HUNTING IN THE DAYLIGHT.
ALL THE MORE REASON DR. NEMESIS NEEDS HIS SPECIMEN.
THERE ARE TOO MANY QUESTIONS.
I'M TIRED OF WASTING TIME ON THIS UGLY MUG.
HOW HARD CAN IT BE TO BAG *ONE LOUSY VAMP?*
ME AND MY BIG MOUTH.

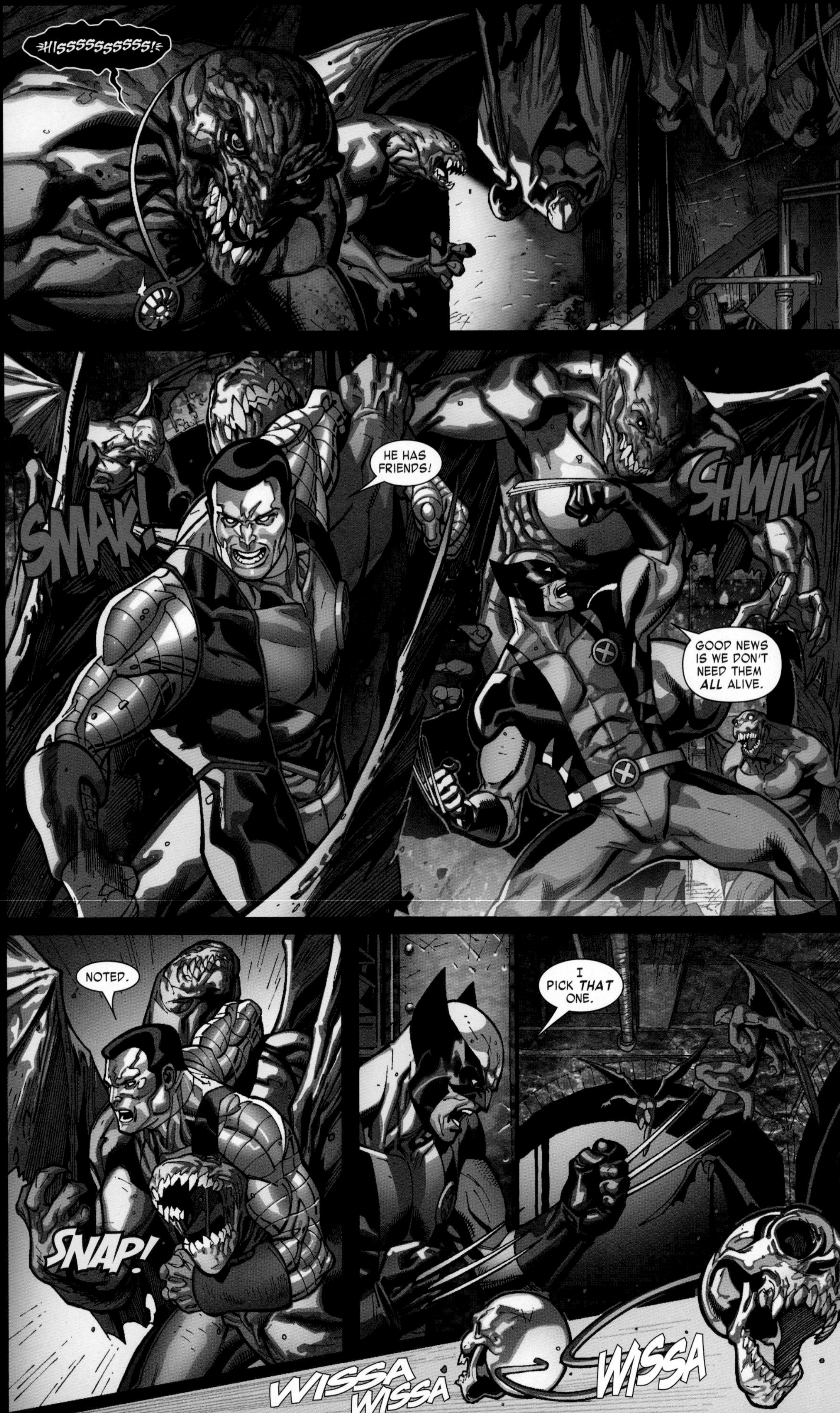
HISSSSSSSSSS!
HE HAS FRIENDS!
SMAK!
SHWIK!
GOOD NEWS IS WE DON'T NEED THEM ALL ALIVE.
NOTED.
SNAP!
I PICK THAT ONE.
WISSA
WISSA
WISSA

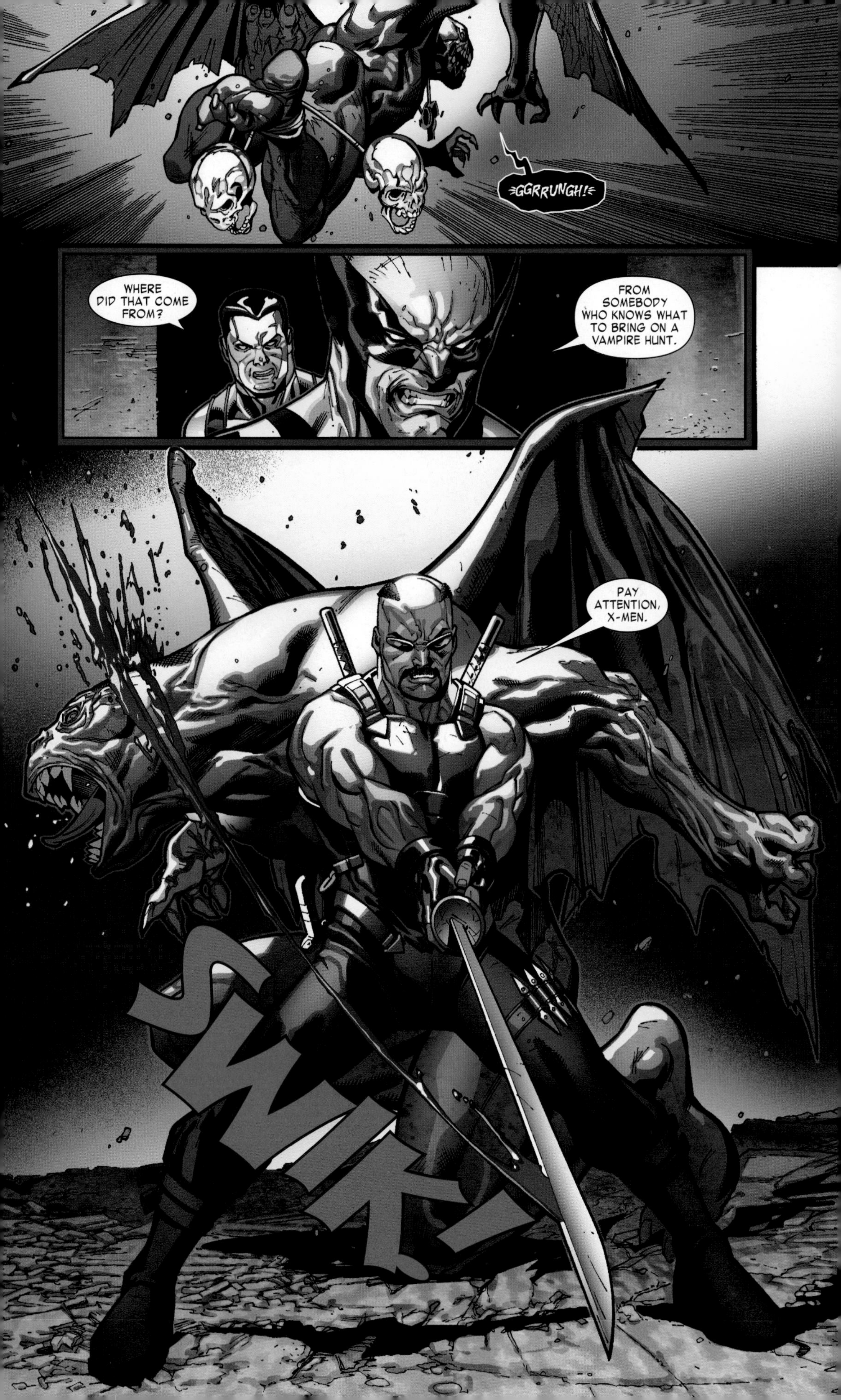
GGRRUNGH!
WHERE DID THAT COME FROM?
FROM SOMEBODY WHO KNOWS WHAT TO BRING ON A VAMPIRE HUNT.
PAY ATTENTION, X-MEN.
SWIK!

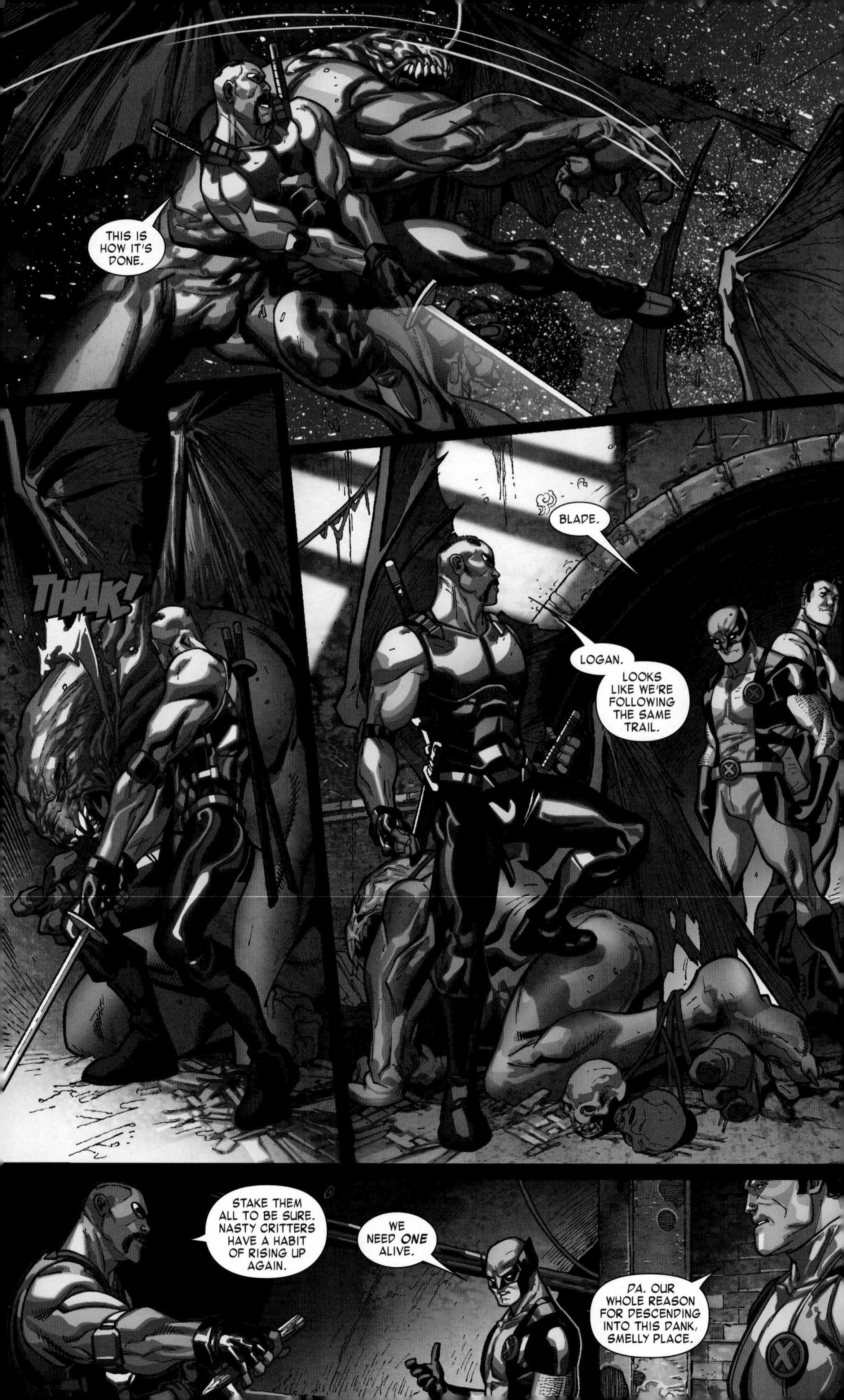
THIS IS HOW IT'S DONE.
THAK!
BLADE.
LOGAN.
LOOKS LIKE WE'RE FOLLOWING THE SAME TRAIL.
STAKE THEM ALL TO BE SURE. NASTY CRITTERS HAVE A HABIT OF RISING UP AGAIN.
WE NEED ONE ALIVE.
DA. OUR WHOLE REASON FOR DESCENDING INTO THIS DANK, SMELLY PLACE.

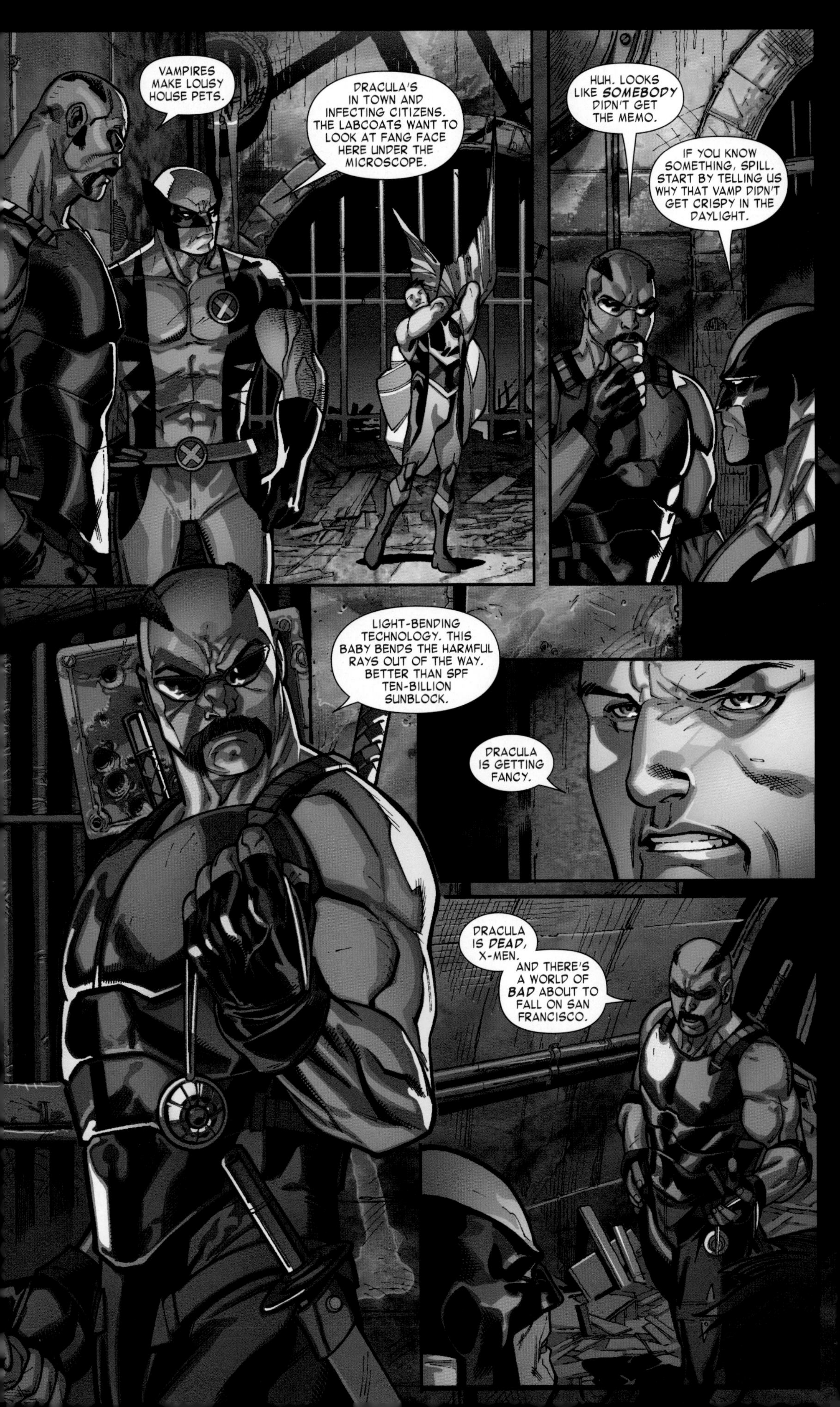

VAMPIRES MAKE LOUSY HOUSE PETS.
DRACULA'S IN TOWN AND INFECTING CITIZENS. THE LABCOATS WANT TO LOOK AT FANG FACE HERE UNDER THE MICROSCOPE.
HUH. LOOKS LIKE *SOMEBODY* DIDN'T GET THE MEMO.
IF YOU KNOW SOMETHING, SPILL. START BY TELLING US WHY THAT VAMP DIDN'T GET CRISPY IN THE DAYLIGHT.
LIGHT-BENDING TECHNOLOGY. THIS BABY BENDS THE HARMFUL RAYS OUT OF THE WAY. BETTER THAN SPF TEN-BILLION SUNBLOCK.
DRACULA IS GETTING FANCY.
DRACULA IS *DEAD*, X-MEN.
AND THERE'S A WORLD OF *BAD* ABOUT TO FALL ON SAN FRANCISCO.

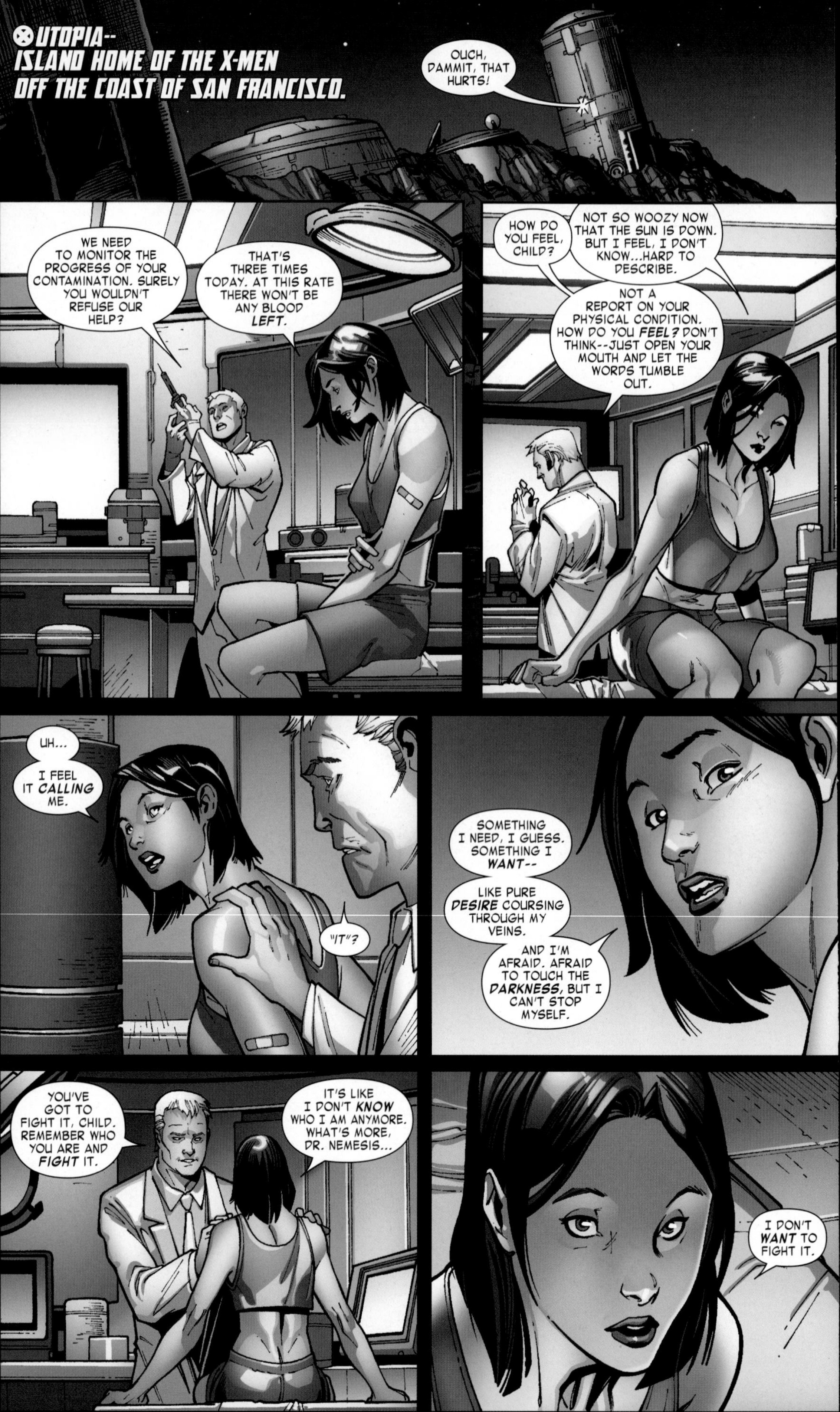
UTOPIA--
ISLAND HOME OF THE X-MEN
OFF THE COAST OF SAN FRANCISCO.
OUCH, DAMMIT, THAT HURTS!
WE NEED TO MONITOR THE PROGRESS OF YOUR CONTAMINATION. SURELY YOU WOULDN'T REFUSE OUR HELP?
THAT'S THREE TIMES TODAY. AT THIS RATE THERE WON'T BE ANY BLOOD LEFT.
HOW DO YOU FEEL, CHILD?
NOT SO WOOZY NOW THAT THE SUN IS DOWN. BUT I FEEL, I DON'T KNOW...HARD TO DESCRIBE.
NOT A REPORT ON YOUR PHYSICAL CONDITION. HOW DO YOU FEEL? DON'T THINK--JUST OPEN YOUR MOUTH AND LET THE WORDS TUMBLE OUT.
UH...
I FEEL IT CALLING ME.
"IT"?
SOMETHING I NEED, I GUESS. SOMETHING I WANT--
LIKE PURE DESIRE COURSING THROUGH MY VEINS.
AND I'M AFRAID. AFRAID TO TOUCH THE DARKNESS, BUT I CAN'T STOP MYSELF.
YOU'VE GOT TO FIGHT IT, CHILD. REMEMBER WHO YOU ARE AND FIGHT IT.
IT'S LIKE I DON'T KNOW WHO I AM ANYMORE. WHAT'S MORE, DR. NEMESIS...
I DON'T WANT TO FIGHT IT.

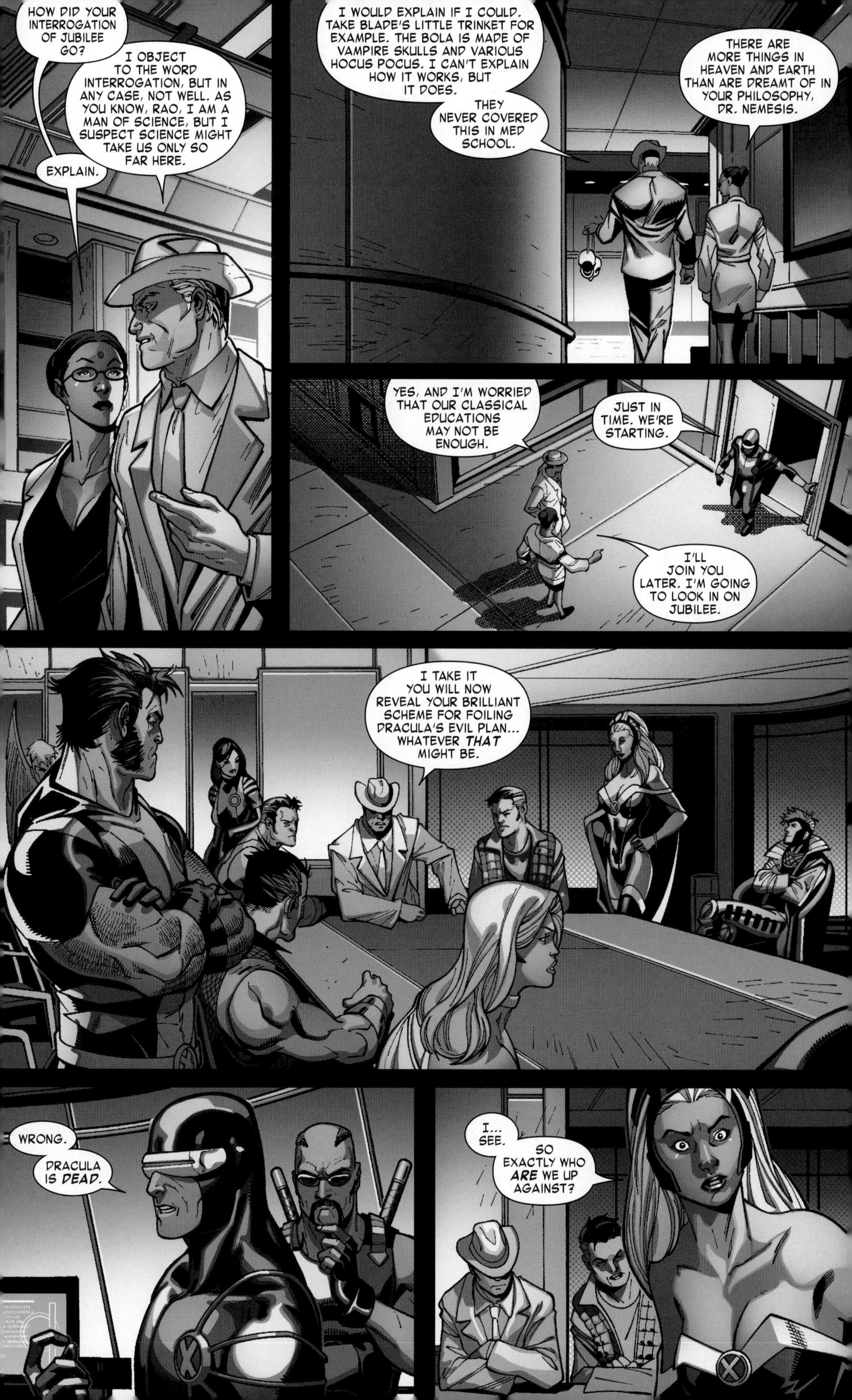
HOW DID YOUR INTERROGATION OF JUBILEE GO?
I OBJECT TO THE WORD INTERROGATION, BUT IN ANY CASE, NOT WELL. AS YOU KNOW, RAO, I AM A MAN OF SCIENCE, BUT I SUSPECT SCIENCE MIGHT TAKE US ONLY SO FAR HERE.
EXPLAIN.
I WOULD EXPLAIN IF I COULD. TAKE BLADE'S LITTLE TRINKET FOR EXAMPLE. THE BOLA IS MADE OF VAMPIRE SKULLS AND VARIOUS HOCUS POCUS. I CAN'T EXPLAIN HOW IT WORKS, BUT IT DOES.
THEY NEVER COVERED THIS IN MED SCHOOL.
THERE ARE MORE THINGS IN HEAVEN AND EARTH THAN ARE DREAMT OF IN YOUR PHILOSOPHY, DR. NEMESIS.
YES, AND I'M WORRIED THAT OUR CLASSICAL EDUCATIONS MAY NOT BE ENOUGH.
JUST IN TIME. WE'RE STARTING.
I'LL JOIN YOU LATER. I'M GOING TO LOOK IN ON JUBILEE.
I TAKE IT YOU WILL NOW REVEAL YOUR BRILLIANT SCHEME FOR FOILING DRACULA'S EVIL PLAN... WHATEVER *THAT* MIGHT BE.
WRONG.
DRACULA IS *DEAD*.
I... SEE.
SO EXACTLY WHO *ARE* WE UP AGAINST?

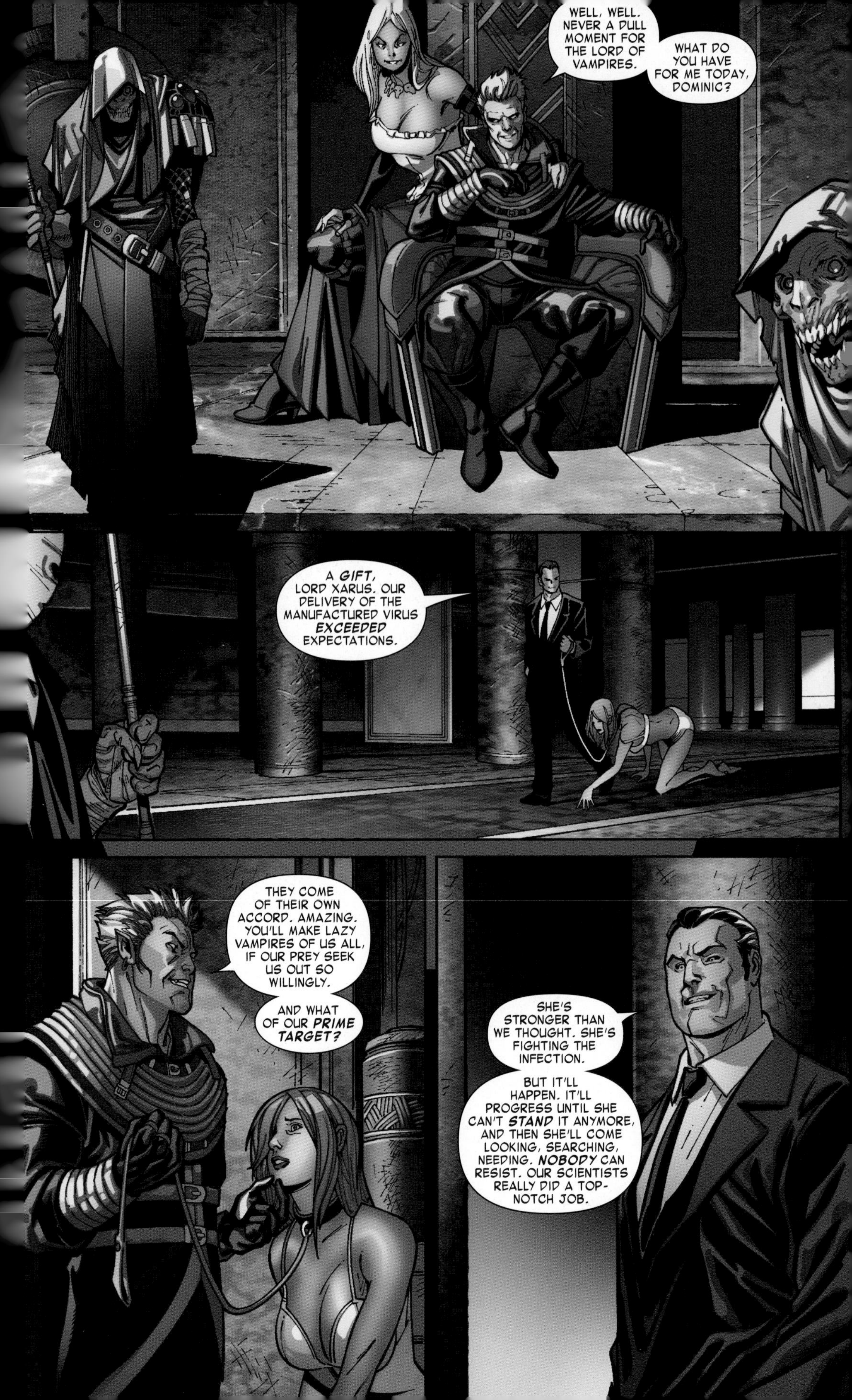
WELL, WELL. NEVER A DULL MOMENT FOR THE LORD OF VAMPIRES.
WHAT DO YOU HAVE FOR ME TODAY, DOMINIC?
A *GIFT*, LORD XARUS. OUR DELIVERY OF THE MANUFACTURED VIRUS *EXCEEDED* EXPECTATIONS.
THEY COME OF THEIR OWN ACCORD. AMAZING. YOU'LL MAKE LAZY VAMPIRES OF US ALL, IF OUR PREY SEEK US OUT SO WILLINGLY.
AND WHAT OF OUR *PRIME TARGET?*
SHE'S STRONGER THAN WE THOUGHT. SHE'S FIGHTING THE INFECTION.
BUT IT'LL HAPPEN. IT'LL PROGRESS UNTIL SHE CAN'T *STAND* IT ANYMORE, AND THEN SHE'LL COME LOOKING, SEARCHING, NEEDING. *NOBODY* CAN RESIST. OUR SCIENTISTS REALLY DID A TOP-NOTCH JOB.

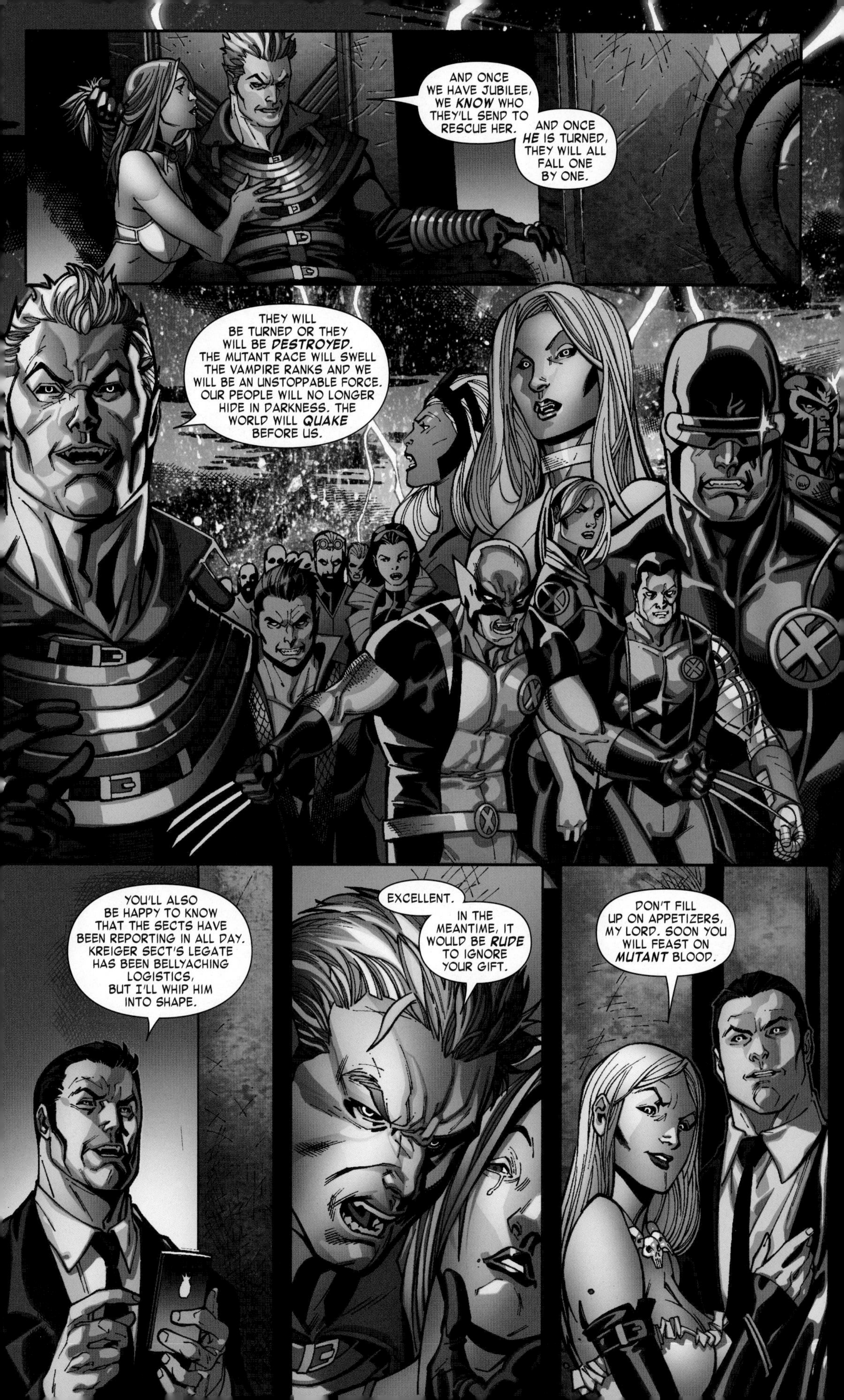
AND ONCE WE HAVE JUBILEE, WE KNOW WHO THEY'LL SEND TO RESCUE HER.
AND ONCE HE IS TURNED, THEY WILL ALL FALL ONE BY ONE.
THEY WILL BE TURNED OR THEY WILL BE DESTROYED. THE MUTANT RACE WILL SWELL THE VAMPIRE RANKS AND WE WILL BE AN UNSTOPPABLE FORCE. OUR PEOPLE WILL NO LONGER HIDE IN DARKNESS. THE WORLD WILL QUAKE BEFORE US.
YOU'LL ALSO BE HAPPY TO KNOW THAT THE SECTS HAVE BEEN REPORTING IN ALL DAY. KREIGER SECT'S LEGATE HAS BEEN BELLYACHING LOGISTICS, BUT I'LL WHIP HIM INTO SHAPE.
EXCELLENT.
IN THE MEANTIME, IT WOULD BE RUDE TO IGNORE YOUR GIFT.
DON'T FILL UP ON APPETIZERS, MY LORD. SOON YOU WILL FEAST ON MUTANT BLOOD.

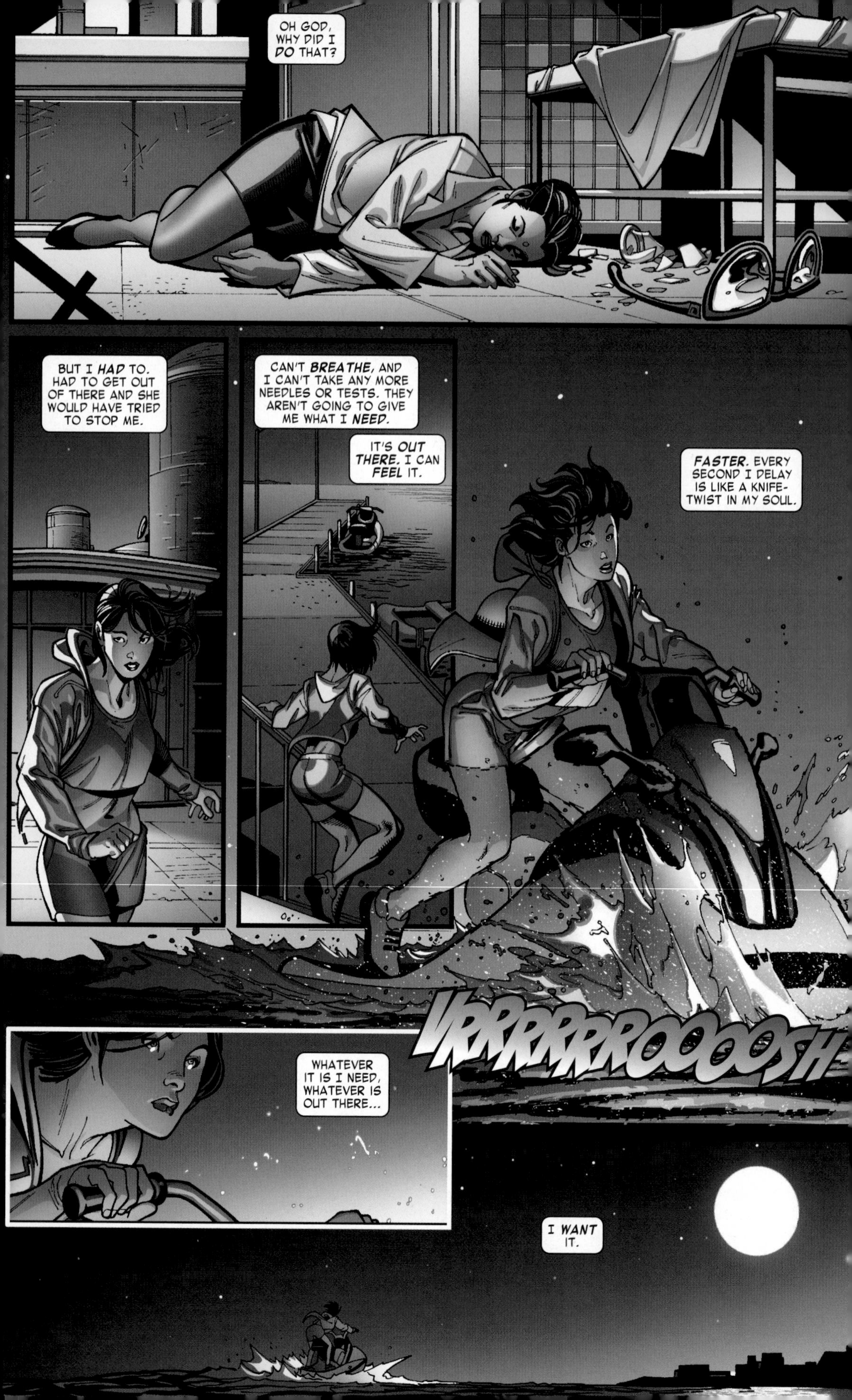
OH GOD, WHY DID I *DO* THAT?
BUT I *HAD* TO. HAD TO GET OUT OF THERE AND SHE WOULD HAVE TRIED TO STOP ME.
CAN'T *BREATHE*, AND I CAN'T TAKE ANY MORE NEEDLES OR TESTS. THEY AREN'T GOING TO GIVE ME WHAT I *NEED*.
IT'S *OUT THERE*. I CAN *FEEL* IT.
FASTER. EVERY SECOND I DELAY IS LIKE A KNIFE-TWIST IN MY SOUL.
VRRRRRRROOOOOSH
WHATEVER IT IS I NEED, WHATEVER IS OUT THERE...
I *WANT* IT.

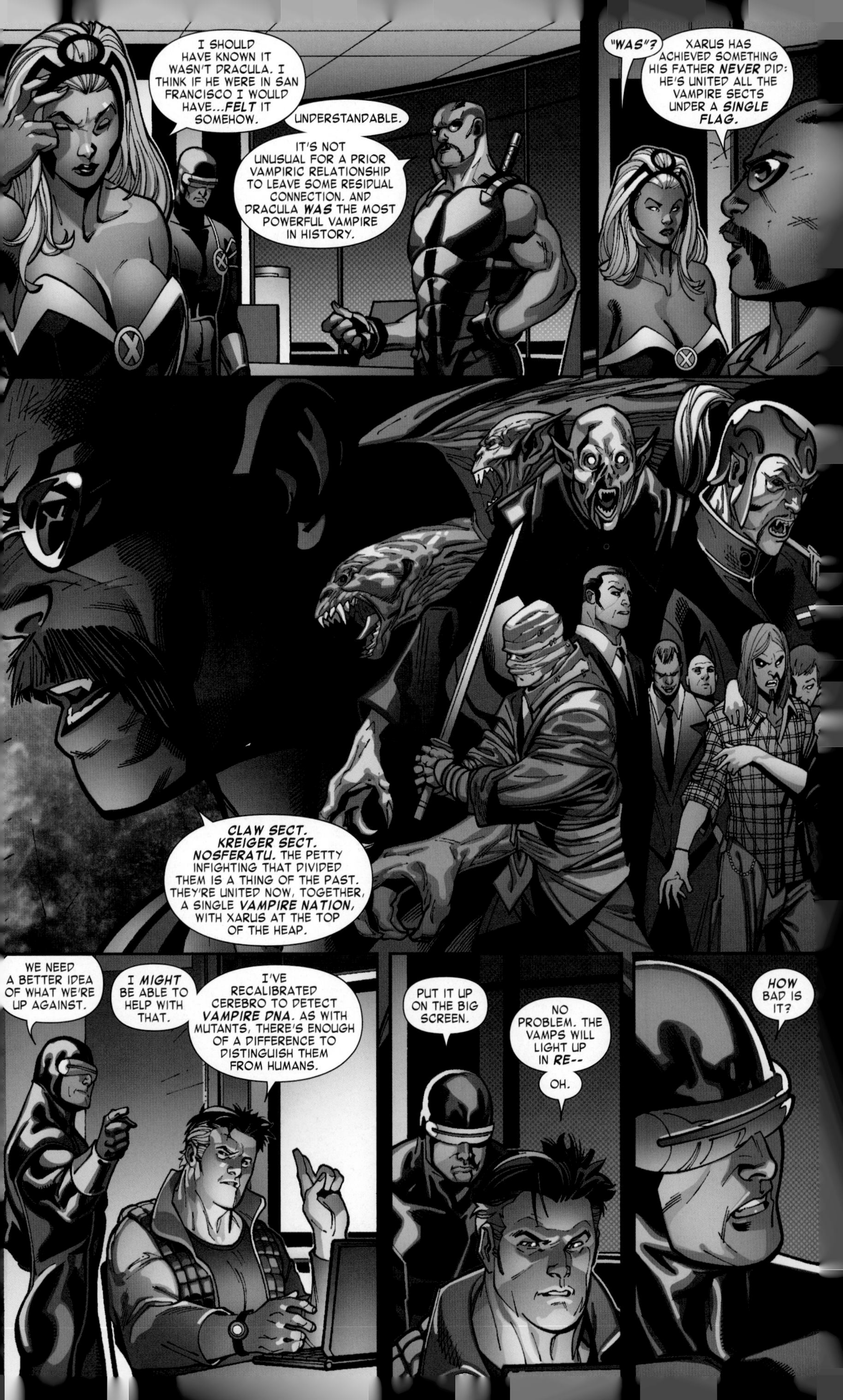

I SHOULD HAVE KNOWN IT WASN'T DRACULA. I THINK IF HE WERE IN SAN FRANCISCO I WOULD HAVE...FELT IT SOMEHOW.
UNDERSTANDABLE.
IT'S NOT UNUSUAL FOR A PRIOR VAMPIRIC RELATIONSHIP TO LEAVE SOME RESIDUAL CONNECTION. AND DRACULA WAS THE MOST POWERFUL VAMPIRE IN HISTORY.
"WAS"?
XARUS HAS ACHIEVED SOMETHING HIS FATHER NEVER DID: HE'S UNITED ALL THE VAMPIRE SECTS UNDER A SINGLE FLAG.
CLAW SECT. KREIGER SECT. NOSFERATU. THE PETTY INFIGHTING THAT DIVIDED THEM IS A THING OF THE PAST. THEY'RE UNITED NOW, TOGETHER, A SINGLE VAMPIRE NATION, WITH XARUS AT THE TOP OF THE HEAP.
WE NEED A BETTER IDEA OF WHAT WE'RE UP AGAINST.
I MIGHT BE ABLE TO HELP WITH THAT.
I'VE RECALIBRATED CEREBRO TO DETECT VAMPIRE DNA. AS WITH MUTANTS, THERE'S ENOUGH OF A DIFFERENCE TO DISTINGUISH THEM FROM HUMANS.
PUT IT UP ON THE BIG SCREEN.
NO PROBLEM. THE VAMPS WILL LIGHT UP IN RE--
OH.
HOW BAD IS IT?

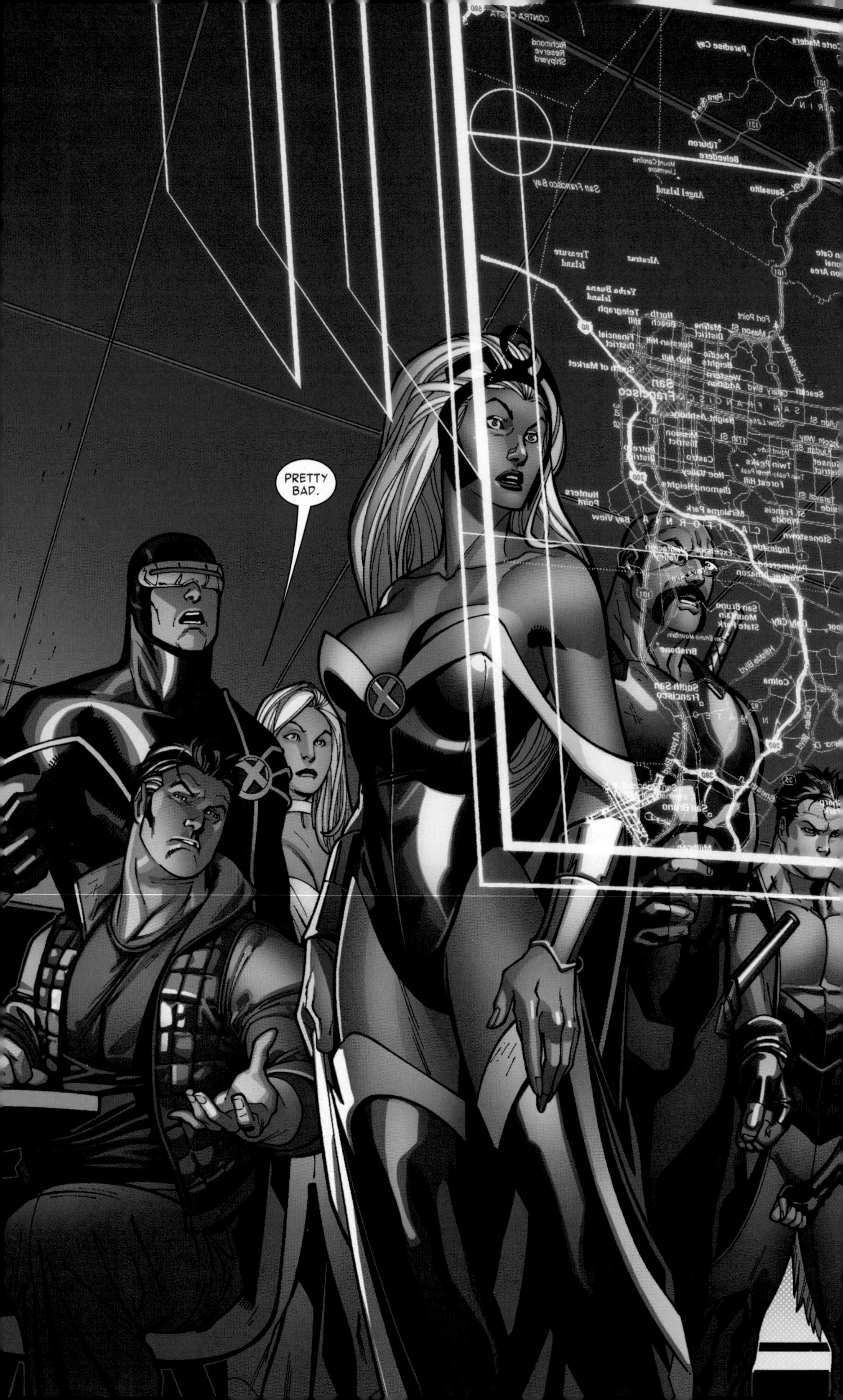
PRETTY BAD.

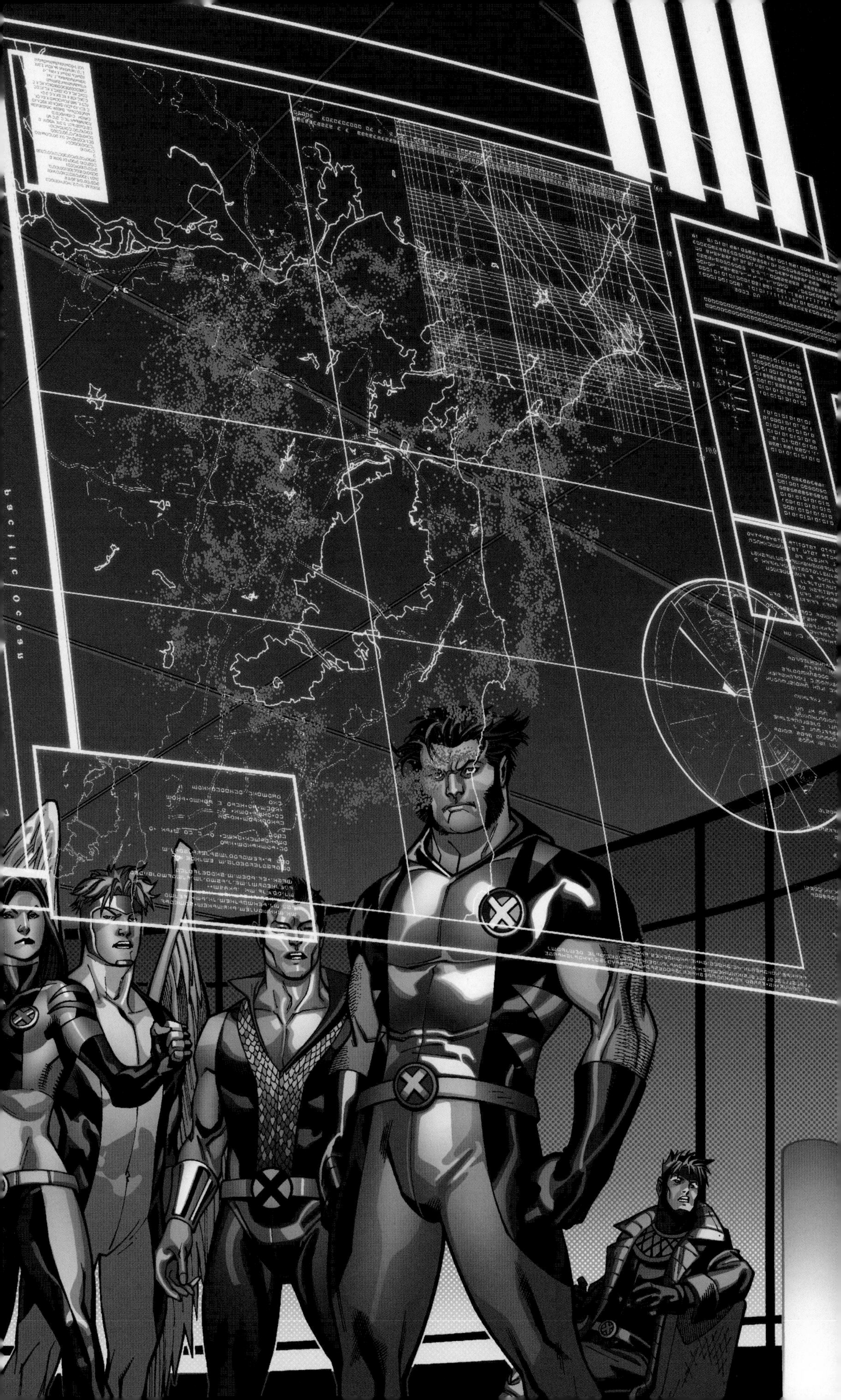

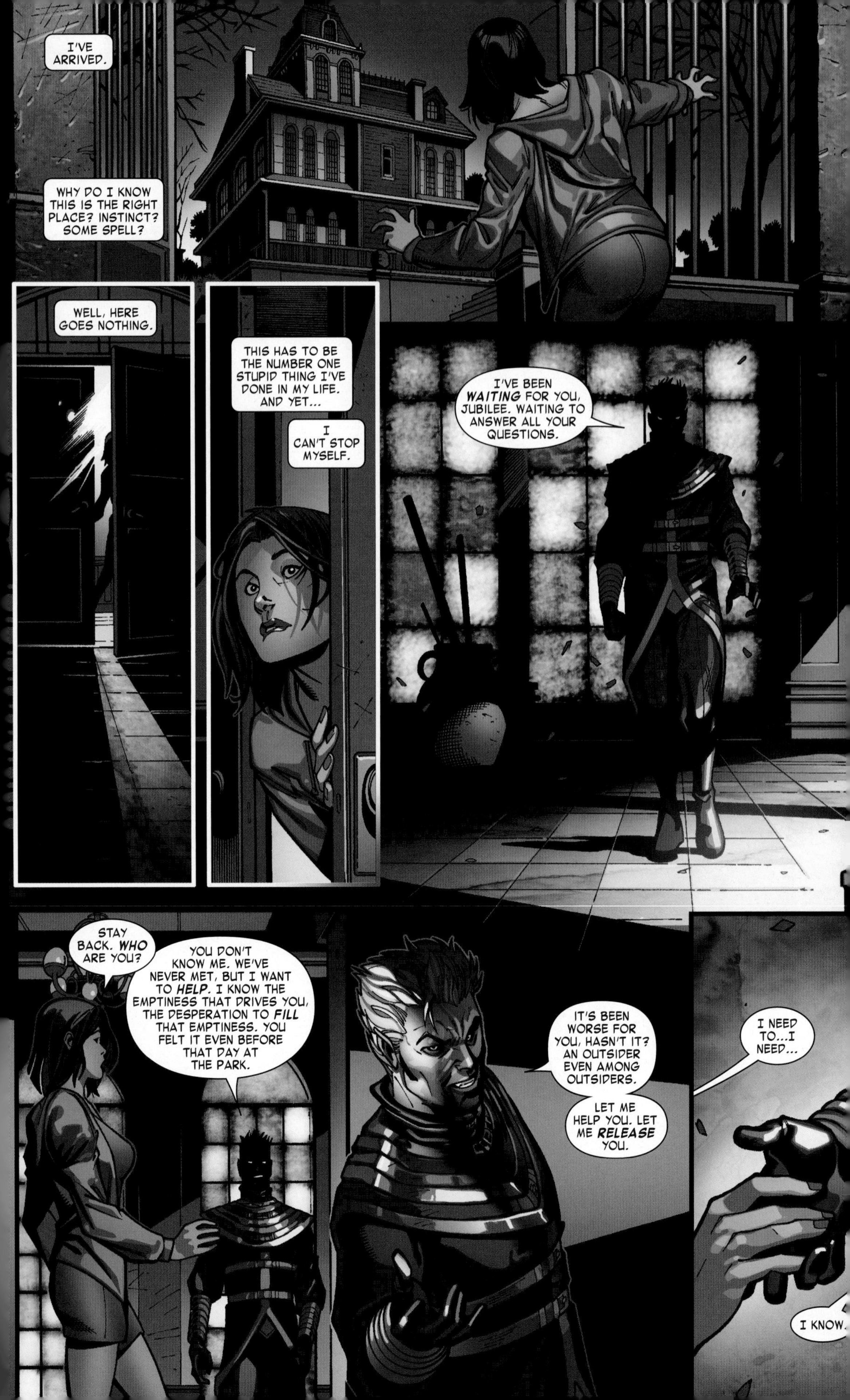
I'VE ARRIVED.
WHY DO I KNOW THIS IS THE RIGHT PLACE? INSTINCT? SOME SPELL?
WELL, HERE GOES NOTHING.
THIS HAS TO BE THE NUMBER ONE STUPID THING I'VE DONE IN MY LIFE. AND YET...
I CAN'T STOP MYSELF.
I'VE BEEN WAITING FOR YOU, JUBILEE. WAITING TO ANSWER ALL YOUR QUESTIONS.
STAY BACK. WHO ARE YOU?
YOU DON'T KNOW ME. WE'VE NEVER MET, BUT I WANT TO HELP. I KNOW THE EMPTINESS THAT DRIVES YOU, THE DESPERATION TO FILL THAT EMPTINESS. YOU FELT IT EVEN BEFORE THAT DAY AT THE PARK.
IT'S BEEN WORSE FOR YOU, HASN'T IT? AN OUTSIDER EVEN AMONG OUTSIDERS.
LET ME HELP YOU. LET ME RELEASE YOU.
I NEED TO...I NEED...
I KNOW.

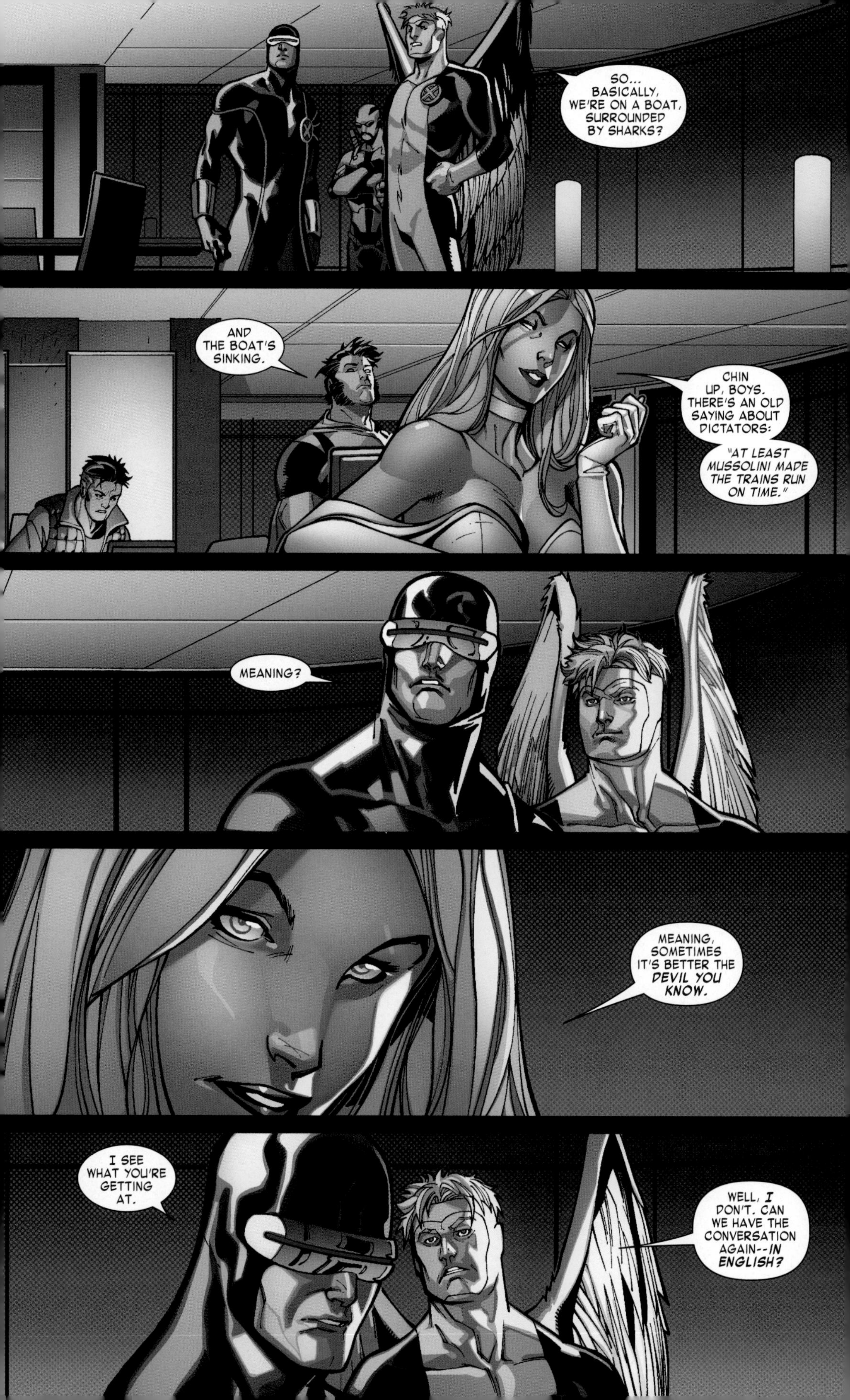
SO... BASICALLY, WE'RE ON A BOAT, SURROUNDED BY SHARKS?
AND THE BOAT'S SINKING.
CHIN UP, BOYS. THERE'S AN OLD SAYING ABOUT DICTATORS:
"AT LEAST MUSSOLINI MADE THE TRAINS RUN ON TIME."
MEANING?
MEANING, SOMETIMES IT'S BETTER THE DEVIL YOU KNOW.
I SEE WHAT YOU'RE GETTING AT.
WELL, I DON'T. CAN WE HAVE THE CONVERSATION AGAIN--IN ENGLISH?

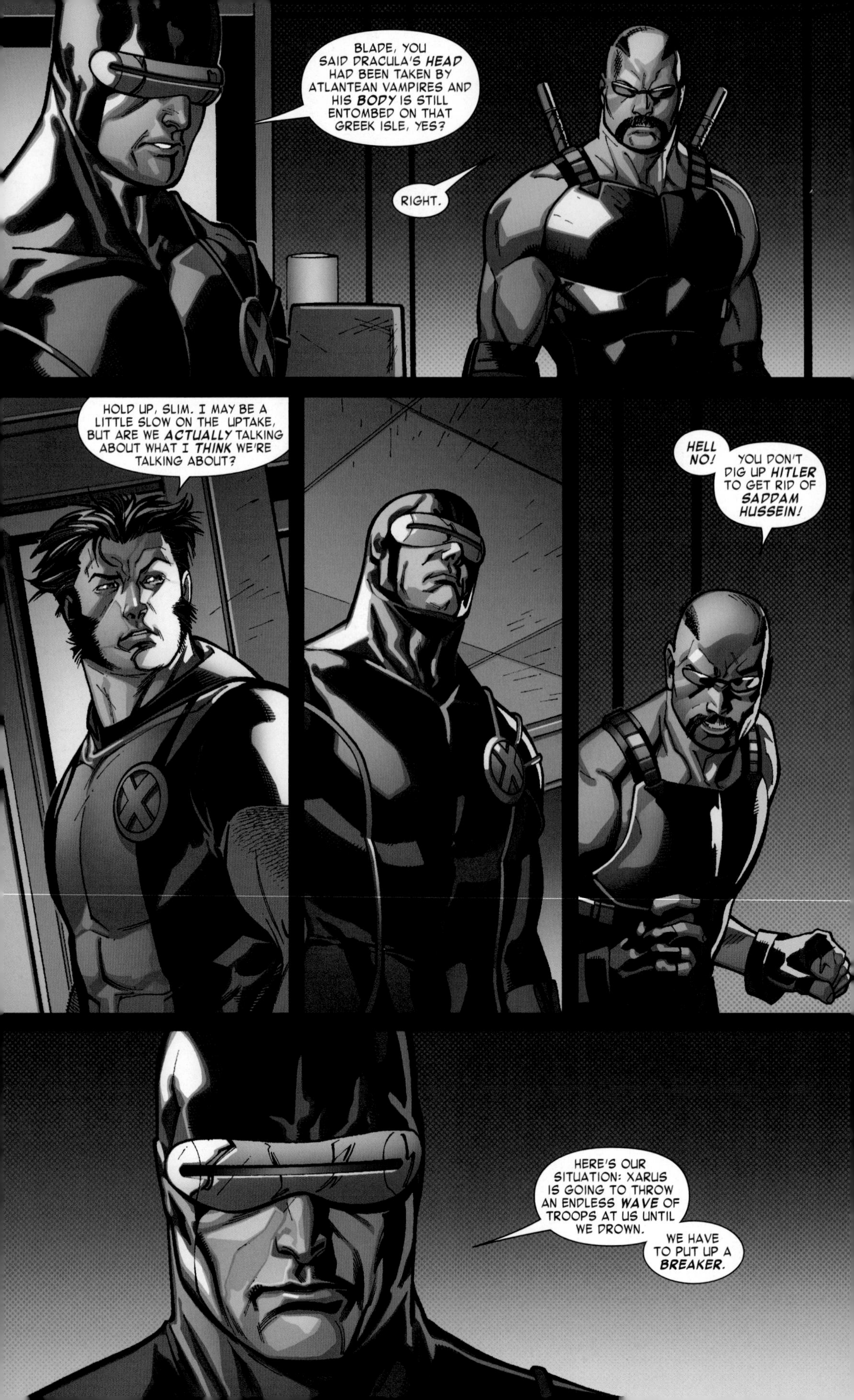

BLADE, YOU SAID DRACULA'S HEAD HAD BEEN TAKEN BY ATLANTEAN VAMPIRES AND HIS BODY IS STILL ENTOMBED ON THAT GREEK ISLE, YES?
RIGHT.
HOLD UP, SLIM. I MAY BE A LITTLE SLOW ON THE UPTAKE, BUT ARE WE ACTUALLY TALKING ABOUT WHAT I THINK WE'RE TALKING ABOUT?
HELL NO!
YOU DON'T DIG UP HITLER TO GET RID OF SADDAM HUSSEIN!
HERE'S OUR SITUATION: XARUS IS GOING TO THROW AN ENDLESS WAVE OF TROOPS AT US UNTIL WE DROWN.
WE HAVE TO PUT UP A BREAKER.

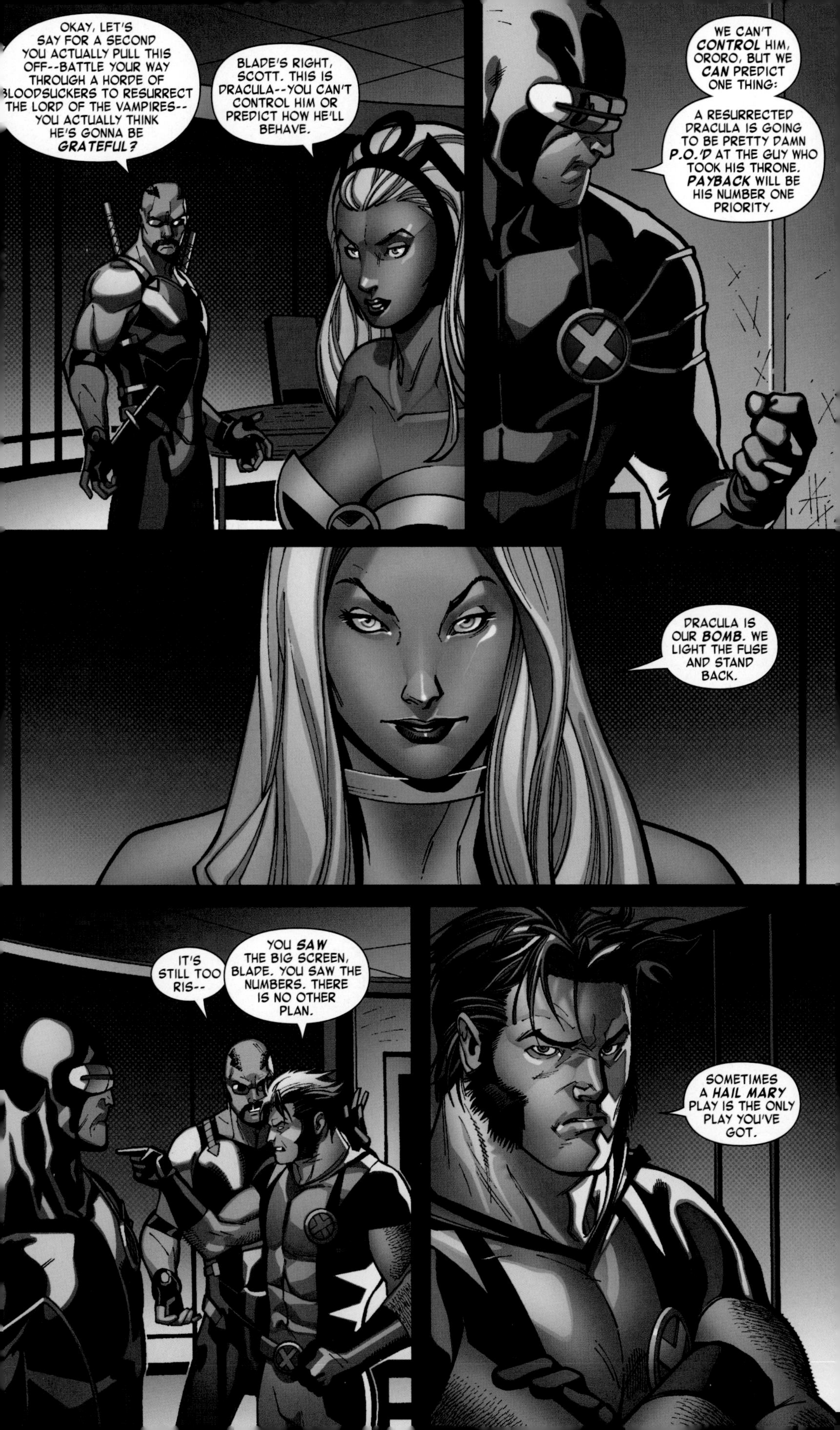
OKAY, LET'S SAY FOR A SECOND YOU ACTUALLY PULL THIS OFF--BATTLE YOUR WAY THROUGH A HORDE OF BLOODSUCKERS TO RESURRECT THE LORD OF THE VAMPIRES--YOU ACTUALLY THINK HE'S GONNA BE GRATEFUL?
BLADE'S RIGHT, SCOTT. THIS IS DRACULA--YOU CAN'T CONTROL HIM OR PREDICT HOW HE'LL BEHAVE.
WE CAN'T CONTROL HIM, ORORO, BUT WE CAN PREDICT ONE THING:
A RESURRECTED DRACULA IS GOING TO BE PRETTY DAMN P.O.'D AT THE GUY WHO TOOK HIS THRONE. PAYBACK WILL BE HIS NUMBER ONE PRIORITY.
DRACULA IS OUR BOMB. WE LIGHT THE FUSE AND STAND BACK.
IT'S STILL TOO RIS--
YOU SAW THE BIG SCREEN, BLADE. YOU SAW THE NUMBERS. THERE IS NO OTHER PLAN.
SOMETIMES A HAIL MARY PLAY IS THE ONLY PLAY YOU'VE GOT.

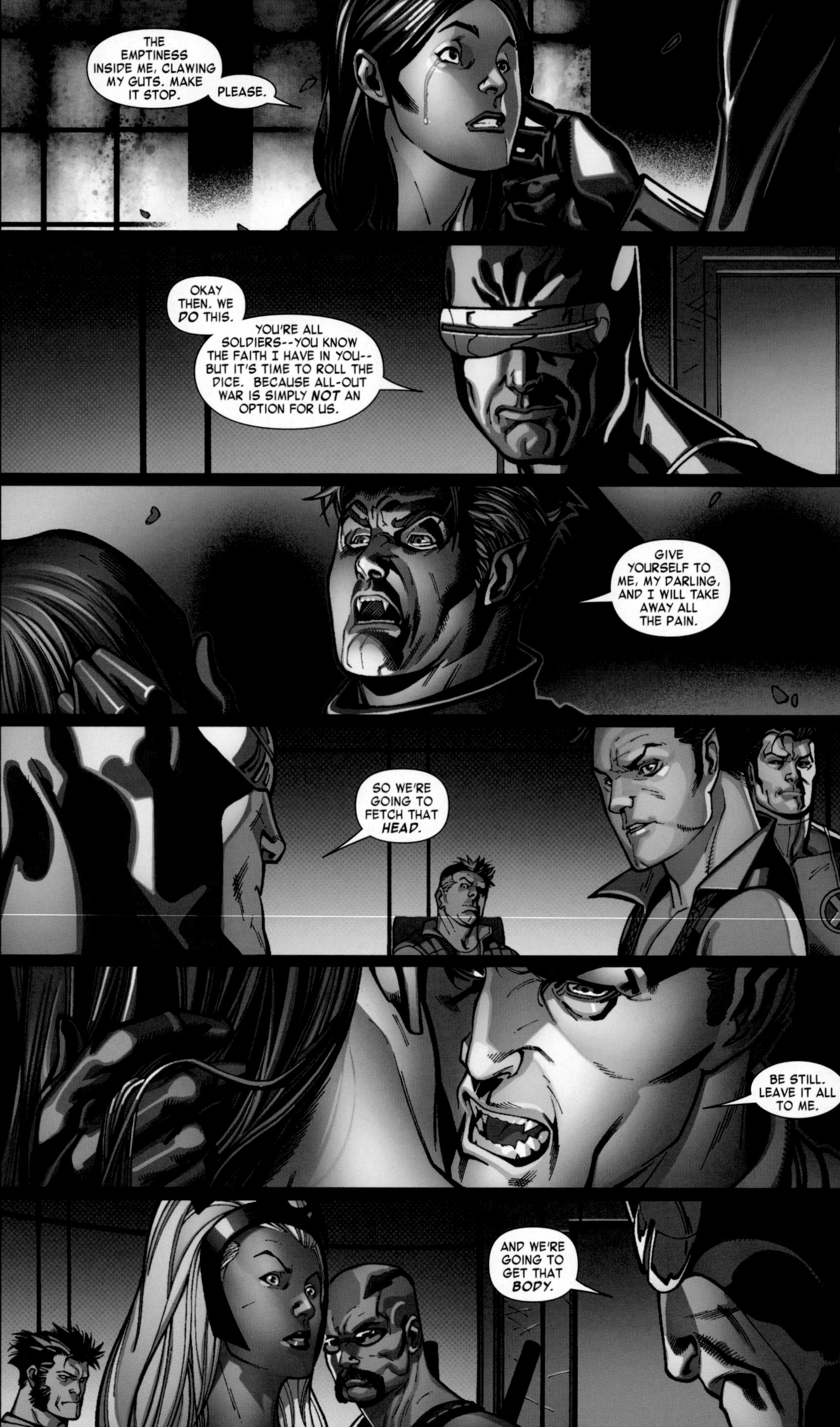

THE EMPTINESS INSIDE ME, CLAWING MY GUTS. MAKE IT STOP.
PLEASE.
OKAY THEN. WE DO THIS.
YOU'RE ALL SOLDIERS--YOU KNOW THE FAITH I HAVE IN YOU--BUT IT'S TIME TO ROLL THE DICE. BECAUSE ALL-OUT WAR IS SIMPLY NOT AN OPTION FOR US.
GIVE YOURSELF TO ME, MY DARLING, AND I WILL TAKE AWAY ALL THE PAIN.
SO WE'RE GOING TO FETCH THAT HEAD.
BE STILL. LEAVE IT ALL TO ME.
AND WE'RE GOING TO GET THAT BODY.

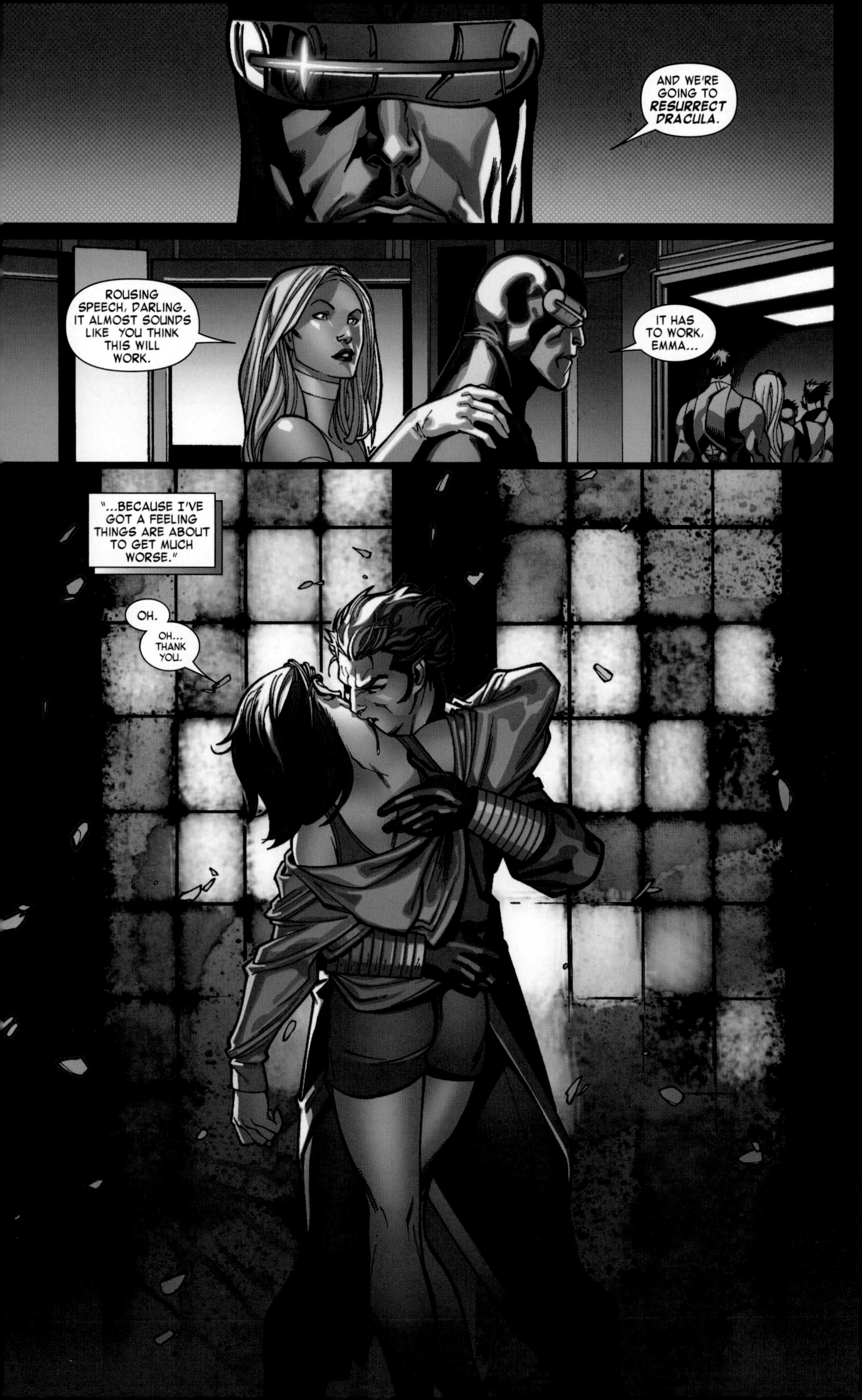
AND WE'RE GOING TO RESURRECT DRACULA.
ROUSING SPEECH, DARLING. IT ALMOST SOUNDS LIKE YOU THINK THIS WILL WORK.
IT HAS TO WORK, EMMA...
"...BECAUSE I'VE GOT A FEELING THINGS ARE ABOUT TO GET MUCH WORSE."
OH.
OH... THANK YOU.

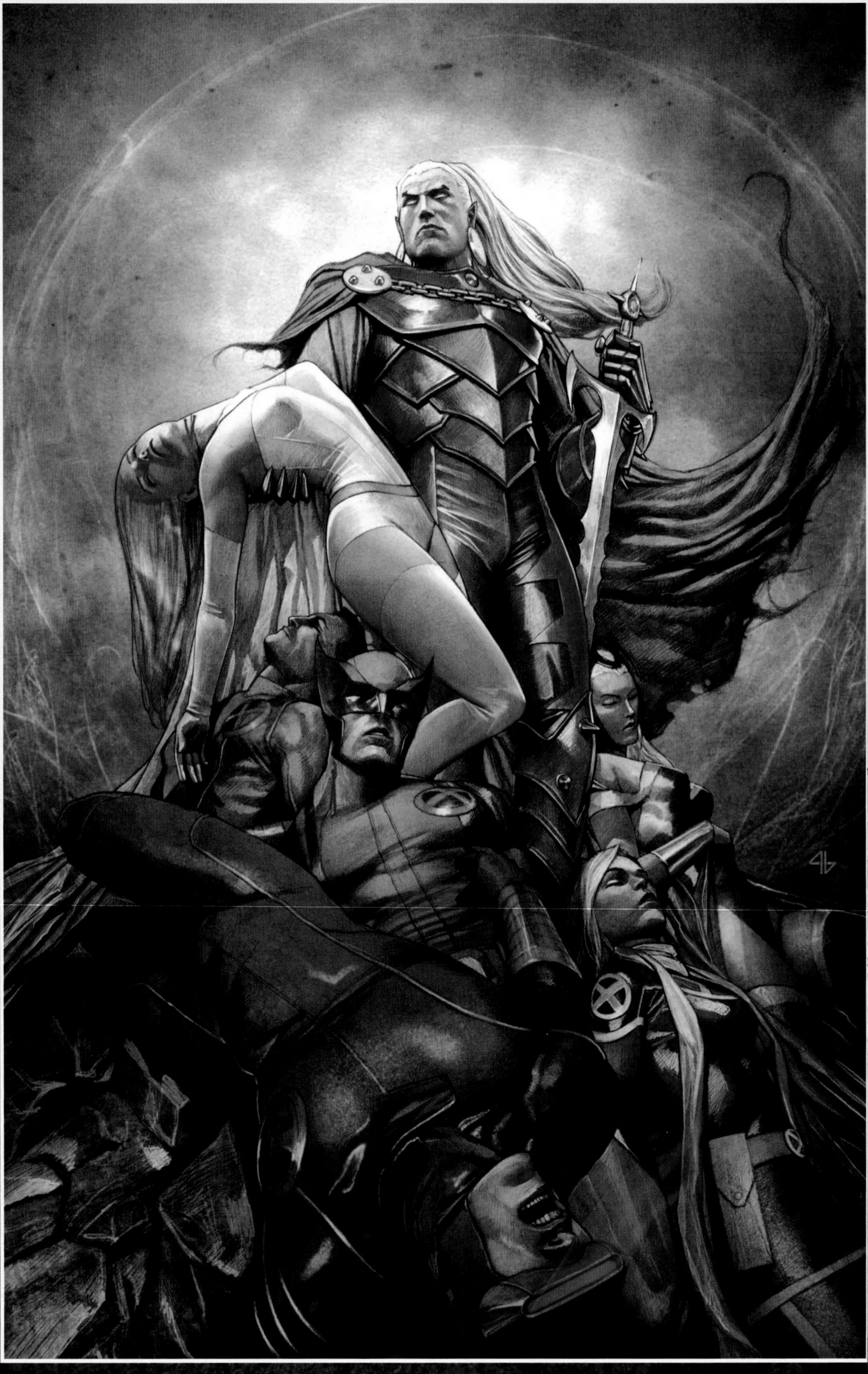

‹THREE›

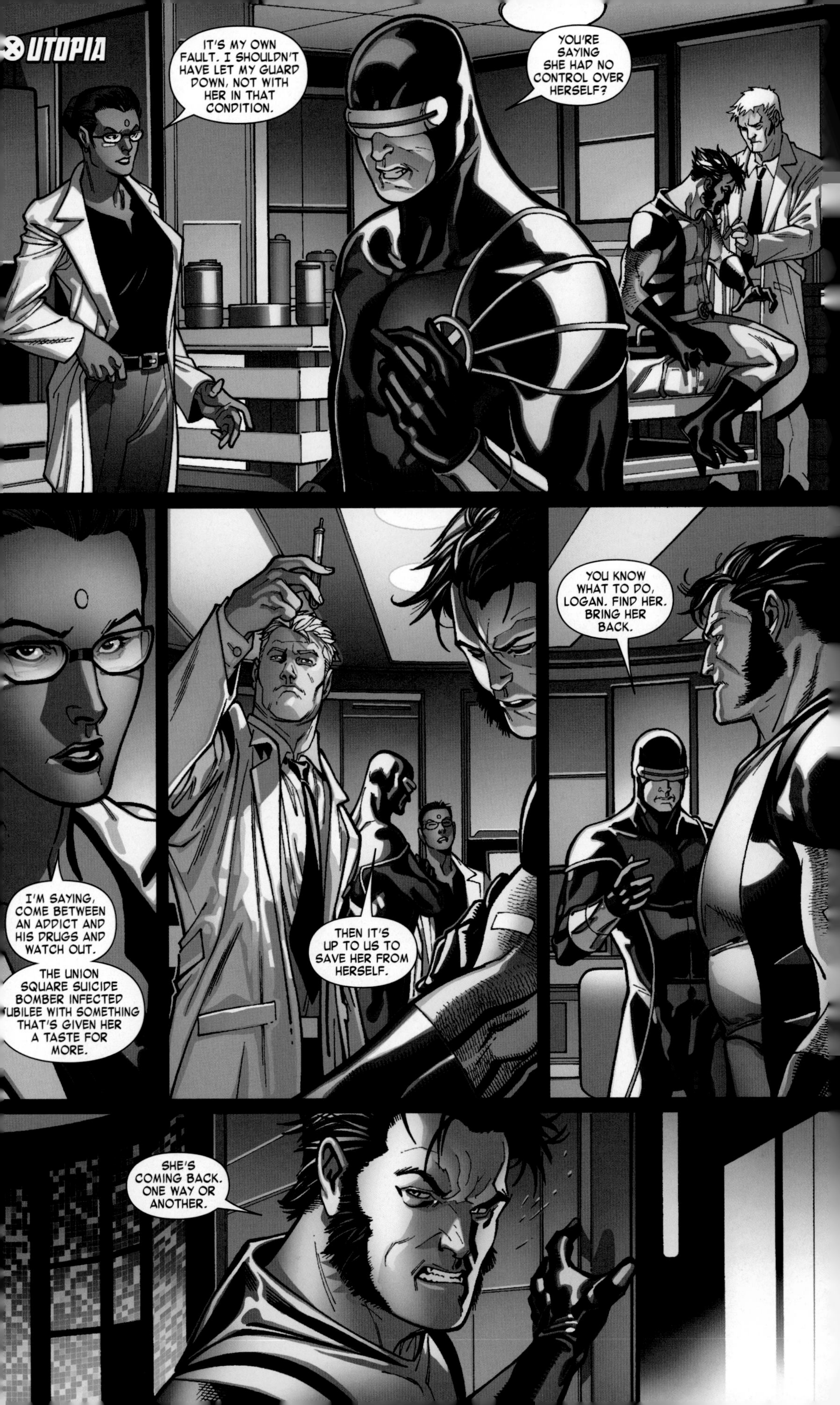

UTOPIA
IT'S MY OWN FAULT. I SHOULDN'T HAVE LET MY GUARD DOWN, NOT WITH HER IN THAT CONDITION.
YOU'RE SAYING SHE HAD NO CONTROL OVER HERSELF?
I'M SAYING, COME BETWEEN AN ADDICT AND HIS DRUGS AND WATCH OUT.
THE UNION SQUARE SUICIDE BOMBER INFECTED JUBILEE WITH SOMETHING THAT'S GIVEN HER A TASTE FOR MORE.
THEN IT'S UP TO US TO SAVE HER FROM HERSELF.
YOU KNOW WHAT TO DO, LOGAN. FIND HER. BRING HER BACK.
SHE'S COMING BACK. ONE WAY OR ANOTHER.

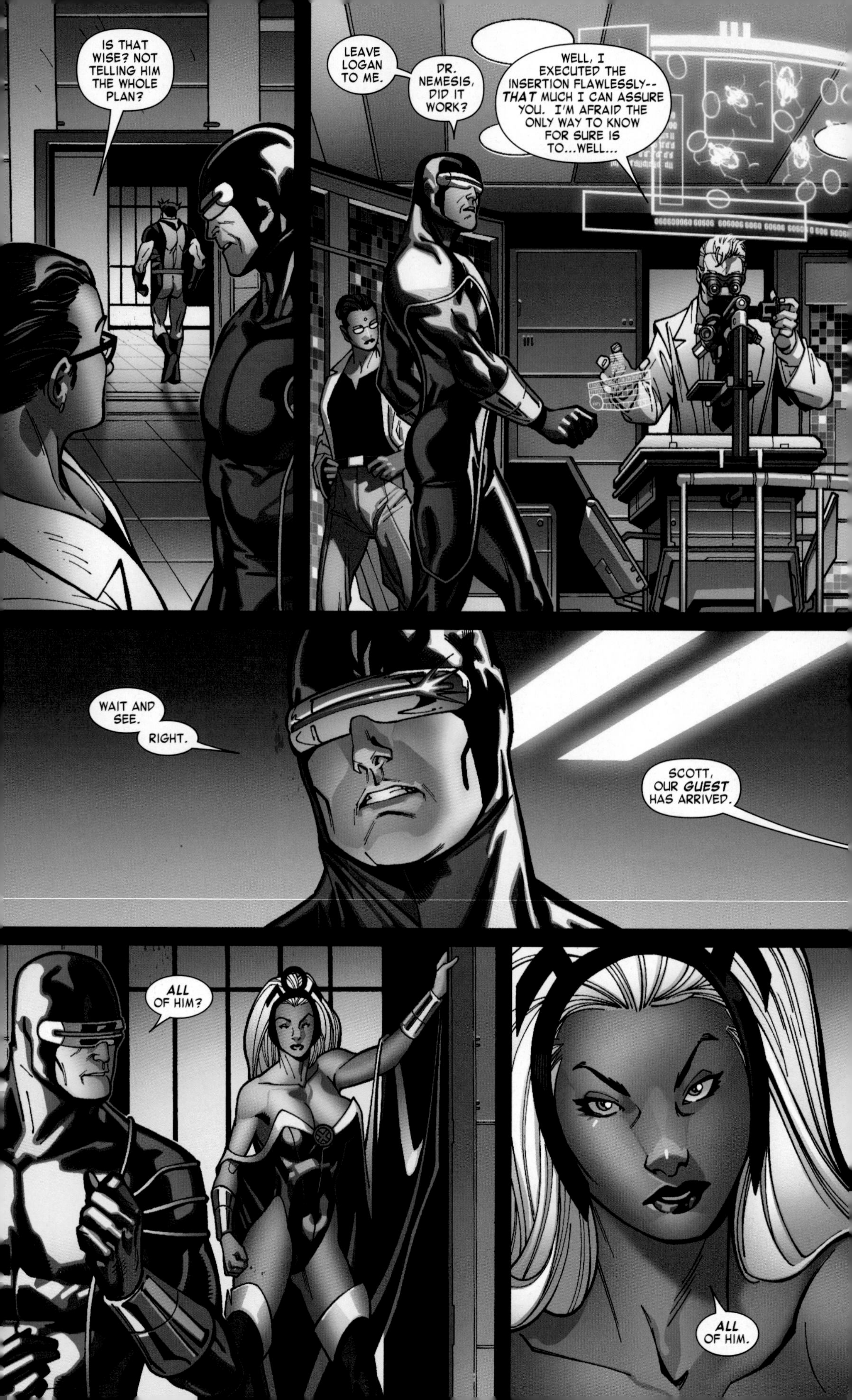
IS THAT WISE? NOT TELLING HIM THE WHOLE PLAN?
LEAVE LOGAN TO ME.
DR. NEMESIS, DID IT WORK?
WELL, I EXECUTED THE INSERTION FLAWLESSLY-- THAT MUCH I CAN ASSURE YOU. I'M AFRAID THE ONLY WAY TO KNOW FOR SURE IS TO...WELL...
WAIT AND SEE.
RIGHT.
SCOTT, OUR GUEST HAS ARRIVED.
ALL OF HIM?
ALL OF HIM.

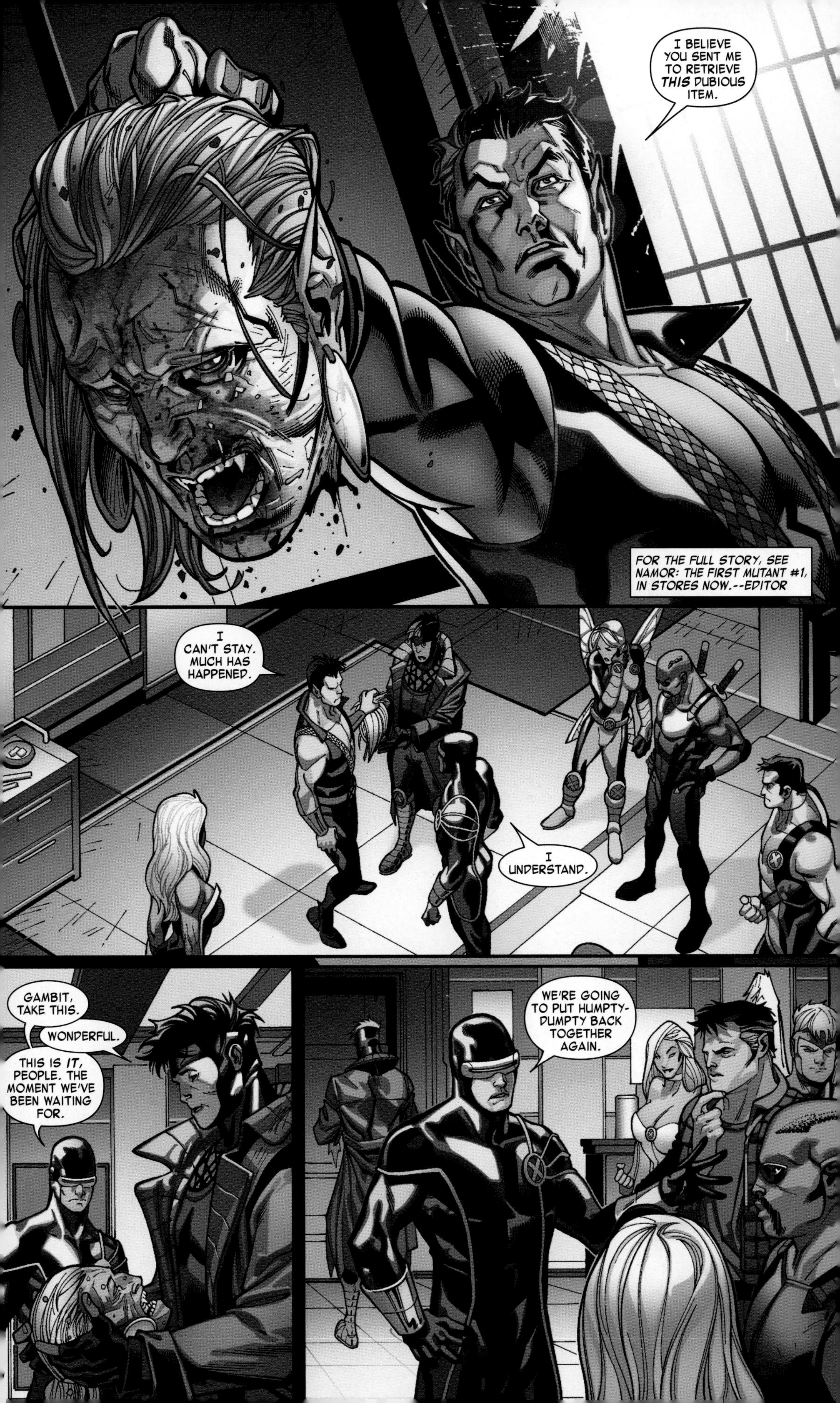
I BELIEVE YOU SENT ME TO RETRIEVE THIS DUBIOUS ITEM.
FOR THE FULL STORY, SEE NAMOR: THE FIRST MUTANT #1, IN STORES NOW.--EDITOR
I CAN'T STAY. MUCH HAS HAPPENED.
I UNDERSTAND.
GAMBIT, TAKE THIS.
WONDERFUL.
THIS IS IT, PEOPLE. THE MOMENT WE'VE BEEN WAITING FOR.
WE'RE GOING TO PUT HUMPTY-DUMPTY BACK TOGETHER AGAIN.

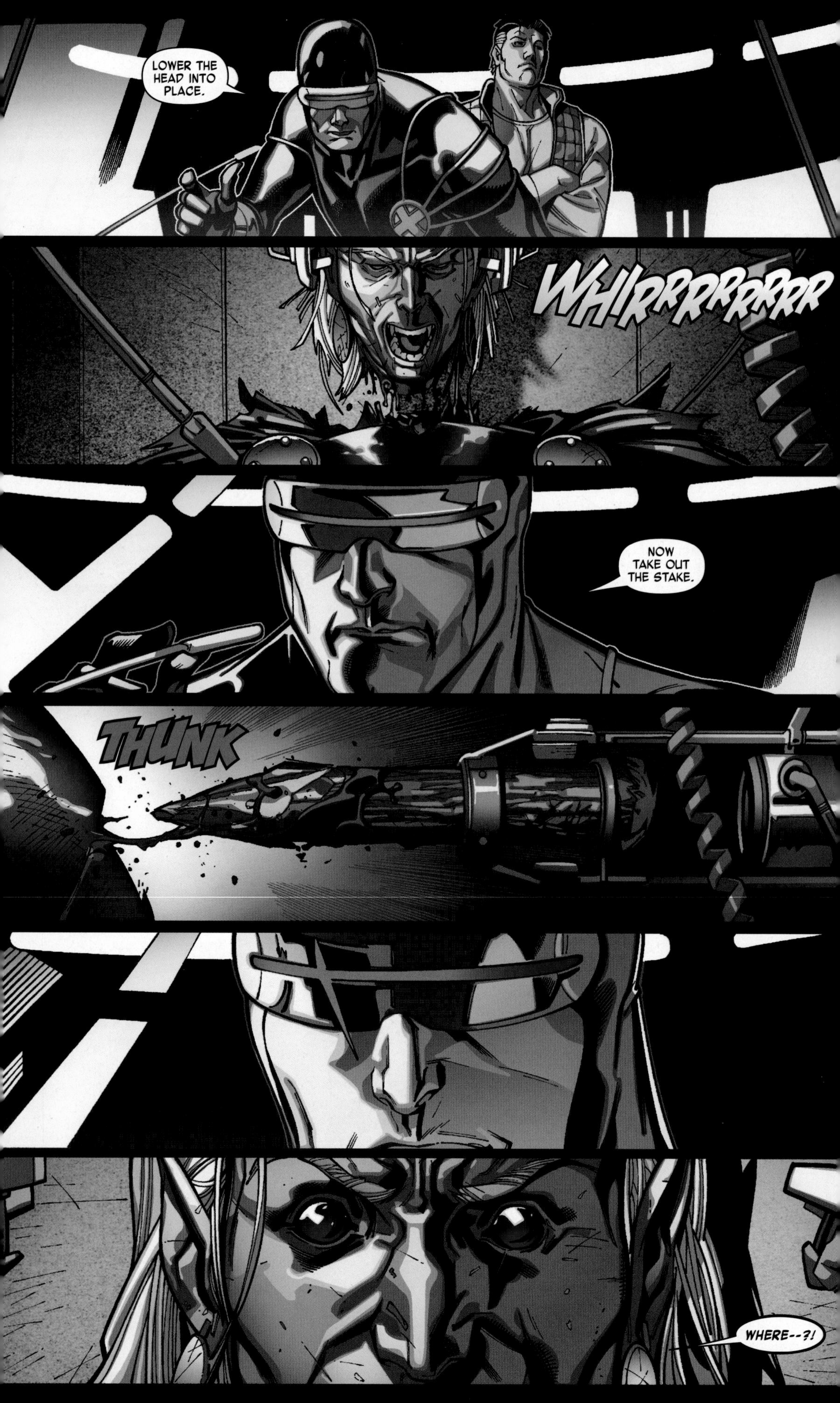
LOWER THE HEAD INTO PLACE.
WHIRRRRRRRR
NOW TAKE OUT THE STAKE.
THUNK
WHERE--?!

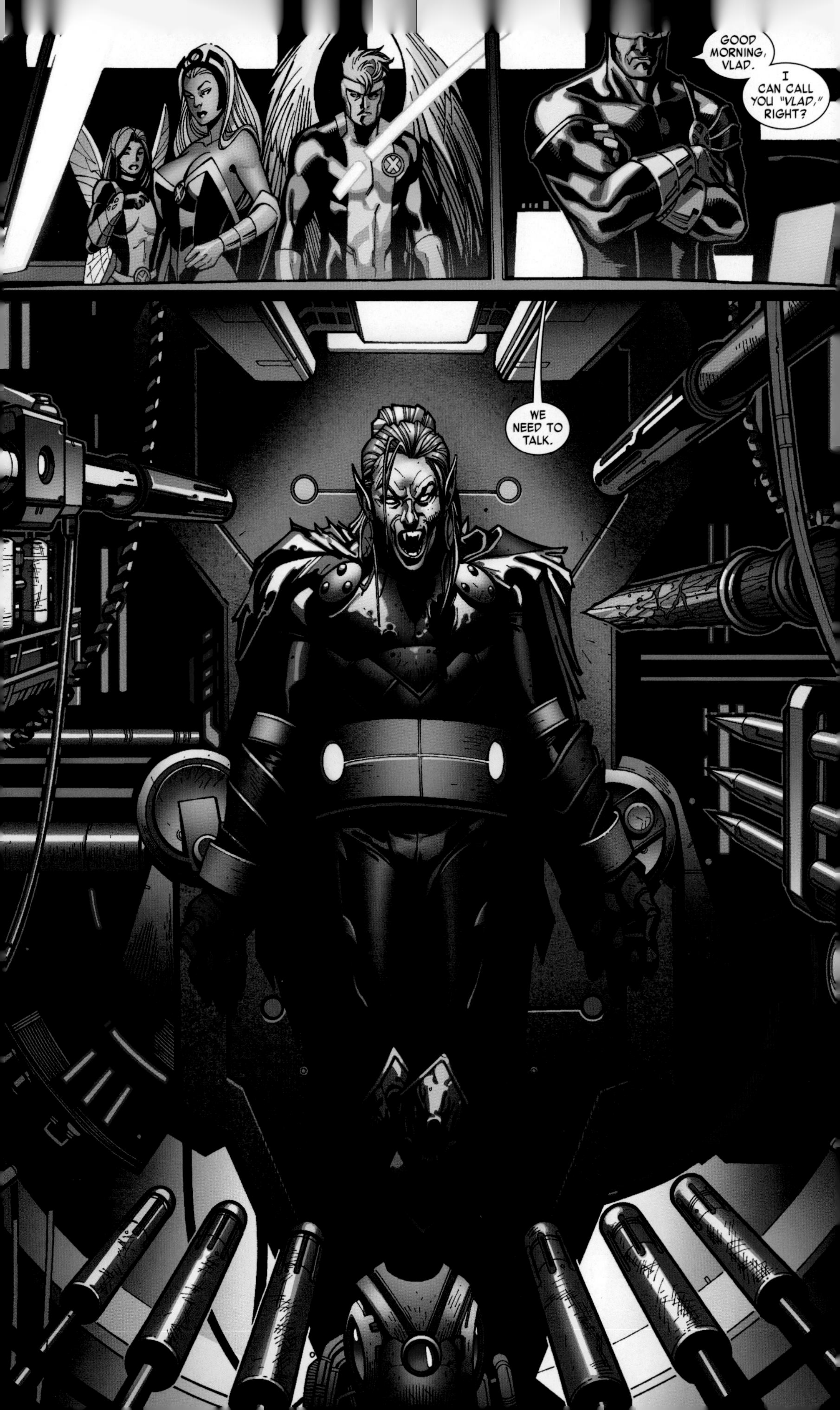
GOOD MORNING, VLAD.
I CAN CALL YOU "VLAD," RIGHT?
WE NEED TO TALK.

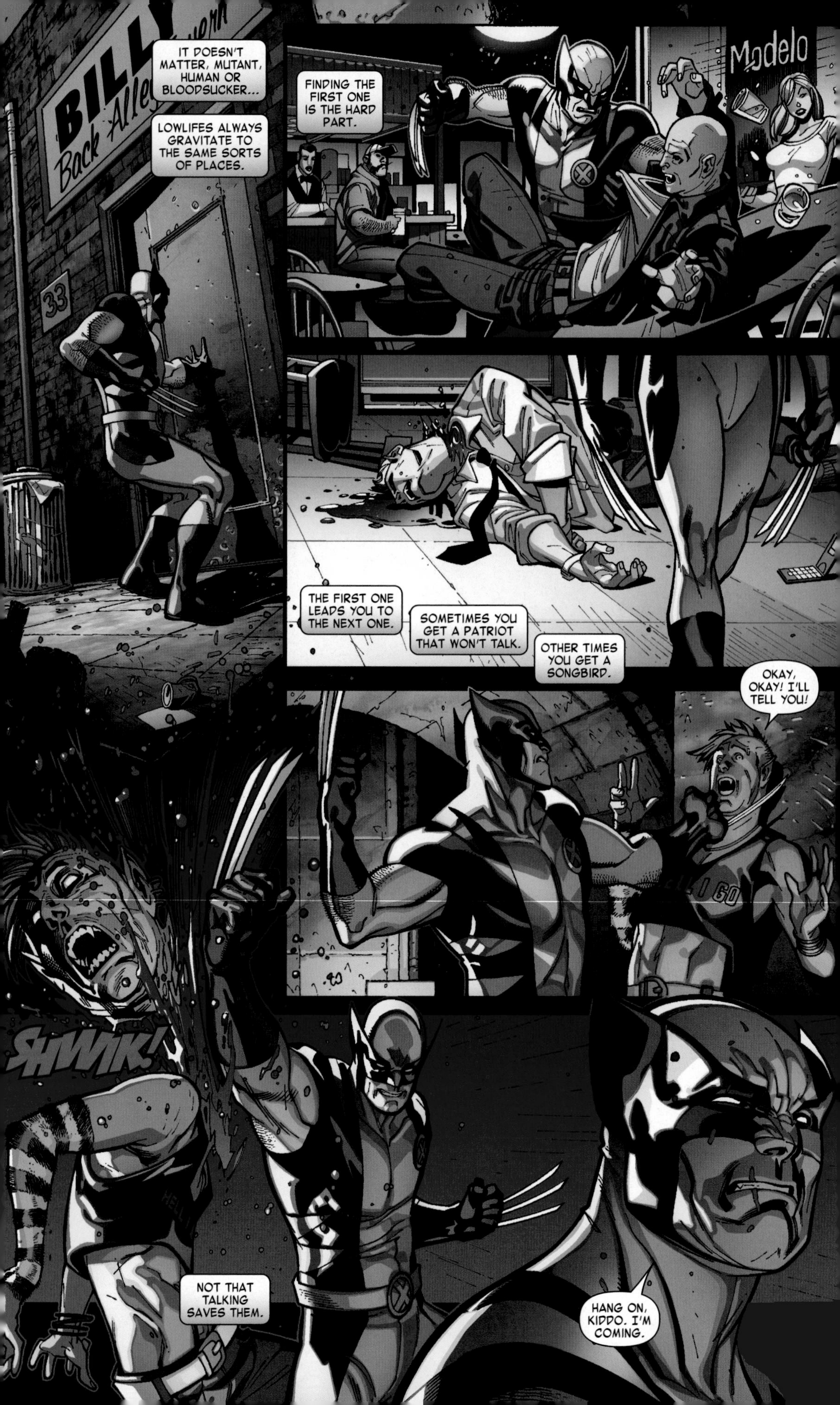
BILLY
Back Alley Tavern
33
IT DOESN'T MATTER, MUTANT, HUMAN OR BLOODSUCKER...
LOWLIFES ALWAYS GRAVITATE TO THE SAME SORTS OF PLACES.
Modelo
FINDING THE FIRST ONE IS THE HARD PART.
THE FIRST ONE LEADS YOU TO THE NEXT ONE.
SOMETIMES YOU GET A PATRIOT THAT WON'T TALK.
OTHER TIMES YOU GET A SONGBIRD.
OKAY, OKAY! I'LL TELL YOU!
SHWIK!
NOT THAT TALKING SAVES THEM.
HANG ON, KIDDO. I'M COMING.

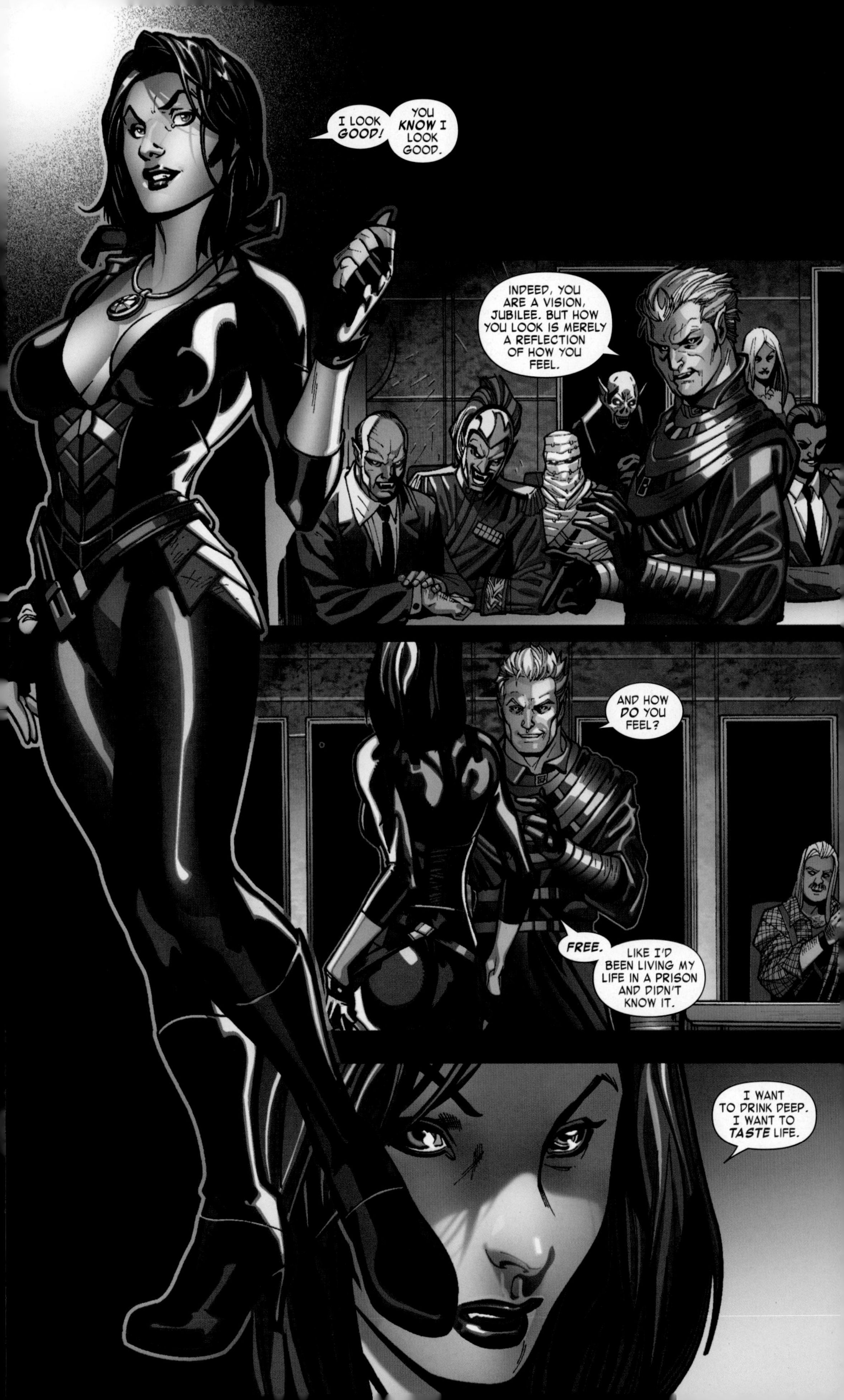

I LOOK GOOD!
YOU KNOW I LOOK GOOD.
INDEED, YOU ARE A VISION, JUBILEE. BUT HOW YOU LOOK IS MERELY A REFLECTION OF HOW YOU FEEL.
AND HOW DO YOU FEEL?
FREE.
LIKE I'D BEEN LIVING MY LIFE IN A PRISON AND DIDN'T KNOW IT.
I WANT TO DRINK DEEP. I WANT TO TASTE LIFE.

LOOK AT ME, JUBILEE. *LISTEN.* WHEN WE INFECTED YOU IN UNION SQUARE THAT DAY, YOU WERE HALF IN YOUR WORLD AND HALF IN OURS. THE VIRUS PREPARED YOU, READIED YOU, MADE YOU *RECEPTIVE* TO YOUR DESTINY.

MY BITE BROUGHT YOU FULLY INTO THE VAMPIRE WORLD.

YOU ARE *ONE* OF US.

I WANT TO OFFER THIS NEW LIFE TO ALL THE X-MEN. THAT'S WHY WE'VE COME TO THIS CITY.

MUTANTS AND VAMPIRES ARE NOT SO DIFFERENT. WE ARE *FEARED* AND *HATED* BY HUMANITY. BUT *UNITED,* WE COULD BE UNSTOPPABLE.

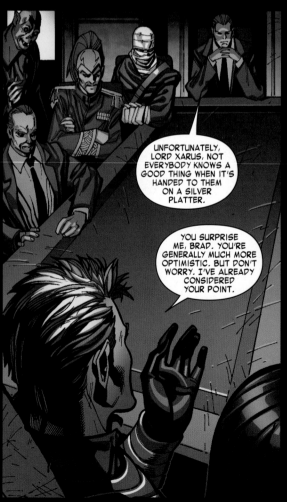

UNFORTUNATELY, LORD XARUS, NOT EVERYBODY KNOWS A GOOD THING WHEN IT'S HANDED TO THEM ON A SILVER PLATTER.

YOU SURPRISE ME, BRAD. YOU'RE GENERALLY MUCH MORE OPTIMISTIC. BUT DON'T WORRY. I'VE ALREADY CONSIDERED YOUR POINT.

FOR EVERY CARROT THERE MUST ALSO BE A *STICK.*

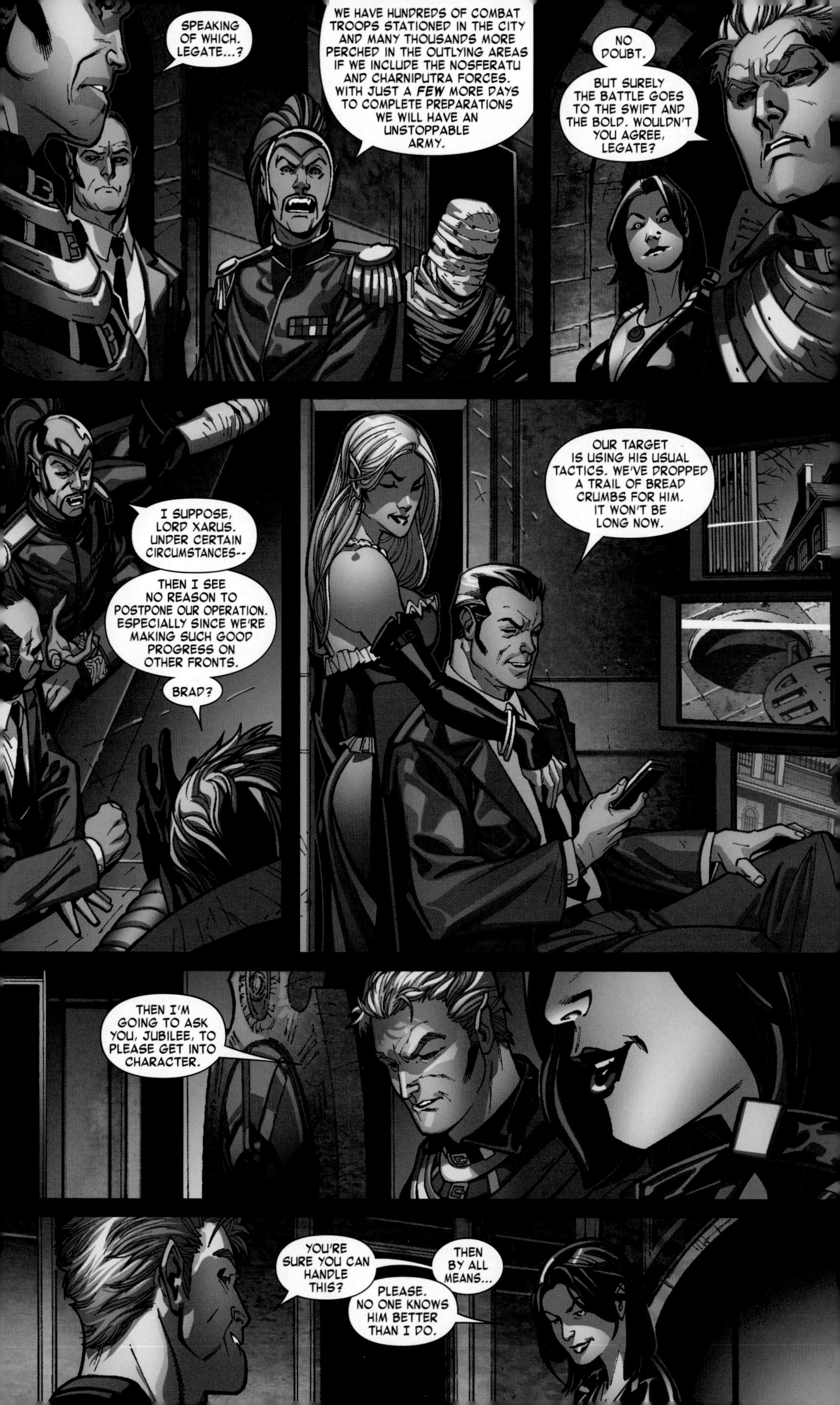
SPEAKING OF WHICH. LEGATE...?
WE HAVE HUNDREDS OF COMBAT TROOPS STATIONED IN THE CITY AND MANY THOUSANDS MORE PERCHED IN THE OUTLYING AREAS IF WE INCLUDE THE NOSFERATU AND CHARNIPUTRA FORCES. WITH JUST A *FEW* MORE DAYS TO COMPLETE PREPARATIONS WE WILL HAVE AN UNSTOPPABLE ARMY.
NO DOUBT.
BUT SURELY THE BATTLE GOES TO THE SWIFT AND THE BOLD. WOULDN'T YOU AGREE, LEGATE?
I SUPPOSE, LORD XARUS. UNDER CERTAIN CIRCUMSTANCES--
THEN I SEE NO REASON TO POSTPONE OUR OPERATION. ESPECIALLY SINCE WE'RE MAKING SUCH GOOD PROGRESS ON OTHER FRONTS.
BRAD?
OUR TARGET IS USING HIS USUAL TACTICS. WE'VE DROPPED A TRAIL OF BREAD CRUMBS FOR HIM. IT WON'T BE LONG NOW.
THEN I'M GOING TO ASK YOU, JUBILEE, TO PLEASE GET INTO CHARACTER.
YOU'RE SURE YOU CAN HANDLE THIS?
THEN BY ALL MEANS...
PLEASE. NO ONE KNOWS HIM BETTER THAN I DO.

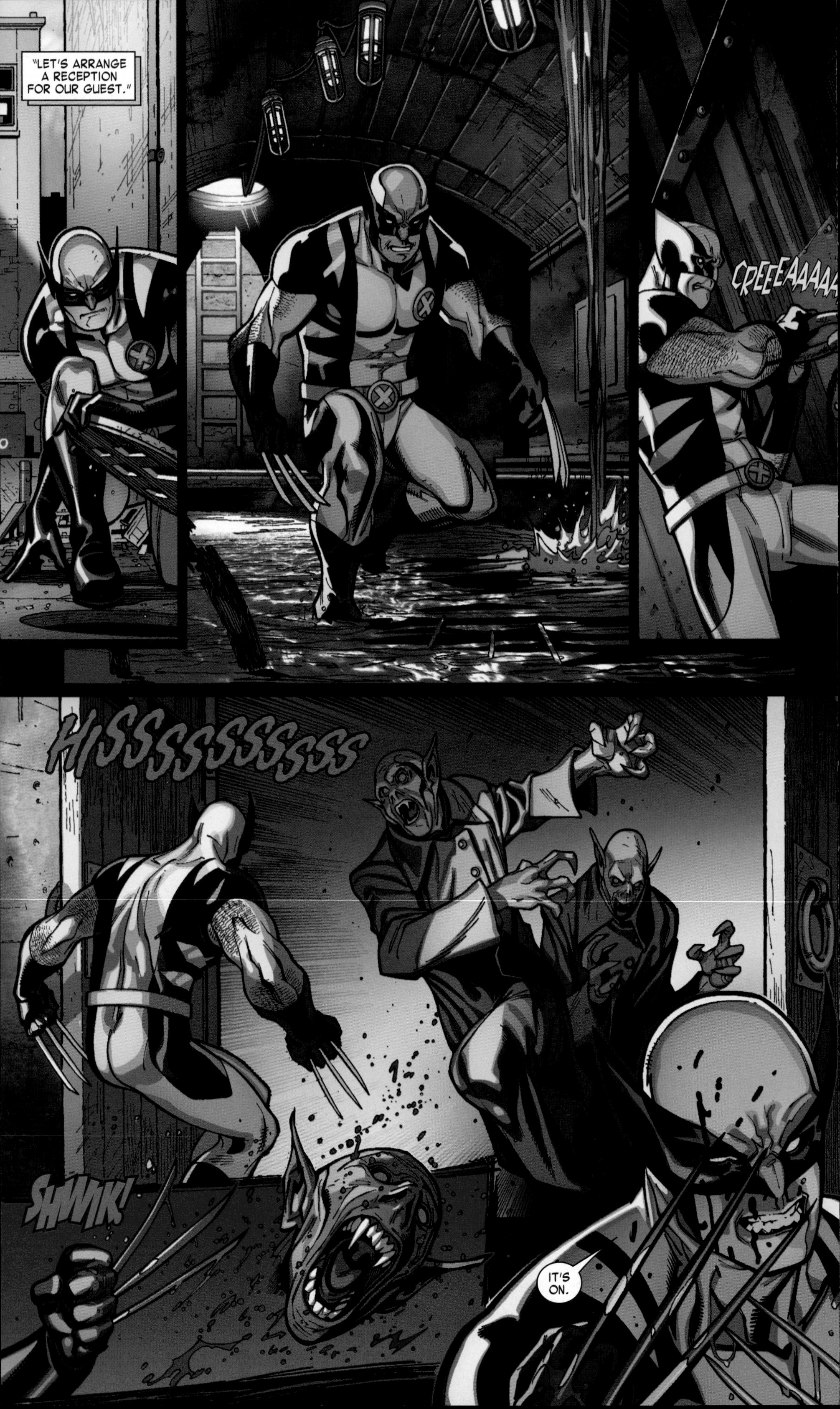
"LET'S ARRANGE A RECEPTION FOR OUR GUEST."
CREEEAAAAA
HISSSSSSSSS
SHWIK!
IT'S ON.

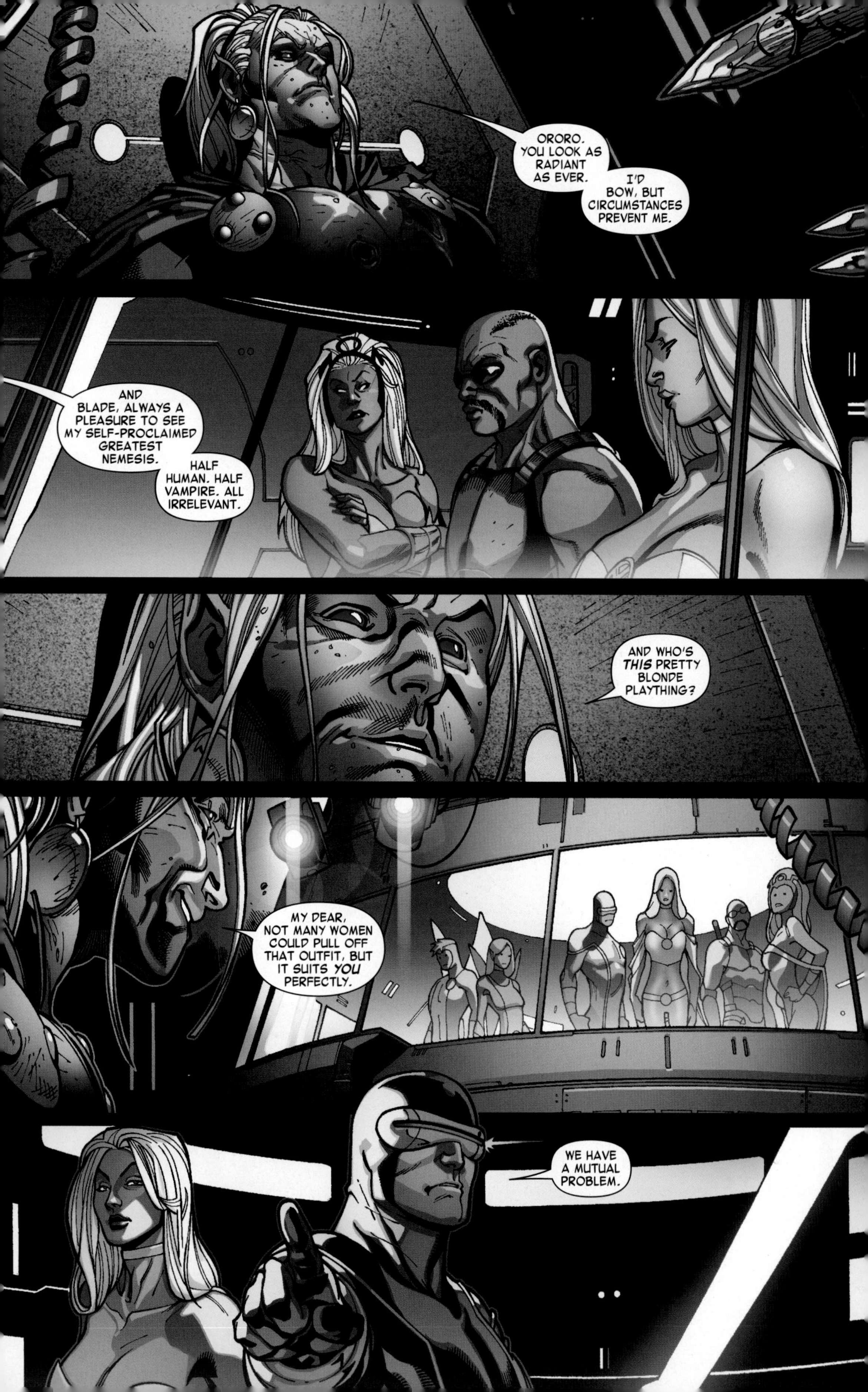

ORORO. YOU LOOK AS RADIANT AS EVER.
I'D BOW, BUT CIRCUMSTANCES PREVENT ME.
AND BLADE, ALWAYS A PLEASURE TO SEE MY SELF-PROCLAIMED GREATEST NEMESIS.
HALF HUMAN. HALF VAMPIRE. ALL IRRELEVANT.
AND WHO'S *THIS* PRETTY BLONDE PLAYTHING?
MY DEAR, NOT MANY WOMEN COULD PULL OFF THAT OUTFIT, BUT IT SUITS *YOU* PERFECTLY.
WE HAVE A MUTUAL PROBLEM.

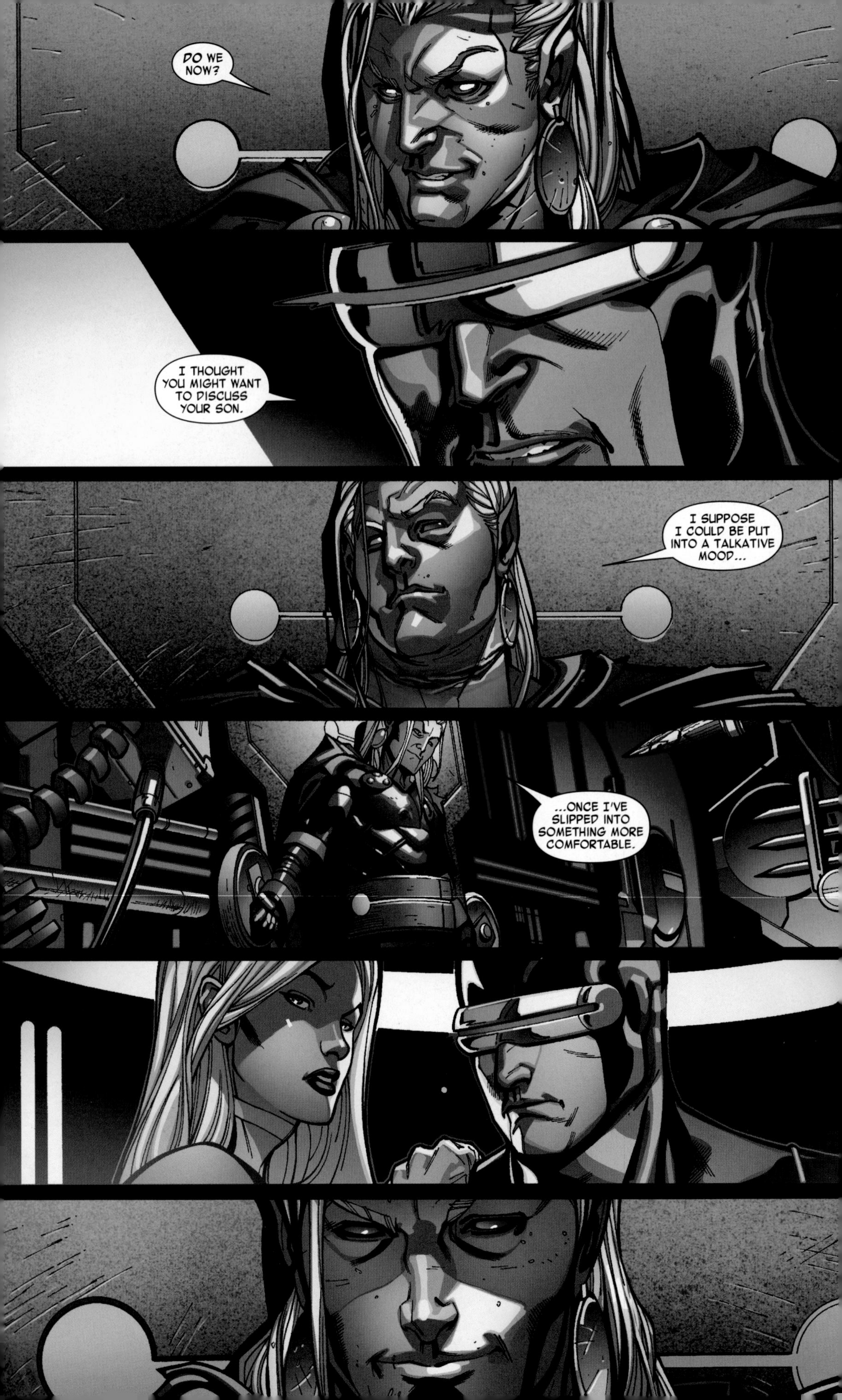
DO WE NOW?
I THOUGHT YOU MIGHT WANT TO DISCUSS YOUR SON.
I SUPPOSE I COULD BE PUT INTO A TALKATIVE MOOD...
...ONCE I'VE SLIPPED INTO SOMETHING MORE COMFORTABLE.

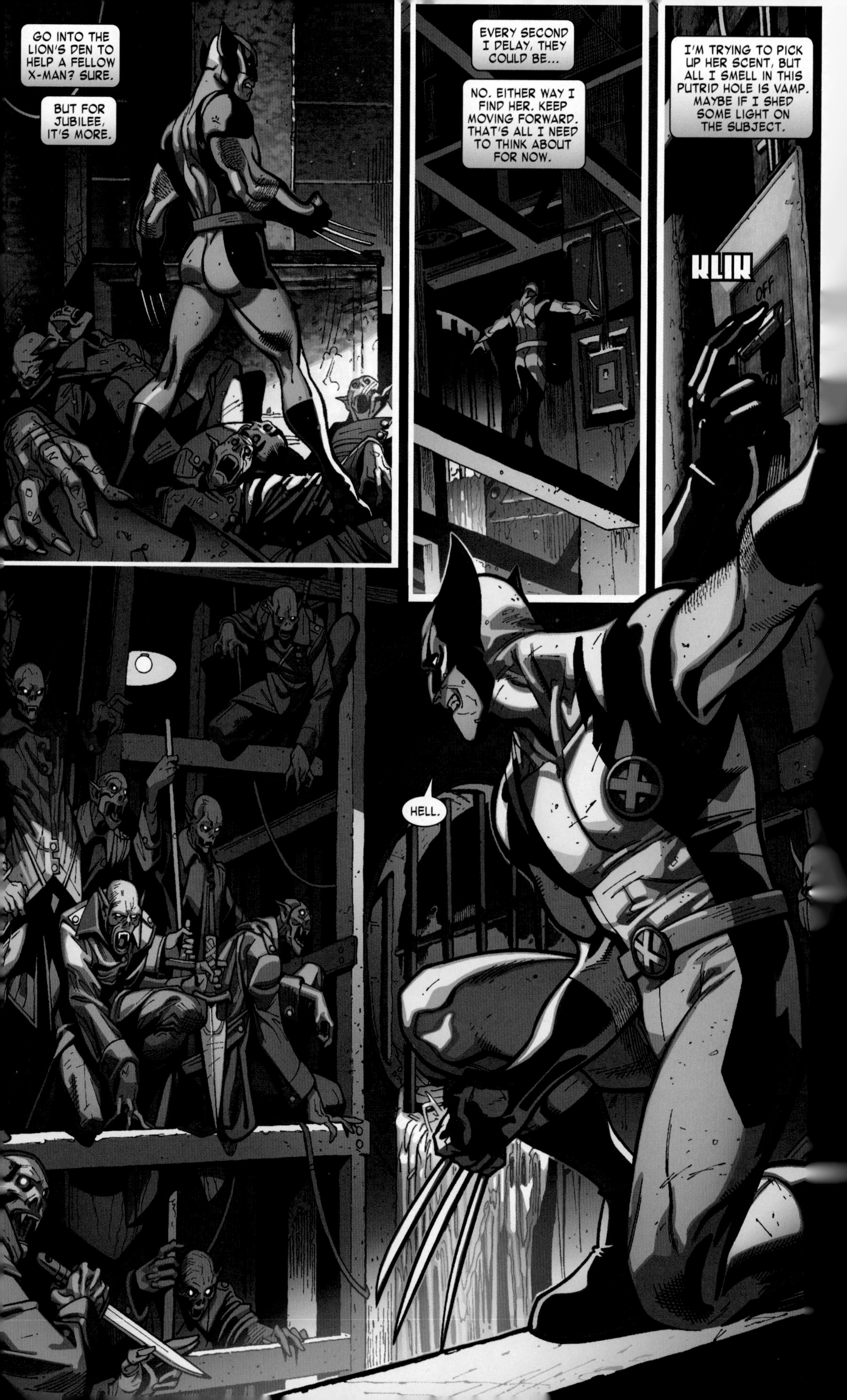
GO INTO THE LION'S DEN TO HELP A FELLOW X-MAN? SURE.
BUT FOR JUBILEE, IT'S MORE.
EVERY SECOND I DELAY, THEY COULD BE...
NO. EITHER WAY I FIND HER. KEEP MOVING FORWARD. THAT'S ALL I NEED TO THINK ABOUT FOR NOW.
I'M TRYING TO PICK UP HER SCENT, BUT ALL I SMELL IN THIS PUTRID HOLE IS VAMP. MAYBE IF I SHED SOME LIGHT ON THE SUBJECT.
KLIK
OFF
HELL.

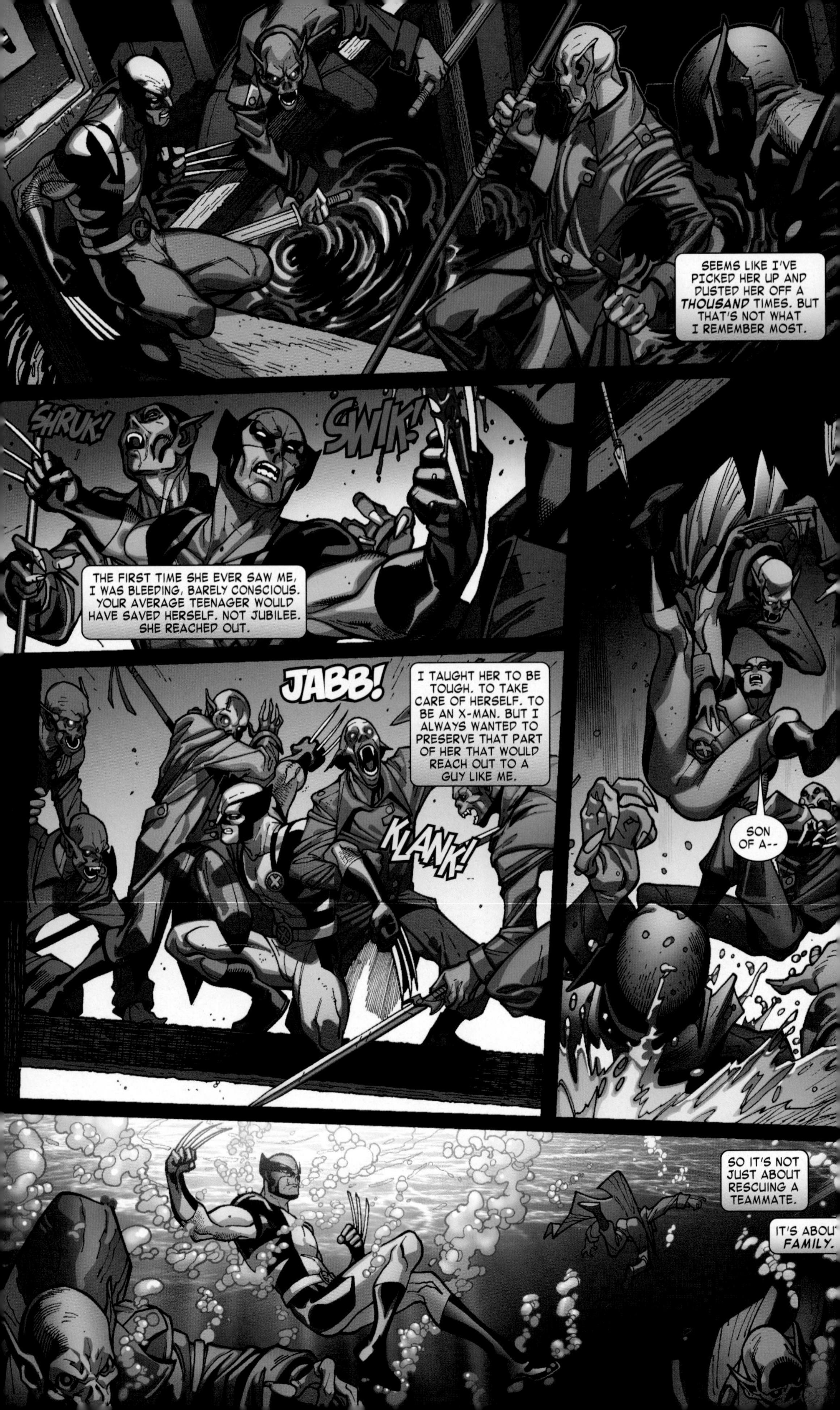
SEEMS LIKE I'VE PICKED HER UP AND DUSTED HER OFF A *THOUSAND* TIMES. BUT THAT'S NOT WHAT I REMEMBER MOST.
SHRUK!
SWIK!
THE FIRST TIME SHE EVER SAW ME, I WAS BLEEDING, BARELY CONSCIOUS. YOUR AVERAGE TEENAGER WOULD HAVE SAVED HERSELF. NOT JUBILEE. SHE REACHED OUT.
JABB!
I TAUGHT HER TO BE TOUGH. TO TAKE CARE OF HERSELF. TO BE AN X-MAN. BUT I ALWAYS WANTED TO PRESERVE THAT PART OF HER THAT WOULD REACH OUT TO A GUY LIKE ME.
KLANK!
SON OF A--
SO IT'S NOT JUST ABOUT RESCUING A TEAMMATE.
IT'S ABOUT *FAMILY.*

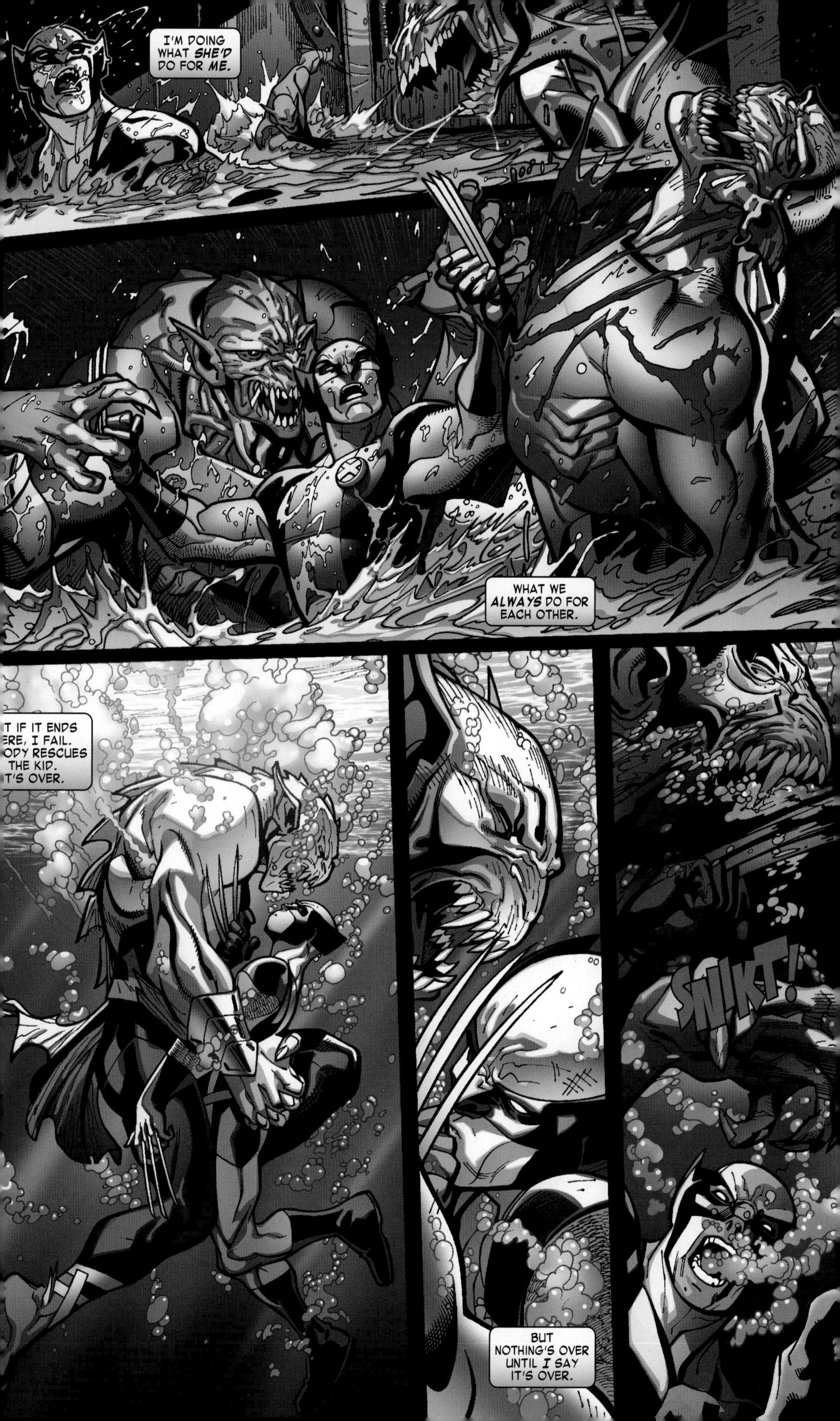
I'M DOING WHAT *SHE'D* DO FOR *ME.*
WHAT WE *ALWAYS* DO FOR EACH OTHER.
T IF IT ENDS ERE, I FAIL. ODY RESCUES THE KID. T'S OVER.
SNIKT!
BUT NOTHING'S OVER UNTIL *I* SAY IT'S OVER.

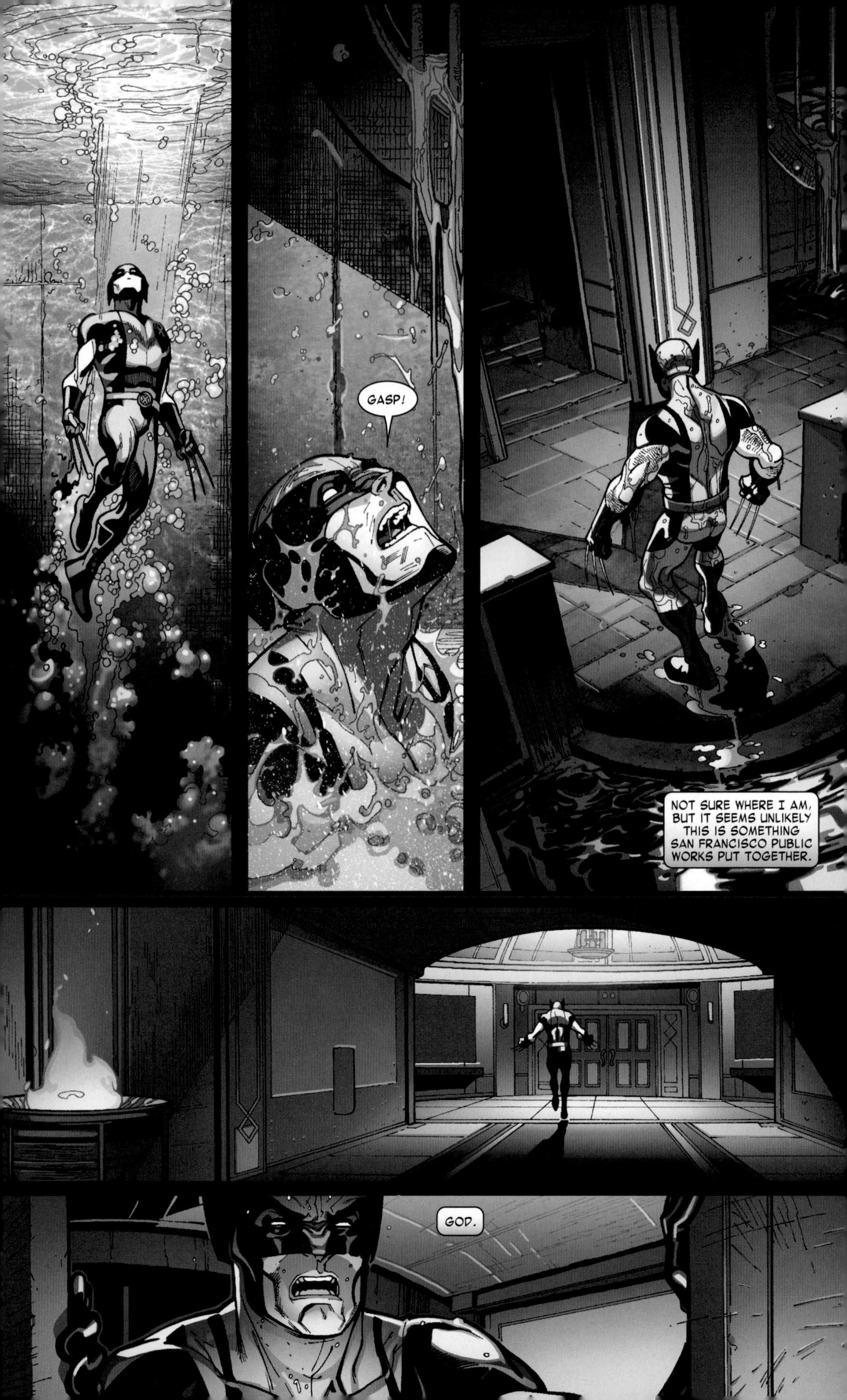
GASP!
NOT SURE WHERE I AM, BUT IT SEEMS UNLIKELY THIS IS SOMETHING SAN FRANCISCO PUBLIC WORKS PUT TOGETHER.
GOD.

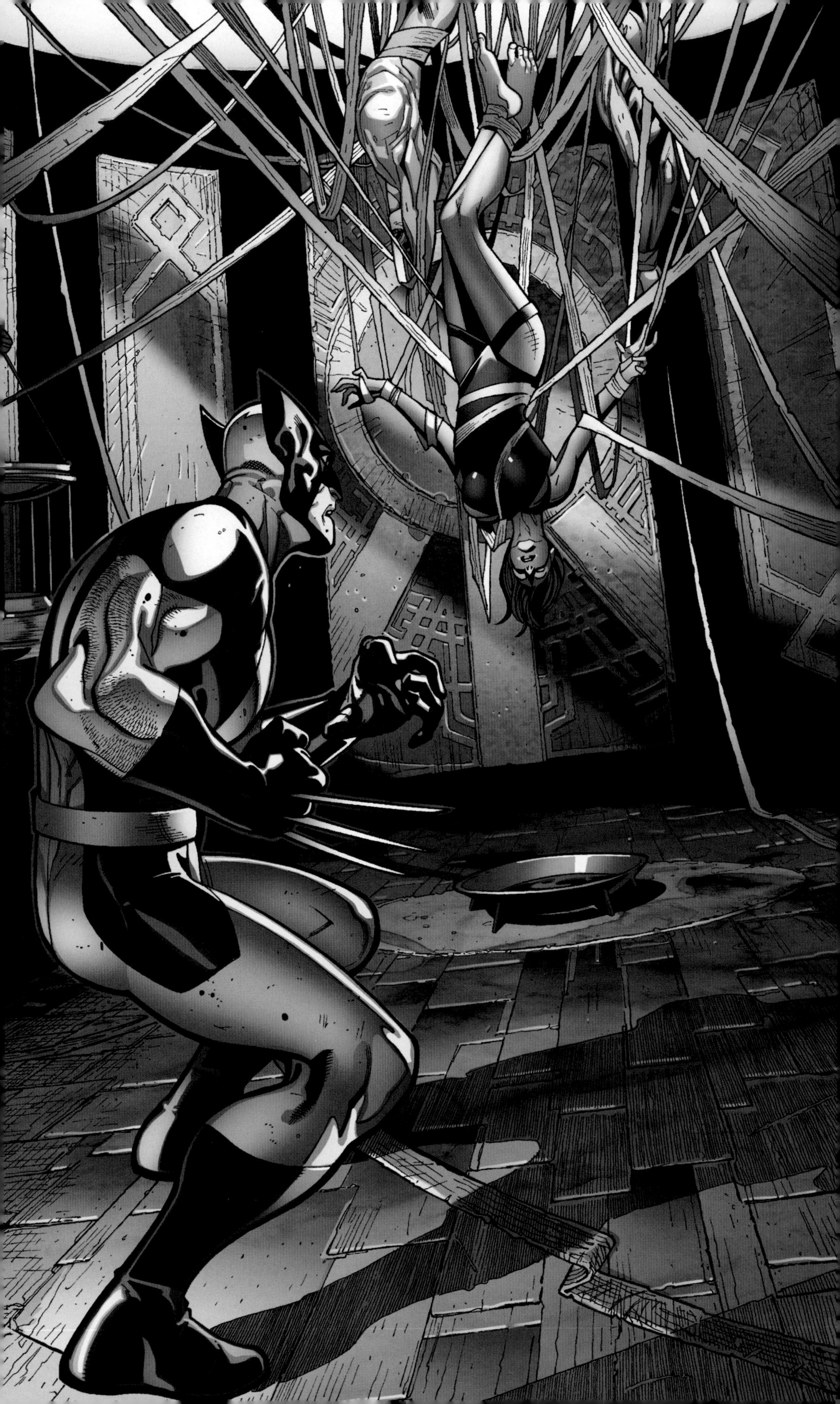

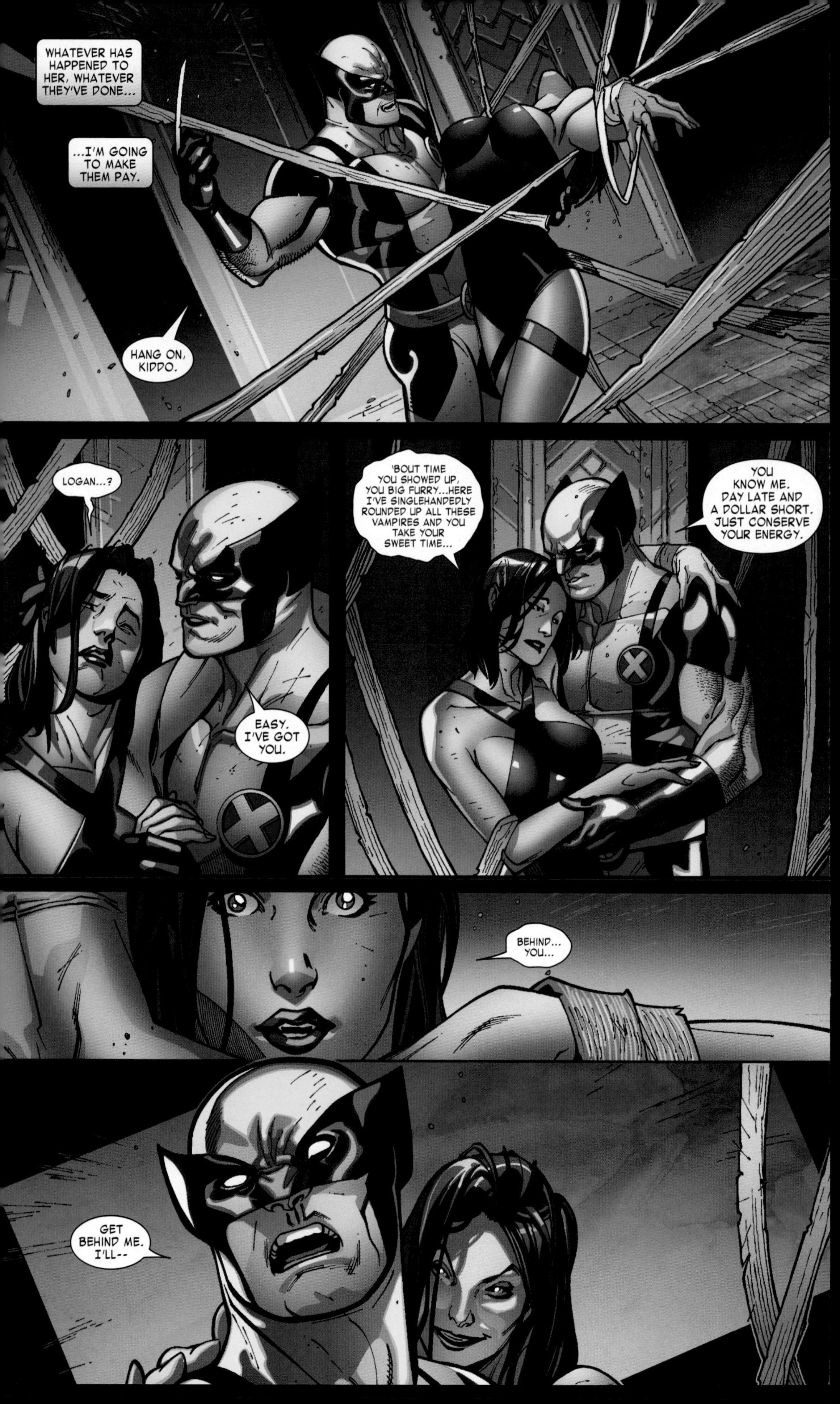

WHATEVER HAS HAPPENED TO HER, WHATEVER THEY'VE DONE...
...I'M GOING TO MAKE THEM PAY.
HANG ON, KIDDO.
LOGAN...?
EASY. I'VE GOT YOU.
'BOUT TIME YOU SHOWED UP, YOU BIG FURRY...HERE I'VE SINGLEHANDEDLY ROUNDED UP ALL THESE VAMPIRES AND YOU TAKE YOUR SWEET TIME...
YOU KNOW ME. DAY LATE AND A DOLLAR SHORT. JUST CONSERVE YOUR ENERGY.
BEHIND... YOU...
GET BEHIND ME. I'LL--

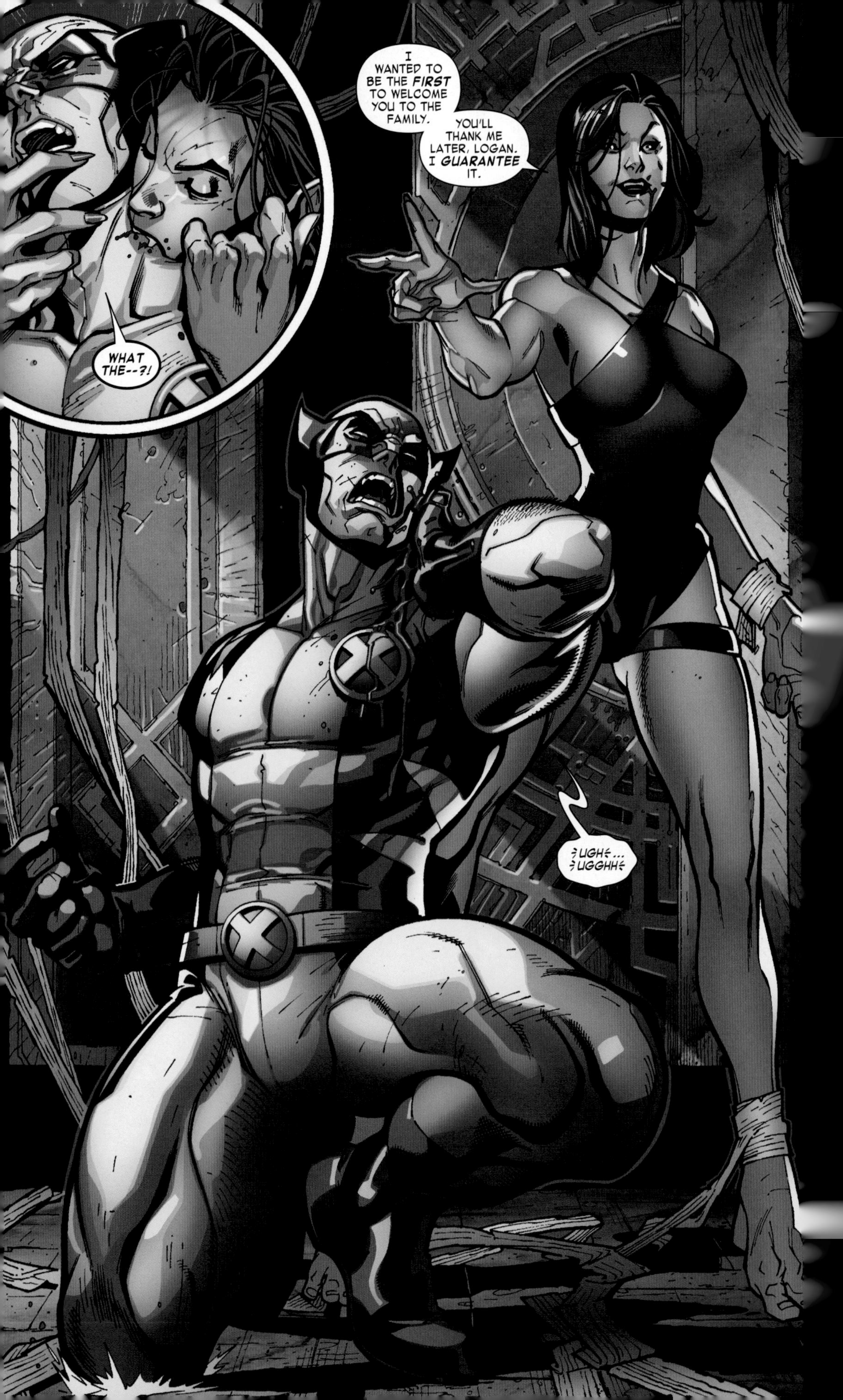
WHAT THE--?!
I WANTED TO BE THE FIRST TO WELCOME YOU TO THE FAMILY.
YOU'LL THANK ME LATER, LOGAN. I GUARANTEE IT.
UGH... UGGHH

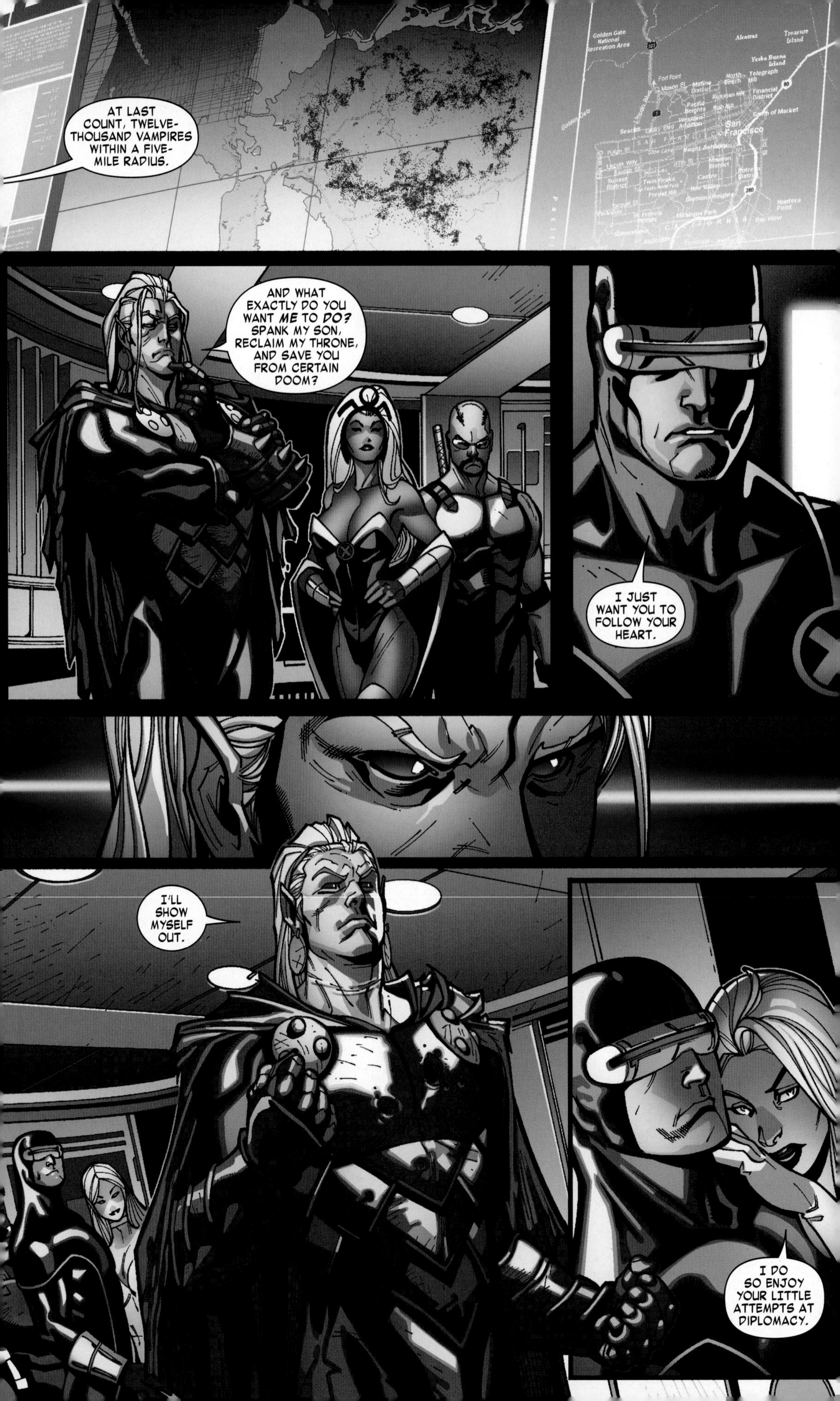
AT LAST COUNT, TWELVE-THOUSAND VAMPIRES WITHIN A FIVE-MILE RADIUS.
AND WHAT EXACTLY DO YOU WANT *ME* TO *DO?* SPANK MY SON, RECLAIM MY THRONE, AND SAVE YOU FROM CERTAIN DOOM?
I JUST WANT YOU TO FOLLOW YOUR HEART.
I'LL SHOW MYSELF OUT.
I DO SO ENJOY YOUR LITTLE ATTEMPTS AT DIPLOMACY.

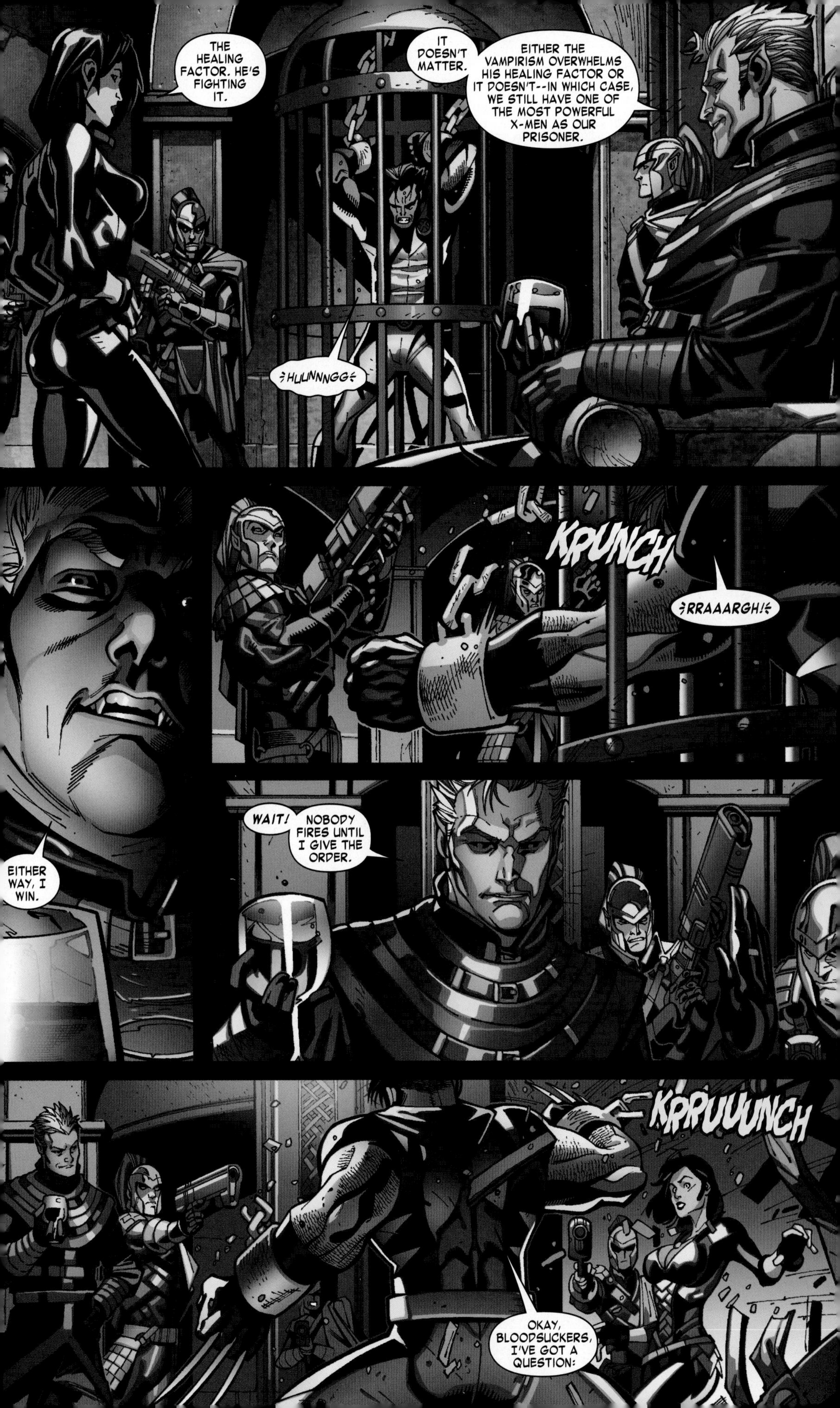
THE HEALING FACTOR. HE'S FIGHTING IT.
IT DOESN'T MATTER.
EITHER THE VAMPIRISM OVERWHELMS HIS HEALING FACTOR OR IT DOESN'T--IN WHICH CASE, WE STILL HAVE ONE OF THE MOST POWERFUL X-MEN AS OUR PRISONER.
HUUNNNGG
EITHER WAY, I WIN.
KRUNCH
RRAAARGH!
WAIT!
NOBODY FIRES UNTIL I GIVE THE ORDER.
KRRUUUNCH
OKAY, BLOODSUCKERS, I'VE GOT A QUESTION:

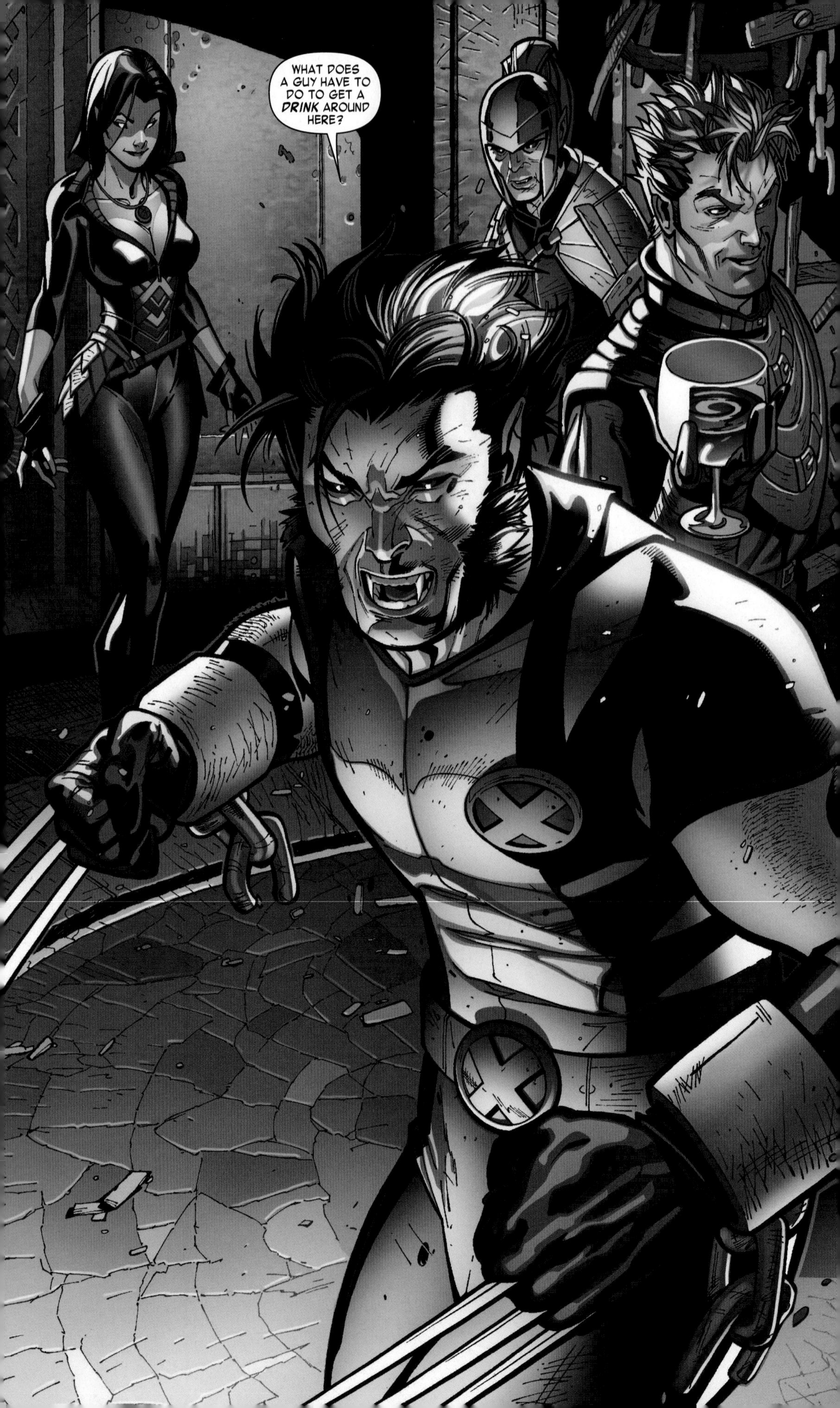
WHAT DOES A GUY HAVE TO DO TO GET A *DRINK* AROUND HERE?

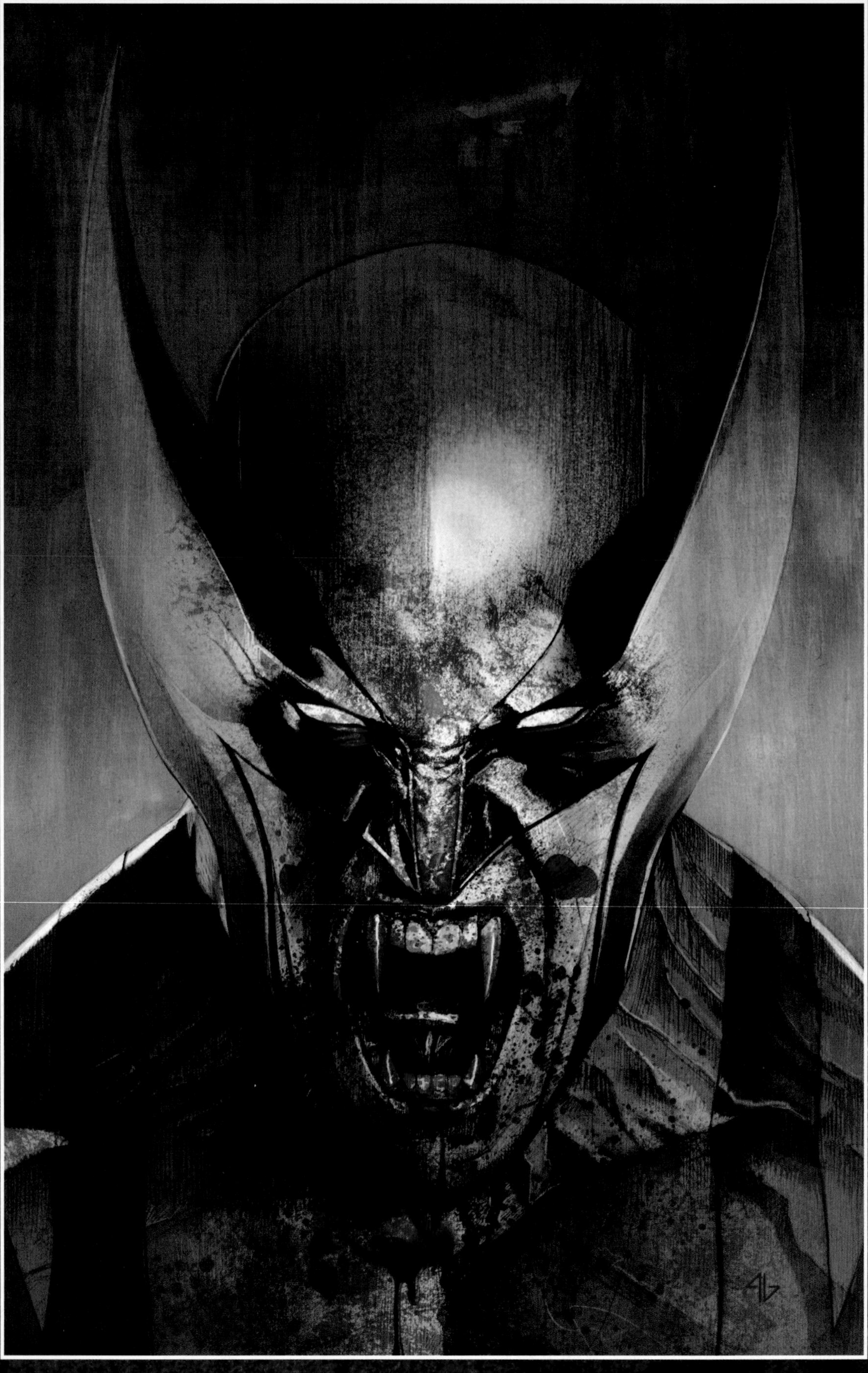

FOUR

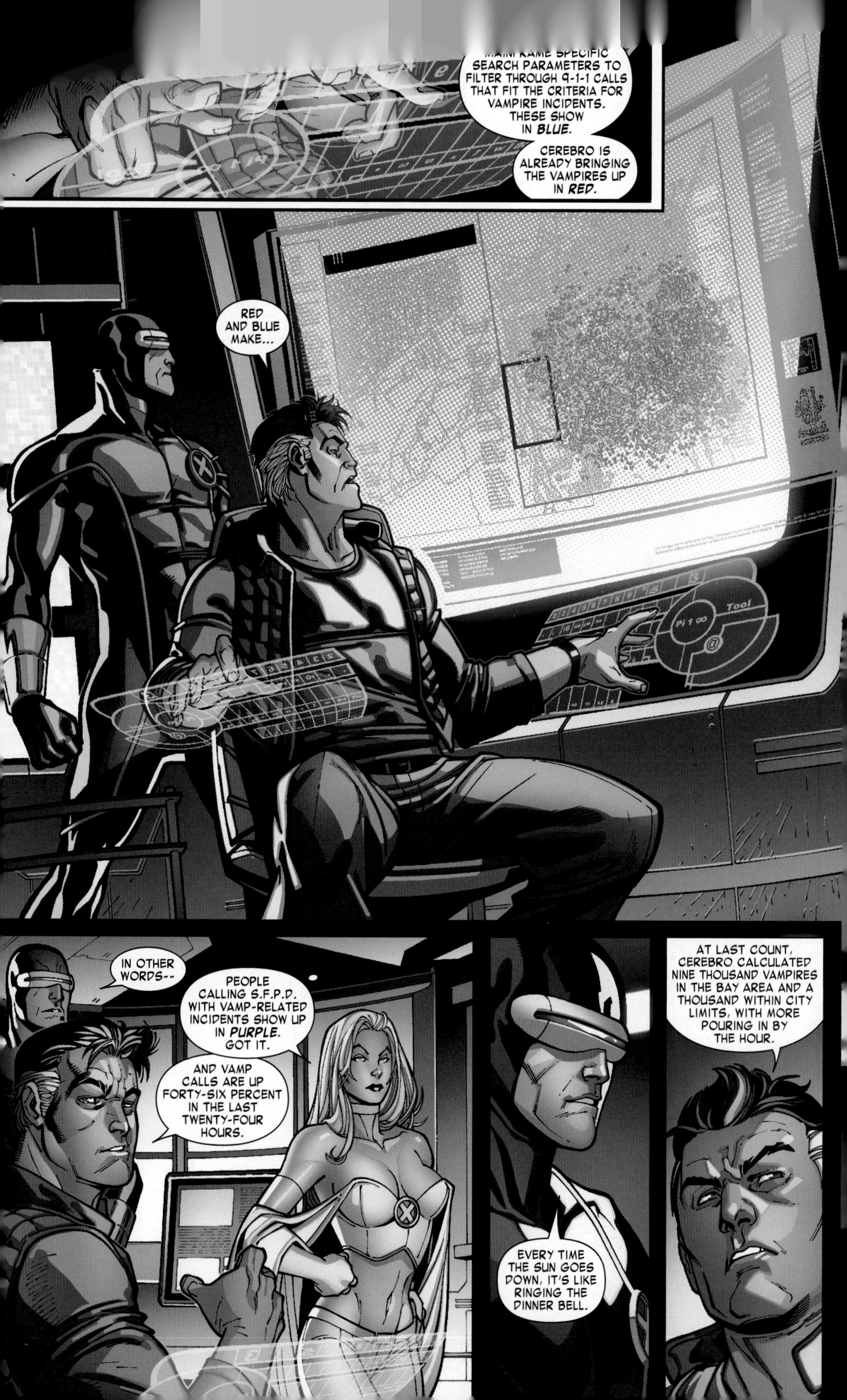
SEARCH PARAMETERS TO FILTER THROUGH 9-1-1 CALLS THAT FIT THE CRITERIA FOR VAMPIRE INCIDENTS. THESE SHOW IN BLUE.
CEREBRO IS ALREADY BRINGING THE VAMPIRES UP IN RED.
RED AND BLUE MAKE...
IN OTHER WORDS--
PEOPLE CALLING S.F.P.D. WITH VAMP-RELATED INCIDENTS SHOW UP IN PURPLE. GOT IT.
AND VAMP CALLS ARE UP FORTY-SIX PERCENT IN THE LAST TWENTY-FOUR HOURS.
AT LAST COUNT, CEREBRO CALCULATED NINE THOUSAND VAMPIRES IN THE BAY AREA AND A THOUSAND WITHIN CITY LIMITS, WITH MORE POURING IN BY THE HOUR.
EVERY TIME THE SUN GOES DOWN, IT'S LIKE RINGING THE DINNER BELL.

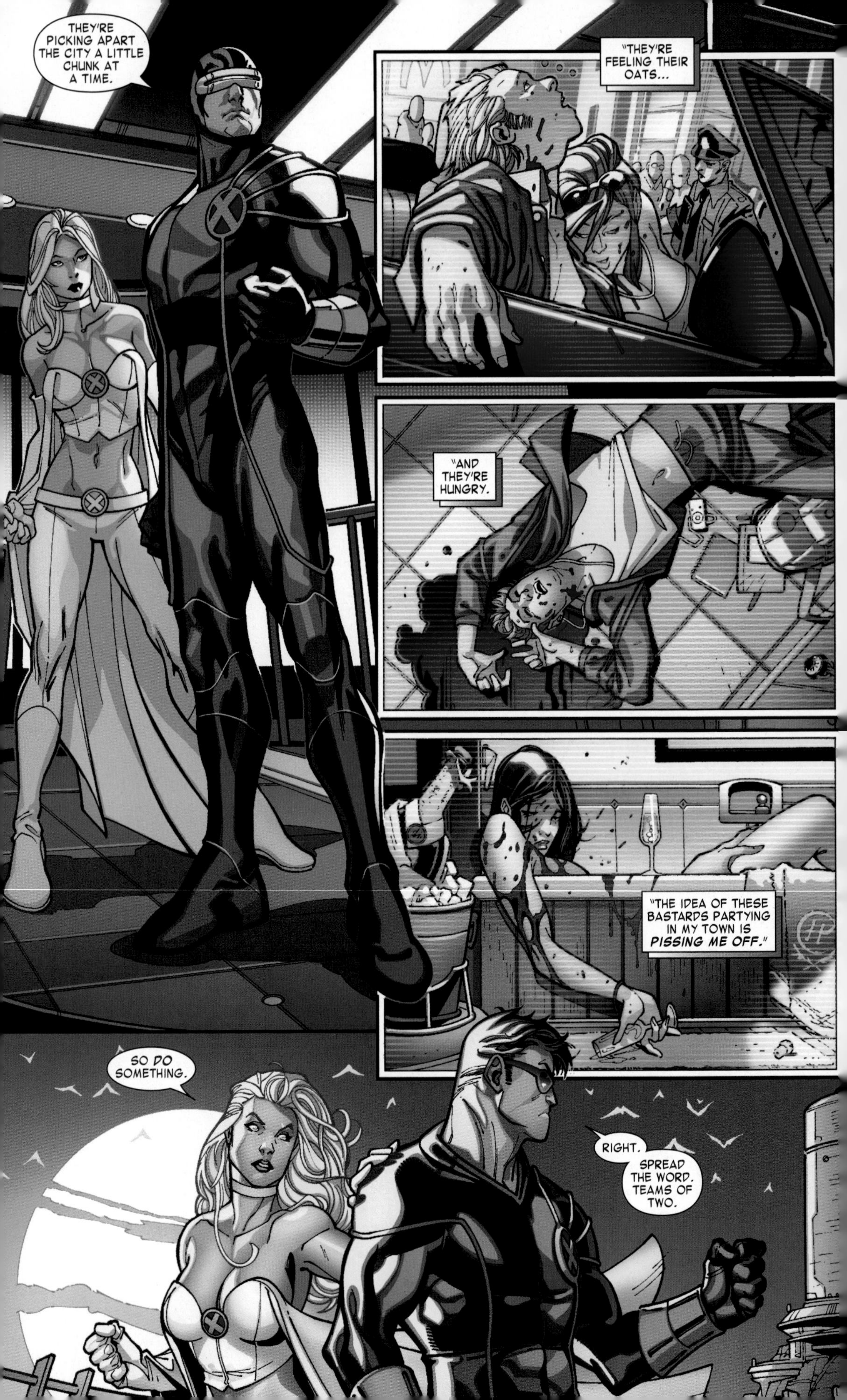
THEY'RE PICKING APART THE CITY A LITTLE CHUNK AT A TIME.
"THEY'RE FEELING THEIR OATS...
"AND THEY'RE HUNGRY.
"THE IDEA OF THESE BASTARDS PARTYING IN MY TOWN IS PISSING ME OFF."
SO DO SOMETHING.
RIGHT.
SPREAD THE WORD. TEAMS OF TWO.

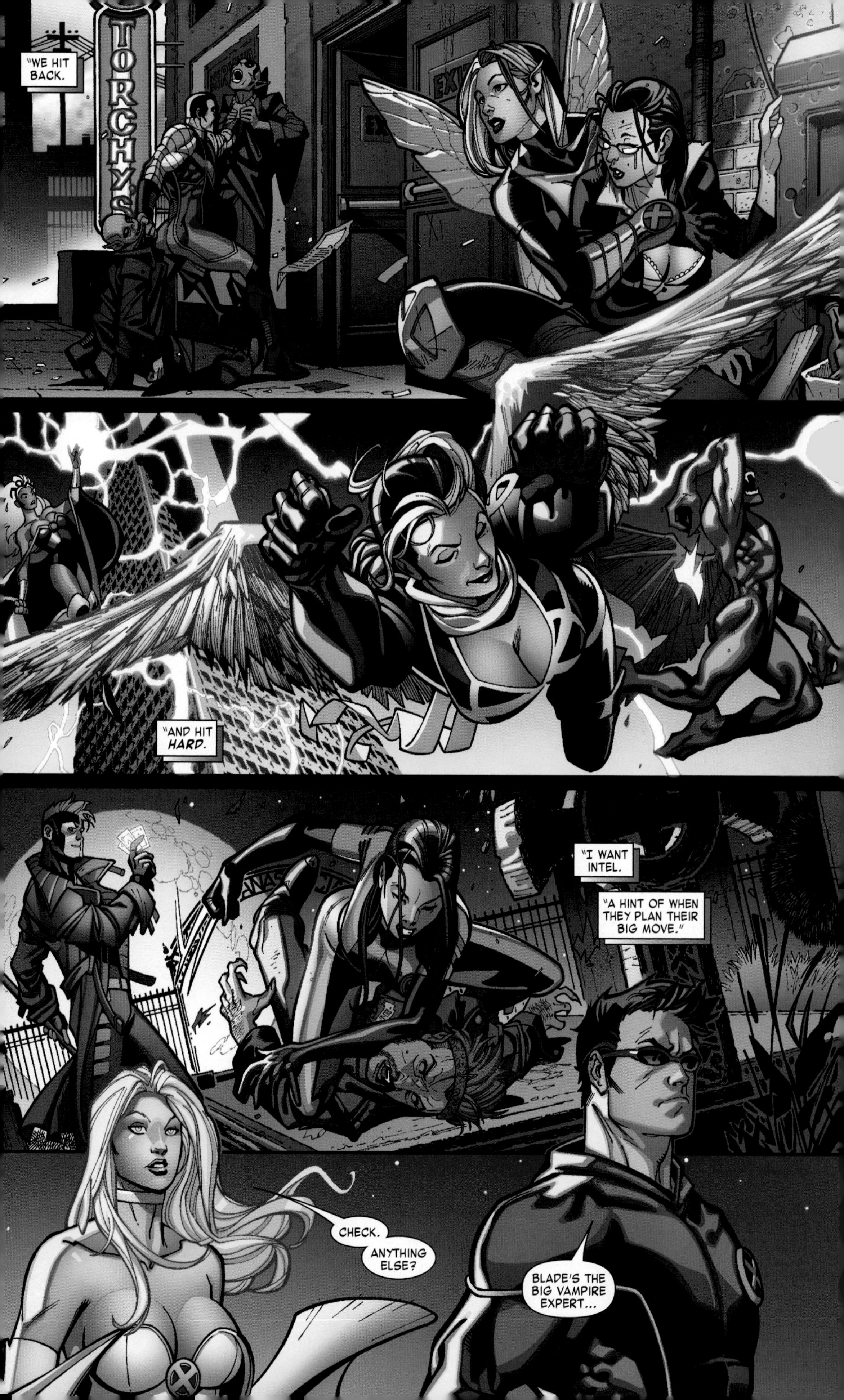

"WE HIT BACK.
TORCHY'S
EXIT
"AND HIT *HARD*.
"I WANT INTEL.
"A HINT OF WHEN THEY PLAN THEIR BIG MOVE."
CHECK.
ANYTHING ELSE?
BLADE'S THE BIG VAMPIRE EXPERT...

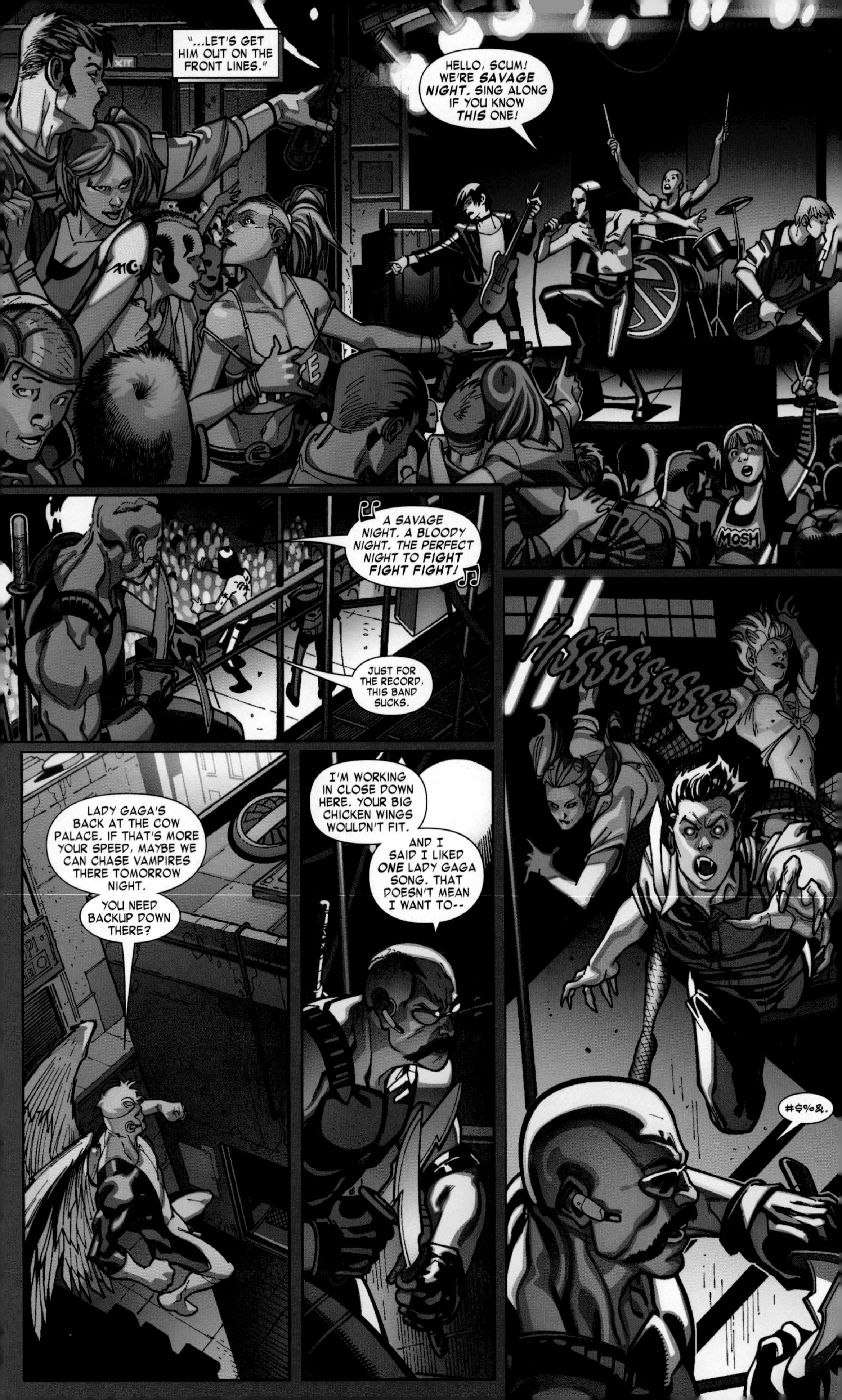

"...LET'S GET HIM OUT ON THE FRONT LINES."
HELLO, SCUM! WE'RE SAVAGE NIGHT. SING ALONG IF YOU KNOW THIS ONE!
MOSH
A SAVAGE NIGHT. A BLOODY NIGHT. THE PERFECT NIGHT TO FIGHT FIGHT FIGHT!
JUST FOR THE RECORD, THIS BAND SUCKS.
HISSSSSSSSSS
LADY GAGA'S BACK AT THE COW PALACE. IF THAT'S MORE YOUR SPEED, MAYBE WE CAN CHASE VAMPIRES THERE TOMORROW NIGHT.
YOU NEED BACKUP DOWN THERE?
I'M WORKING IN CLOSE DOWN HERE. YOUR BIG CHICKEN WINGS WOULDN'T FIT.
AND I SAID I LIKED ONE LADY GAGA SONG. THAT DOESN'T MEAN I WANT TO--
#$%&.

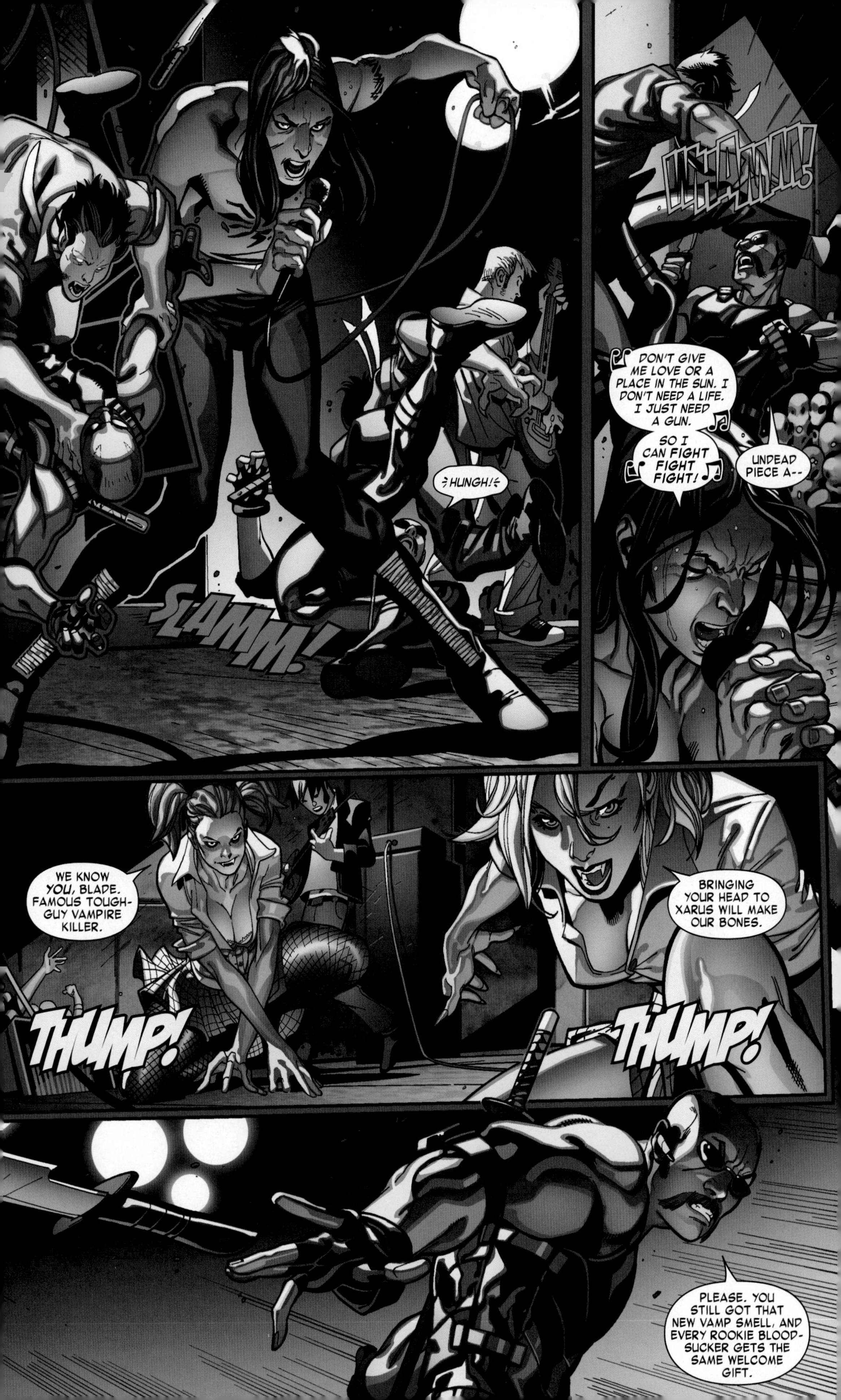
HUNGH!
SLAMM!
WHAMM!
DON'T GIVE ME LOVE OR A PLACE IN THE SUN. I DON'T NEED A LIFE. I JUST NEED A GUN.
SO I CAN FIGHT FIGHT FIGHT!
UNDEAD PIECE A--
WE KNOW YOU, BLADE. FAMOUS TOUGH-GUY VAMPIRE KILLER.
BRINGING YOUR HEAD TO XARUS WILL MAKE OUR BONES.
THUMP!
THUMP!
PLEASE. YOU STILL GOT THAT NEW VAMP SMELL, AND EVERY ROOKIE BLOOD-SUCKER GETS THE SAME WELCOME GIFT.

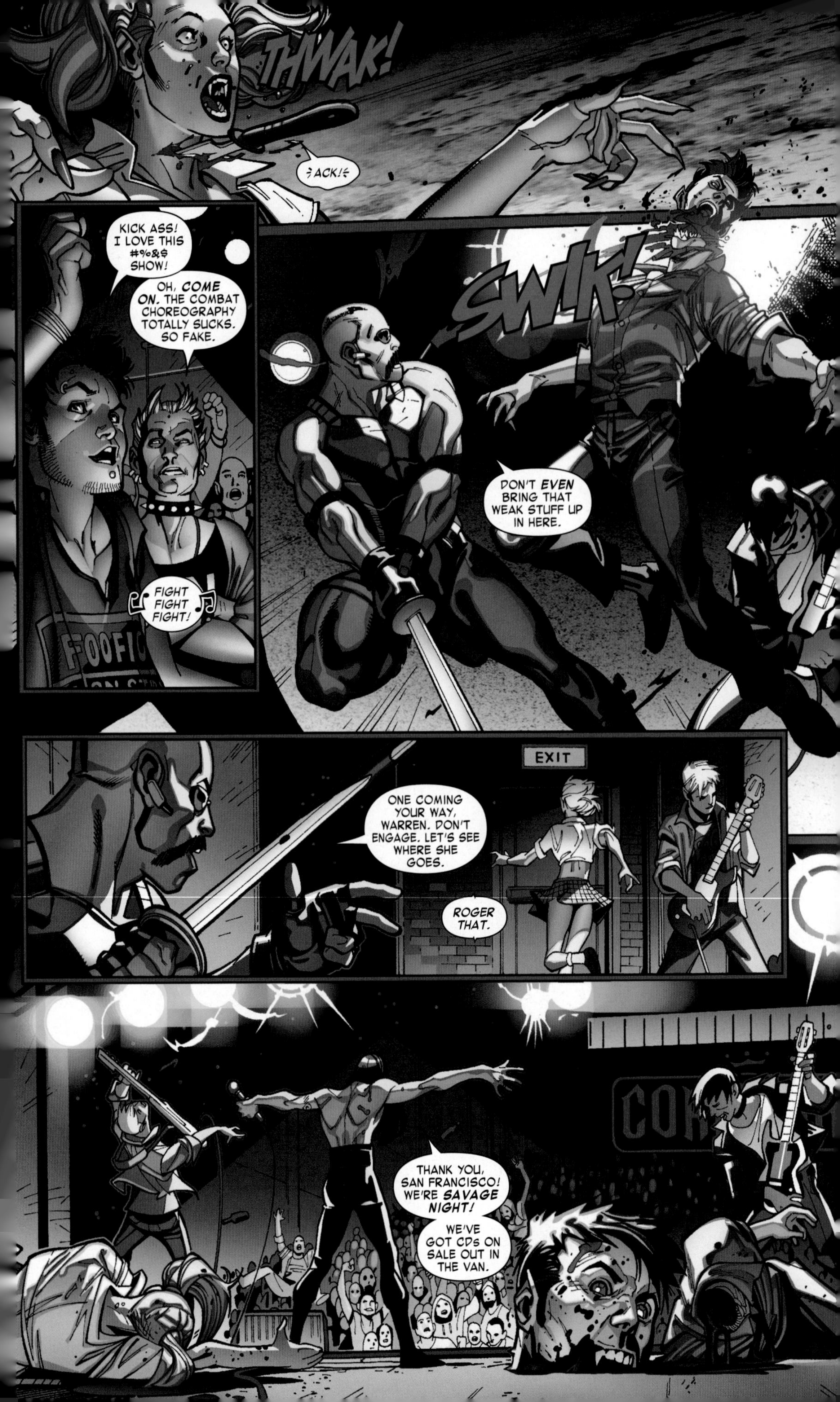
THWAK!
ACK!
KICK ASS! I LOVE THIS #%&$ SHOW!
OH, COME ON. THE COMBAT CHOREOGRAPHY TOTALLY SUCKS. SO FAKE.
FIGHT FIGHT FIGHT!
SWIK!
DON'T EVEN BRING THAT WEAK STUFF UP IN HERE.
EXIT
ONE COMING YOUR WAY, WARREN. DON'T ENGAGE. LET'S SEE WHERE SHE GOES.
ROGER THAT.
THANK YOU, SAN FRANCISCO! WE'RE SAVAGE NIGHT!
WE'VE GOT CDs ON SALE OUT IN THE VAN.

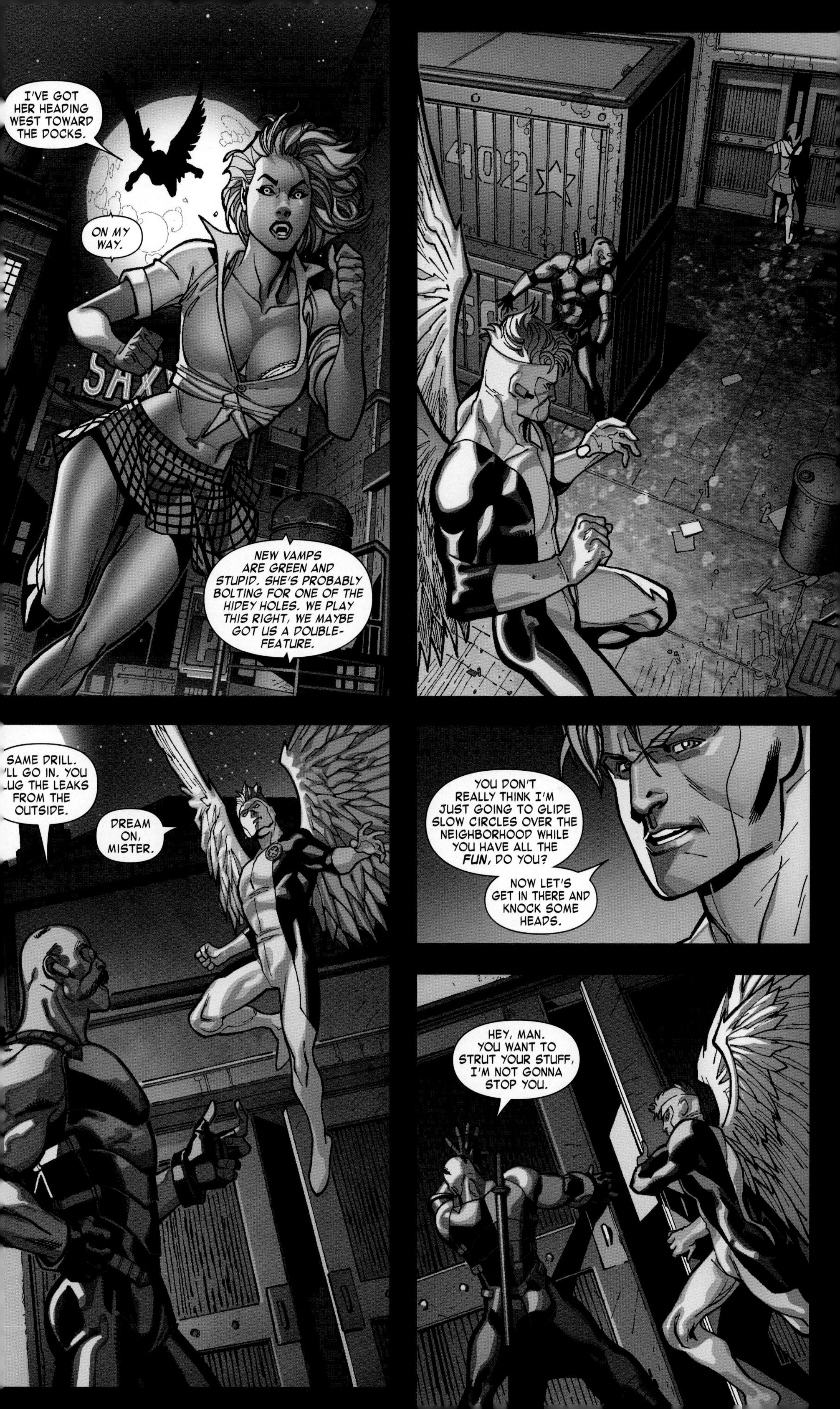

I'VE GOT HER HEADING WEST TOWARD THE DOCKS.
ON MY WAY.
NEW VAMPS ARE GREEN AND STUPID. SHE'S PROBABLY BOLTING FOR ONE OF THE HIDEY HOLES. WE PLAY THIS RIGHT, WE MAYBE GOT US A DOUBLE-FEATURE.
SAME DRILL. 'LL GO IN. YOU LUG THE LEAKS FROM THE OUTSIDE.
DREAM ON, MISTER.
YOU DON'T REALLY THINK I'M JUST GOING TO GLIDE SLOW CIRCLES OVER THE NEIGHBORHOOD WHILE YOU HAVE ALL THE FUN, DO YOU?
NOW LET'S GET IN THERE AND KNOCK SOME HEADS.
HEY, MAN. YOU WANT TO STRUT YOUR STUFF, I'M NOT GONNA STOP YOU.

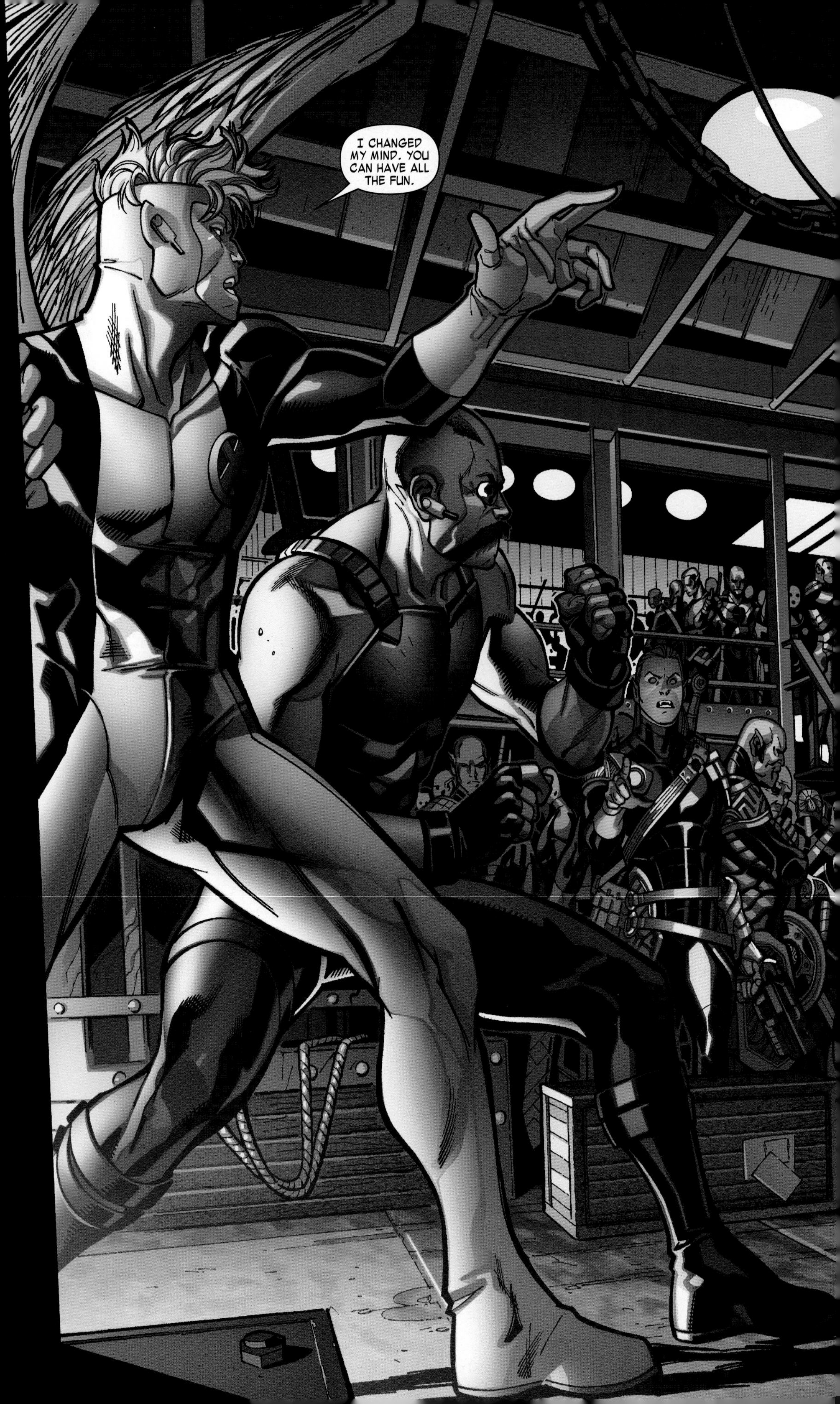
I CHANGED MY MIND. YOU CAN HAVE ALL THE FUN.

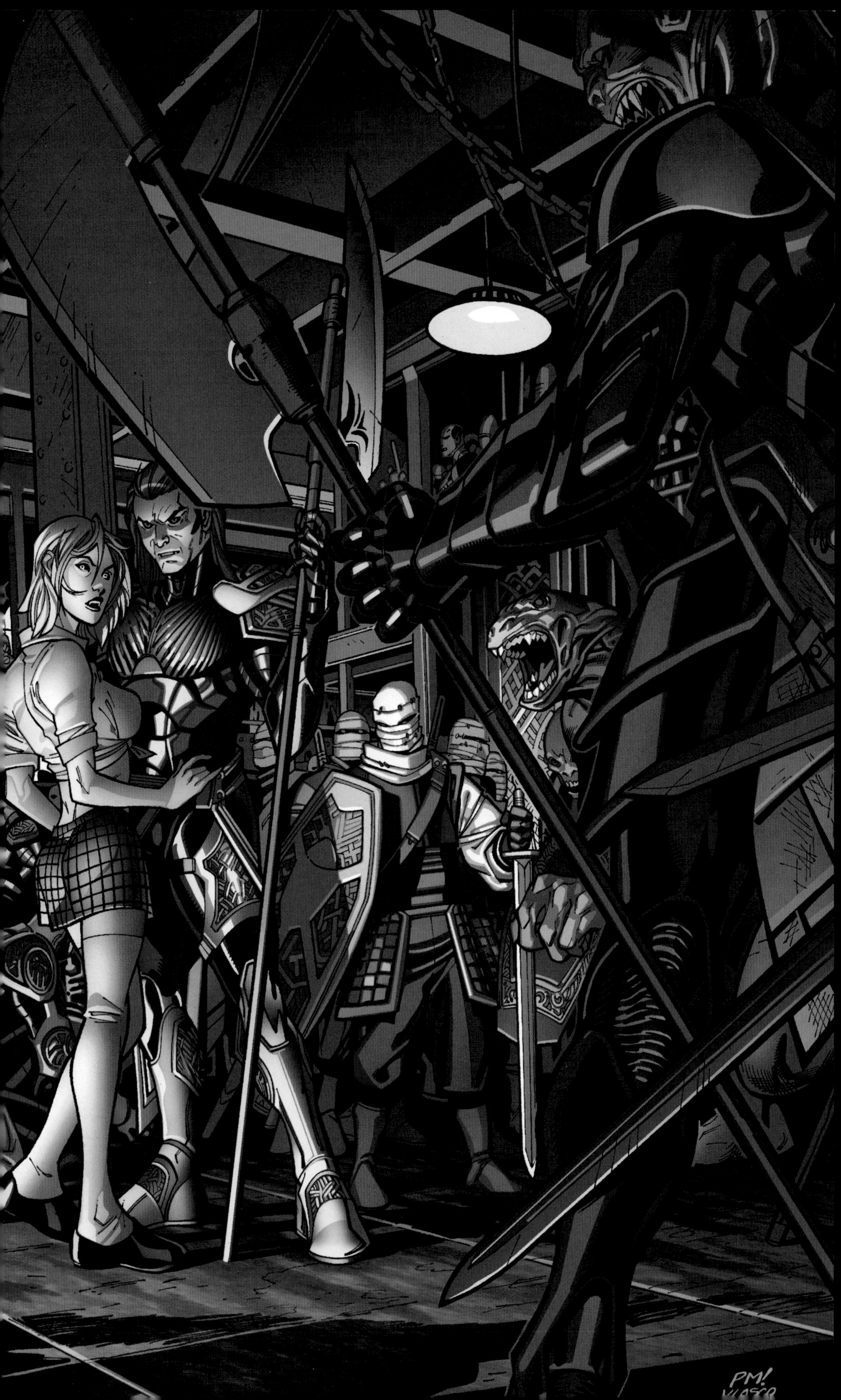
PM!

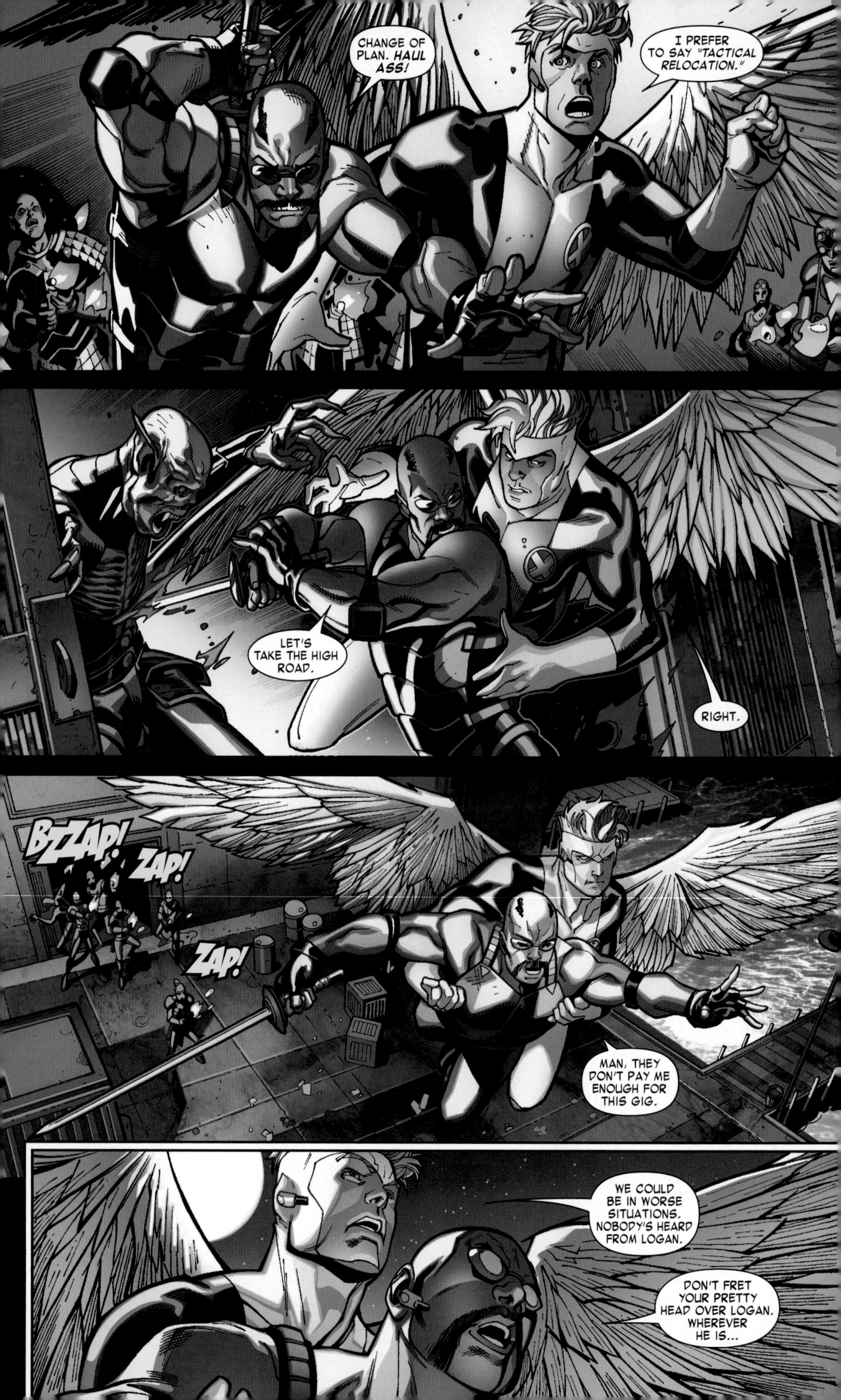

CHANGE OF PLAN. HAUL ASS!
I PREFER TO SAY "TACTICAL RELOCATION."
LET'S TAKE THE HIGH ROAD.
RIGHT.
BZZAP!
ZAP!
ZAP!
MAN, THEY DON'T PAY ME ENOUGH FOR THIS GIG.
WE COULD BE IN WORSE SITUATIONS. NOBODY'S HEARD FROM LOGAN.
DON'T FRET YOUR PRETTY HEAD OVER LOGAN. WHEREVER HE IS...

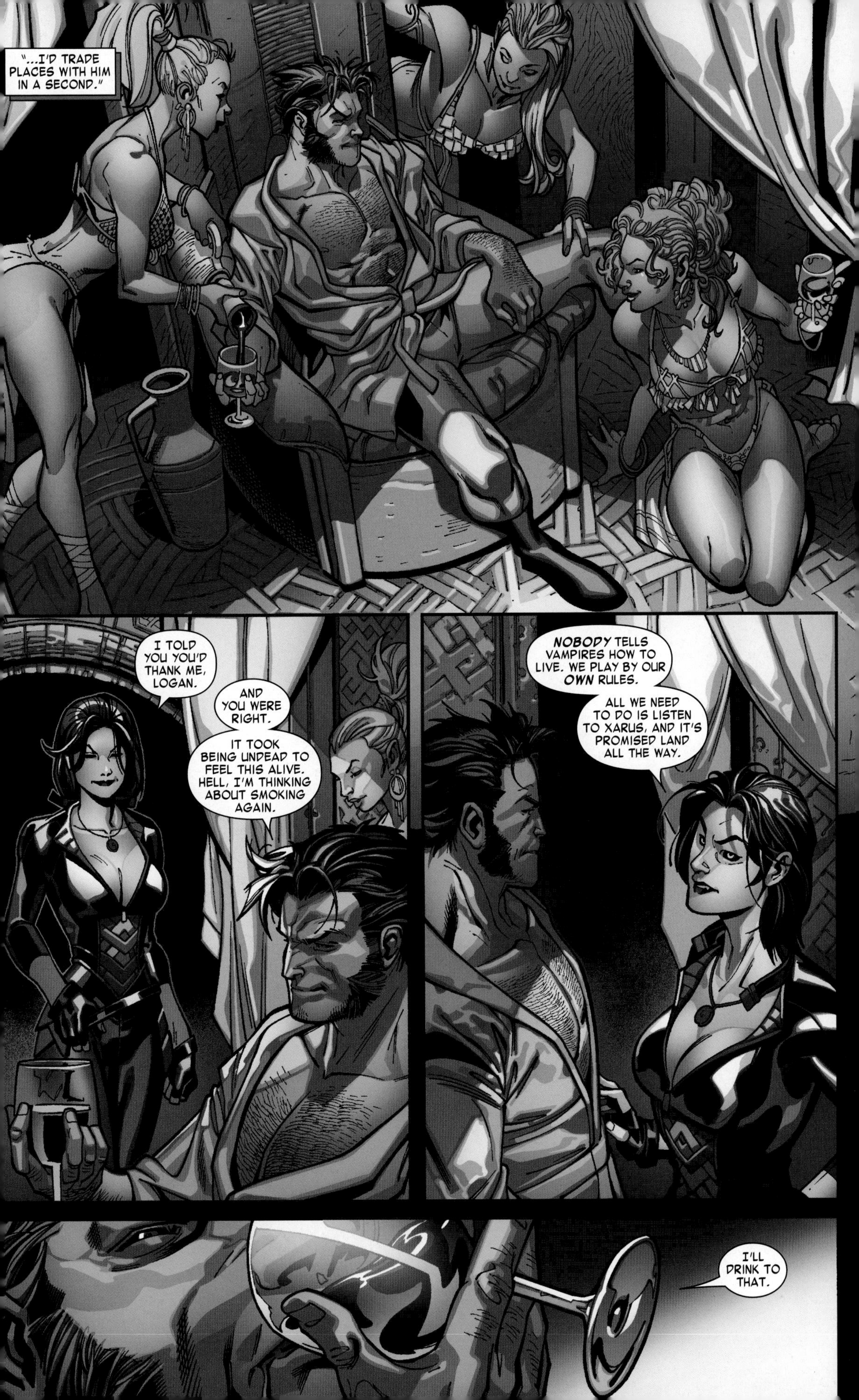
"...I'D TRADE PLACES WITH HIM IN A SECOND."
I TOLD YOU YOU'D THANK ME, LOGAN.
AND YOU WERE RIGHT.
IT TOOK BEING UNDEAD TO FEEL THIS ALIVE. HELL, I'M THINKING ABOUT SMOKING AGAIN.
NOBODY TELLS VAMPIRES HOW TO LIVE. WE PLAY BY OUR OWN RULES.
ALL WE NEED TO DO IS LISTEN TO XARUS, AND IT'S PROMISED LAND ALL THE WAY.
I'LL DRINK TO THAT.

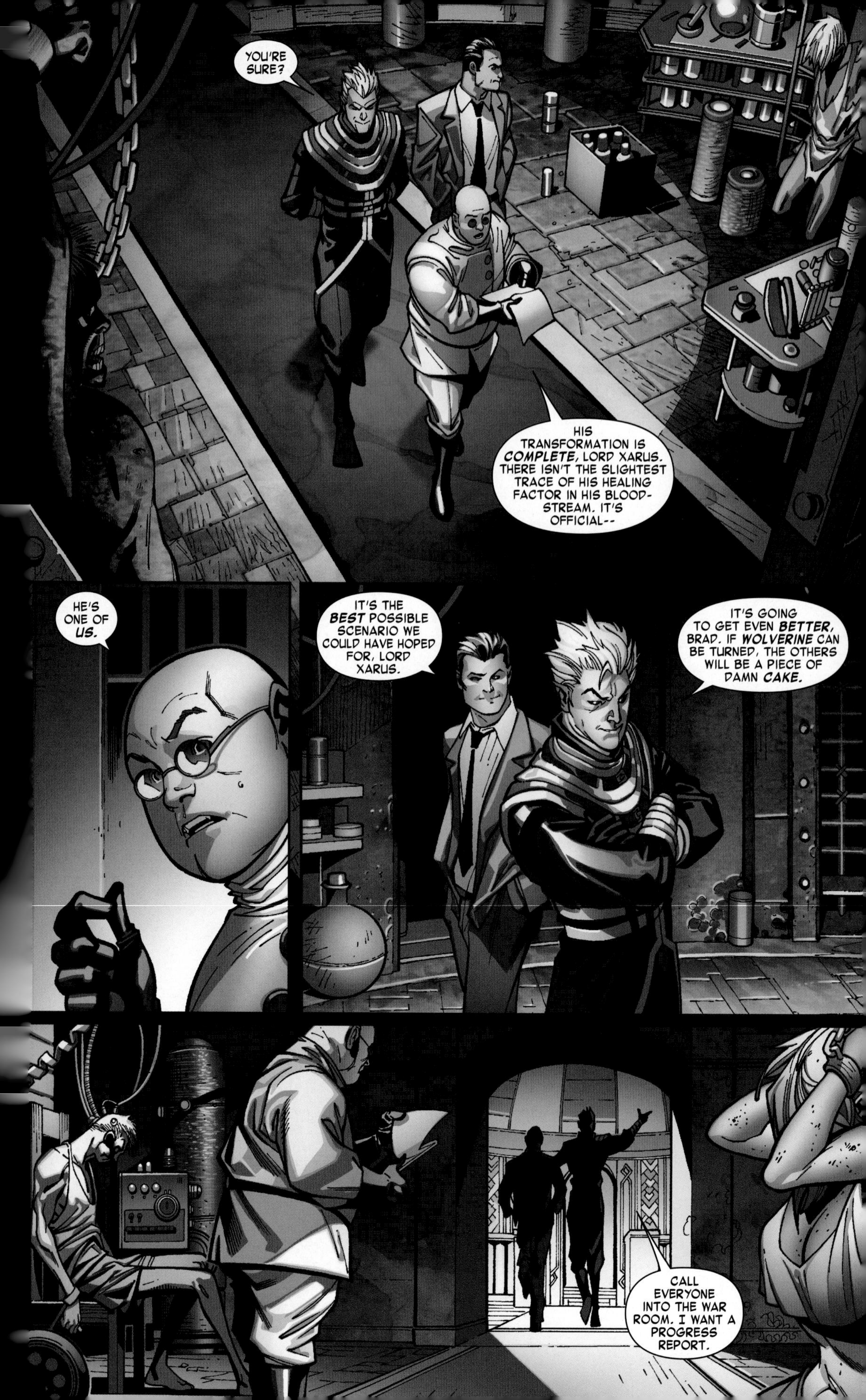
YOU'RE SURE?
HIS TRANSFORMATION IS COMPLETE, LORD XARUS. THERE ISN'T THE SLIGHTEST TRACE OF HIS HEALING FACTOR IN HIS BLOOD-STREAM. IT'S OFFICIAL--
HE'S ONE OF US.
IT'S THE BEST POSSIBLE SCENARIO WE COULD HAVE HOPED FOR, LORD XARUS.
IT'S GOING TO GET EVEN BETTER, BRAD. IF WOLVERINE CAN BE TURNED, THE OTHERS WILL BE A PIECE OF DAMN CAKE.
CALL EVERYONE INTO THE WAR ROOM. I WANT A PROGRESS REPORT.

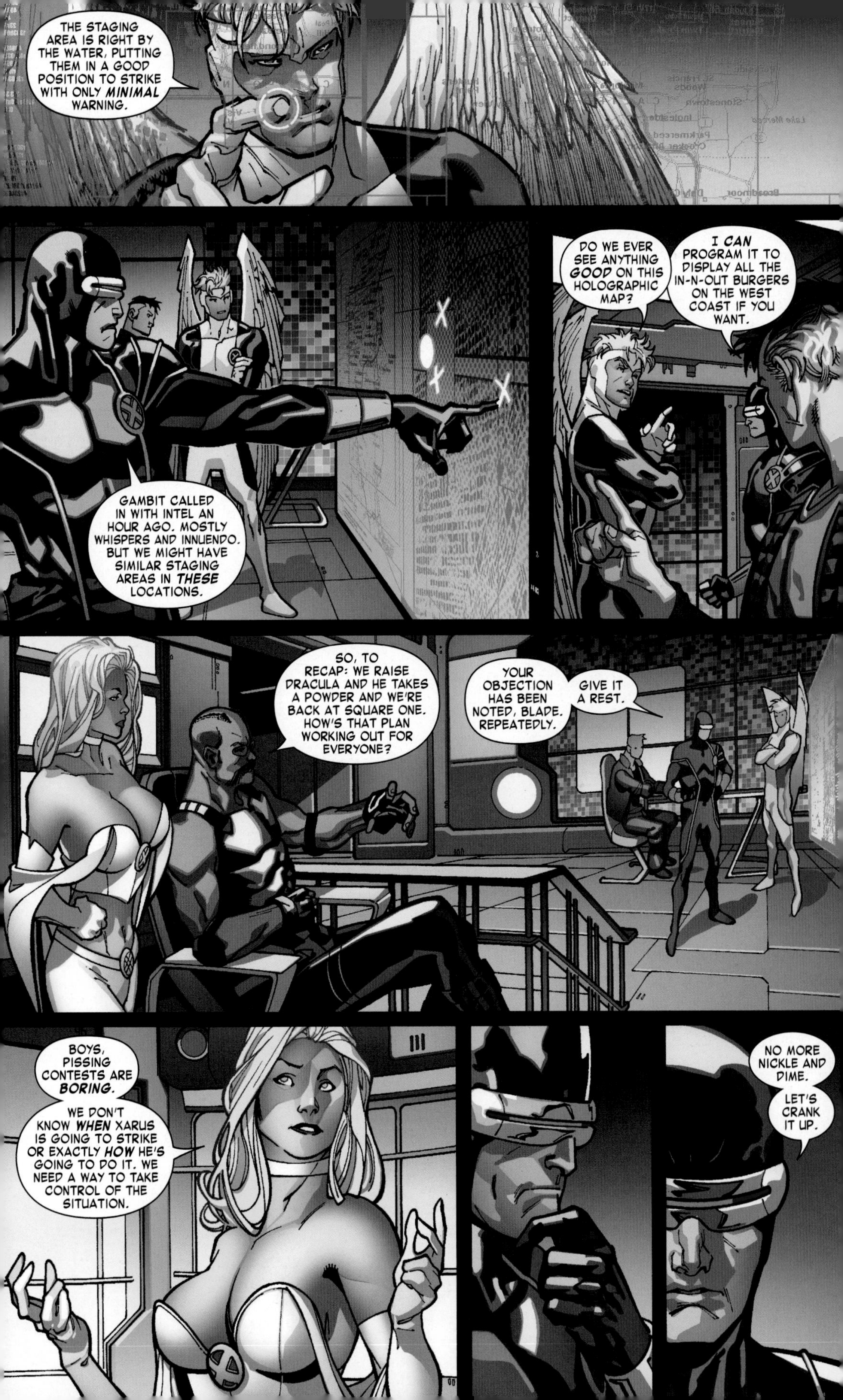
THE STAGING AREA IS RIGHT BY THE WATER, PUTTING THEM IN A GOOD POSITION TO STRIKE WITH ONLY *MINIMAL* WARNING.
GAMBIT CALLED IN WITH INTEL AN HOUR AGO. MOSTLY WHISPERS AND INNUENDO. BUT WE MIGHT HAVE SIMILAR STAGING AREAS IN *THESE* LOCATIONS.
DO WE EVER SEE ANYTHING *GOOD* ON THIS HOLOGRAPHIC MAP?
I *CAN* PROGRAM IT TO DISPLAY ALL THE IN-N-OUT BURGERS ON THE WEST COAST IF YOU WANT.
SO, TO RECAP: WE RAISE DRACULA AND HE TAKES A POWDER AND WE'RE BACK AT SQUARE ONE. HOW'S THAT PLAN WORKING OUT FOR EVERYONE?
YOUR OBJECTION HAS BEEN NOTED, BLADE. REPEATEDLY.
GIVE IT A REST.
BOYS, PISSING CONTESTS ARE *BORING.*
WE DON'T KNOW *WHEN* XARUS IS GOING TO STRIKE OR EXACTLY *HOW* HE'S GOING TO DO IT. WE NEED A WAY TO TAKE CONTROL OF THE SITUATION.
NO MORE NICKLE AND DIME.
LET'S CRANK IT UP.

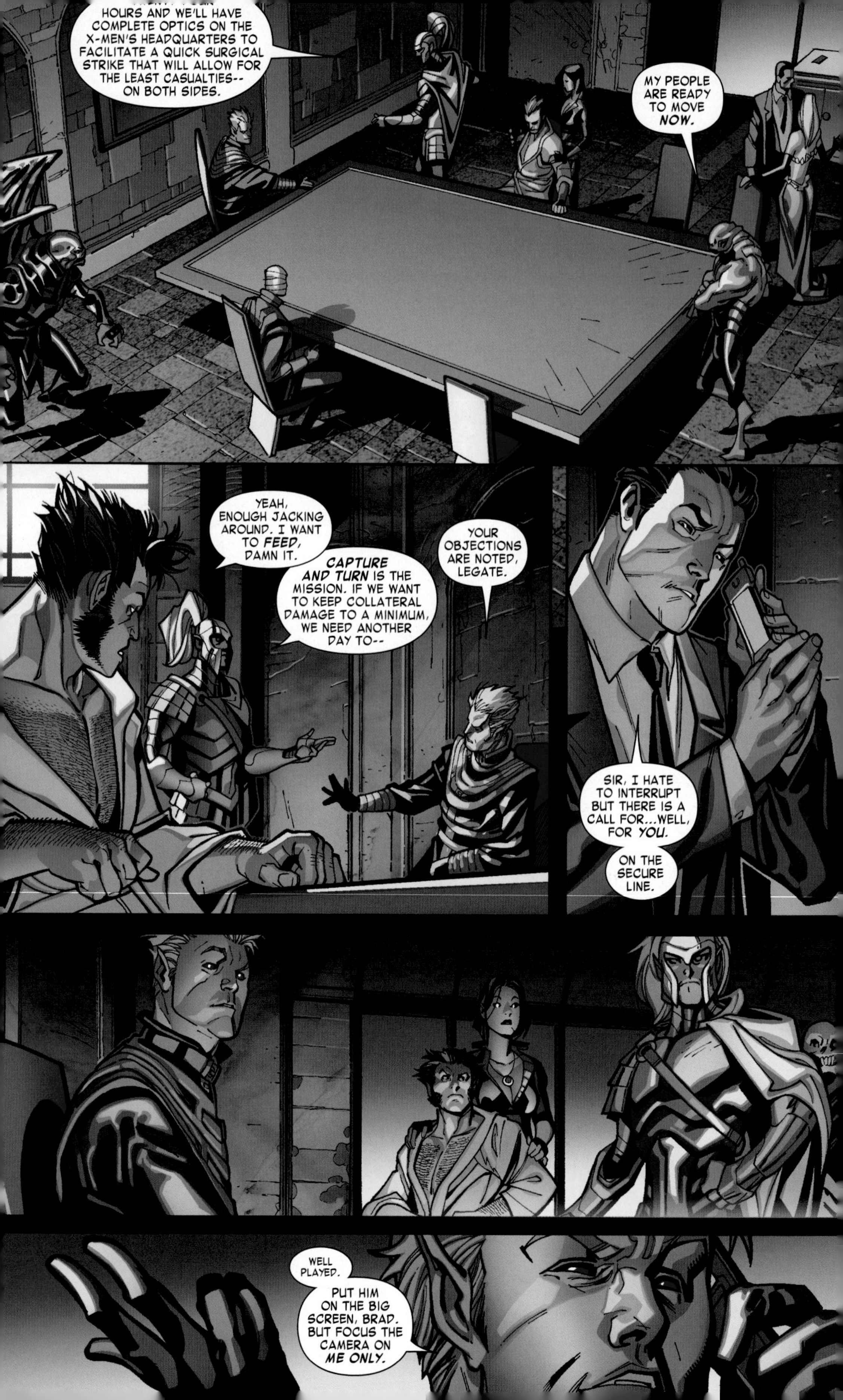

HOURS AND WE'LL HAVE COMPLETE OPTICS ON THE X-MEN'S HEADQUARTERS TO FACILITATE A QUICK SURGICAL STRIKE THAT WILL ALLOW FOR THE LEAST CASUALTIES-- ON BOTH SIDES.
MY PEOPLE ARE READY TO MOVE NOW.
YEAH, ENOUGH JACKING AROUND. I WANT TO FEED, DAMN IT.
CAPTURE AND TURN IS THE MISSION. IF WE WANT TO KEEP COLLATERAL DAMAGE TO A MINIMUM, WE NEED ANOTHER DAY TO--
YOUR OBJECTIONS ARE NOTED, LEGATE.
SIR, I HATE TO INTERRUPT BUT THERE IS A CALL FOR...WELL, FOR YOU.
ON THE SECURE LINE.
WELL PLAYED.
PUT HIM ON THE BIG SCREEN, BRAD. BUT FOCUS THE CAMERA ON ME ONLY.

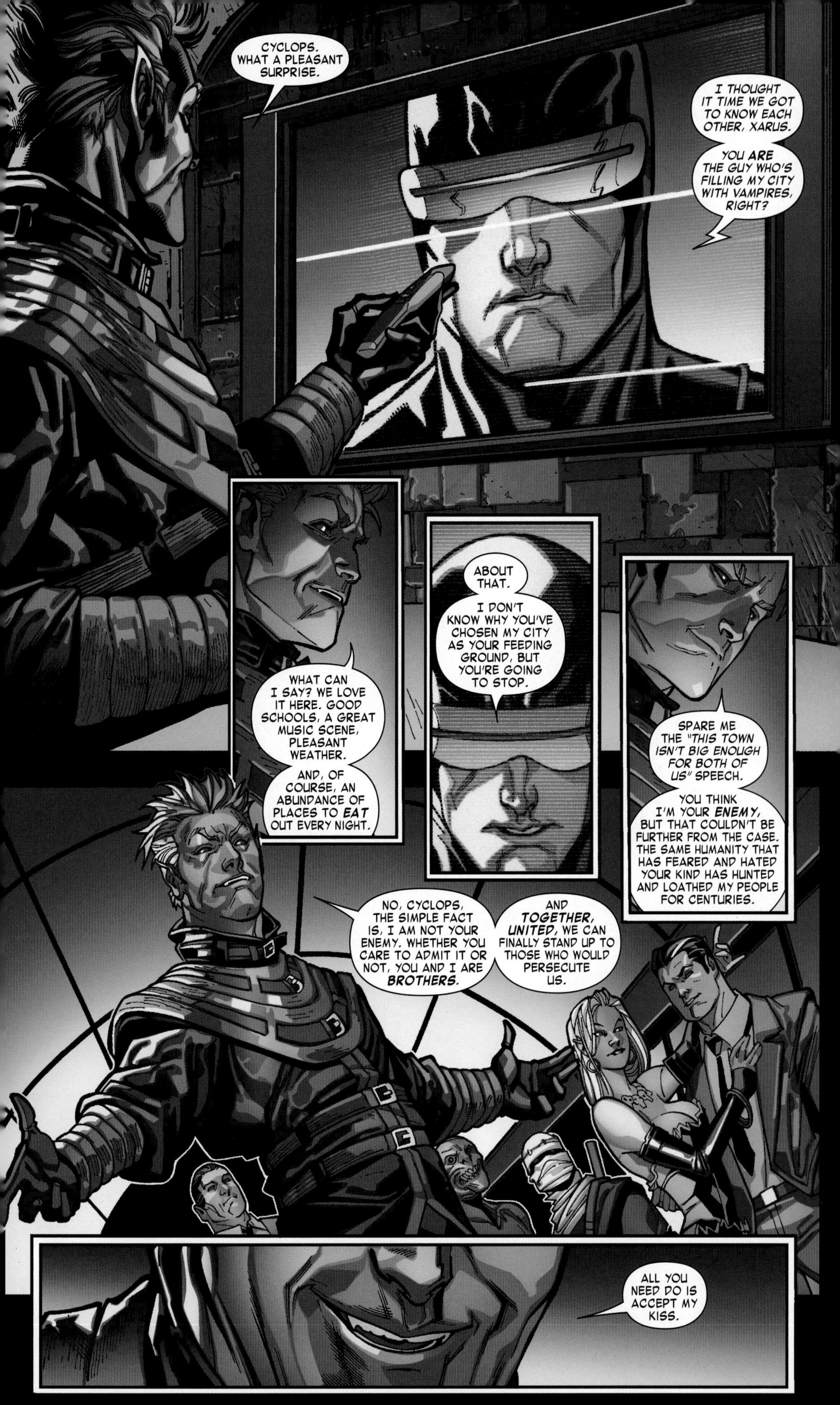
CYCLOPS. WHAT A PLEASANT SURPRISE.
I THOUGHT IT TIME WE GOT TO KNOW EACH OTHER, XARUS.
YOU ARE THE GUY WHO'S FILLING MY CITY WITH VAMPIRES, RIGHT?
WHAT CAN I SAY? WE LOVE IT HERE. GOOD SCHOOLS, A GREAT MUSIC SCENE, PLEASANT WEATHER.
AND, OF COURSE, AN ABUNDANCE OF PLACES TO EAT OUT EVERY NIGHT.
ABOUT THAT.
I DON'T KNOW WHY YOU'VE CHOSEN MY CITY AS YOUR FEEDING GROUND, BUT YOU'RE GOING TO STOP.
SPARE ME THE "THIS TOWN ISN'T BIG ENOUGH FOR BOTH OF US" SPEECH.
YOU THINK I'M YOUR ENEMY, BUT THAT COULDN'T BE FURTHER FROM THE CASE. THE SAME HUMANITY THAT HAS FEARED AND HATED YOUR KIND HAS HUNTED AND LOATHED MY PEOPLE FOR CENTURIES.
NO, CYCLOPS, THE SIMPLE FACT IS, I AM NOT YOUR ENEMY. WHETHER YOU CARE TO ADMIT IT OR NOT, YOU AND I ARE BROTHERS.
AND TOGETHER, UNITED, WE CAN FINALLY STAND UP TO THOSE WHO WOULD PERSECUTE US.
ALL YOU NEED DO IS ACCEPT MY KISS.

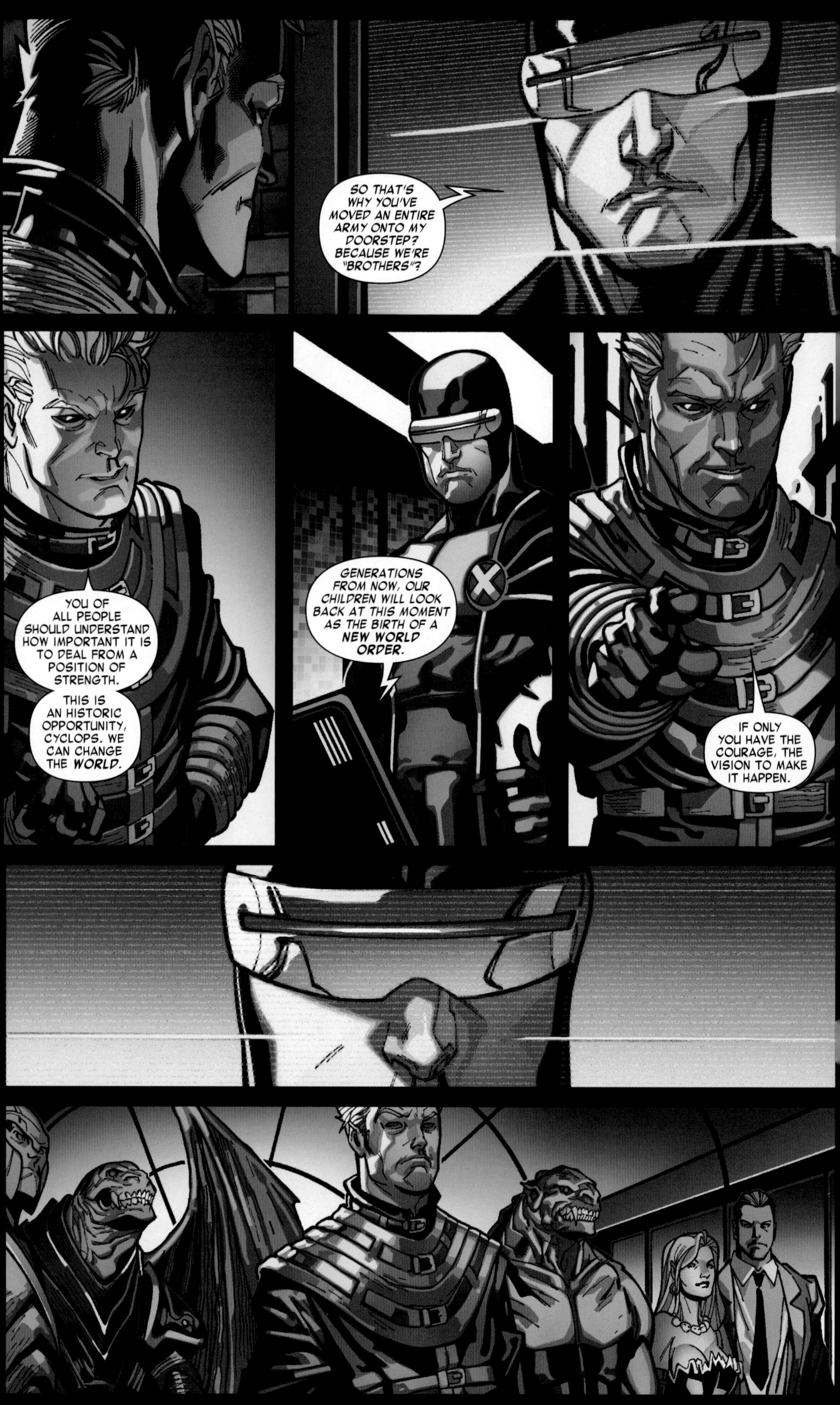

SO THAT'S WHY YOU'VE MOVED AN ENTIRE ARMY ONTO MY DOORSTEP? BECAUSE WE'RE "BROTHERS"?
YOU OF ALL PEOPLE SHOULD UNDERSTAND HOW IMPORTANT IT IS TO DEAL FROM A POSITION OF STRENGTH.
THIS IS AN HISTORIC OPPORTUNITY, CYCLOPS. WE CAN CHANGE THE *WORLD*.
GENERATIONS FROM NOW, OUR CHILDREN WILL LOOK BACK AT THIS MOMENT AS THE BIRTH OF A **NEW WORLD ORDER**.
IF ONLY YOU HAVE THE COURAGE, THE VISION TO MAKE IT HAPPEN.

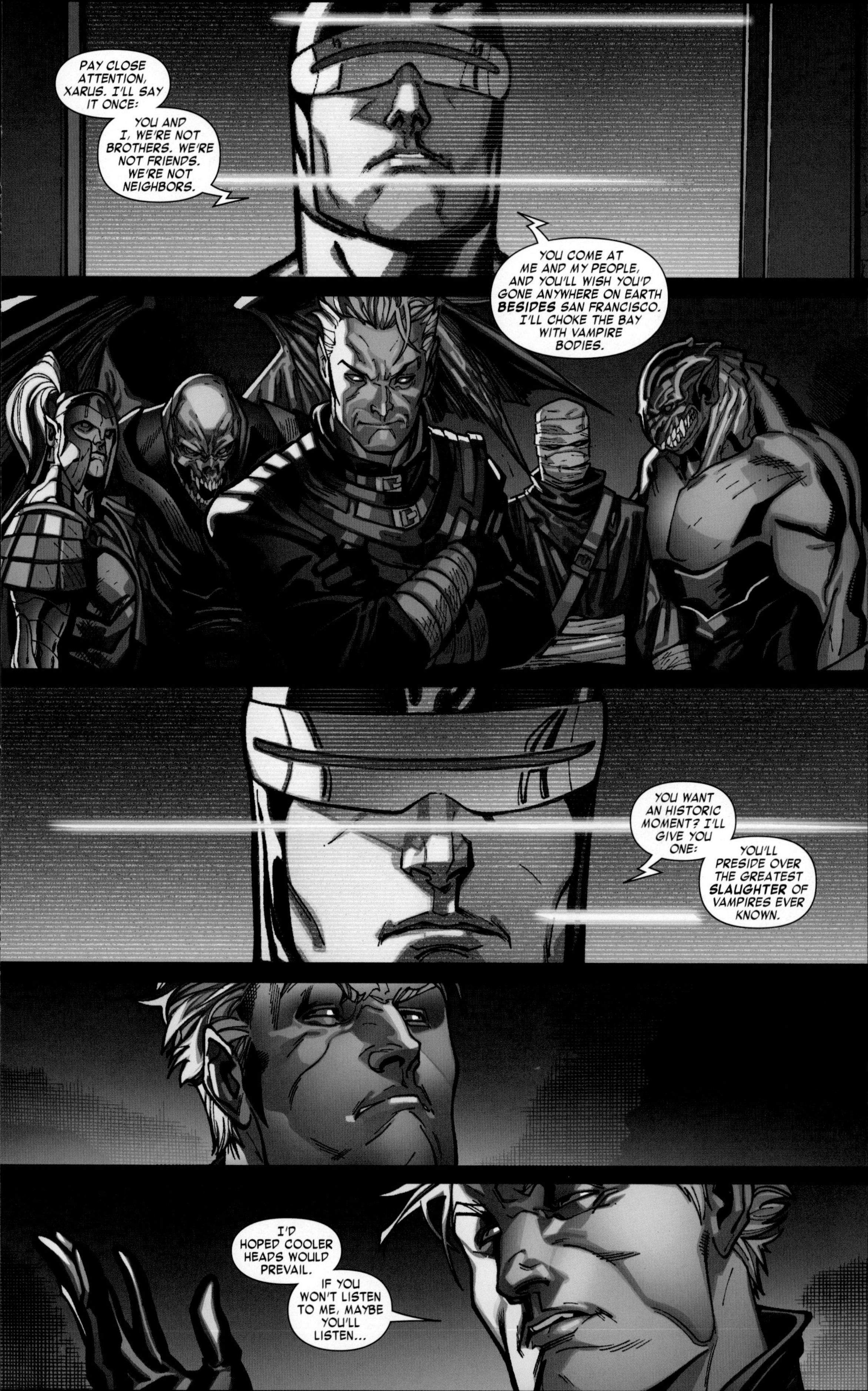
PAY CLOSE ATTENTION, XARUS. I'LL SAY IT ONCE:
YOU AND I, WE'RE NOT BROTHERS. WE'RE NOT FRIENDS. WE'RE NOT NEIGHBORS.
YOU COME AT ME AND MY PEOPLE, AND YOU'LL WISH YOU'D GONE ANYWHERE ON EARTH BESIDES SAN FRANCISCO. I'LL CHOKE THE BAY WITH VAMPIRE BODIES.
YOU WANT AN HISTORIC MOMENT? I'LL GIVE YOU ONE:
YOU'LL PRESIDE OVER THE GREATEST SLAUGHTER OF VAMPIRES EVER KNOWN.
I'D HOPED COOLER HEADS WOULD PREVAIL.
IF YOU WON'T LISTEN TO ME, MAYBE YOU'LL LISTEN...

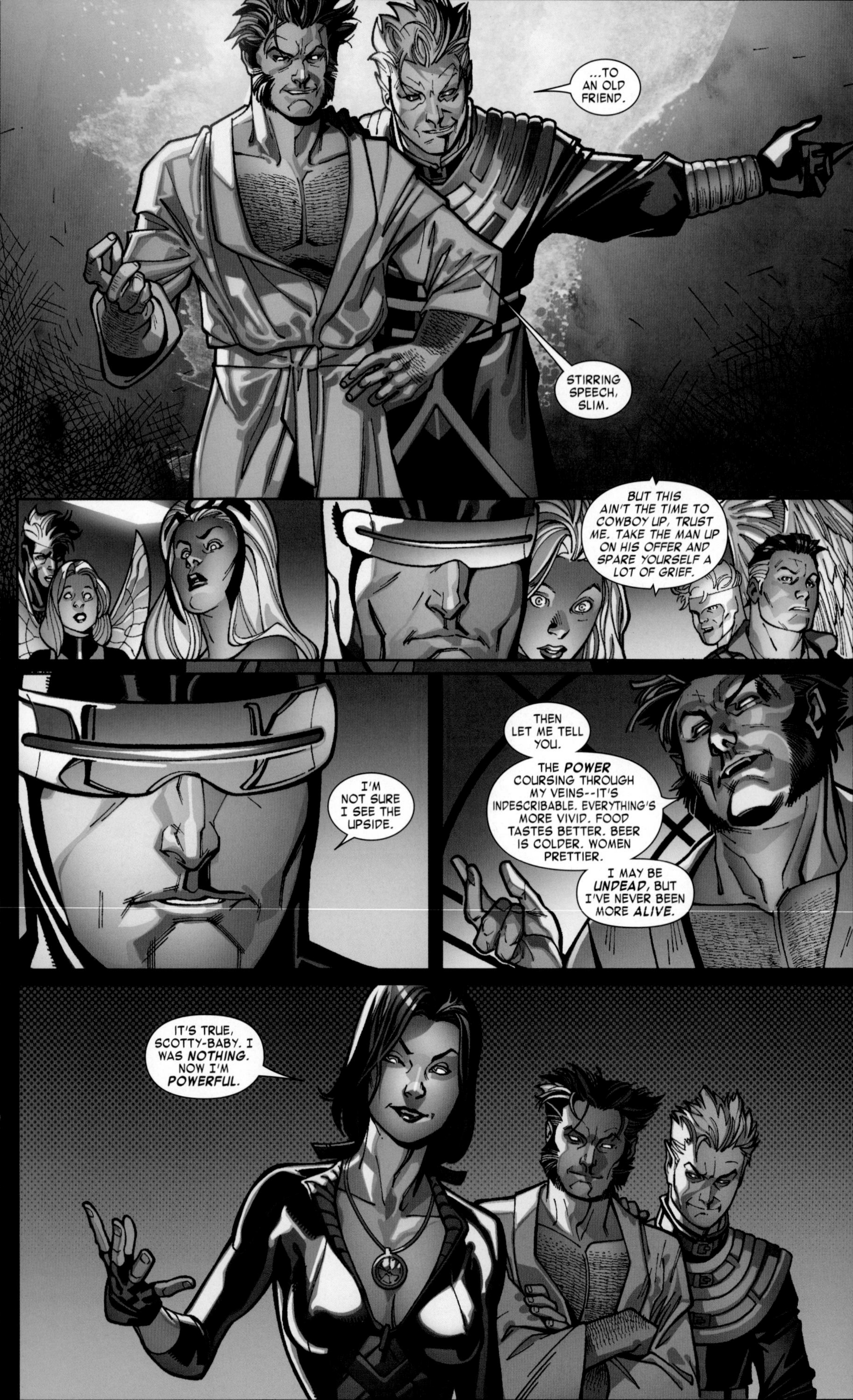
...TO AN OLD FRIEND.
STIRRING SPEECH, SLIM.
BUT THIS AIN'T THE TIME TO COWBOY UP, TRUST ME. TAKE THE MAN UP ON HIS OFFER AND SPARE YOURSELF A LOT OF GRIEF.
I'M NOT SURE I SEE THE UPSIDE.
THEN LET ME TELL YOU.
THE POWER COURSING THROUGH MY VEINS--IT'S INDESCRIBABLE. EVERYTHING'S MORE VIVID. FOOD TASTES BETTER. BEER IS COLDER. WOMEN PRETTIER.
I MAY BE UNDEAD, BUT I'VE NEVER BEEN MORE ALIVE.
IT'S TRUE, SCOTTY-BABY. I WAS NOTHING. NOW I'M POWERFUL.

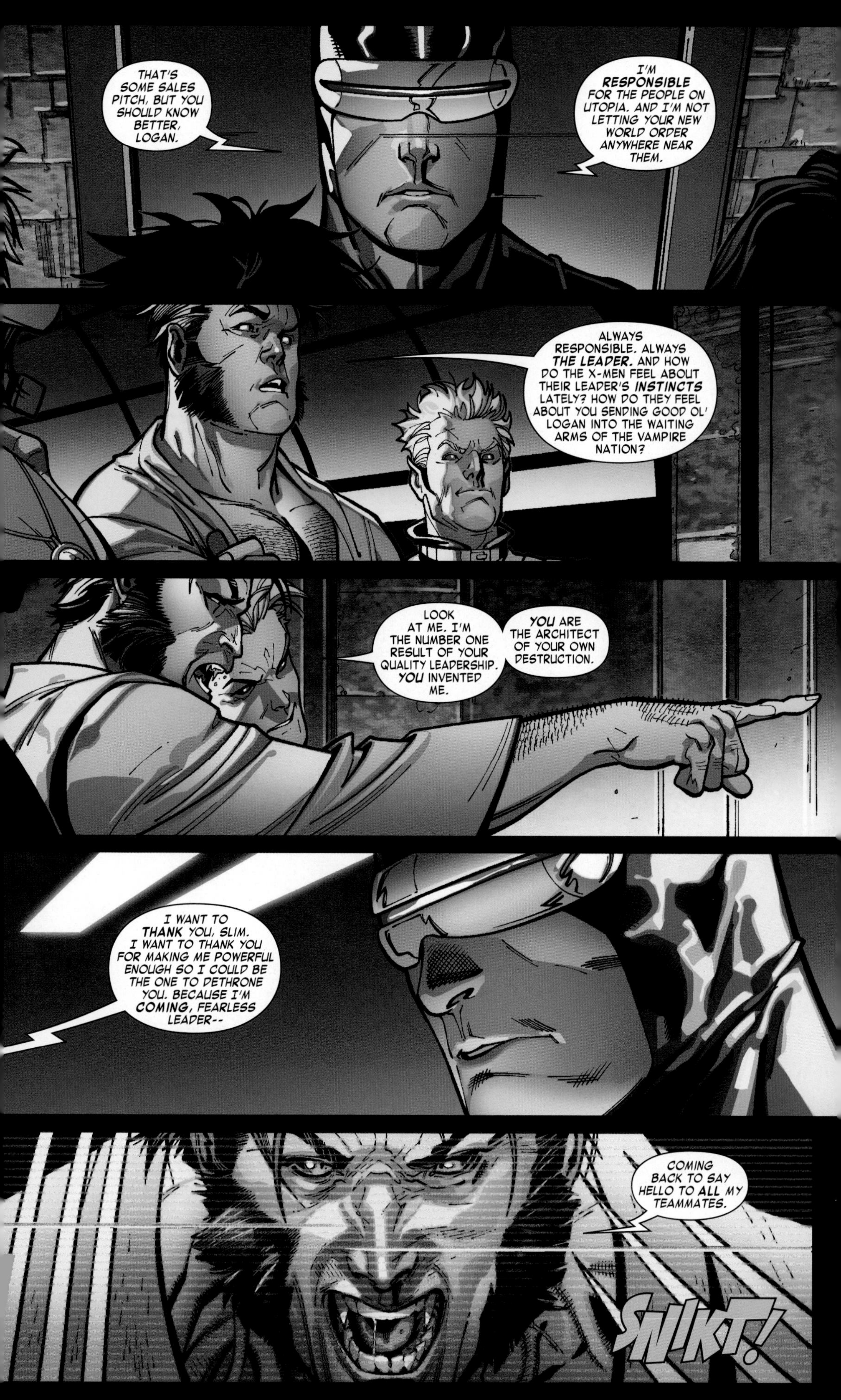
THAT'S SOME SALES PITCH, BUT YOU SHOULD KNOW BETTER, LOGAN.
I'M RESPONSIBLE FOR THE PEOPLE ON UTOPIA. AND I'M NOT LETTING YOUR NEW WORLD ORDER ANYWHERE NEAR THEM.
ALWAYS RESPONSIBLE. ALWAYS THE LEADER. AND HOW DO THE X-MEN FEEL ABOUT THEIR LEADER'S INSTINCTS LATELY? HOW DO THEY FEEL ABOUT YOU SENDING GOOD OL' LOGAN INTO THE WAITING ARMS OF THE VAMPIRE NATION?
LOOK AT ME. I'M THE NUMBER ONE RESULT OF YOUR QUALITY LEADERSHIP. YOU INVENTED ME.
YOU ARE THE ARCHITECT OF YOUR OWN DESTRUCTION.
I WANT TO THANK YOU, SLIM. I WANT TO THANK YOU FOR MAKING ME POWERFUL ENOUGH SO I COULD BE THE ONE TO DETHRONE YOU. BECAUSE I'M COMING, FEARLESS LEADER--
COMING BACK TO SAY HELLO TO ALL MY TEAMMATES.
SNIKT!

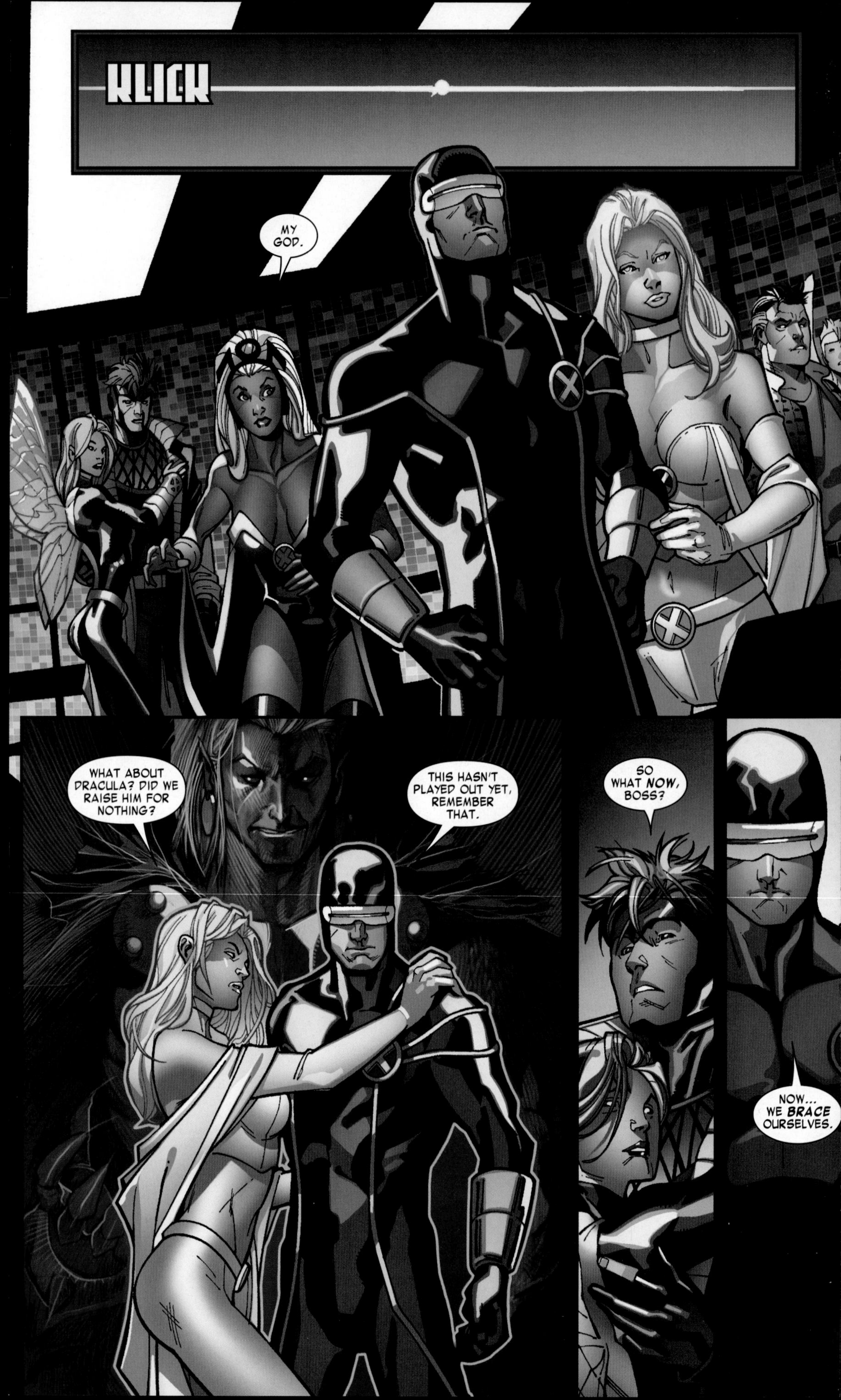
KLICK
MY GOD.
WHAT ABOUT DRACULA? DID WE RAISE HIM FOR NOTHING?
THIS HASN'T PLAYED OUT YET, REMEMBER THAT.
SO WHAT NOW, BOSS?
NOW... WE BRACE OURSELVES.

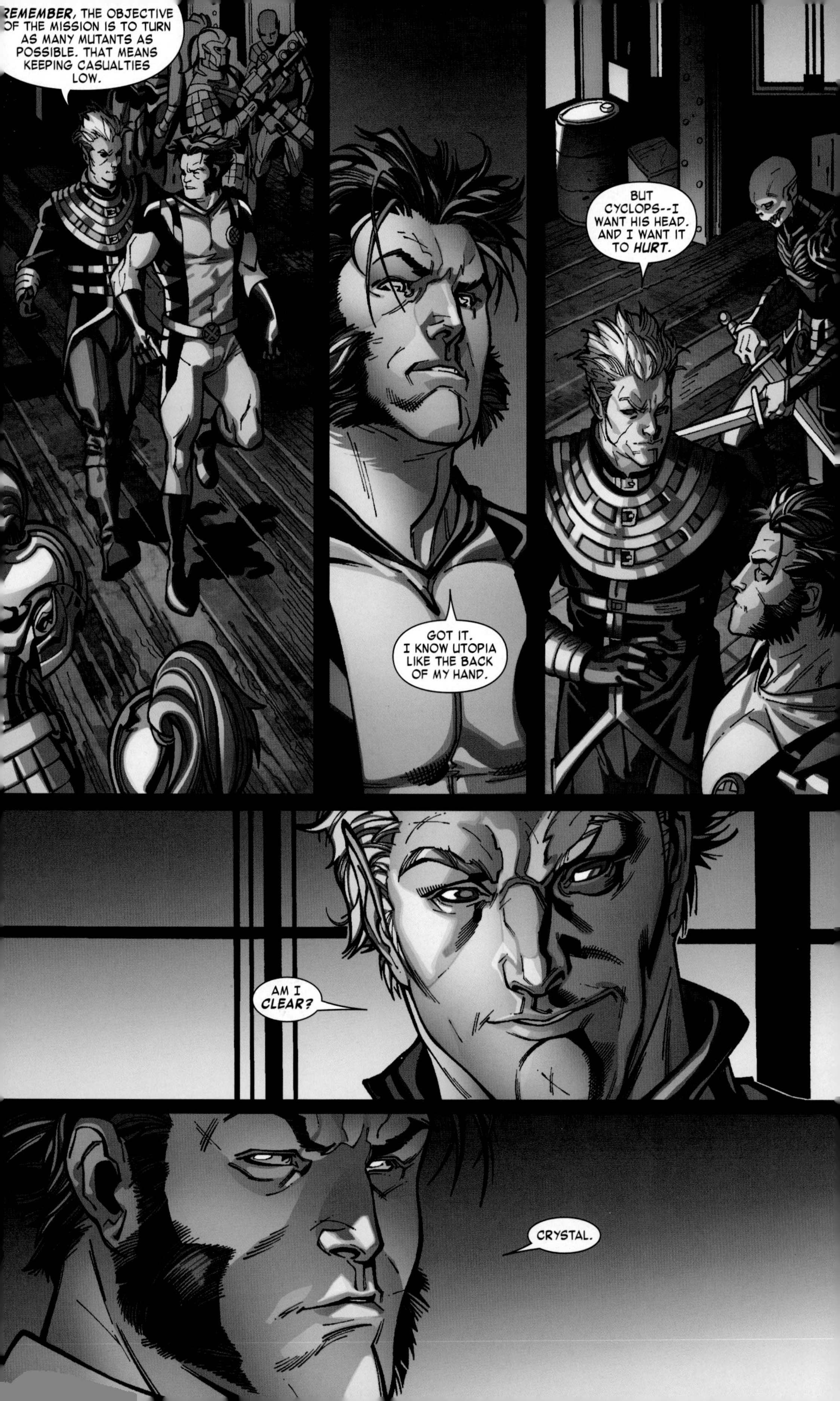
REMEMBER, THE OBJECTIVE OF THE MISSION IS TO TURN AS MANY MUTANTS AS POSSIBLE. THAT MEANS KEEPING CASUALTIES LOW.
GOT IT. I KNOW UTOPIA LIKE THE BACK OF MY HAND.
BUT CYCLOPS--I WANT HIS HEAD. AND I WANT IT TO HURT.
AM I CLEAR?
CRYSTAL.

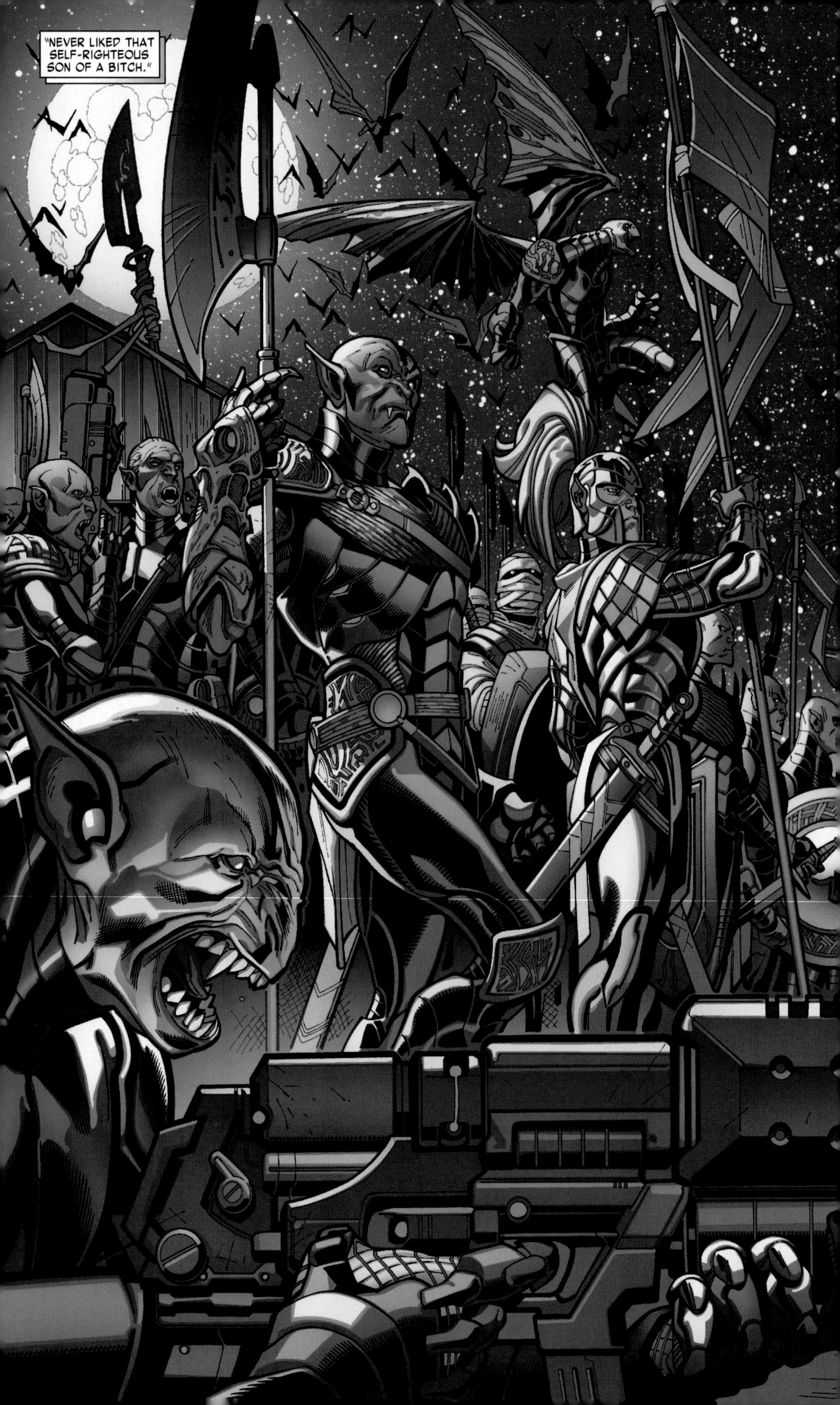
"NEVER LIKED THAT SELF-RIGHTEOUS SON OF A BITCH."

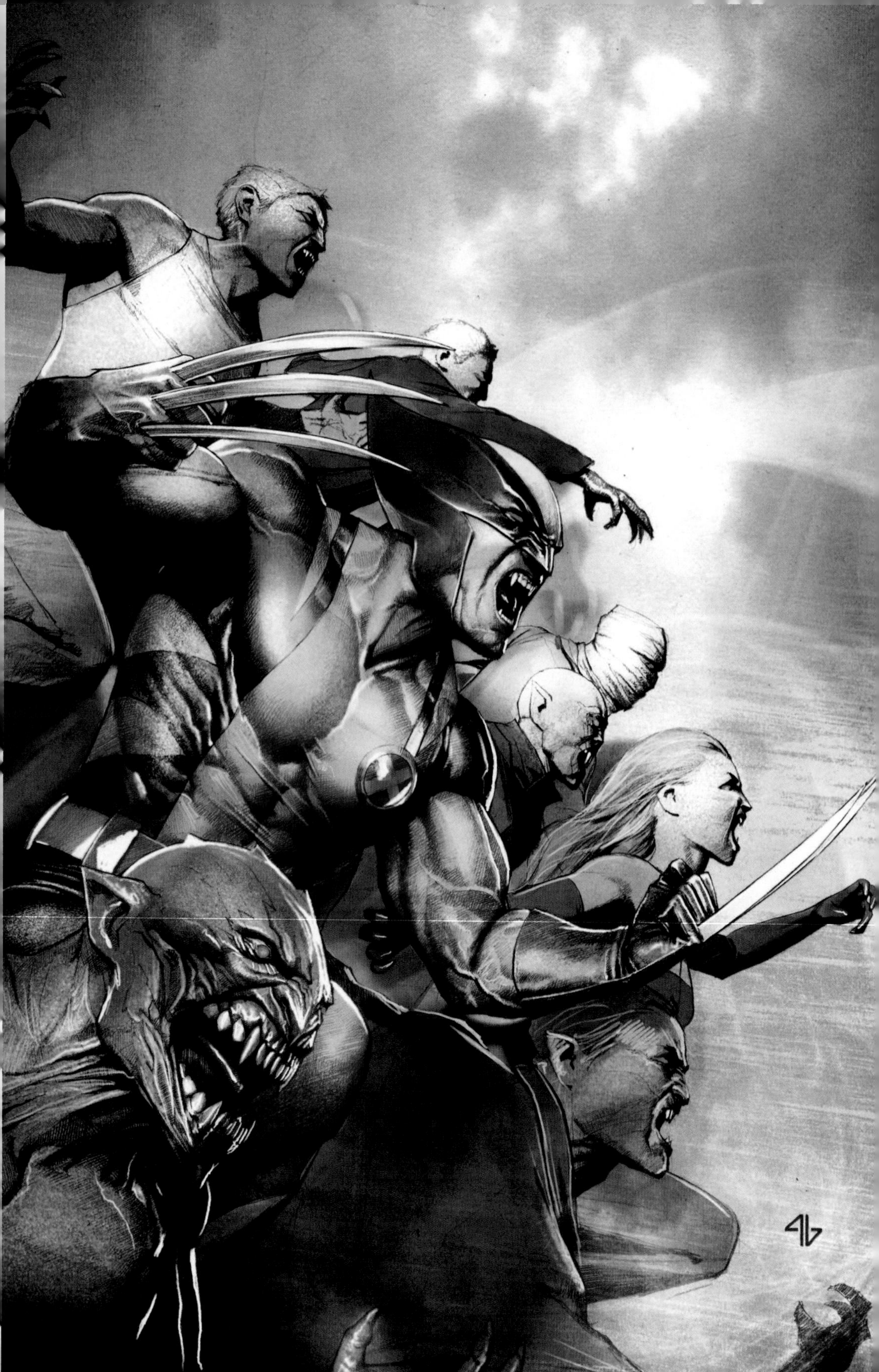

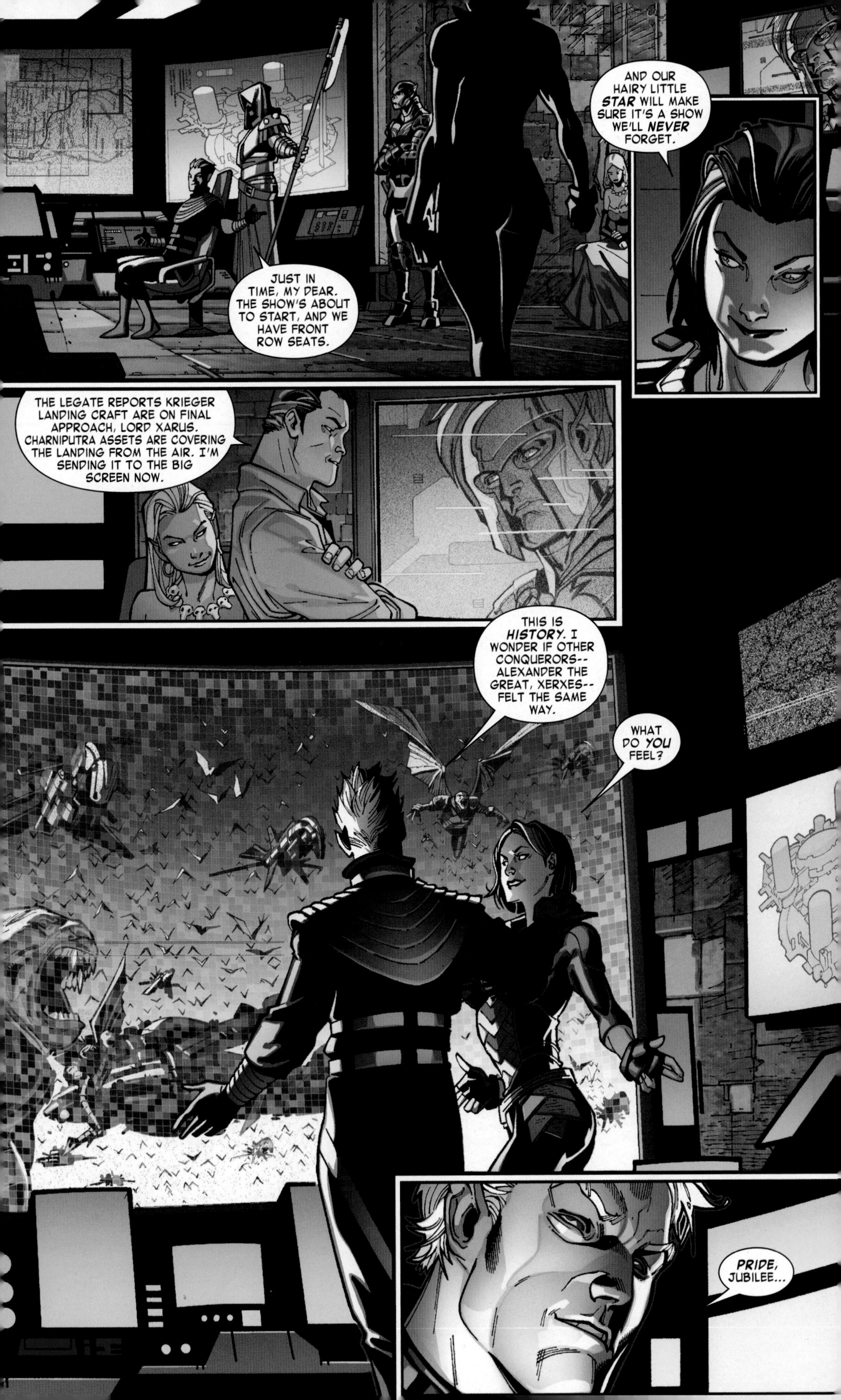
AND OUR HAIRY LITTLE STAR WILL MAKE SURE IT'S A SHOW WE'LL NEVER FORGET.
JUST IN TIME, MY DEAR. THE SHOW'S ABOUT TO START, AND WE HAVE FRONT ROW SEATS.
THE LEGATE REPORTS KRIEGER LANDING CRAFT ARE ON FINAL APPROACH, LORD XARUS. CHARNIPUTRA ASSETS ARE COVERING THE LANDING FROM THE AIR. I'M SENDING IT TO THE BIG SCREEN NOW.
THIS IS HISTORY. I WONDER IF OTHER CONQUERORS-- ALEXANDER THE GREAT, XERXES-- FELT THE SAME WAY.
WHAT DO YOU FEEL?
PRIDE, JUBILEE...

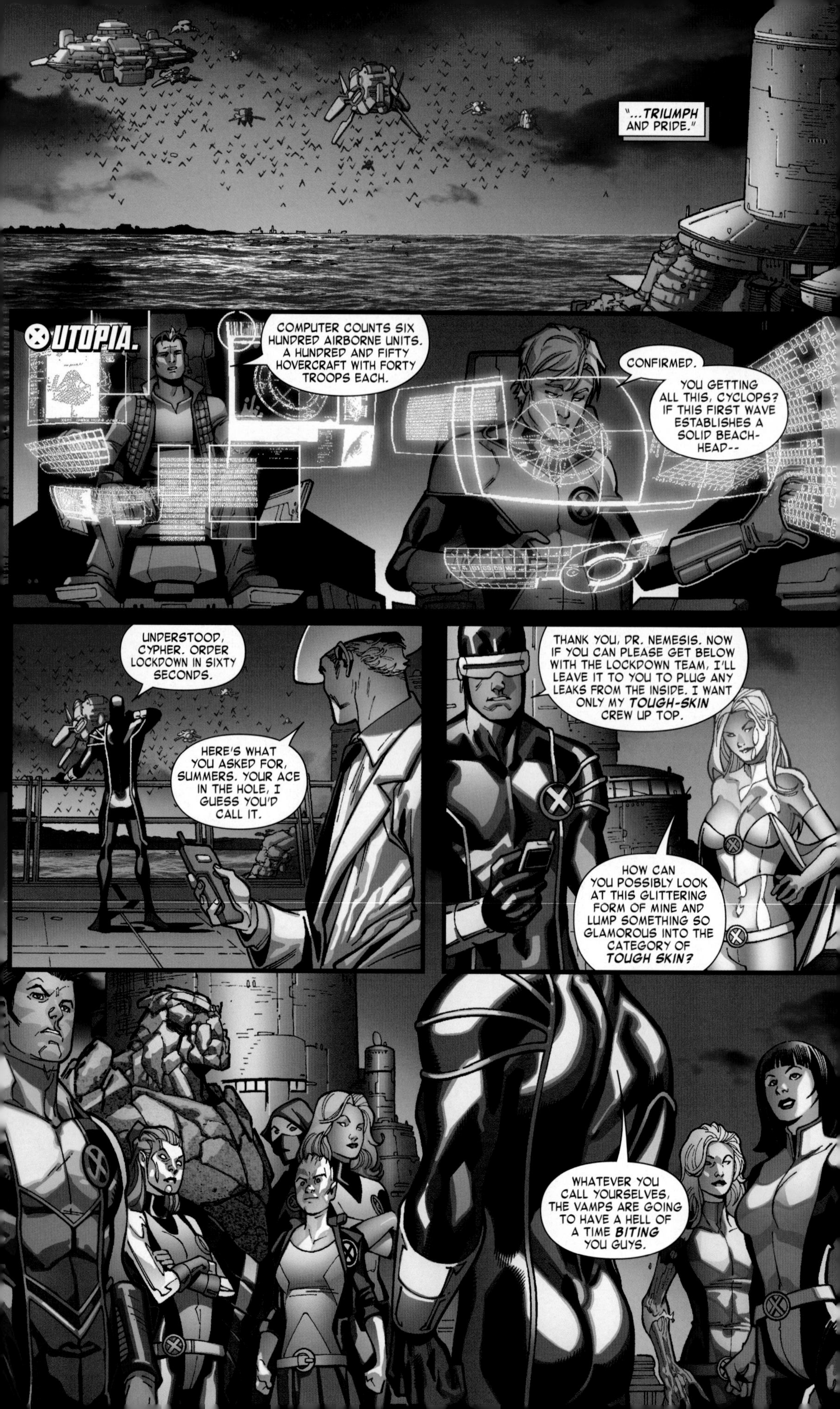
"...TRIUMPH AND PRIDE."
UTOPIA.
COMPUTER COUNTS SIX HUNDRED AIRBORNE UNITS. A HUNDRED AND FIFTY HOVERCRAFT WITH FORTY TROOPS EACH.
CONFIRMED.
YOU GETTING ALL THIS, CYCLOPS? IF THIS FIRST WAVE ESTABLISHES A SOLID BEACH-HEAD--
UNDERSTOOD, CYPHER. ORDER LOCKDOWN IN SIXTY SECONDS.
HERE'S WHAT YOU ASKED FOR, SUMMERS. YOUR ACE IN THE HOLE, I GUESS YOU'D CALL IT.
THANK YOU, DR. NEMESIS. NOW IF YOU CAN PLEASE GET BELOW WITH THE LOCKDOWN TEAM, I'LL LEAVE IT TO YOU TO PLUG ANY LEAKS FROM THE INSIDE. I WANT ONLY MY TOUGH-SKIN CREW UP TOP.
HOW CAN YOU POSSIBLY LOOK AT THIS GLITTERING FORM OF MINE AND LUMP SOMETHING SO GLAMOROUS INTO THE CATEGORY OF TOUGH SKIN?
WHATEVER YOU CALL YOURSELVES, THE VAMPS ARE GOING TO HAVE A HELL OF A TIME BITING YOU GUYS.

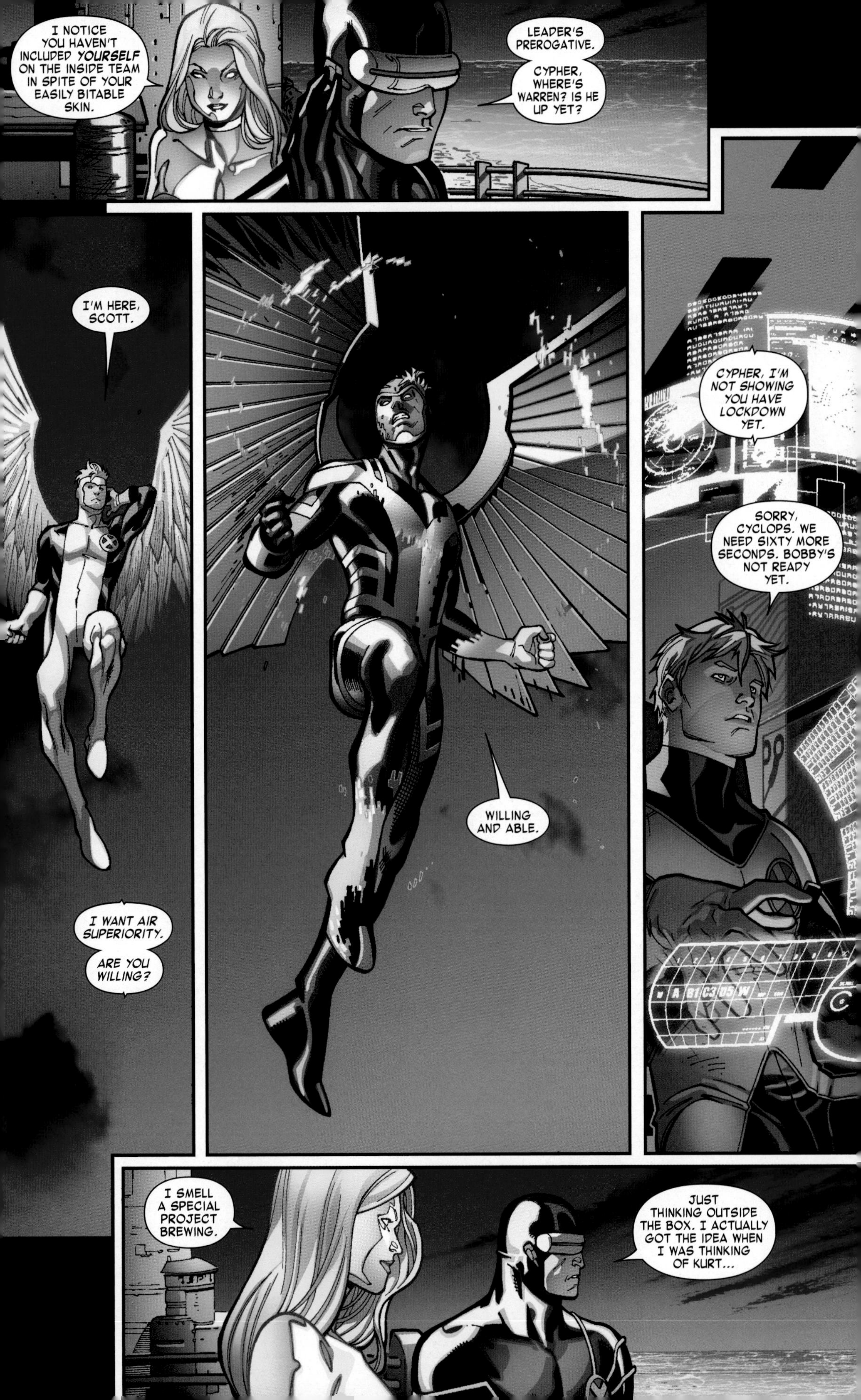
I NOTICE YOU HAVEN'T INCLUDED *YOURSELF* ON THE INSIDE TEAM IN SPITE OF YOUR EASILY BITABLE SKIN.
LEADER'S PREROGATIVE.
CYPHER, WHERE'S WARREN? IS HE UP YET?
I'M HERE, SCOTT.
I WANT AIR SUPERIORITY.
ARE YOU WILLING?
WILLING AND ABLE.
CYPHER, I'M NOT SHOWING YOU HAVE LOCKDOWN YET.
SORRY, CYCLOPS. WE NEED SIXTY MORE SECONDS. BOBBY'S NOT READY YET.
I SMELL A SPECIAL PROJECT BREWING.
JUST THINKING OUTSIDE THE BOX. I ACTUALLY GOT THE IDEA WHEN I WAS THINKING OF KURT...

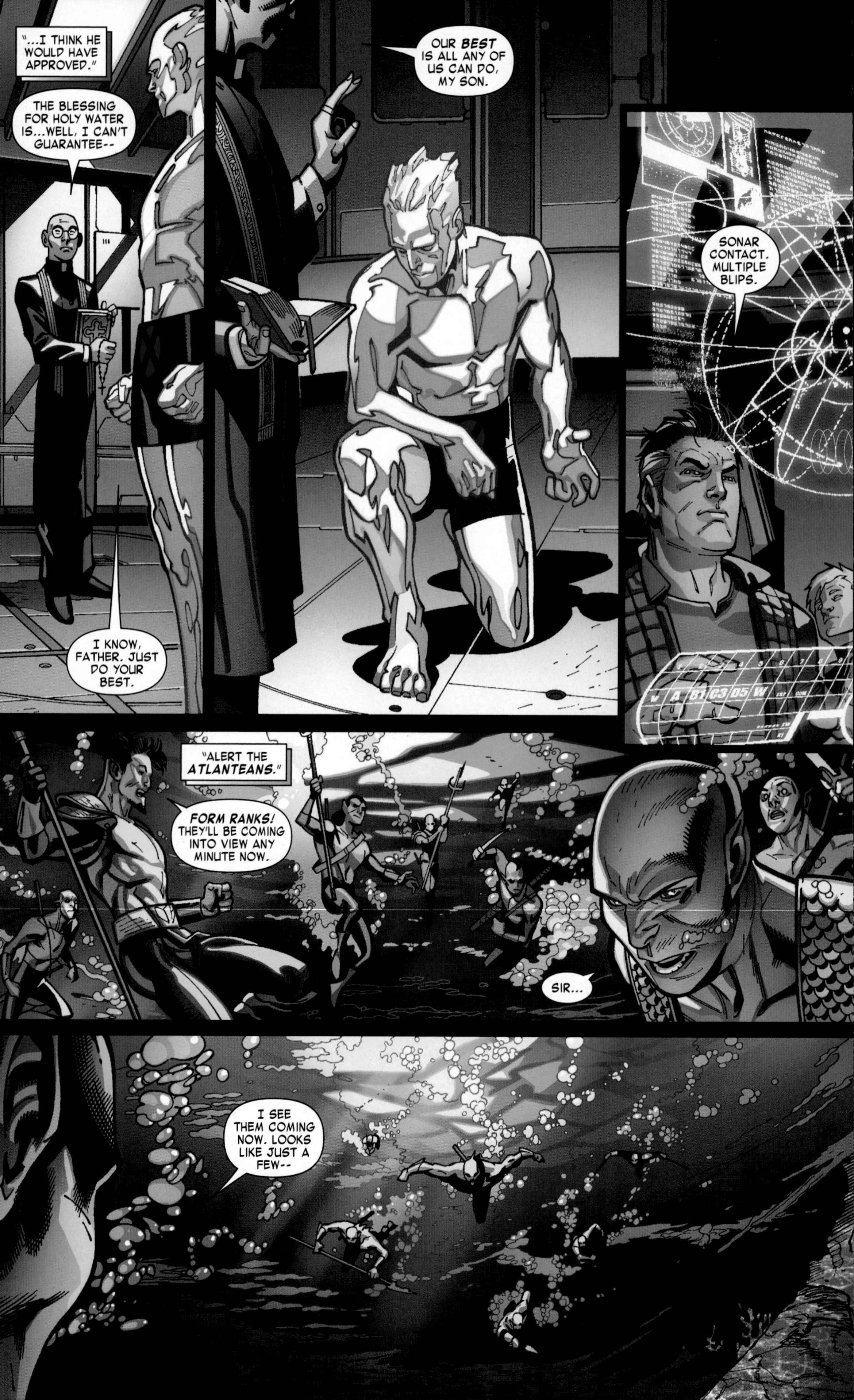
"...I THINK HE WOULD HAVE APPROVED."
THE BLESSING FOR HOLY WATER IS...WELL, I CAN'T GUARANTEE--
I KNOW, FATHER. JUST DO YOUR BEST.
OUR BEST IS ALL ANY OF US CAN DO, MY SON.
SONAR CONTACT. MULTIPLE BLIPS.
"ALERT THE ATLANTEANS."
FORM RANKS! THEY'LL BE COMING INTO VIEW ANY MINUTE NOW.
SIR...
I SEE THEM COMING NOW. LOOKS LIKE JUST A FEW--

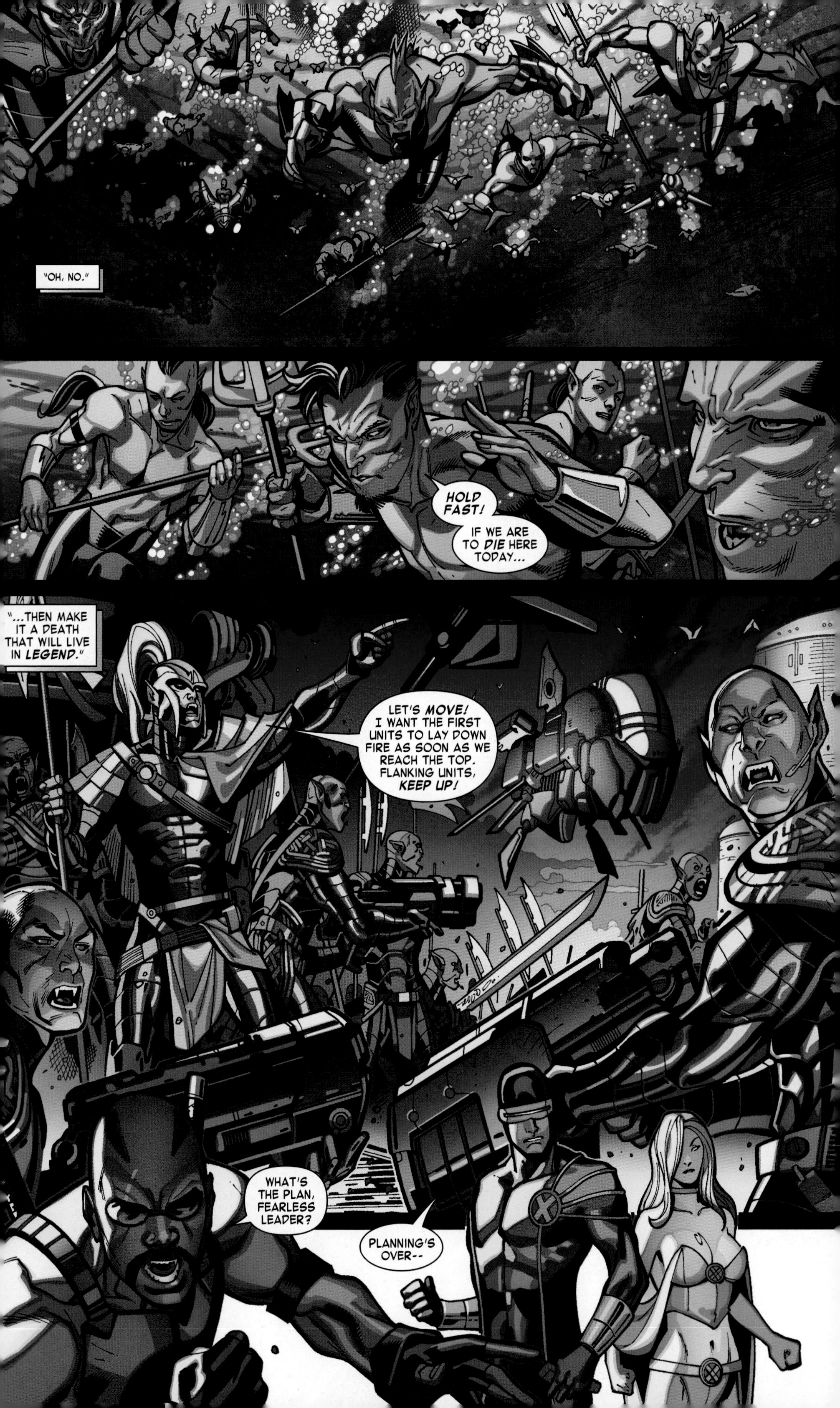
"OH, NO."
HOLD FAST!
IF WE ARE TO DIE HERE TODAY...
"...THEN MAKE IT A DEATH THAT WILL LIVE IN LEGEND."
LET'S MOVE! I WANT THE FIRST UNITS TO LAY DOWN FIRE AS SOON AS WE REACH THE TOP. FLANKING UNITS, KEEP UP!
WHAT'S THE PLAN, FEARLESS LEADER?
PLANNING'S OVER--

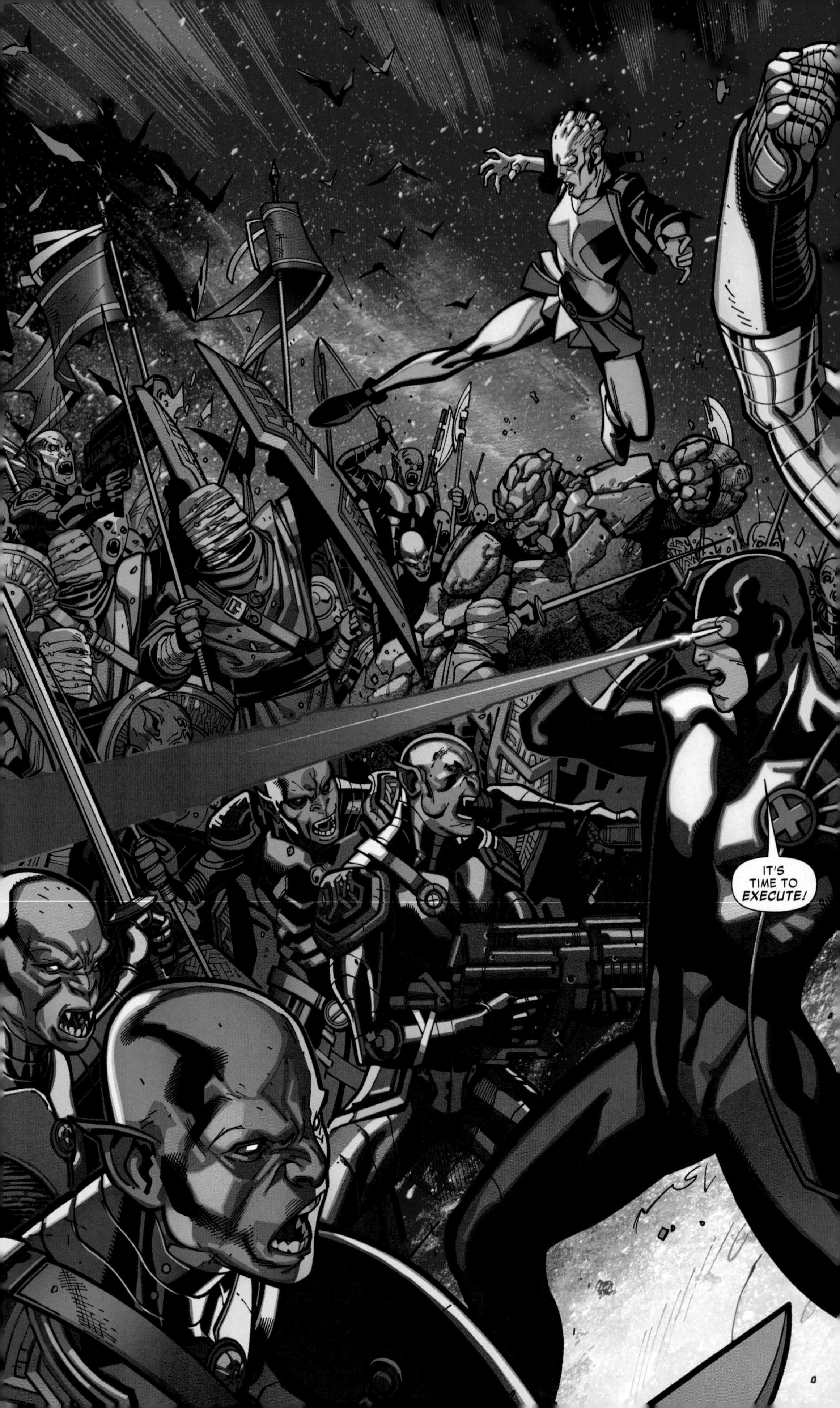
IT'S TIME TO EXECUTE!

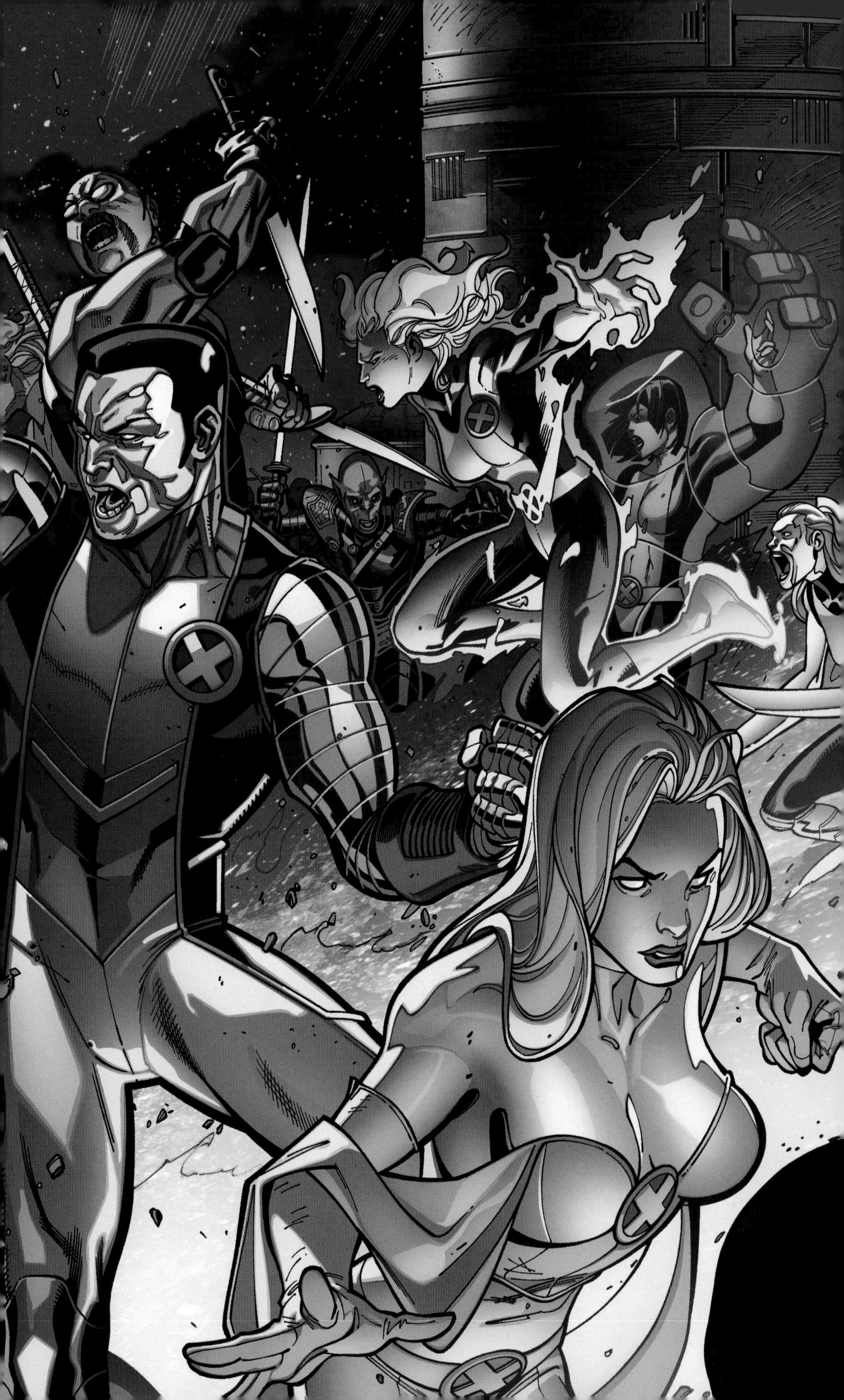

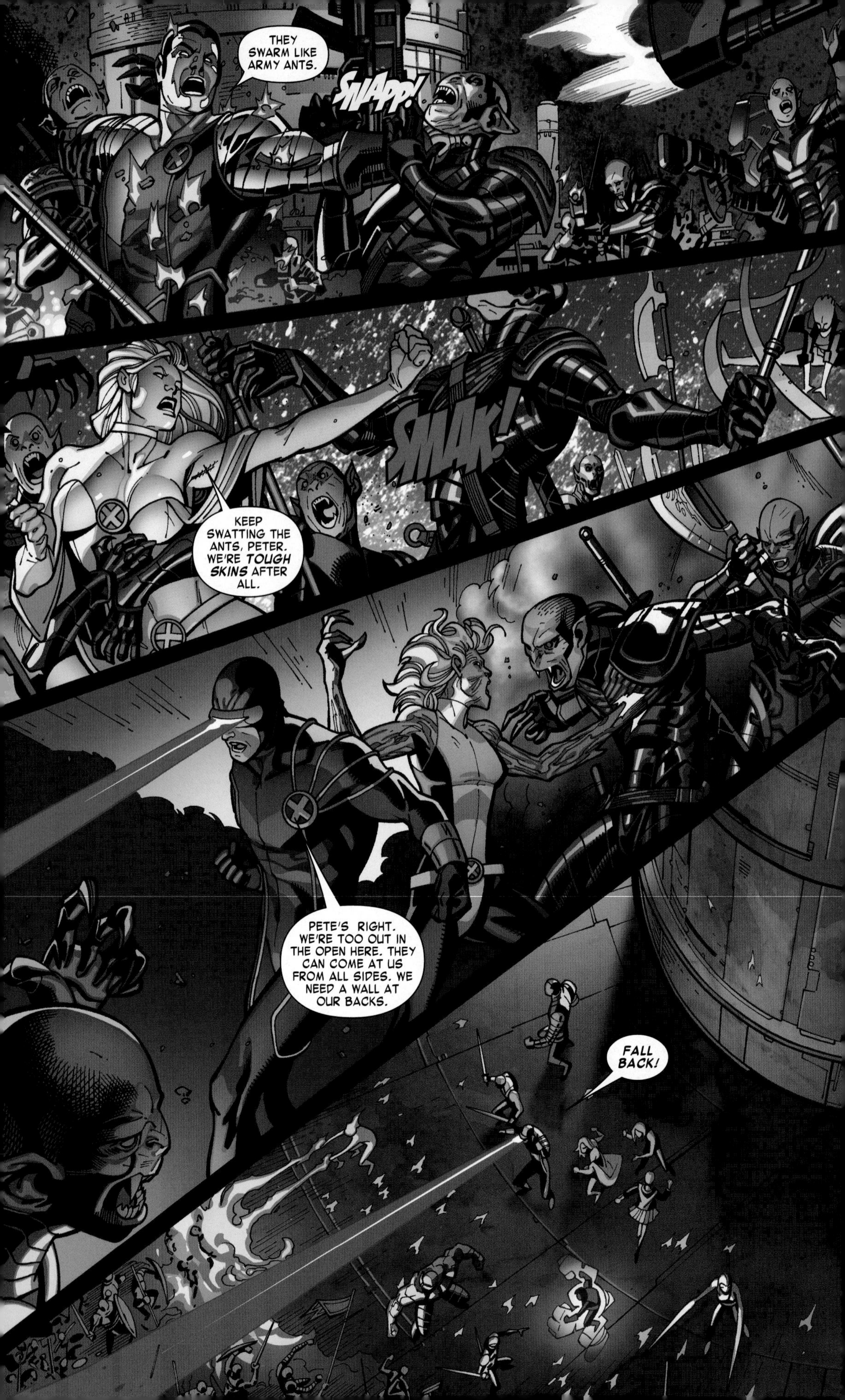
THEY SWARM LIKE ARMY ANTS.
SWAPP!
SMAK!
KEEP SWATTING THE ANTS, PETER. WE'RE TOUGH SKINS AFTER ALL.
PETE'S RIGHT. WE'RE TOO OUT IN THE OPEN HERE. THEY CAN COME AT US FROM ALL SIDES. WE NEED A WALL AT OUR BACKS.
FALL BACK!

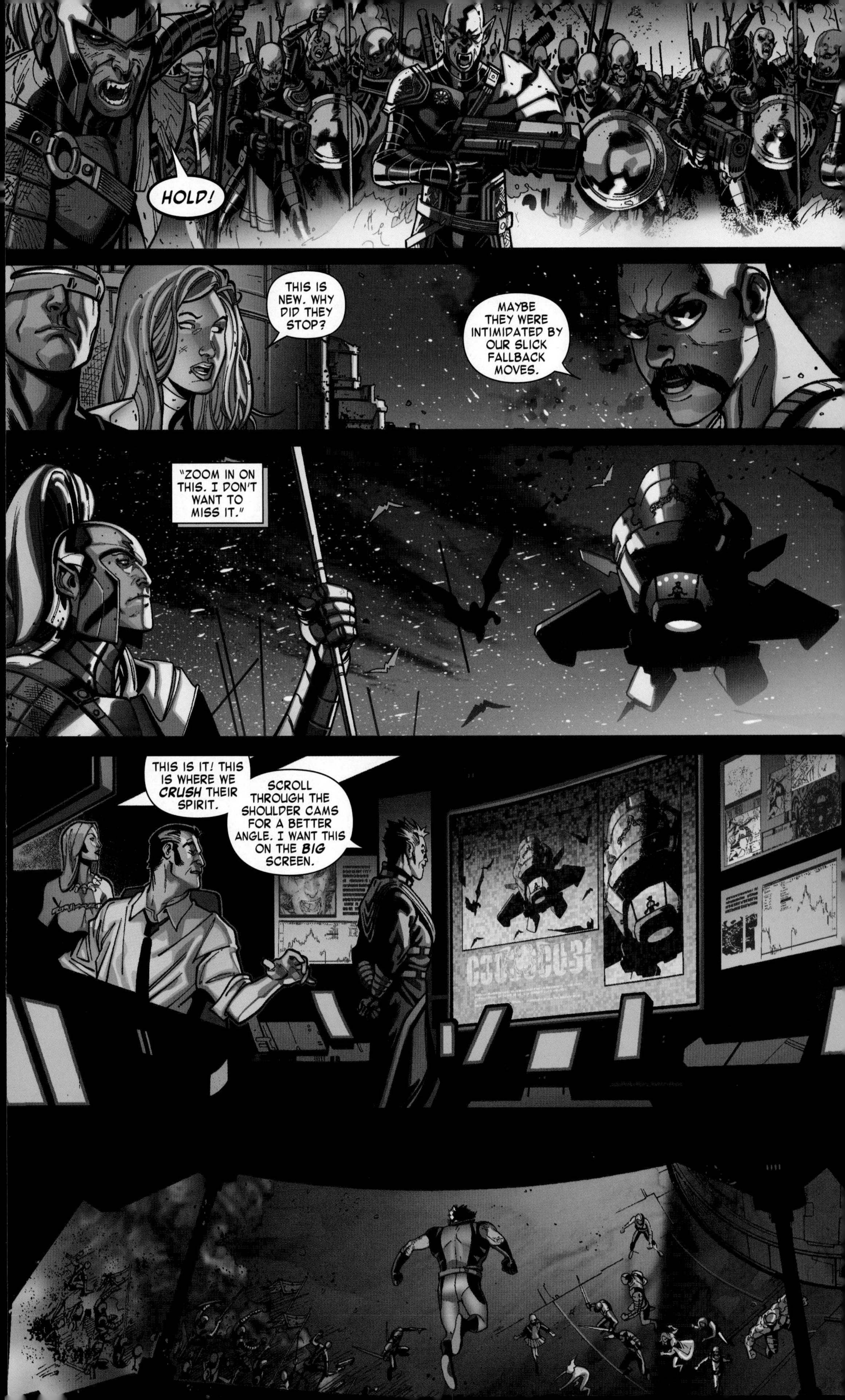

HOLD!
THIS IS NEW. WHY DID THEY STOP?
MAYBE THEY WERE INTIMIDATED BY OUR SLICK FALLBACK MOVES.
"ZOOM IN ON THIS. I DON'T WANT TO MISS IT."
THIS IS IT! THIS IS WHERE WE *CRUSH* THEIR SPIRIT.
SCROLL THROUGH THE SHOULDER CAMS FOR A BETTER ANGLE. I WANT THIS ON THE *BIG* SCREEN.

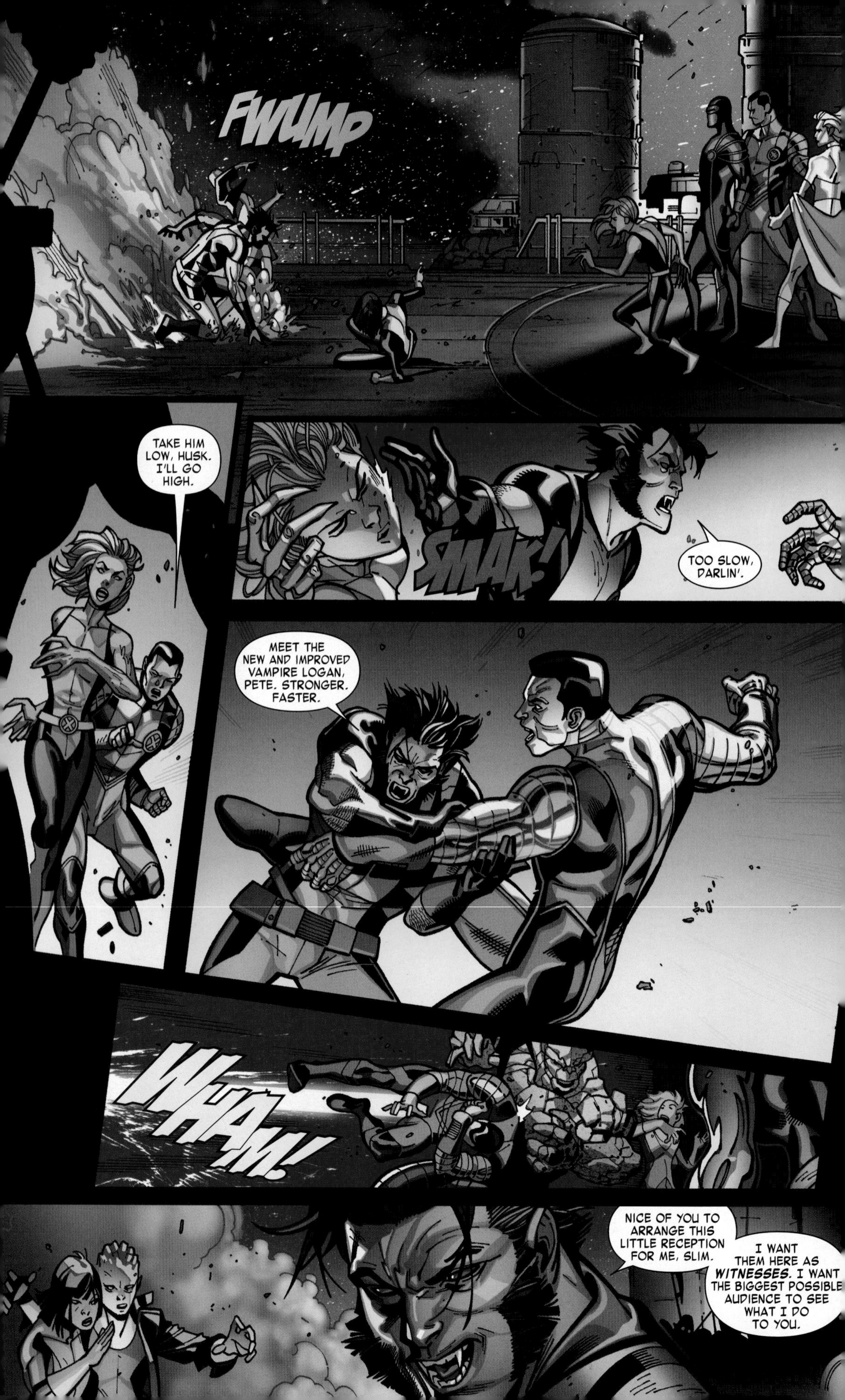
FWUMP
TAKE HIM LOW, HUSK. I'LL GO HIGH.
SMAK!
TOO SLOW, DARLIN'.
MEET THE NEW AND IMPROVED VAMPIRE LOGAN, PETE. STRONGER. FASTER.
WHAM!
NICE OF YOU TO ARRANGE THIS LITTLE RECEPTION FOR ME, SLIM.
I WANT THEM HERE AS *WITNESSES.* I WANT THE BIGGEST POSSIBLE AUDIENCE TO SEE WHAT I DO TO YOU.

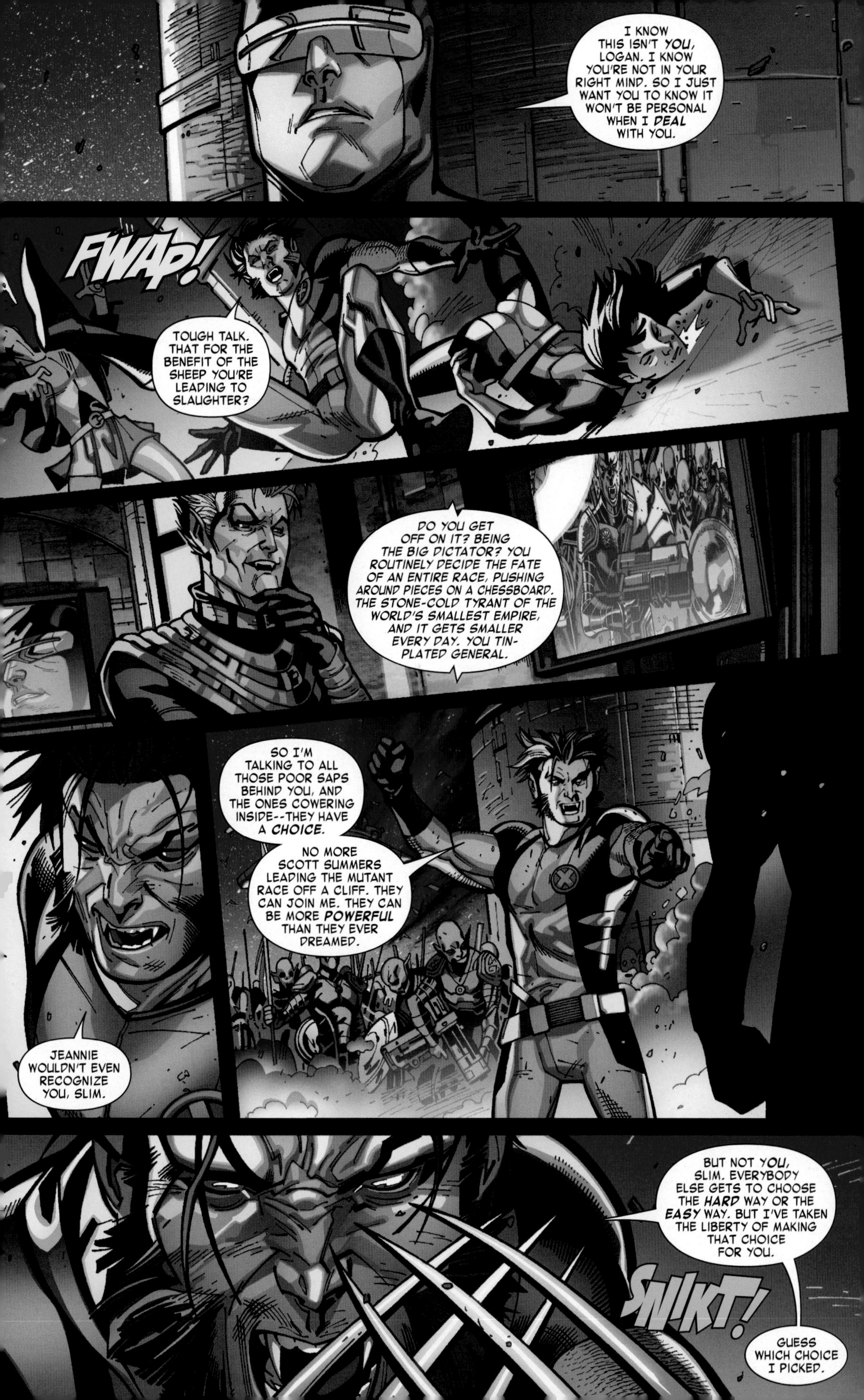
I KNOW THIS ISN'T YOU, LOGAN. I KNOW YOU'RE NOT IN YOUR RIGHT MIND. SO I JUST WANT YOU TO KNOW IT WON'T BE PERSONAL WHEN I DEAL WITH YOU.
FWAP!
TOUGH TALK. THAT FOR THE BENEFIT OF THE SHEEP YOU'RE LEADING TO SLAUGHTER?
DO YOU GET OFF ON IT? BEING THE BIG DICTATOR? YOU ROUTINELY DECIDE THE FATE OF AN ENTIRE RACE, PUSHING AROUND PIECES ON A CHESSBOARD. THE STONE-COLD TYRANT OF THE WORLD'S SMALLEST EMPIRE, AND IT GETS SMALLER EVERY DAY. YOU TIN-PLATED GENERAL.
SO I'M TALKING TO ALL THOSE POOR SAPS BEHIND YOU, AND THE ONES COWERING INSIDE--THEY HAVE A CHOICE.
NO MORE SCOTT SUMMERS LEADING THE MUTANT RACE OFF A CLIFF. THEY CAN JOIN ME. THEY CAN BE MORE POWERFUL THAN THEY EVER DREAMED.
JEANNIE WOULDN'T EVEN RECOGNIZE YOU, SLIM.
BUT NOT YOU, SLIM. EVERYBODY ELSE GETS TO CHOOSE THE HARD WAY OR THE EASY WAY. BUT I'VE TAKEN THE LIBERTY OF MAKING THAT CHOICE FOR YOU.
SNIKT!
GUESS WHICH CHOICE I PICKED.

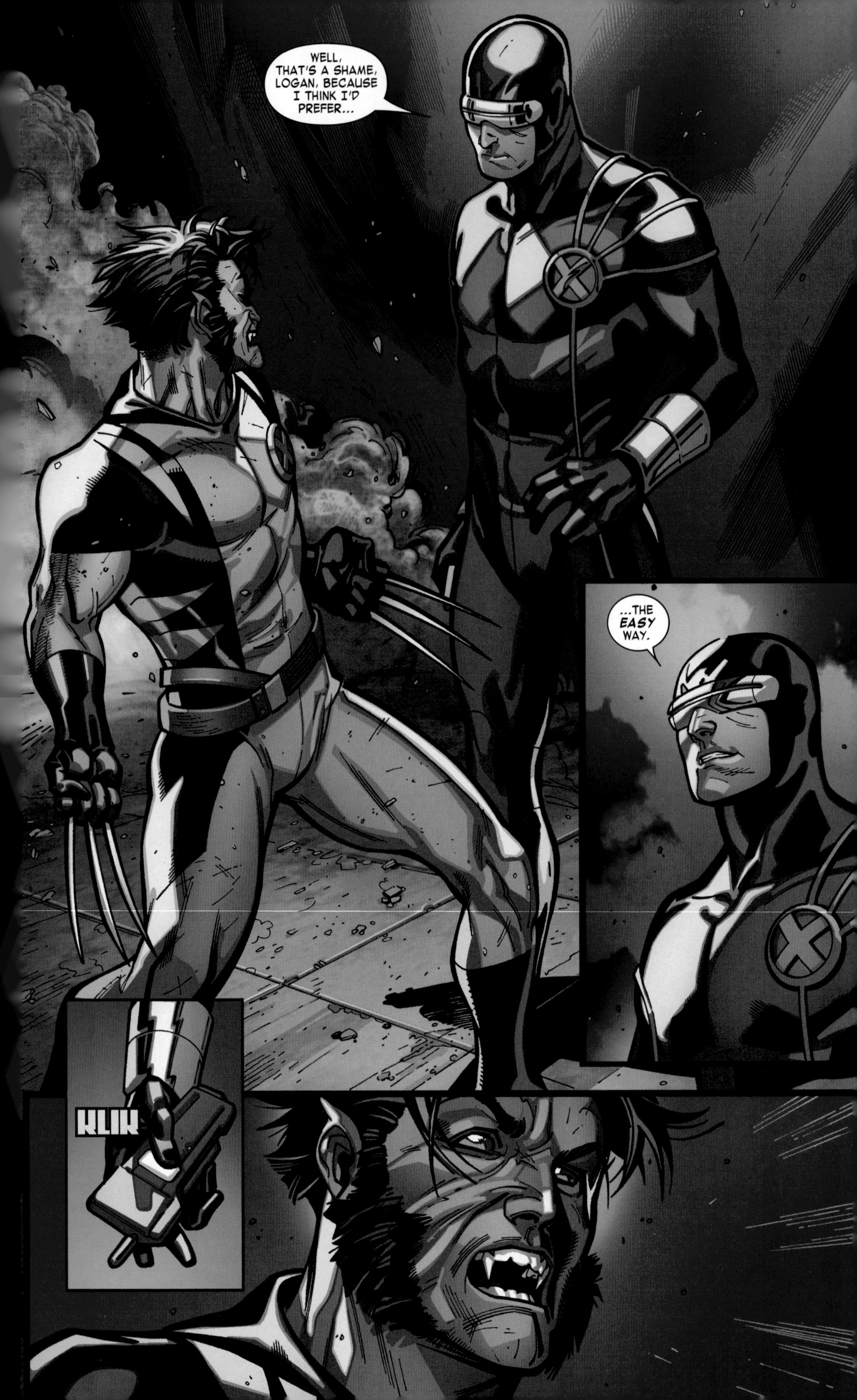
WELL, THAT'S A SHAME, LOGAN, BECAUSE I THINK I'D PREFER...
...THE EASY WAY.
KLIK

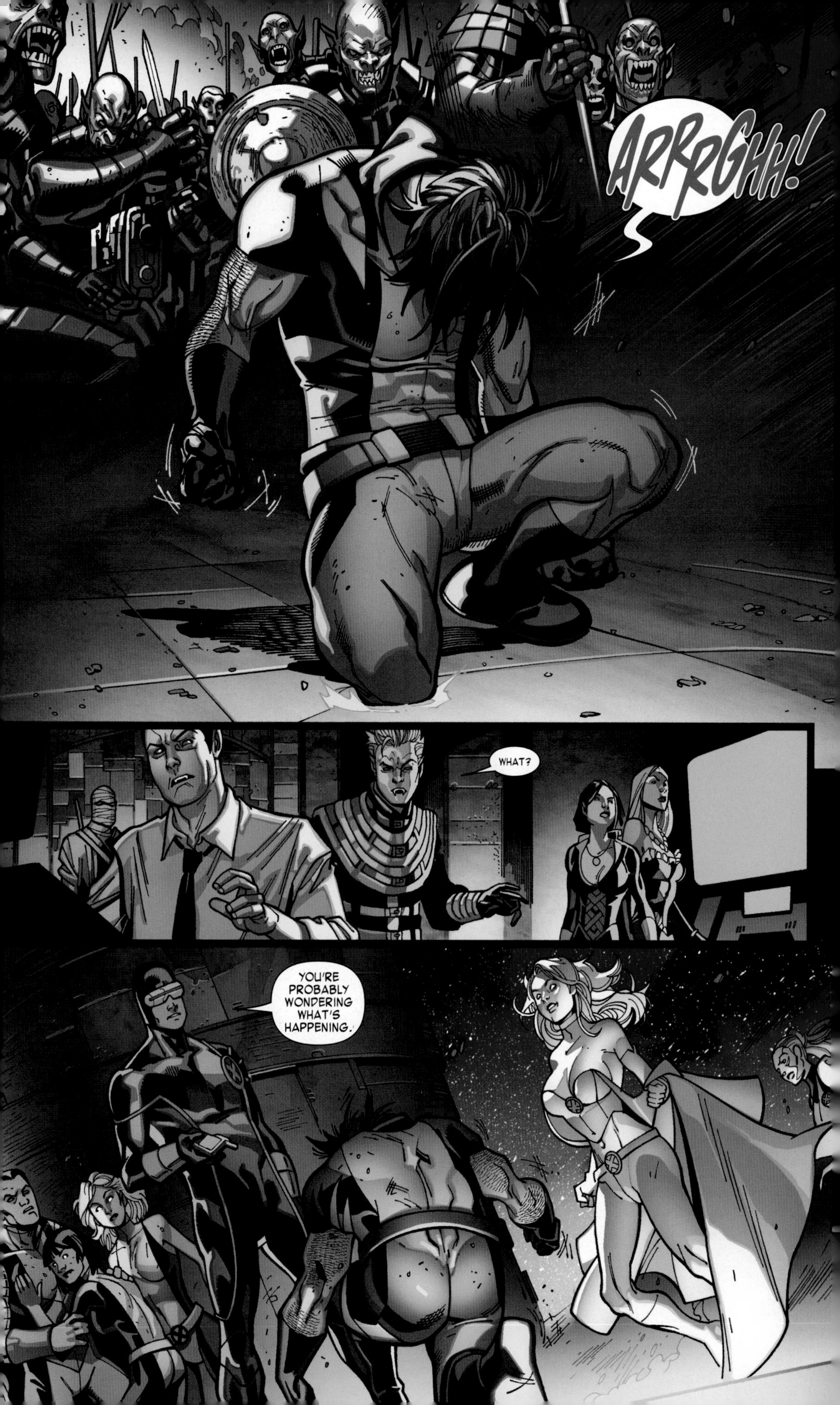
ARRRGHH!
WHAT?
YOU'RE PROBABLY WONDERING WHAT'S HAPPENING.

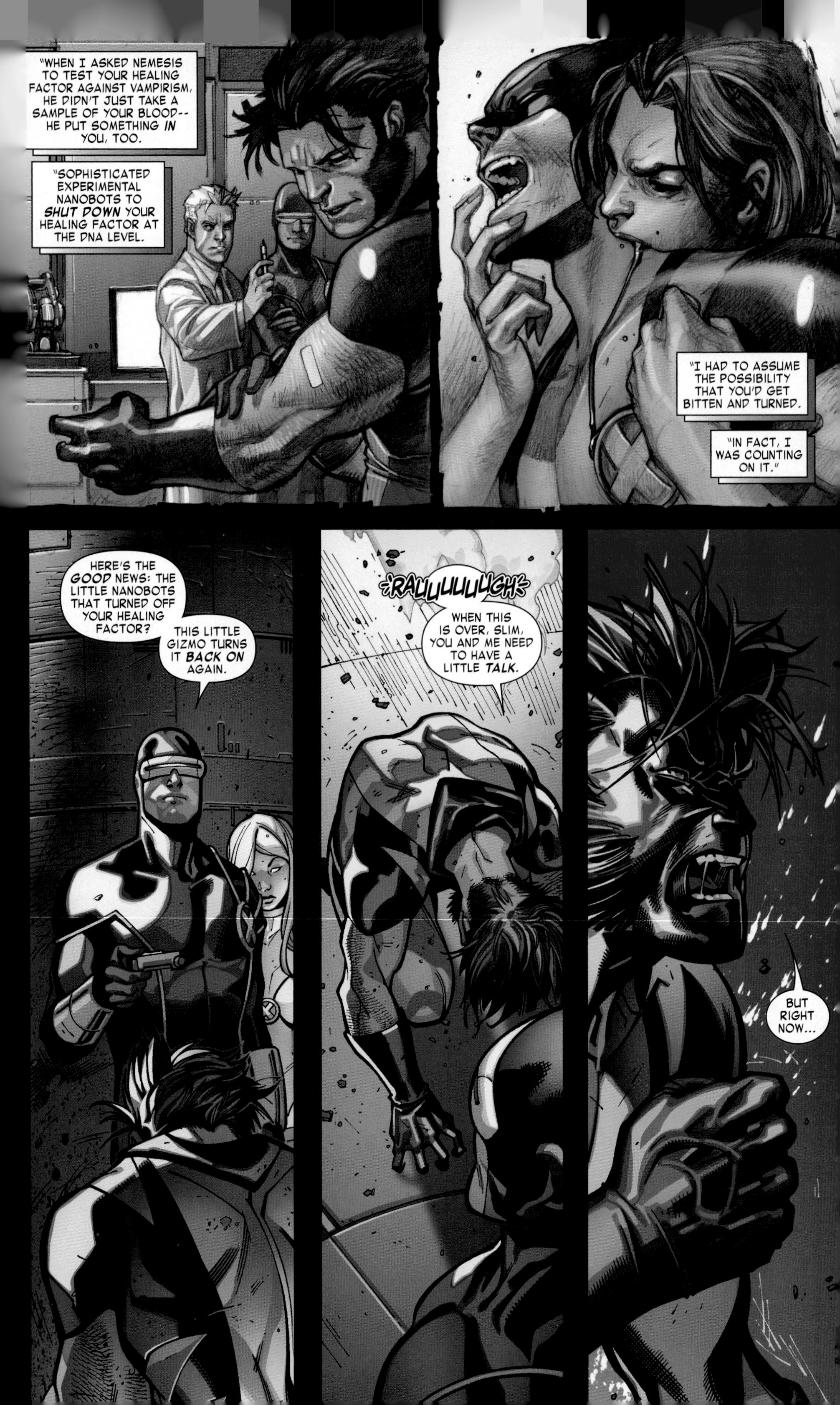
"WHEN I ASKED NEMESIS TO TEST YOUR HEALING FACTOR AGAINST VAMPIRISM, HE DIDN'T JUST TAKE A SAMPLE OF YOUR BLOOD-- HE PUT SOMETHING *IN* YOU, TOO.
"SOPHISTICATED EXPERIMENTAL NANOBOTS TO ***SHUT DOWN*** YOUR HEALING FACTOR AT THE DNA LEVEL.
"I HAD TO ASSUME THE POSSIBILITY THAT YOU'D GET BITTEN AND TURNED.
"IN FACT, I WAS COUNTING ON IT."
HERE'S THE ***GOOD*** NEWS: THE LITTLE NANOBOTS THAT TURNED OFF YOUR HEALING FACTOR?
THIS LITTLE GIZMO TURNS IT ***BACK ON*** AGAIN.
RAUUUUUUGH
WHEN THIS IS OVER, SLIM, YOU AND ME NEED TO HAVE A LITTLE ***TALK***.
BUT RIGHT NOW...

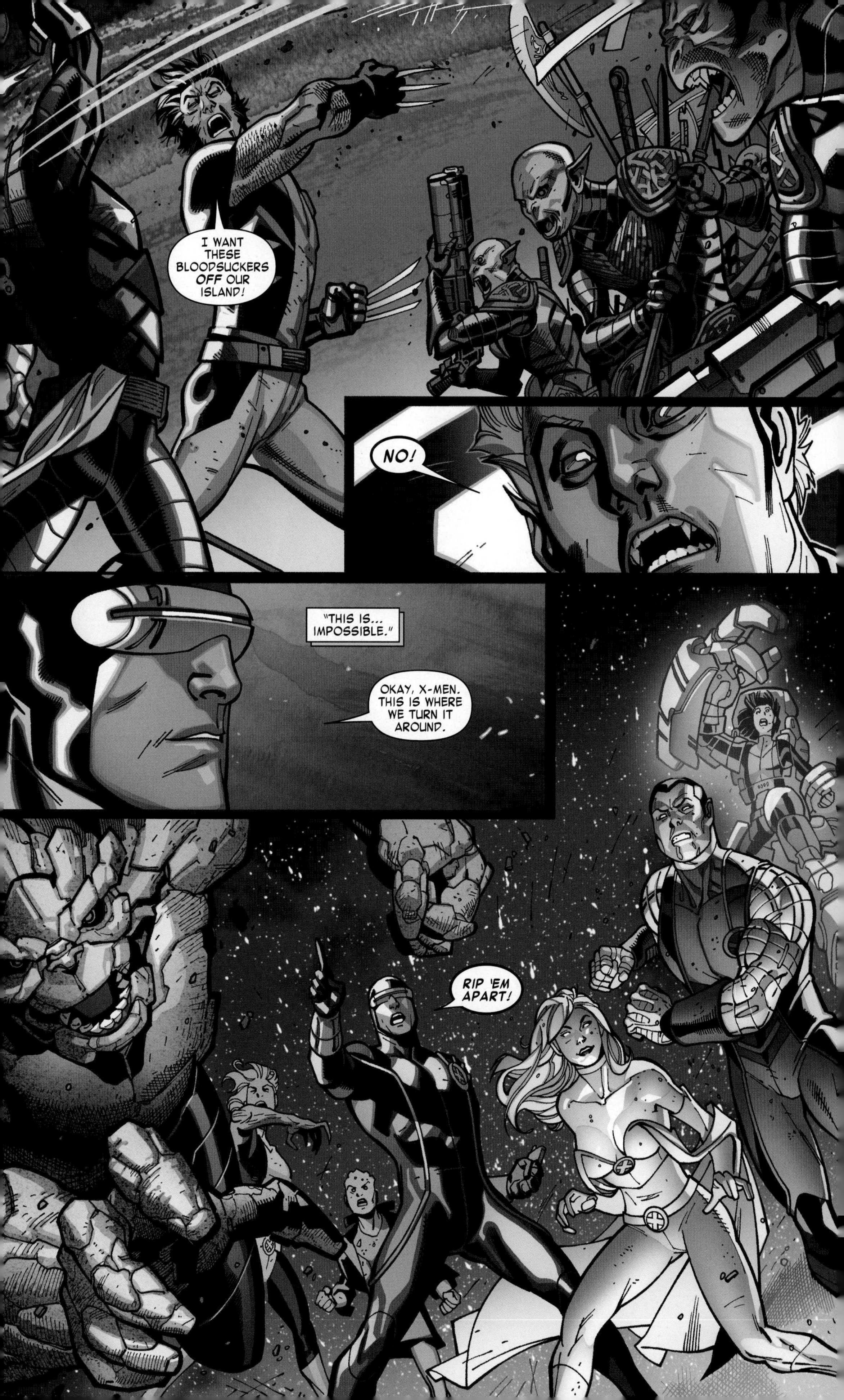
I WANT THESE BLOODSUCKERS OFF OUR ISLAND!
NO!
"THIS IS... IMPOSSIBLE."
OKAY, X-MEN. THIS IS WHERE WE TURN IT AROUND.
RIP 'EM APART!

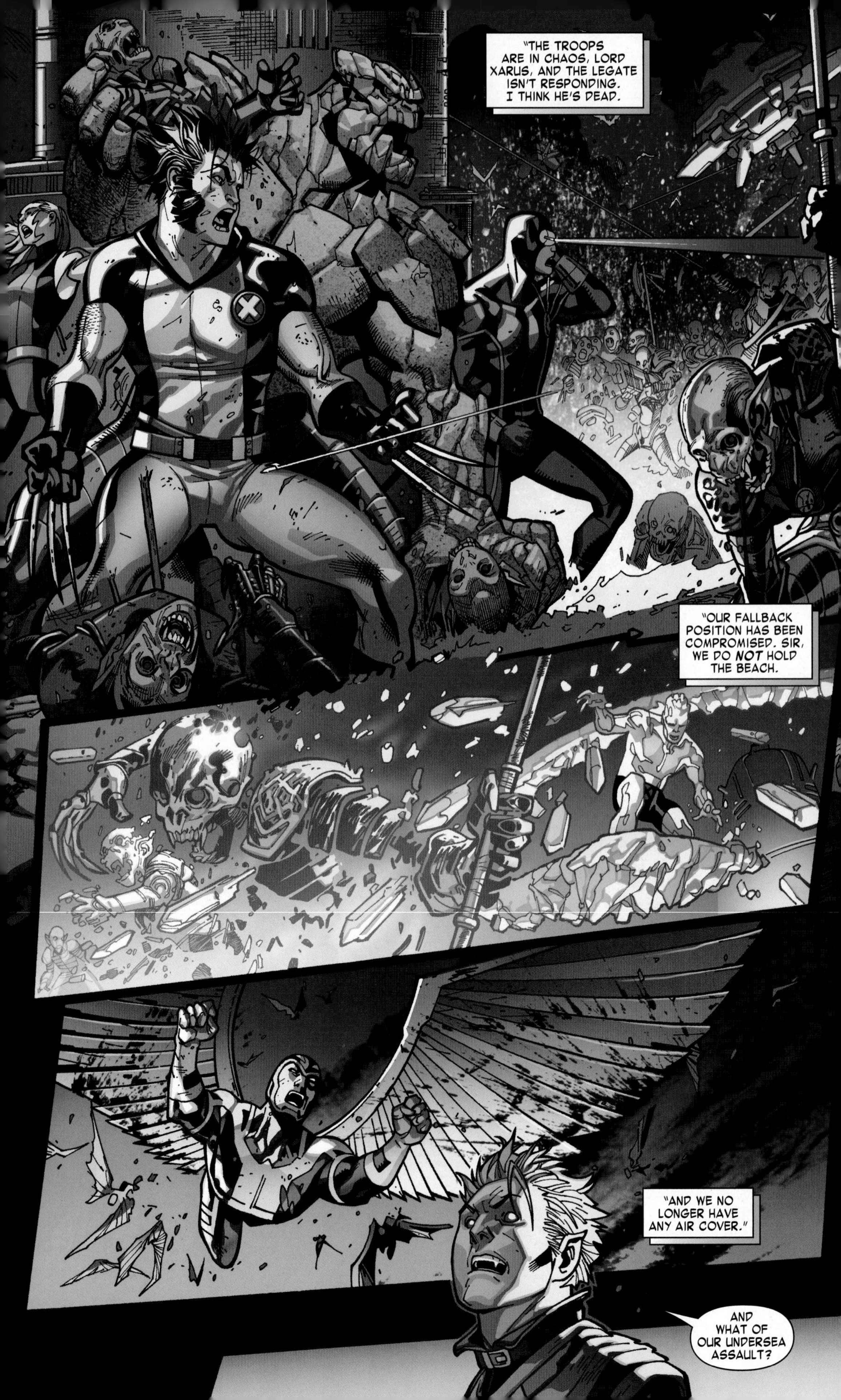
"THE TROOPS ARE IN CHAOS, LORD XARUS, AND THE LEGATE ISN'T RESPONDING. I THINK HE'S DEAD.
"OUR FALLBACK POSITION HAS BEEN COMPROMISED. SIR, WE DO **NOT** HOLD THE BEACH.
"AND WE NO LONGER HAVE ANY AIR COVER."
AND WHAT OF OUR UNDERSEA ASSAULT?

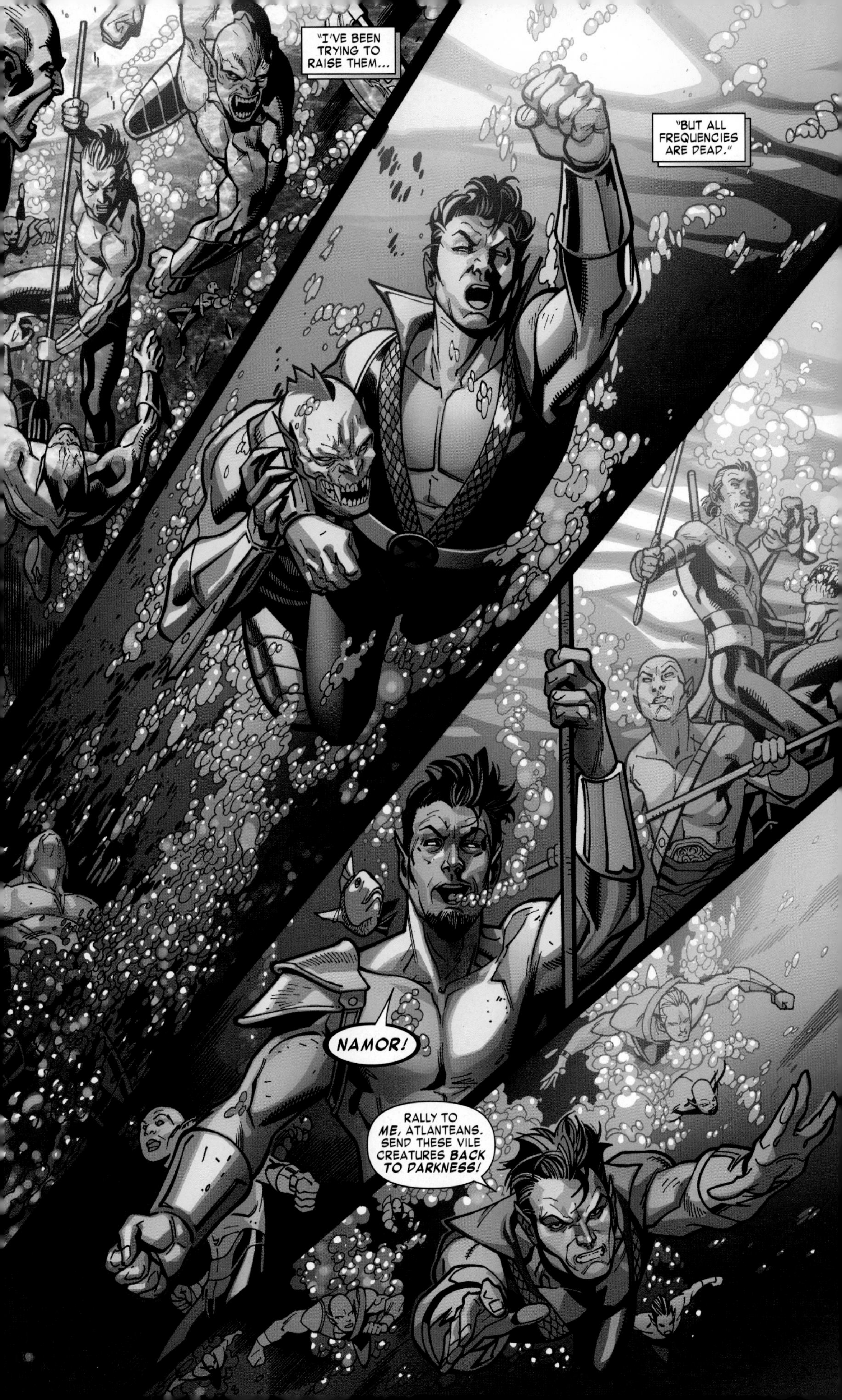
"I'VE BEEN TRYING TO RAISE THEM...
"BUT ALL FREQUENCIES ARE DEAD."
NAMOR!
RALLY TO ME, ATLANTEANS. SEND THESE VILE CREATURES BACK TO DARKNESS!

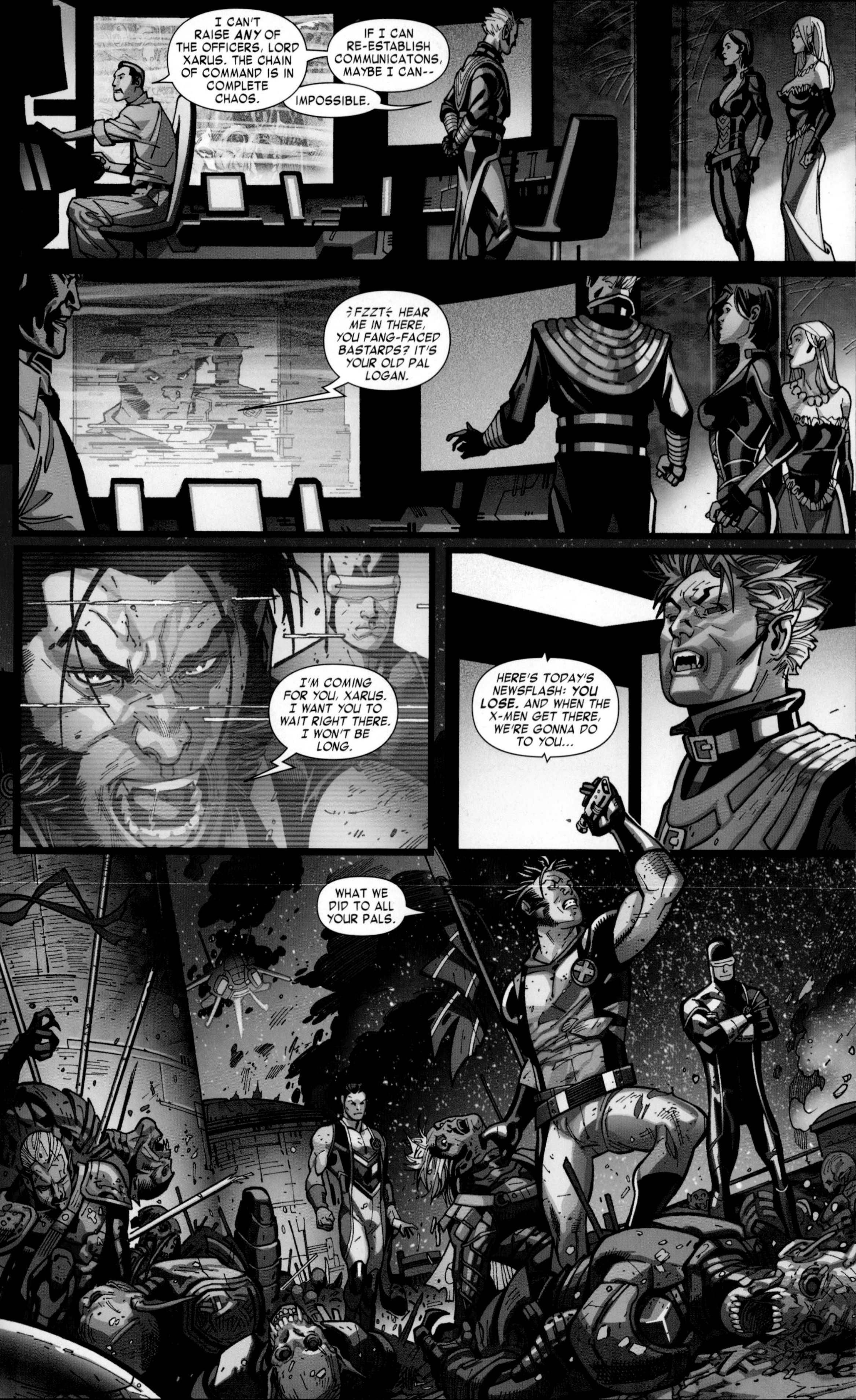
I CAN'T RAISE ANY OF THE OFFICERS, LORD XARUS. THE CHAIN OF COMMAND IS IN COMPLETE CHAOS.
IF I CAN RE-ESTABLISH COMMUNICATONS, MAYBE I CAN--
IMPOSSIBLE.
≠FZZT≠ HEAR ME IN THERE, YOU FANG-FACED BASTARDS? IT'S YOUR OLD PAL LOGAN.
I'M COMING FOR YOU, XARUS. I WANT YOU TO WAIT RIGHT THERE. I WON'T BE LONG.
HERE'S TODAY'S NEWSFLASH: YOU LOSE. AND WHEN THE X-MEN GET THERE, WE'RE GONNA DO TO YOU...
WHAT WE DID TO ALL YOUR PALS.

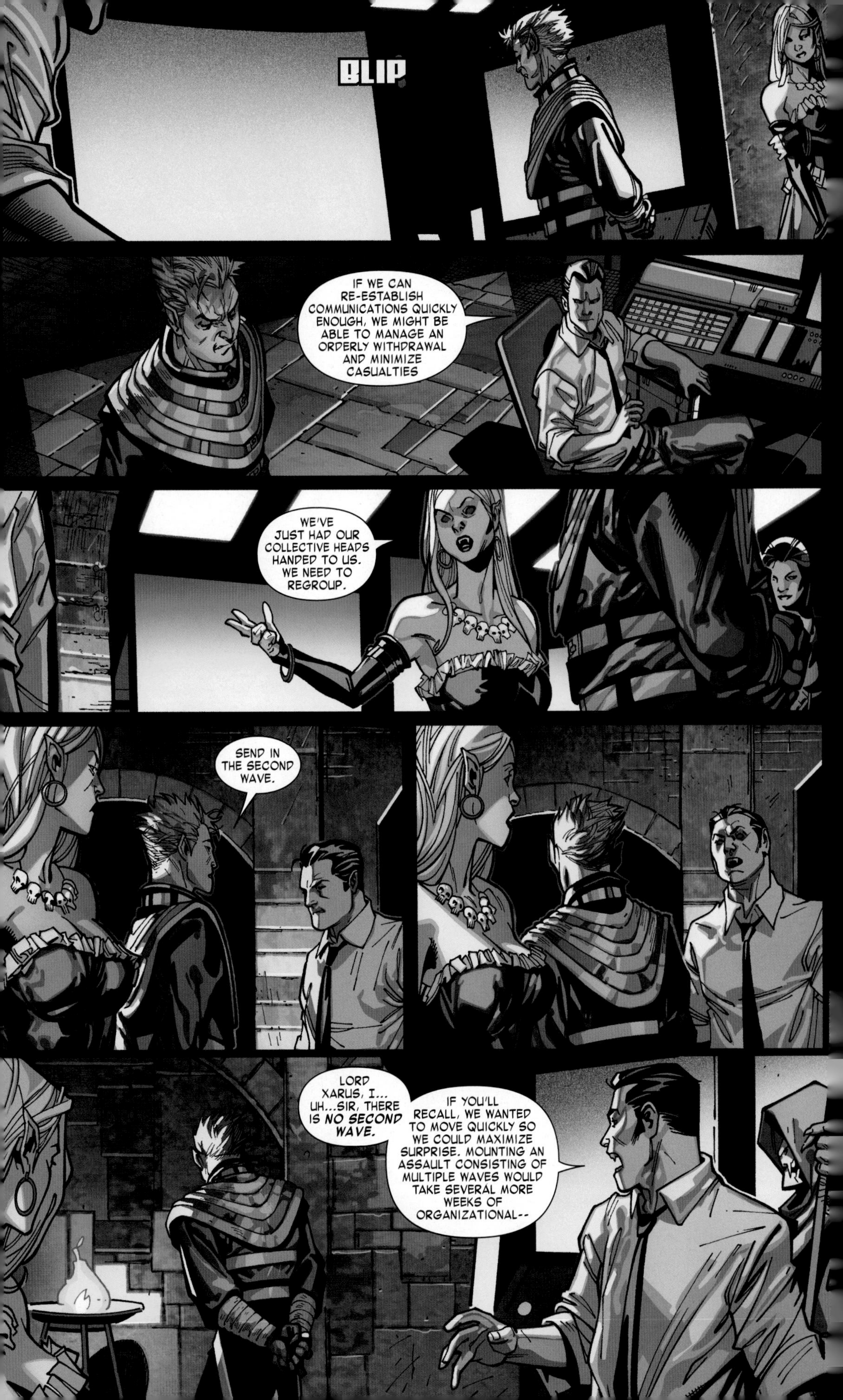
BLIP
IF WE CAN RE-ESTABLISH COMMUNICATIONS QUICKLY ENOUGH, WE MIGHT BE ABLE TO MANAGE AN ORDERLY WITHDRAWAL AND MINIMIZE CASUALTIES
WE'VE JUST HAD OUR COLLECTIVE HEADS HANDED TO US. WE NEED TO REGROUP.
SEND IN THE SECOND WAVE.
LORD XARUS, I... UH...SIR, THERE IS *NO SECOND WAVE.*
IF YOU'LL RECALL, WE WANTED TO MOVE QUICKLY SO WE COULD MAXIMIZE SURPRISE. MOUNTING AN ASSAULT CONSISTING OF MULTIPLE WAVES WOULD TAKE SEVERAL MORE WEEKS OF ORGANIZATIONAL--

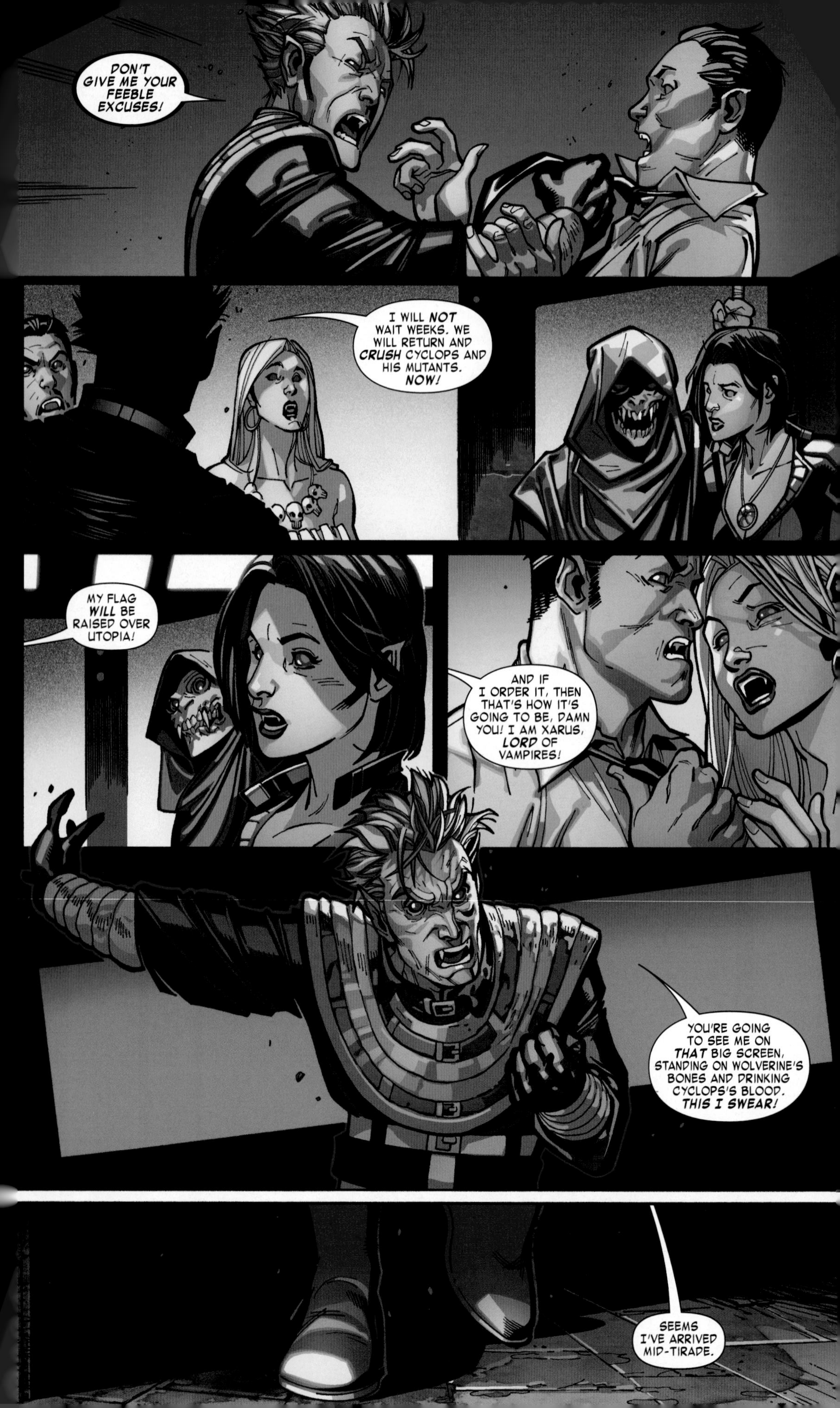
DON'T GIVE ME YOUR FEEBLE EXCUSES!
I WILL NOT WAIT WEEKS. WE WILL RETURN AND CRUSH CYCLOPS AND HIS MUTANTS. NOW!
MY FLAG WILL BE RAISED OVER UTOPIA!
AND IF I ORDER IT, THEN THAT'S HOW IT'S GOING TO BE, DAMN YOU! I AM XARUS, LORD OF VAMPIRES!
YOU'RE GOING TO SEE ME ON THAT BIG SCREEN, STANDING ON WOLVERINE'S BONES AND DRINKING CYCLOPS'S BLOOD. THIS I SWEAR!
SEEMS I'VE ARRIVED MID-TIRADE.

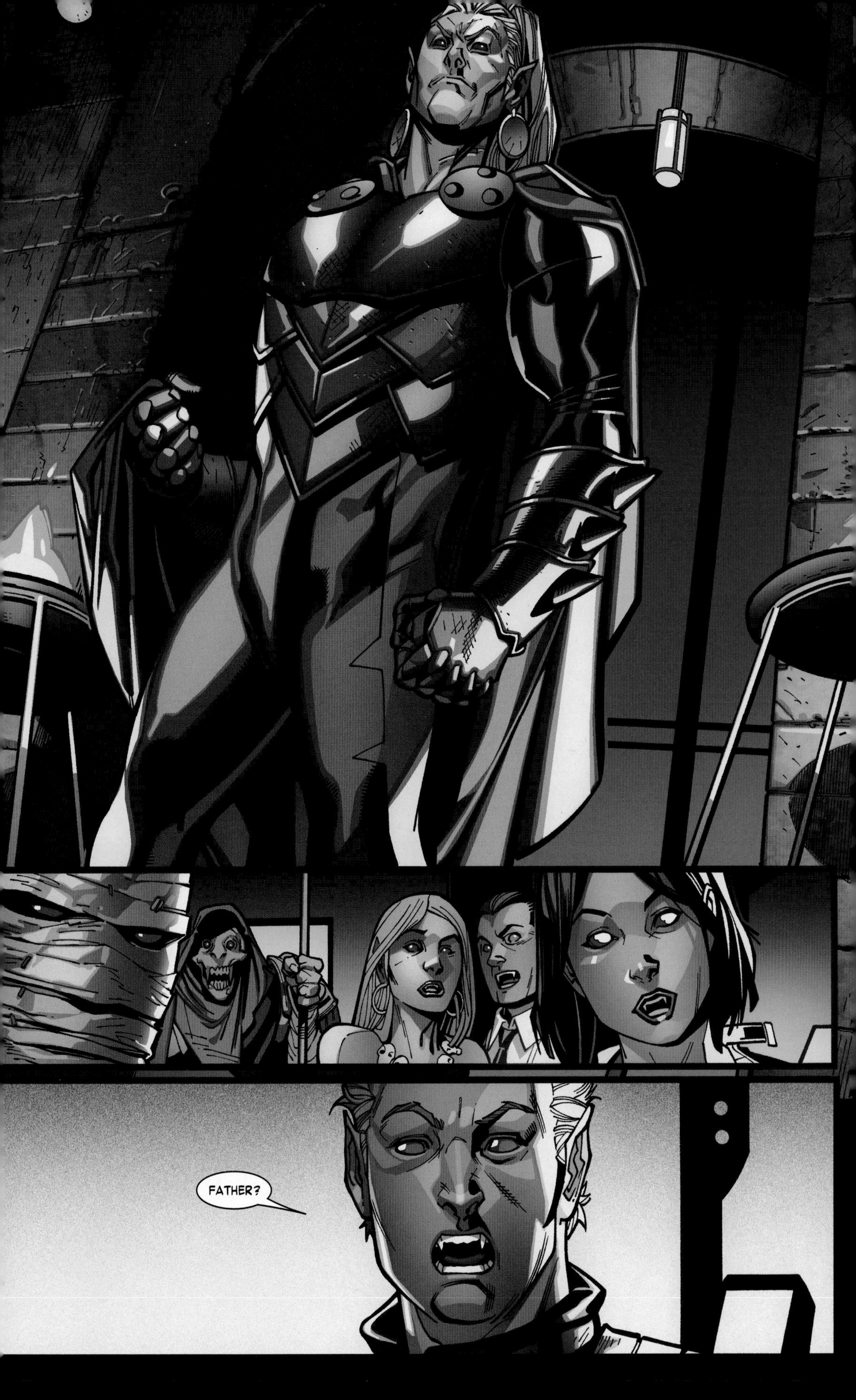
FATHER?

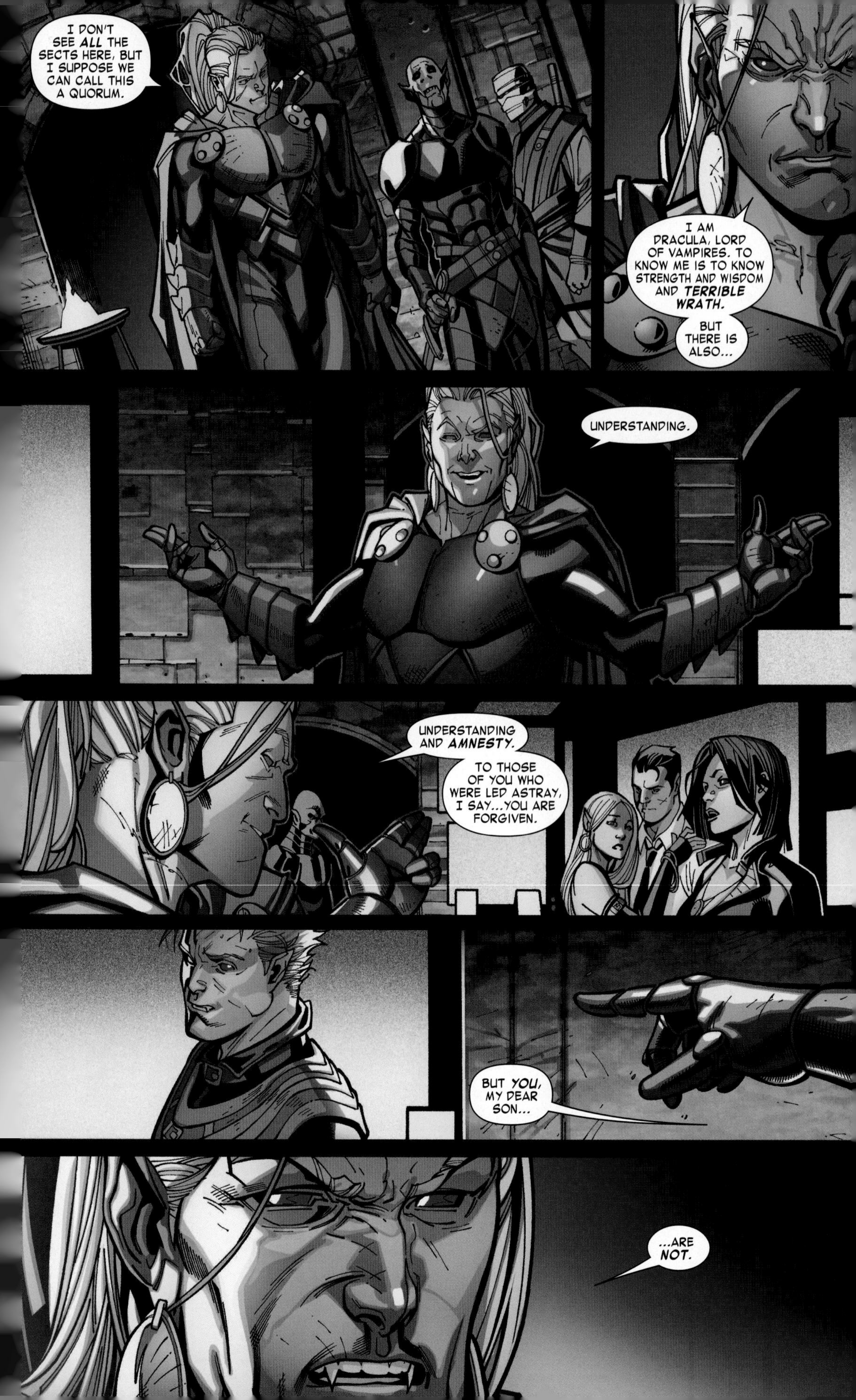
I DON'T SEE ALL THE SECTS HERE, BUT I SUPPOSE WE CAN CALL THIS A QUORUM.
I AM DRACULA, LORD OF VAMPIRES. TO KNOW ME IS TO KNOW STRENGTH AND WISDOM AND TERRIBLE WRATH.
BUT THERE IS ALSO...
UNDERSTANDING.
UNDERSTANDING AND AMNESTY.
TO THOSE OF YOU WHO WERE LED ASTRAY, I SAY...YOU ARE FORGIVEN.
BUT YOU, MY DEAR SON...
...ARE NOT.

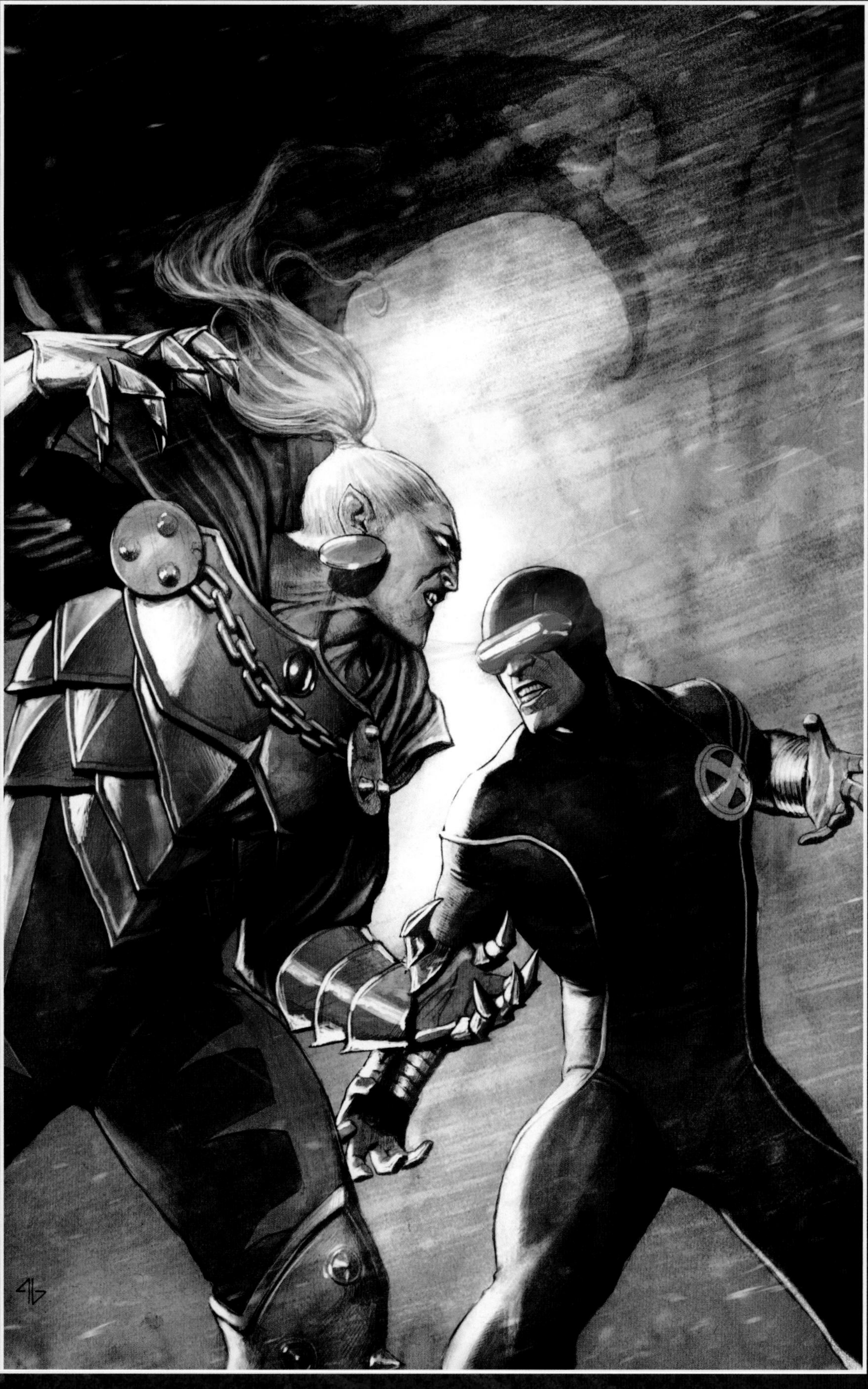

SIX

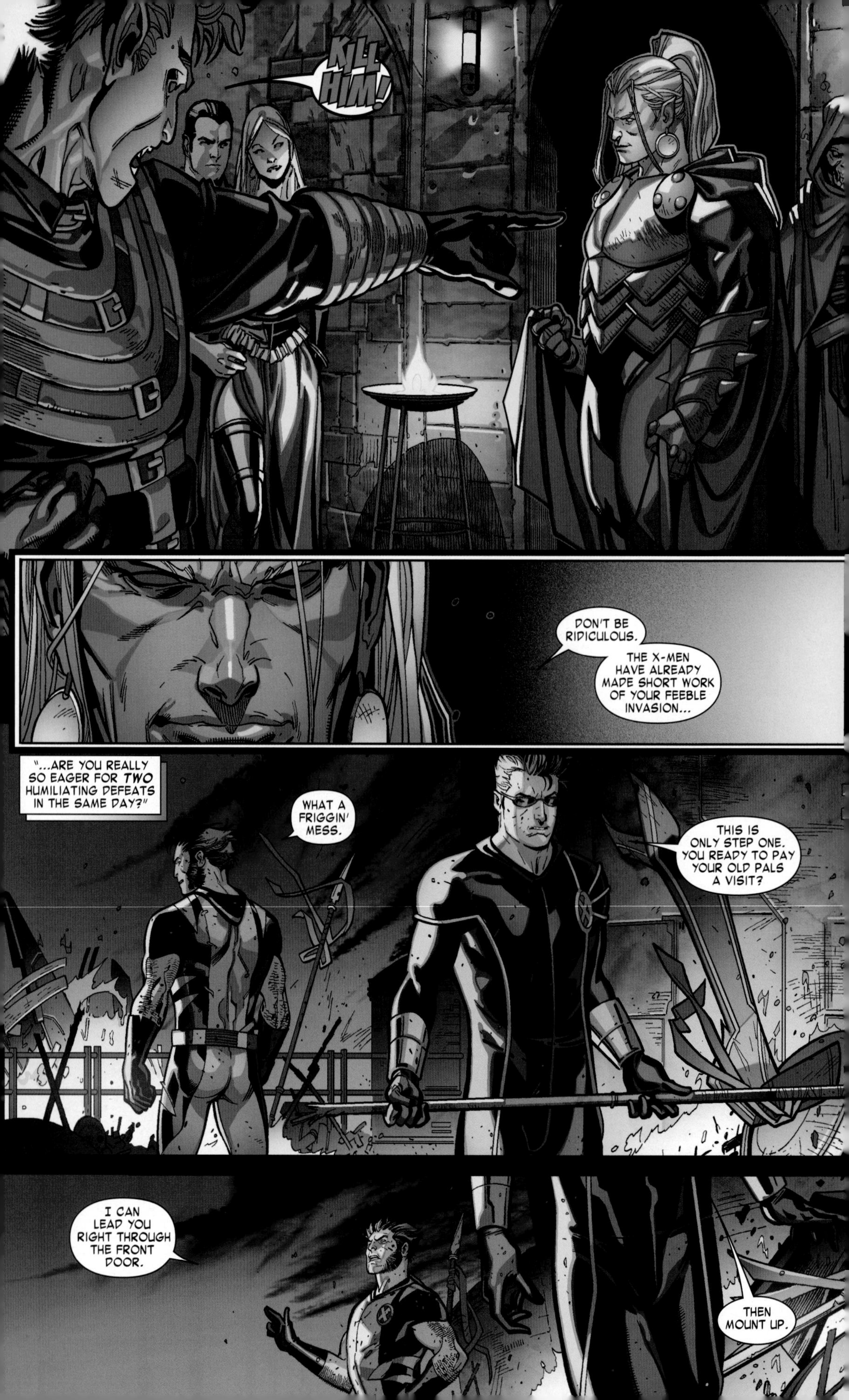
KILL HIM!
DON'T BE RIDICULOUS.
THE X-MEN HAVE ALREADY MADE SHORT WORK OF YOUR FEEBLE INVASION...
"...ARE YOU REALLY SO EAGER FOR TWO HUMILIATING DEFEATS IN THE SAME DAY?"
WHAT A FRIGGIN' MESS.
THIS IS ONLY STEP ONE. YOU READY TO PAY YOUR OLD PALS A VISIT?
I CAN LEAD YOU RIGHT THROUGH THE FRONT DOOR.
THEN MOUNT UP.

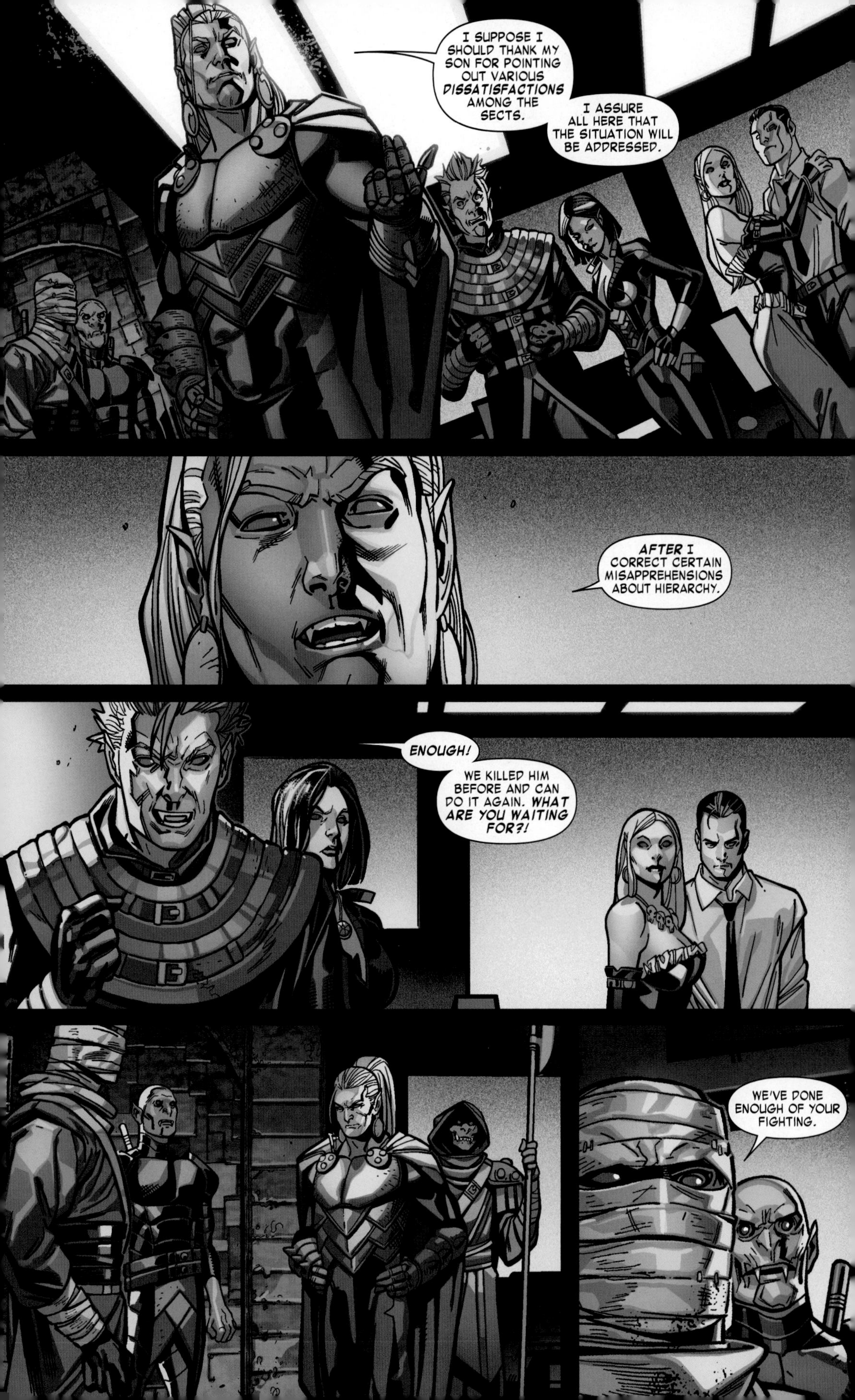
I SUPPOSE I SHOULD THANK MY SON FOR POINTING OUT VARIOUS DISSATISFACTIONS AMONG THE SECTS.
I ASSURE ALL HERE THAT THE SITUATION WILL BE ADDRESSED.
AFTER I CORRECT CERTAIN MISAPPREHENSIONS ABOUT HIERARCHY.
ENOUGH!
WE KILLED HIM BEFORE AND CAN DO IT AGAIN. WHAT ARE YOU WAITING FOR?!
WE'VE DONE ENOUGH OF YOUR FIGHTING.

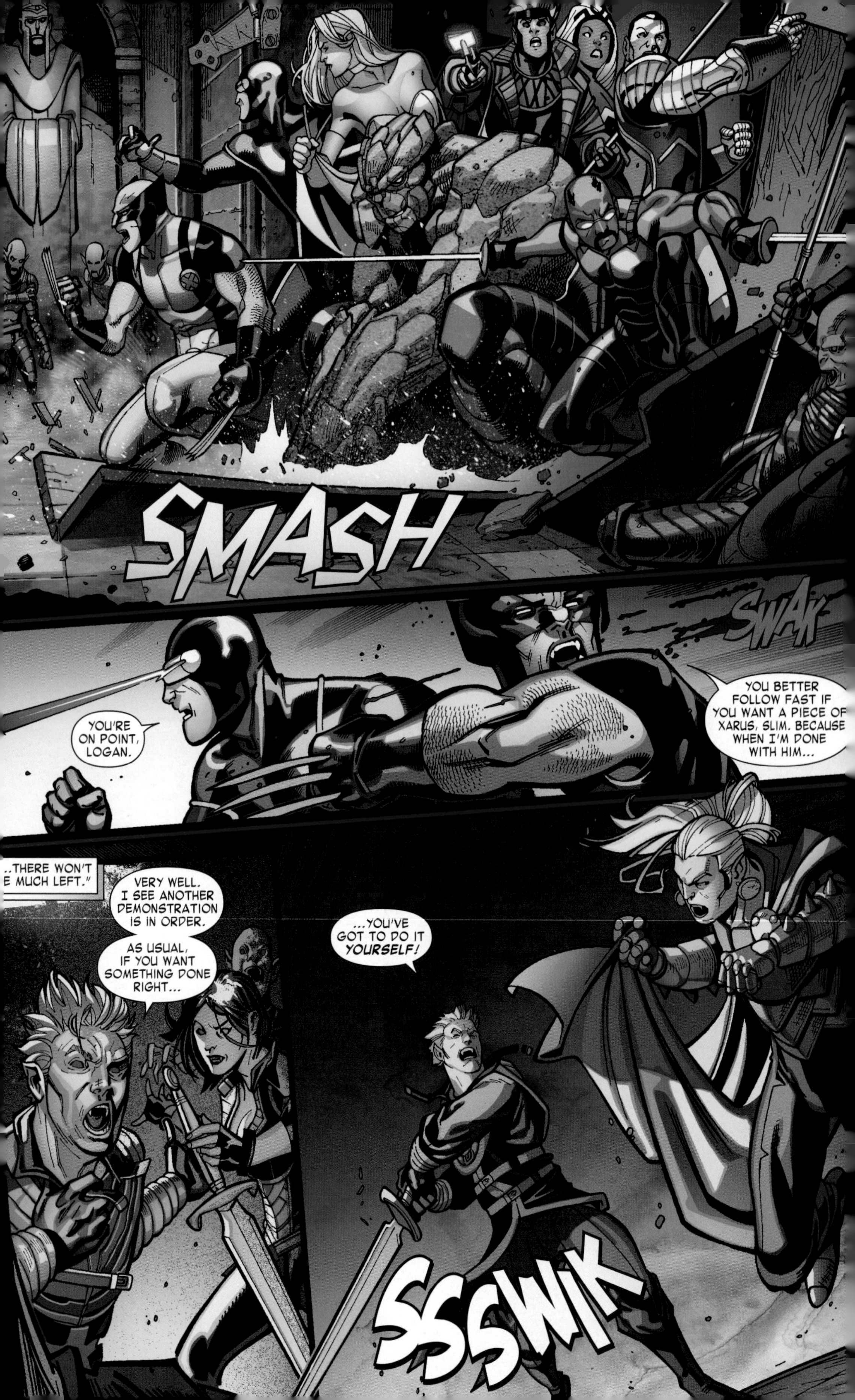
SMASH
SWAK
YOU'RE ON POINT, LOGAN.
YOU BETTER FOLLOW FAST IF YOU WANT A PIECE OF XARUS, SLIM. BECAUSE WHEN I'M DONE WITH HIM...
..THERE WON'T E MUCH LEFT."
VERY WELL. I SEE ANOTHER DEMONSTRATION IS IN ORDER.
AS USUAL, IF YOU WANT SOMETHING DONE RIGHT...
...YOU'VE GOT TO DO IT YOURSELF!
SSSWIK

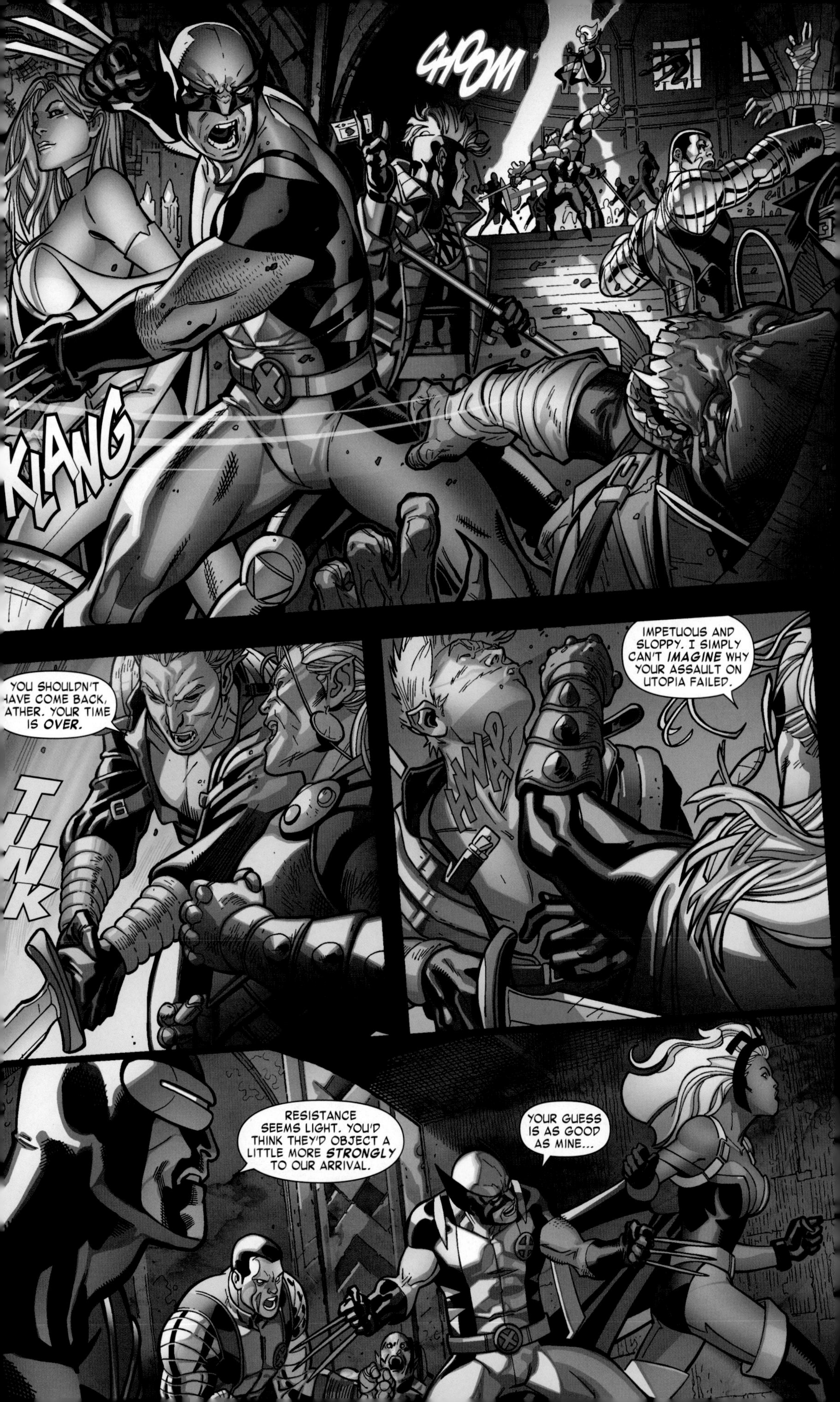

CHOOM
KLANG
YOU SHOULDN'T HAVE COME BACK, FATHER. YOUR TIME IS OVER.
TINK
IMPETUOUS AND SLOPPY. I SIMPLY CAN'T IMAGINE WHY YOUR ASSAULT ON UTOPIA FAILED.
WHAP
RESISTANCE SEEMS LIGHT. YOU'D THINK THEY'D OBJECT A LITTLE MORE STRONGLY TO OUR ARRIVAL.
YOUR GUESS IS AS GOOD AS MINE...

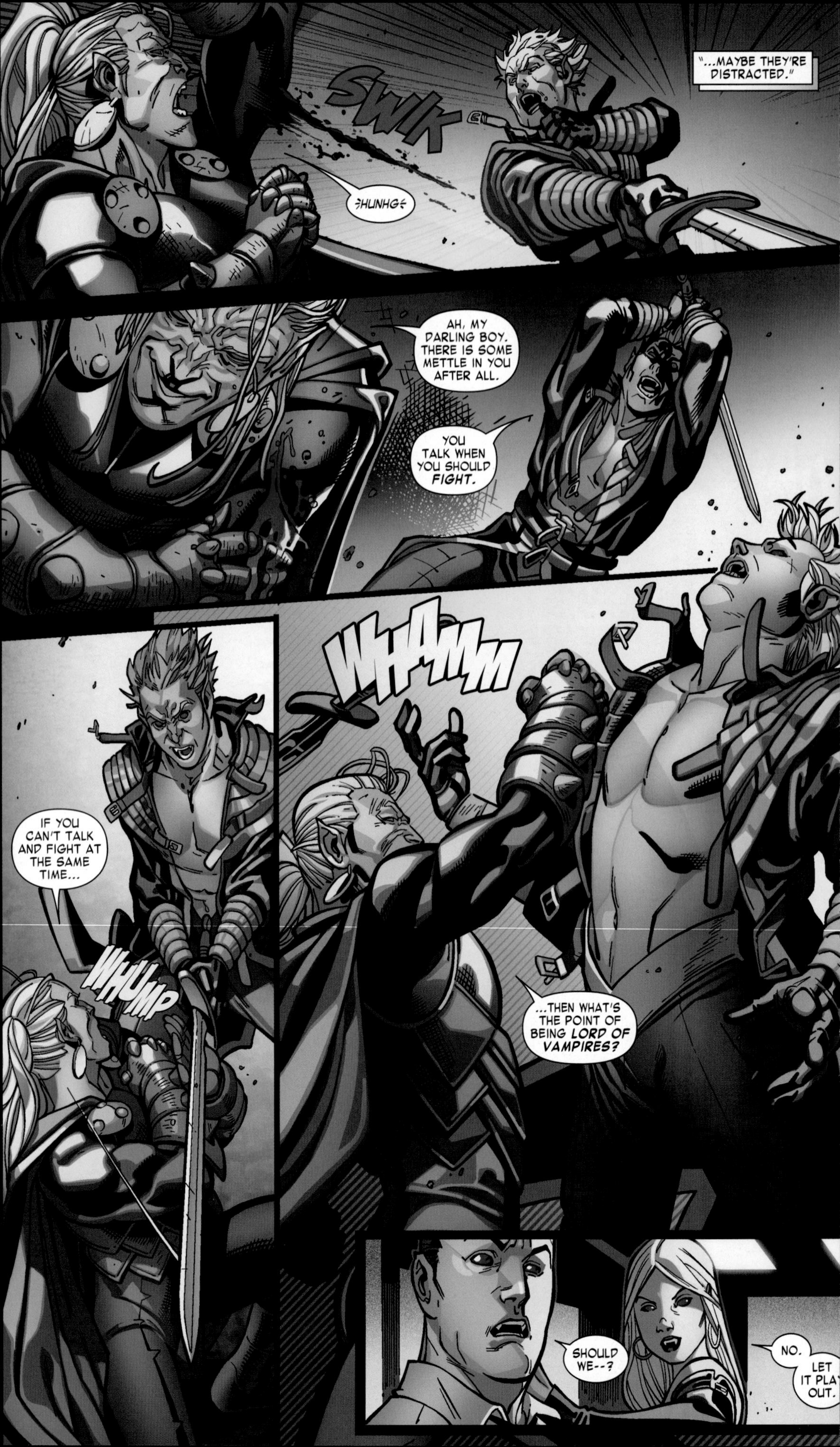
"...MAYBE THEY'RE DISTRACTED."
SWIK
HUNHG
AH, MY DARLING BOY. THERE IS SOME METTLE IN YOU AFTER ALL.
YOU TALK WHEN YOU SHOULD FIGHT.
WHAMM
IF YOU CAN'T TALK AND FIGHT AT THE SAME TIME...
WHUMP
...THEN WHAT'S THE POINT OF BEING LORD OF VAMPIRES?
SHOULD WE--?
NO.
LET IT PLA
OUT.

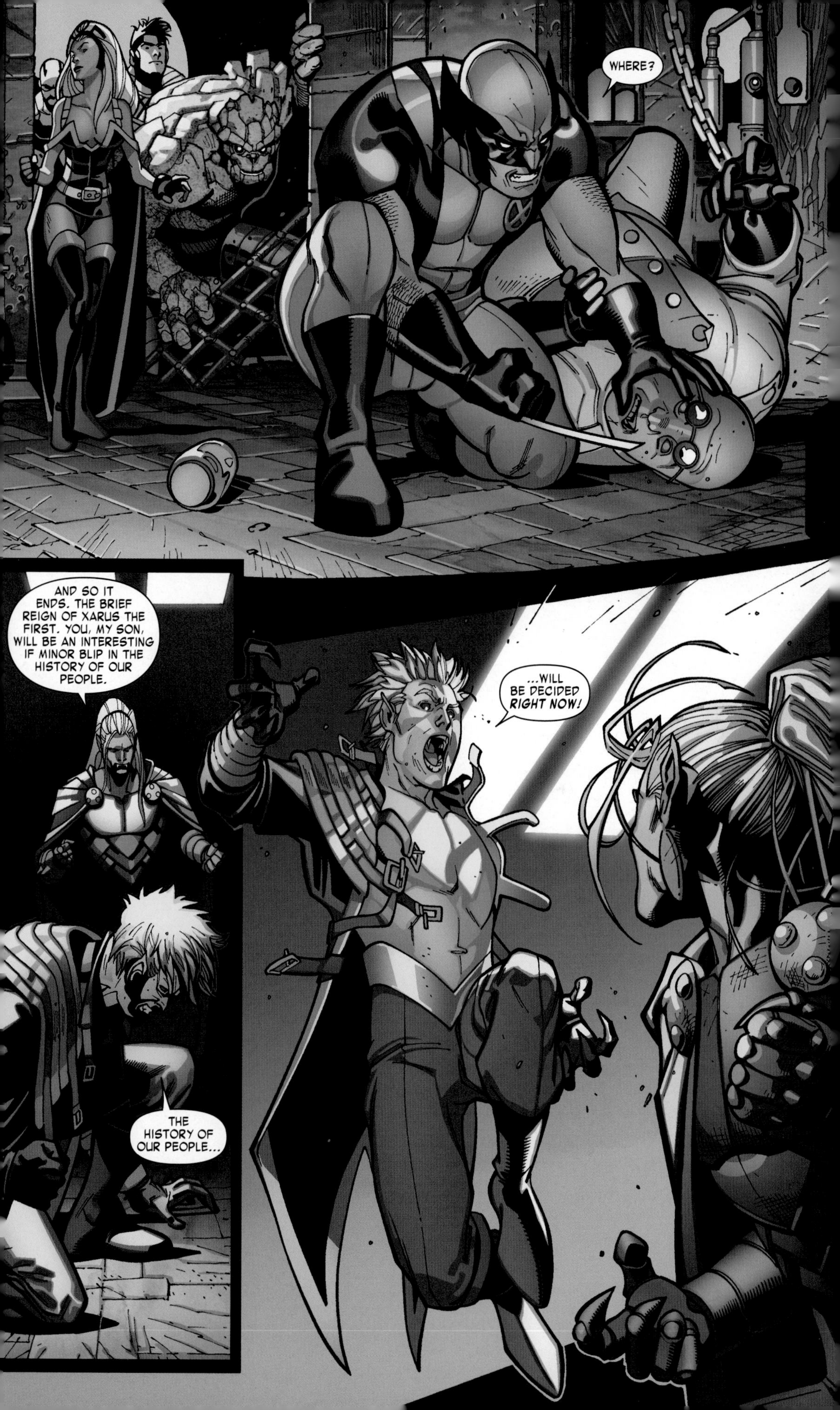
WHERE?
AND SO IT ENDS. THE BRIEF REIGN OF XARUS THE FIRST. YOU, MY SON, WILL BE AN INTERESTING IF MINOR BLIP IN THE HISTORY OF OUR PEOPLE.
THE HISTORY OF OUR PEOPLE...
...WILL BE DECIDED RIGHT NOW!

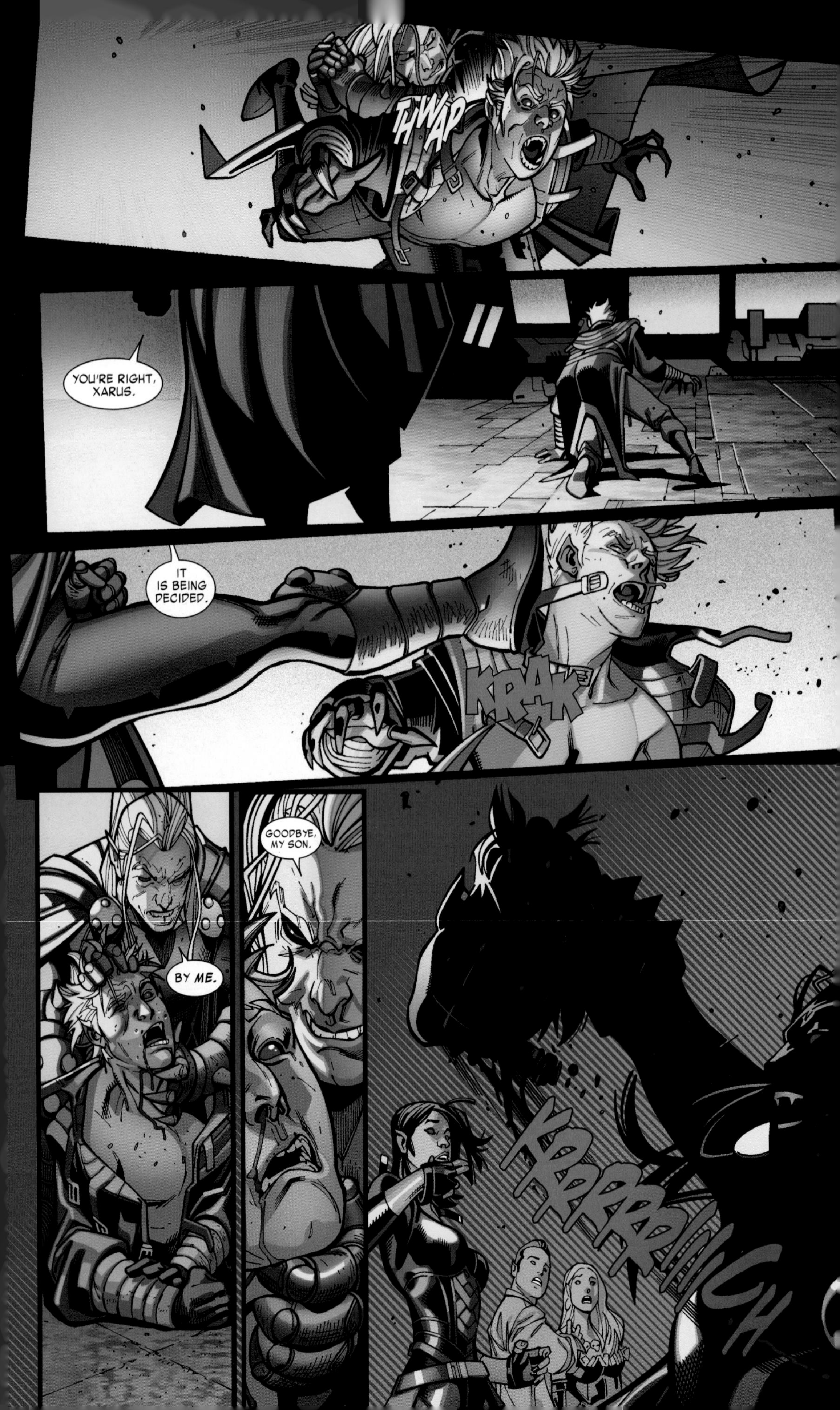
THWAP
YOU'RE RIGHT, XARUS.
IT IS BEING DECIDED.
KRAK
BY ME.
GOODBYE, MY SON.
KRRRRRUNCH

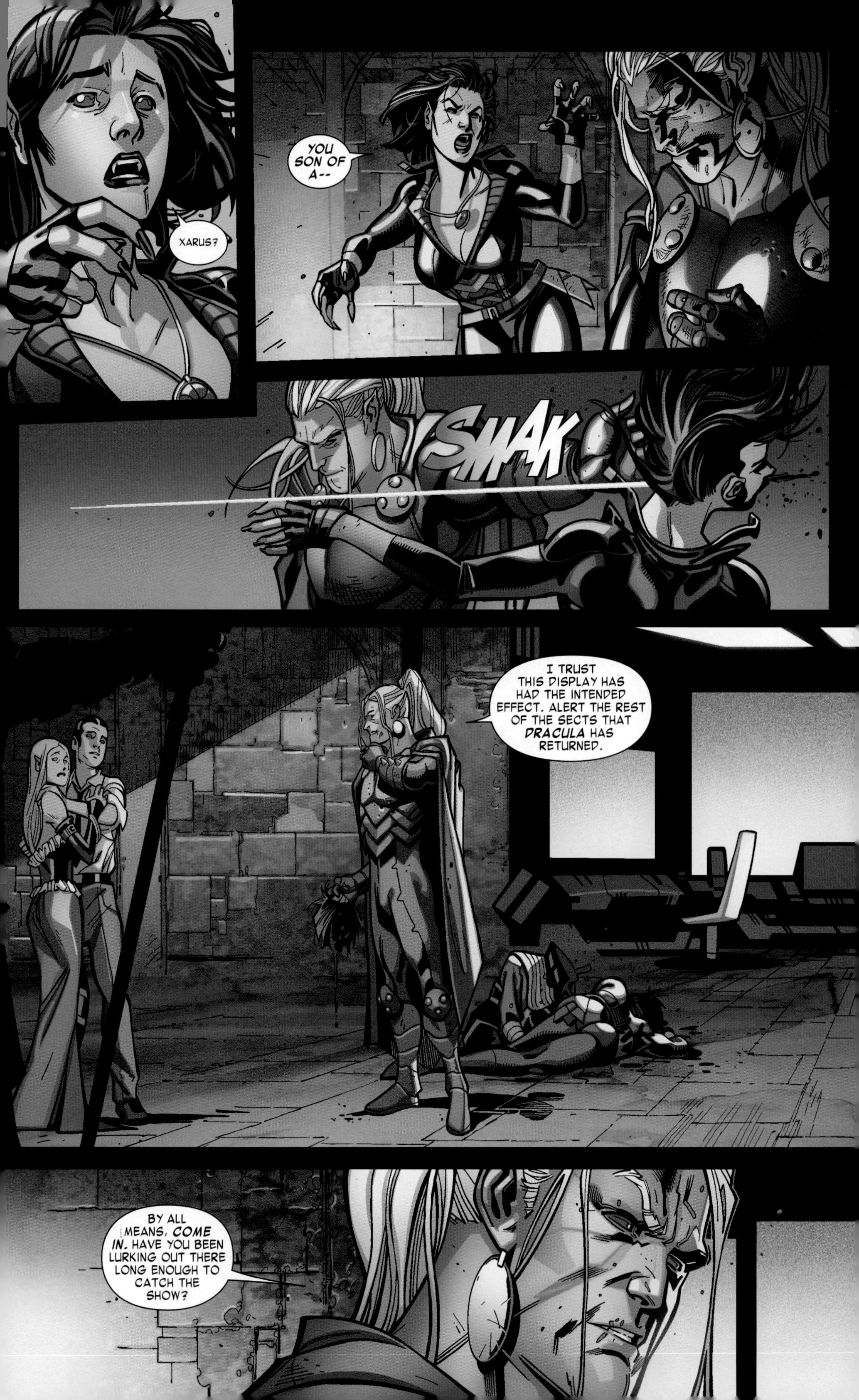
XARUS?
YOU SON OF A--
SMAK
I TRUST THIS DISPLAY HAS HAD THE INTENDED EFFECT. ALERT THE REST OF THE SECTS THAT *DRACULA* HAS RETURNED.
BY ALL MEANS, *COME IN.* HAVE YOU BEEN LURKING OUT THERE LONG ENOUGH TO CATCH THE SHOW?

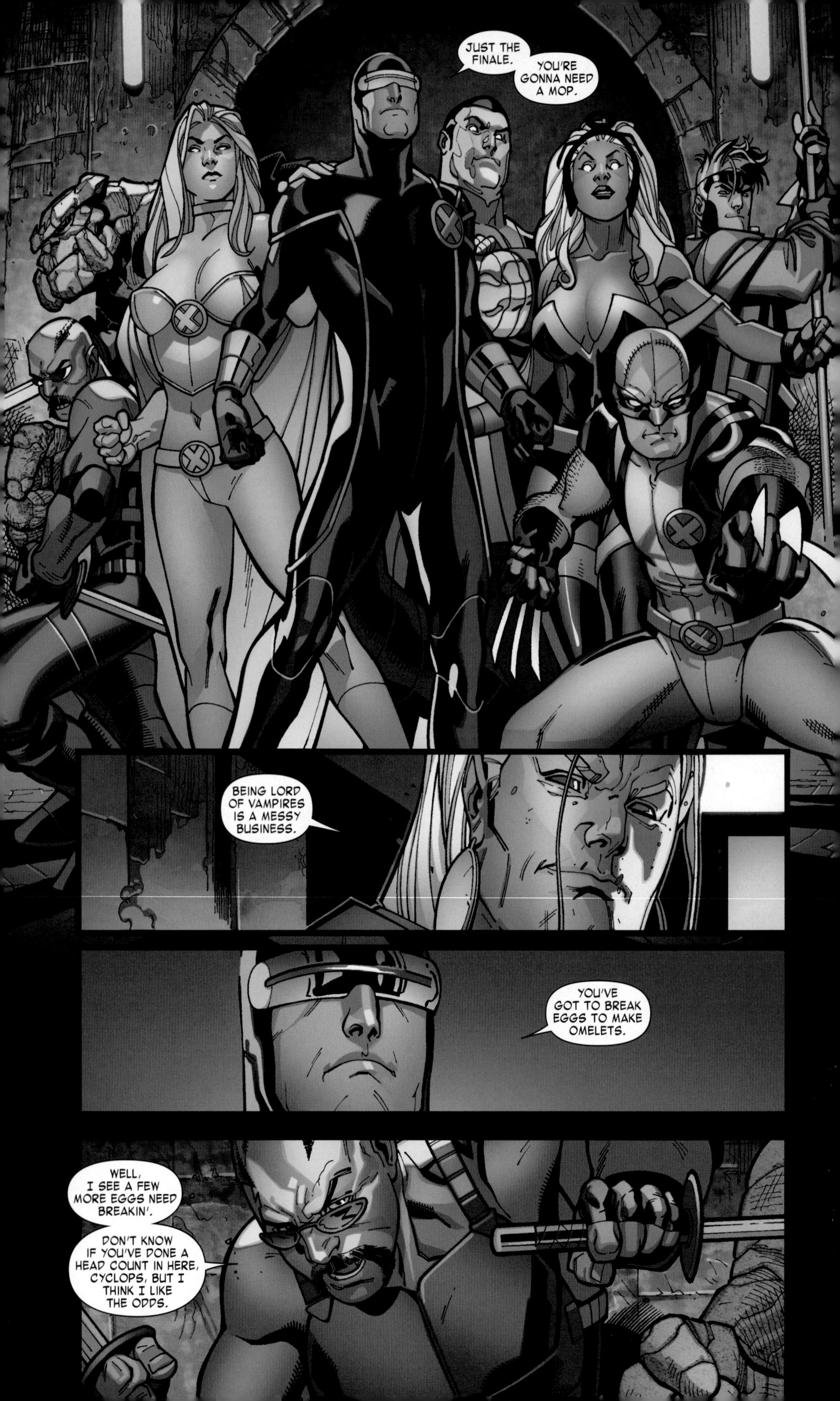
JUST THE FINALE.
YOU'RE GONNA NEED A MOP.
BEING LORD OF VAMPIRES IS A MESSY BUSINESS.
YOU'VE GOT TO BREAK EGGS TO MAKE OMELETS.
WELL, I SEE A FEW MORE EGGS NEED BREAKIN'.
DON'T KNOW IF YOU'VE DONE A HEAD COUNT IN HERE, CYCLOPS, BUT I THINK I LIKE THE ODDS.

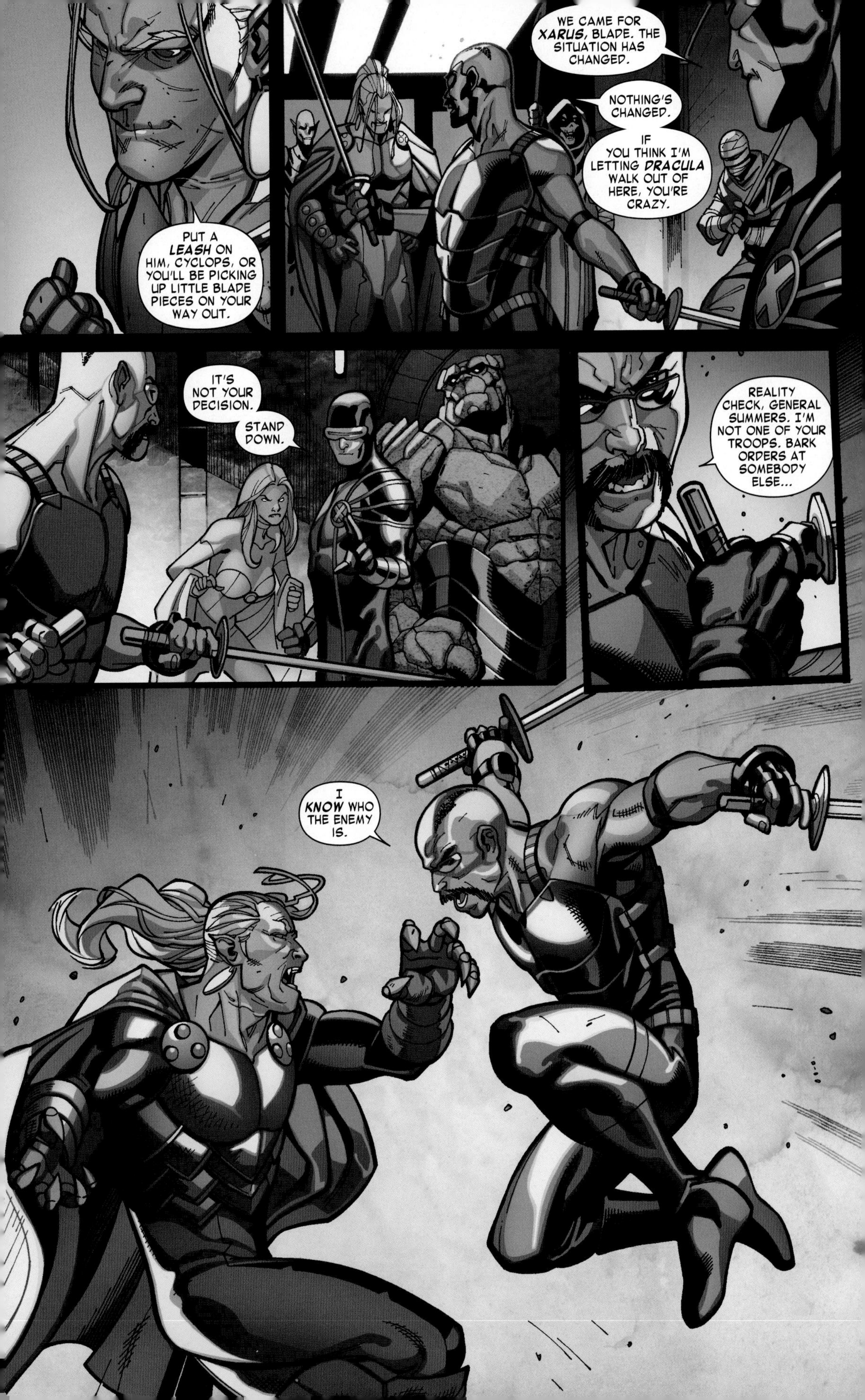

PUT A *LEASH* ON HIM, CYCLOPS, OR YOU'LL BE PICKING UP LITTLE BLADE PIECES ON YOUR WAY OUT.
WE CAME FOR *XARUS*, BLADE. THE SITUATION HAS CHANGED.
NOTHING'S CHANGED.
IF YOU THINK I'M LETTING *DRACULA* WALK OUT OF HERE, YOU'RE CRAZY.
IT'S NOT YOUR DECISION.
STAND DOWN.
REALITY CHECK, GENERAL SUMMERS. I'M NOT ONE OF YOUR TROOPS. BARK ORDERS AT SOMEBODY ELSE...
I *KNOW* WHO THE ENEMY IS.

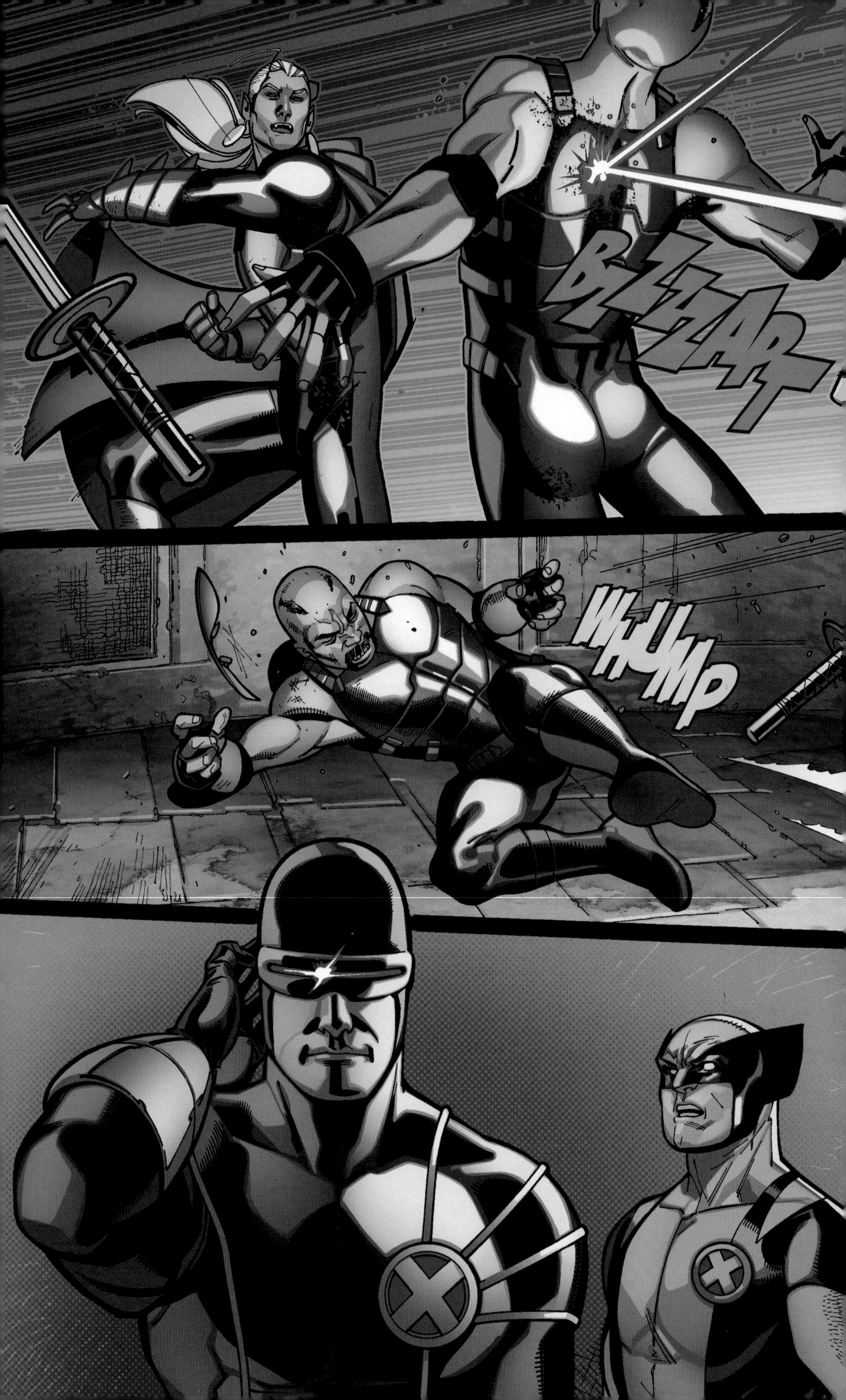
BZZZZART
WHUMP

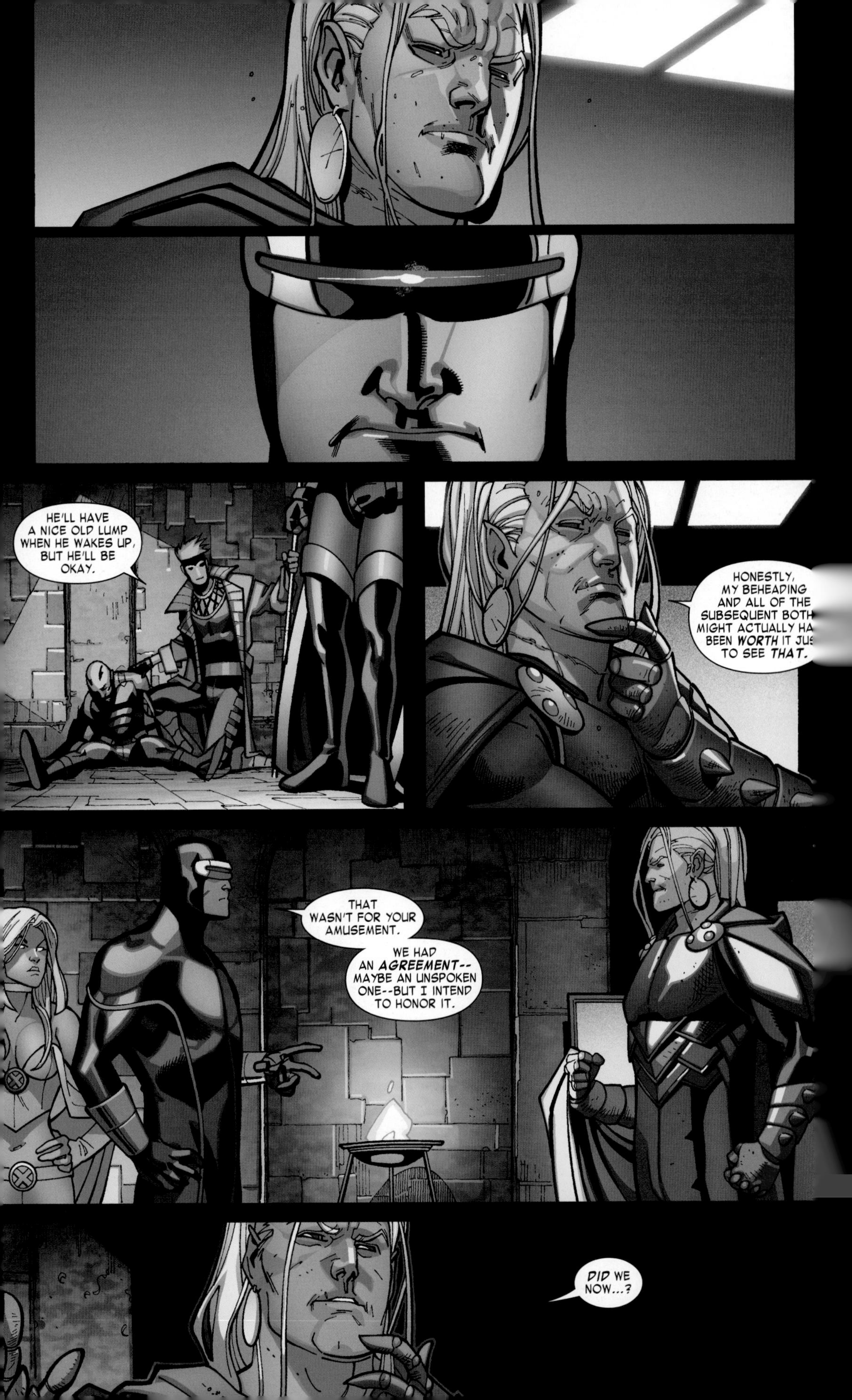
HE'LL HAVE A NICE OLD LUMP WHEN HE WAKES UP, BUT HE'LL BE OKAY.
HONESTLY, MY BEHEADING AND ALL OF THE SUBSEQUENT BOTH MIGHT ACTUALLY HA BEEN WORTH IT JUS TO SEE THAT.
THAT WASN'T FOR YOUR AMUSEMENT.
WE HAD AN AGREEMENT-- MAYBE AN UNSPOKEN ONE--BUT I INTEND TO HONOR IT.
DID WE NOW...?

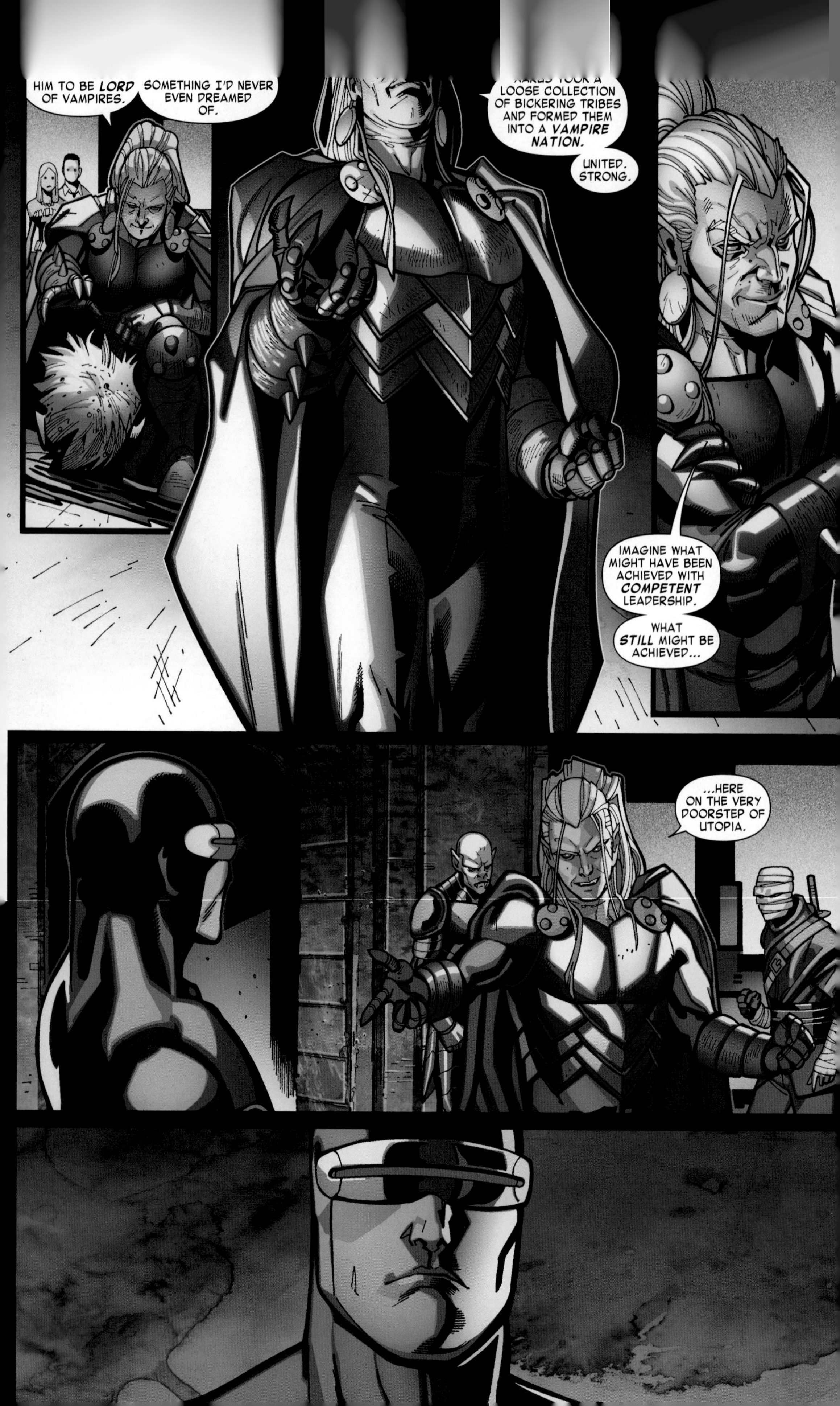

HIM TO BE *LORD* OF VAMPIRES.
SOMETHING I'D NEVER EVEN DREAMED OF.
LOOSE COLLECTION OF BICKERING TRIBES AND FORMED THEM INTO A *VAMPIRE NATION.*
UNITED. STRONG.
IMAGINE WHAT MIGHT HAVE BEEN ACHIEVED WITH *COMPETENT* LEADERSHIP.
WHAT *STILL* MIGHT BE ACHIEVED...
...HERE ON THE VERY DOORSTEP OF UTOPIA.

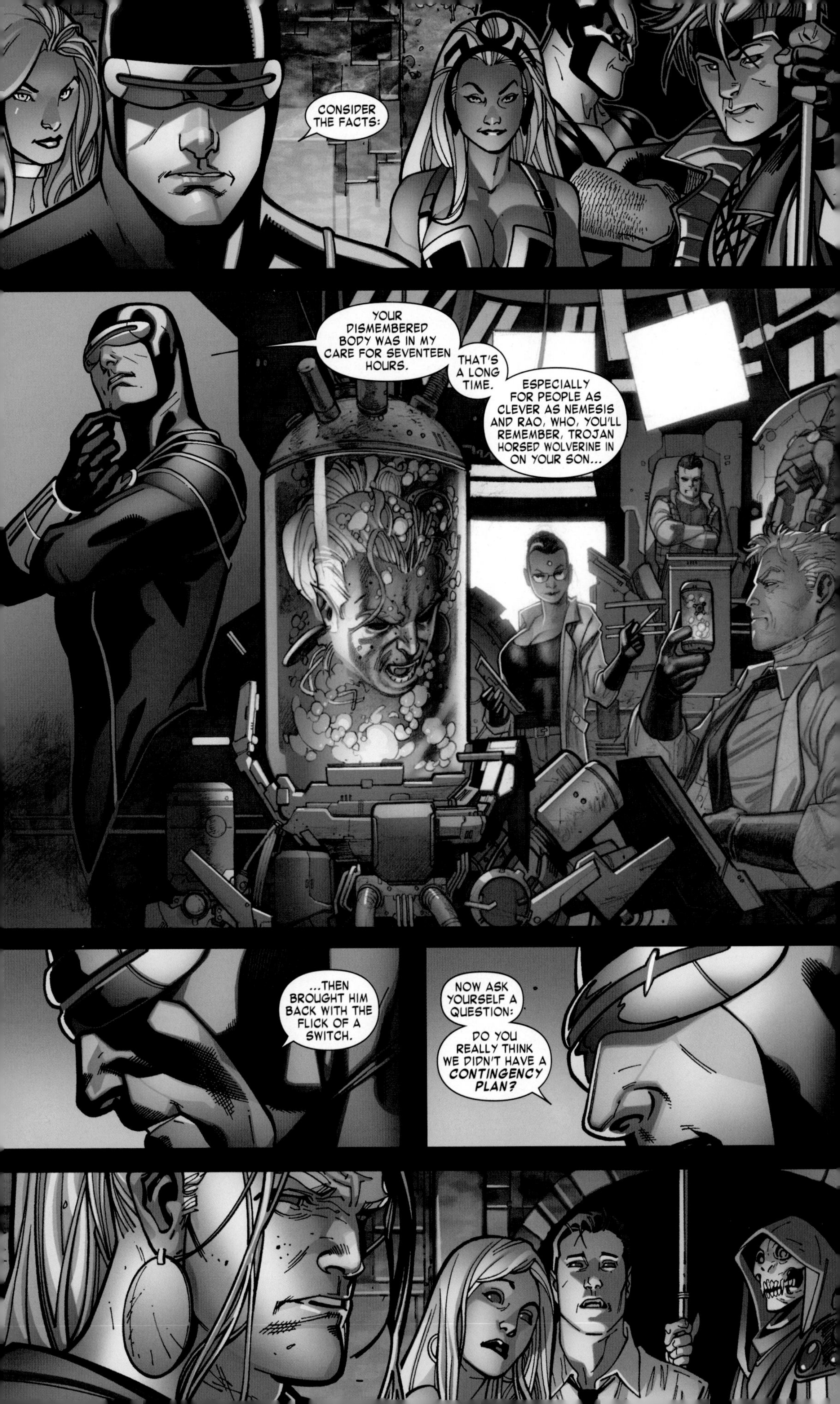
CONSIDER THE FACTS:
YOUR DISMEMBERED BODY WAS IN MY CARE FOR SEVENTEEN HOURS.
THAT'S A LONG TIME.
ESPECIALLY FOR PEOPLE AS CLEVER AS NEMESIS AND RAO, WHO, YOU'LL REMEMBER, TROJAN HORSED WOLVERINE IN ON YOUR SON...
...THEN BROUGHT HIM BACK WITH THE FLICK OF A SWITCH.
NOW ASK YOURSELF A QUESTION:
DO YOU REALLY THINK WE DIDN'T HAVE A CONTINGENCY PLAN?

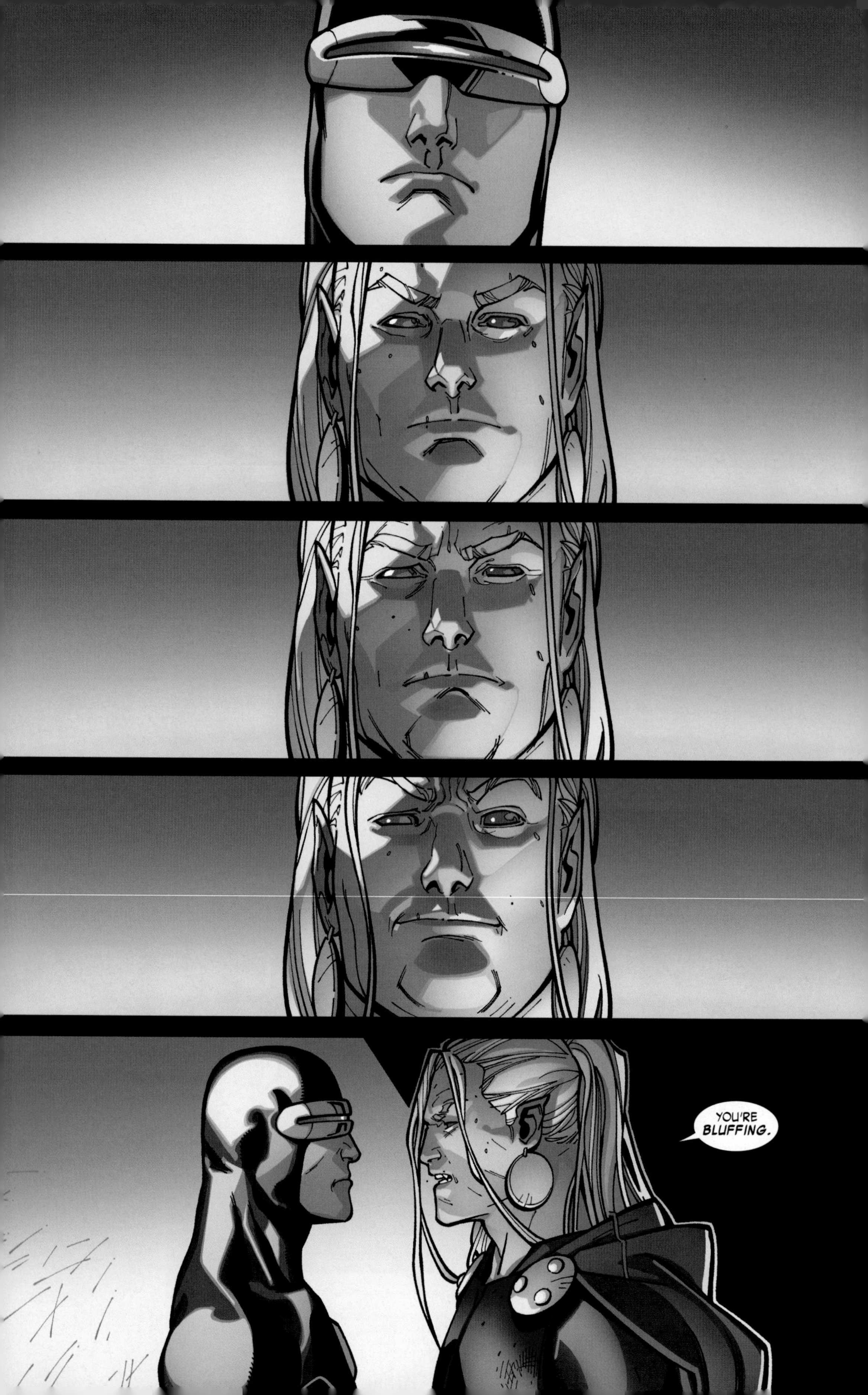
YOU'RE BLUFFING.

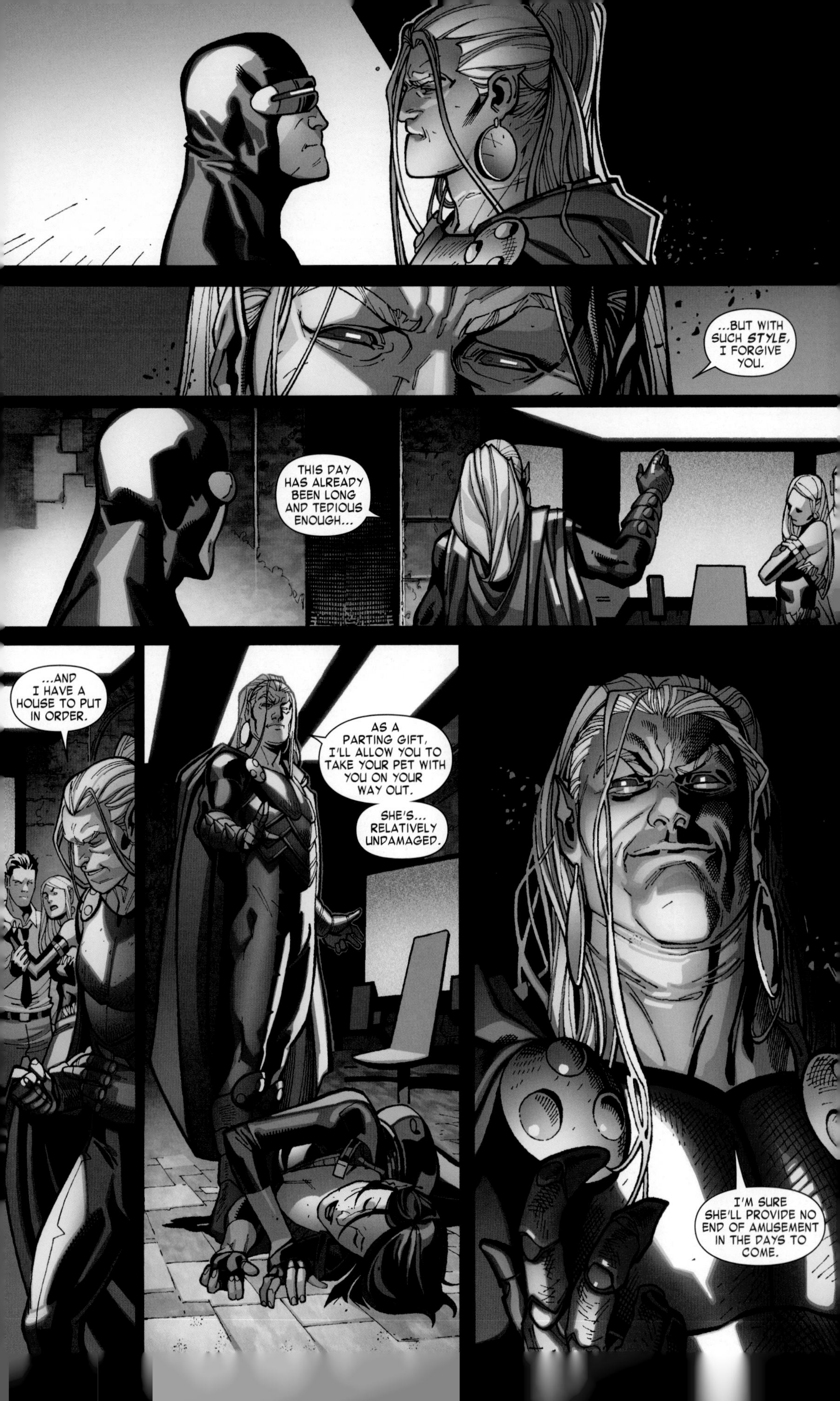
...BUT WITH SUCH STYLE, I FORGIVE YOU.
THIS DAY HAS ALREADY BEEN LONG AND TEDIOUS ENOUGH...
...AND I HAVE A HOUSE TO PUT IN ORDER.
AS A PARTING GIFT, I'LL ALLOW YOU TO TAKE YOUR PET WITH YOU ON YOUR WAY OUT.
SHE'S... RELATIVELY UNDAMAGED.
I'M SURE SHE'LL PROVIDE NO END OF AMUSEMENT IN THE DAYS TO COME.

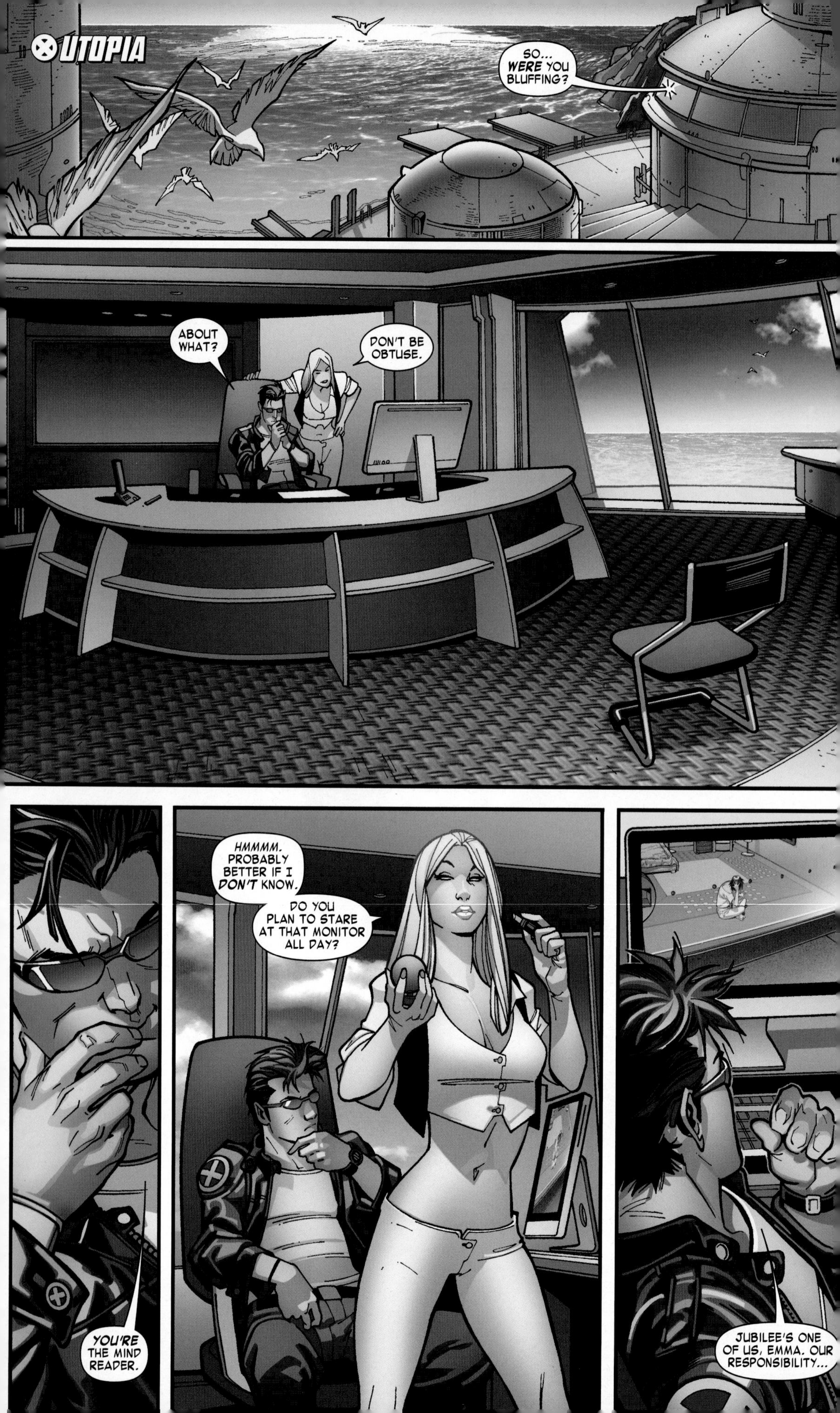
UTOPIA
SO... WERE YOU BLUFFING?
ABOUT WHAT?
DON'T BE OBTUSE.
YOU'RE THE MIND READER.
HMMMM. PROBABLY BETTER IF I DON'T KNOW.
DO YOU PLAN TO STARE AT THAT MONITOR ALL DAY?
JUBILEE'S ONE OF US, EMMA. OUR RESPONSIBILITY...

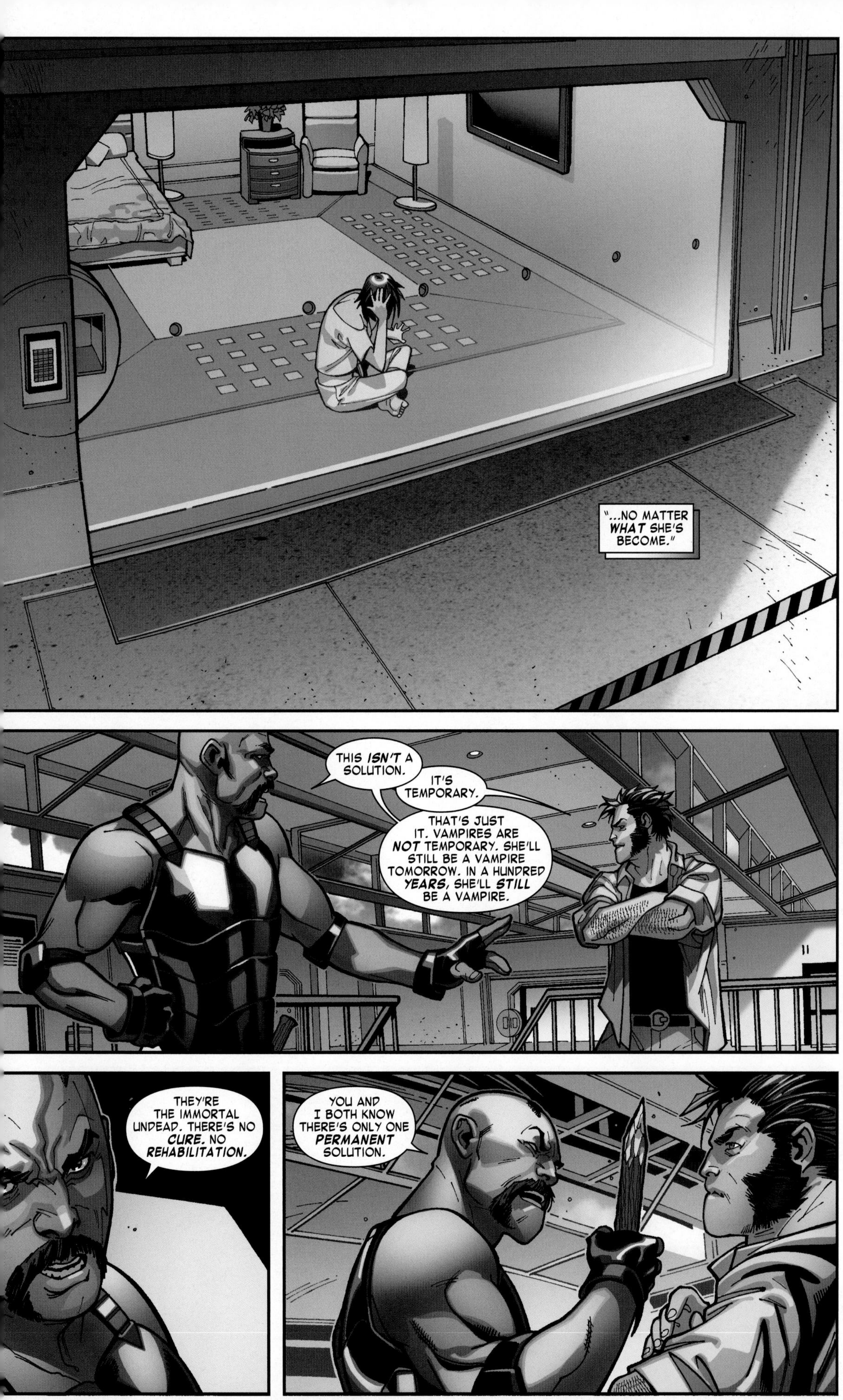

"...NO MATTER WHAT SHE'S BECOME."
THIS ISN'T A SOLUTION.
IT'S TEMPORARY.
THAT'S JUST IT. VAMPIRES ARE NOT TEMPORARY. SHE'LL STILL BE A VAMPIRE TOMORROW. IN A HUNDRED YEARS, SHE'LL STILL BE A VAMPIRE.
THEY'RE THE IMMORTAL UNDEAD. THERE'S NO CURE. NO REHABILITATION.
YOU AND I BOTH KNOW THERE'S ONLY ONE PERMANENT SOLUTION.

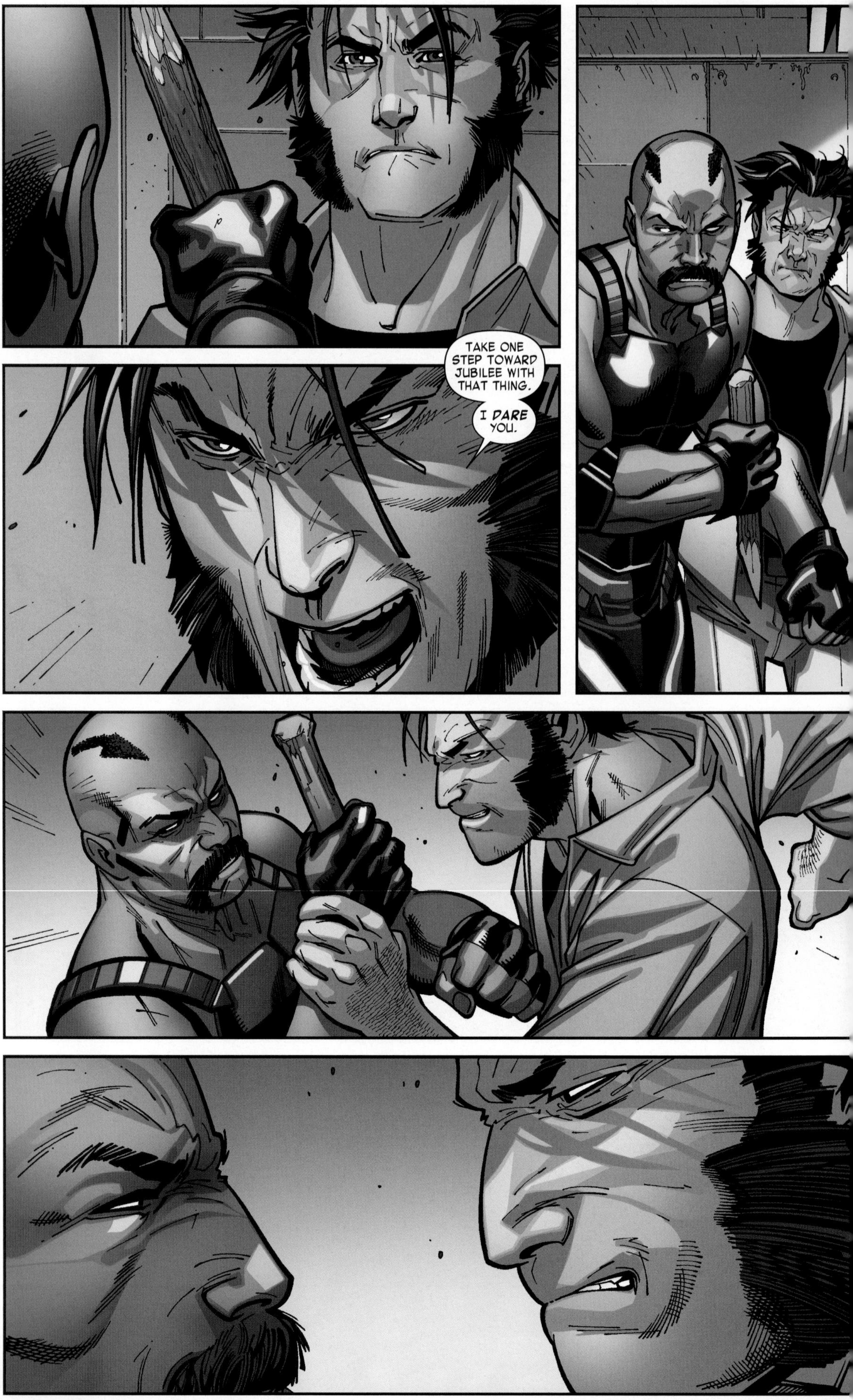

TAKE ONE STEP TOWARD JUBILEE WITH THAT THING.
I *DARE* YOU.

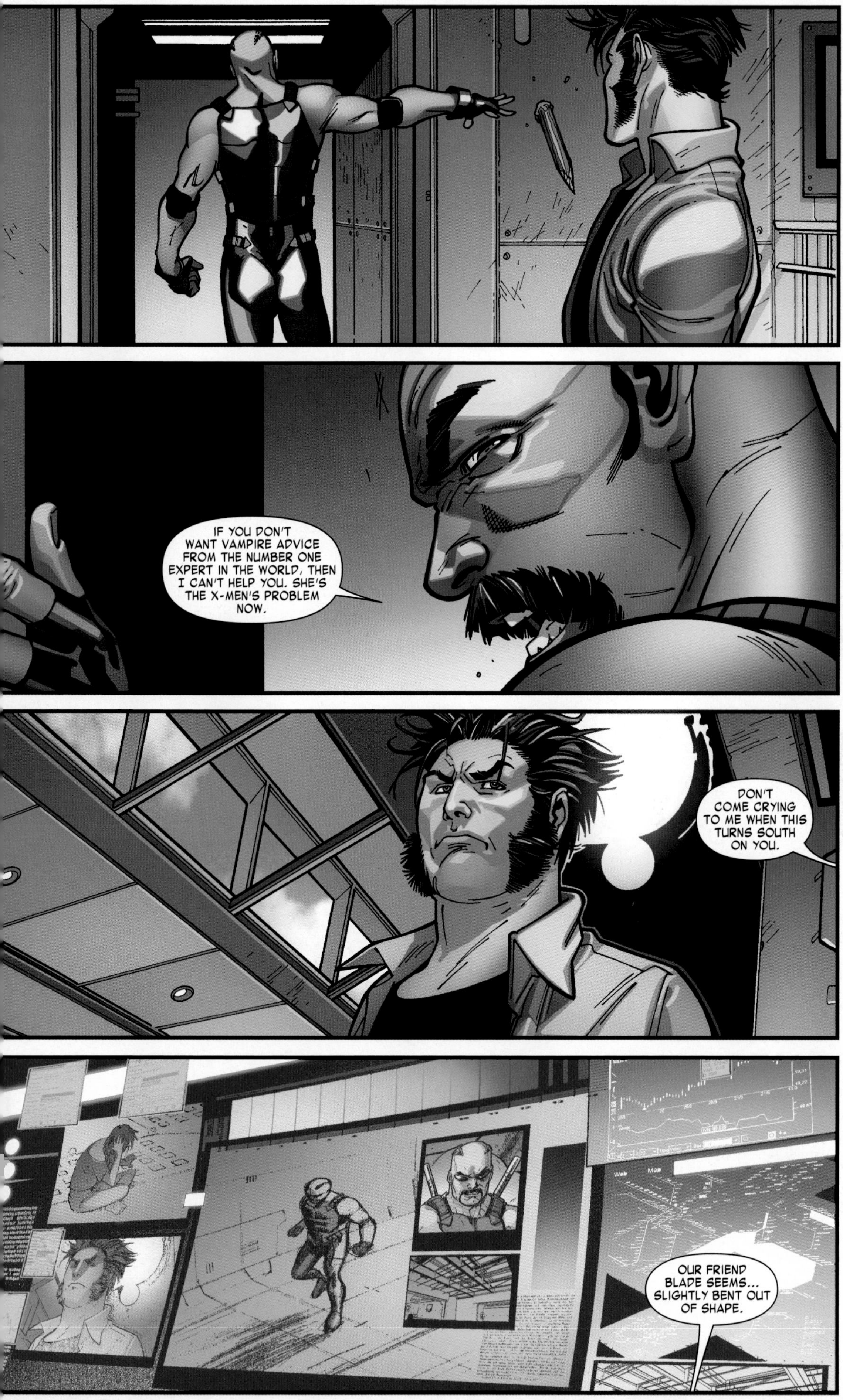
IF YOU DON'T WANT VAMPIRE ADVICE FROM THE NUMBER ONE EXPERT IN THE WORLD, THEN I CAN'T HELP YOU. SHE'S THE X-MEN'S PROBLEM NOW.
DON'T COME CRYING TO ME WHEN THIS TURNS SOUTH ON YOU.
OUR FRIEND BLADE SEEMS... SLIGHTLY BENT OUT OF SHAPE.

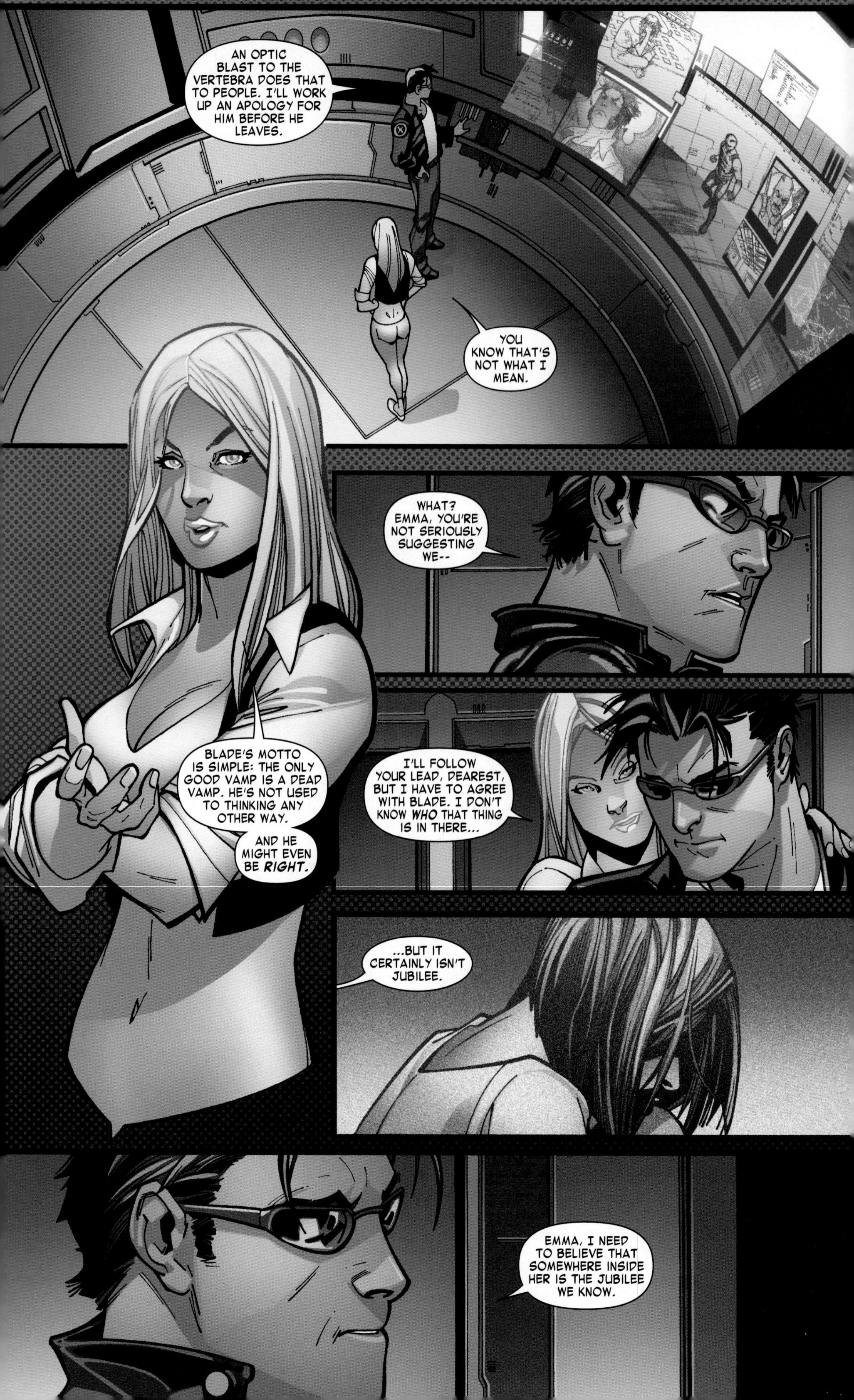
AN OPTIC BLAST TO THE VERTEBRA DOES THAT TO PEOPLE. I'LL WORK UP AN APOLOGY FOR HIM BEFORE HE LEAVES.
YOU KNOW THAT'S NOT WHAT I MEAN.
WHAT? EMMA, YOU'RE NOT SERIOUSLY SUGGESTING WE--
BLADE'S MOTTO IS SIMPLE: THE ONLY GOOD VAMP IS A DEAD VAMP. HE'S NOT USED TO THINKING ANY OTHER WAY.
AND HE MIGHT EVEN BE *RIGHT.*
I'LL FOLLOW YOUR LEAD, DEAREST, BUT I HAVE TO AGREE WITH BLADE. I DON'T KNOW *WHO* THAT THING IS IN THERE...
...BUT IT CERTAINLY ISN'T JUBILEE.
EMMA, I NEED TO BELIEVE THAT SOMEWHERE INSIDE HER IS THE JUBILEE WE KNOW.

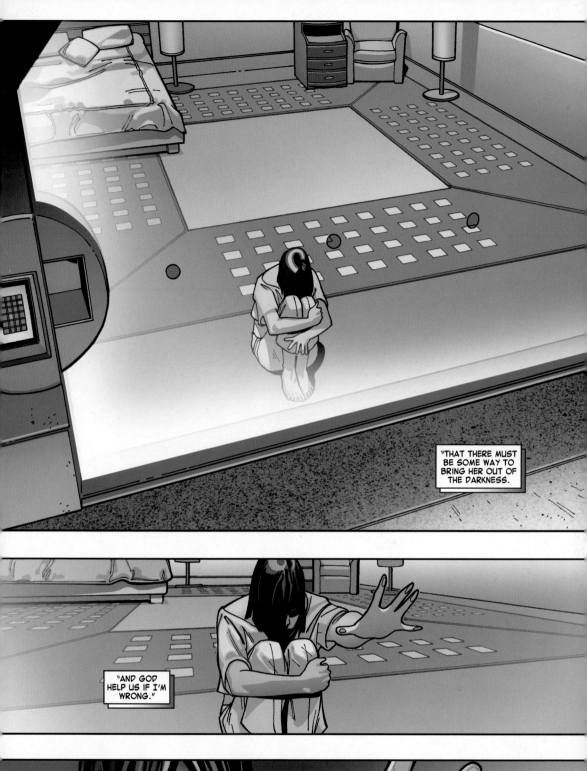

"THAT THERE MUST BE SOME WAY TO BRING HER OUT OF THE DARKNESS.

"AND GOD HELP US IF I'M WRONG."

NEXT: TO SERVE AND PROTECT!

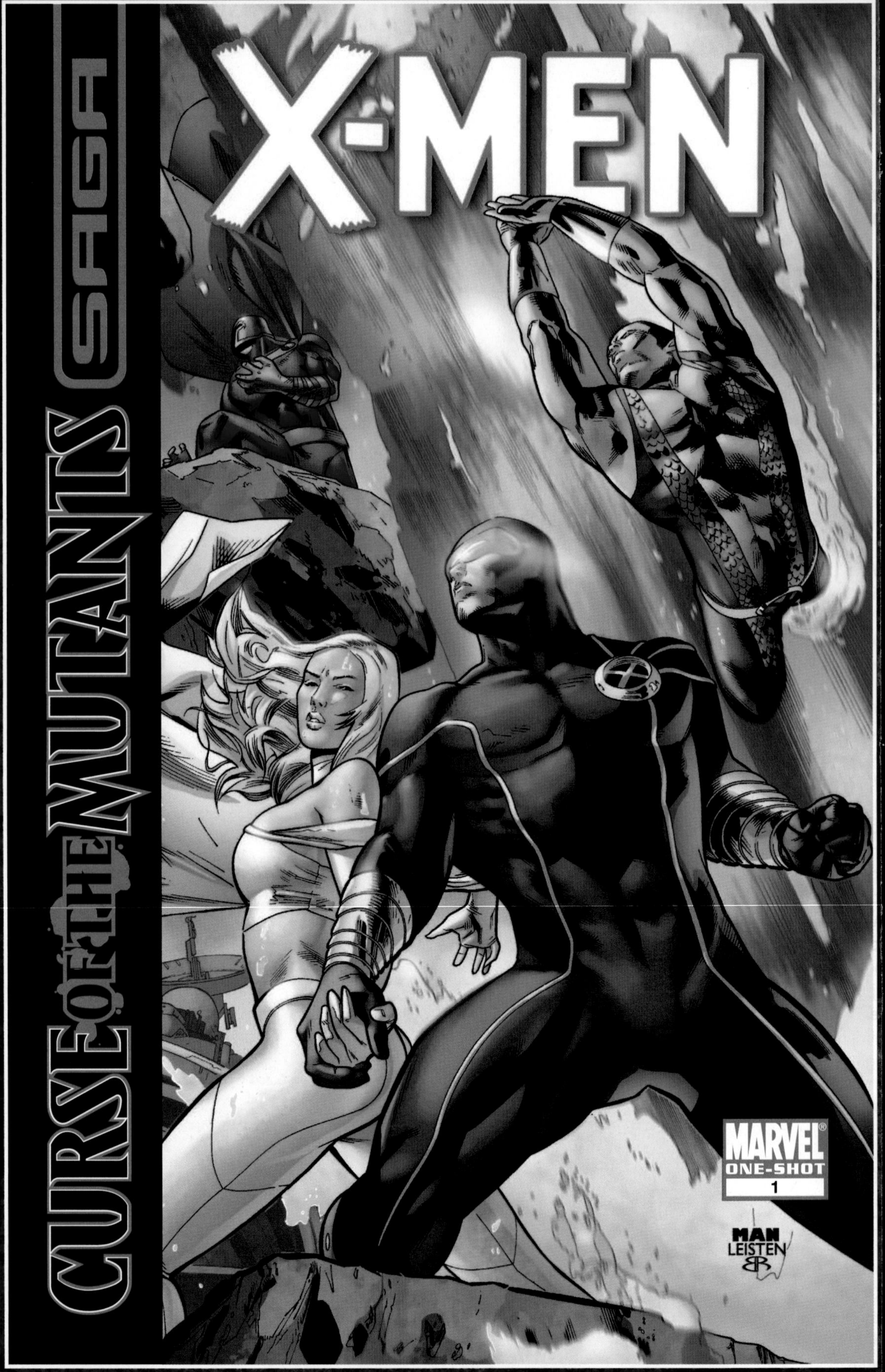

X-MEN
CURSE OF THE MUTANTS SAGA
MARVEL
ONE-SHOT
1
MAN
LEISTEN

X-MEN A GO-GO!

Inside The New X-Men Series By Victor Gischler!

By John Rhett Thomas

Design by Michael Kronenberg

He's written five hard-boiled crime novels, two satirical sci-fi romps, and two more Deadpool series than Marvel's health plan will allow for preexisting conditions! But now, Victor Gischler gets to write a whole lotta mutants in *X-Men*, a new ongoing series featuring the adjectiveless mutants of the Heroic Age! Victor's story starts in San Francisco with the X-Men (most of them, that is) having survived "*Second Coming*," but now facing an ancient yet very familiar threat…familiar, that is, until you see what Victor and Marvel have in store!

MARVEL: Let's get this first question out of the way, since I know it's going to be tops on everyone's mind: When the first issue of *X-Men* hit the stands in 1991, it sold over eight million copies. How much pressure are you putting on yourself to top that?

VICTOR: Honestly, that number is so gigantic that it actually takes the pressure off. Eight million copies? (*Laughs.*) I'm not even going to *think* that's going to happen. But I have heard through the grapevine that the first issue is expected to do well, so I'm optimistic. And I am somewhat nervous to be honest, but not because of sales numbers. I just know that X-Men readers expect a high level of quality, and I want to do right by them.

MARVEL: To take a more serious line of questioning, can you acclimate us to your X-Men as the team comes out of the events of "*Second Coming*"?

VICTOR: We open with the X-Men feeling pretty good about themselves. The Heroic Age is an optimistic time and that goes for the X-Men, too. That's why it hits the X-Men doubly hard

that such a sinister threat drops on them so soon in this first *X-Men* arc.

MARVEL: Can you sum up in a few words what you like about the roster of mutants you'll be dealing with?

VICTOR: The events in the first arc are big enough that the X-Men need all hands on deck, so we haven't settled into the core team just yet. It's still being decided. I can tell you that I have my eye on Gambit and am taking a closer look at Psylocke, but I need to discuss this with the bigwigs back at the X-Office, too. I am also warming up to Pixie. I think she's had the training wheels come off recently and is ready to strut her stuff a little more. I also want to have a few "staples" on the team, but as I said, it's all still being discussed and *nothing* is for sure yet until we battle our way through the first arc.

MARVEL: As a resident of Louisiana, it would seem obvious you might want to get your hands on everyone's favorite Cajun mutant, Gambit. What is it you like about the character and how do you imagine you'd use him?

LOGAN THE VAMPIRE SLAYER: Wolverine faces an eternal threat in *X-Men* #1. (Preview art by Paco Medina.)

VICTOR: Gambit is a great character. I'm not a native of Louisiana, but I've come to really appreciate the culture in the few years I've been here. So, in part, Gambit is like a hometown pick. Also, my sister-in-law is begging me to put Gambit on the team. If he ends up on the team (and there's a good chance), I can dive further into local culture and call it "research." This will involve doubling my intake of gumbo.

MARVEL: Your first storyline is called "*Curse of the Mutants*" and features one of the most well known villains in all of pop culture (and no stranger to the X-Men, as longtime fans know). Can you tell us a little about your *Death of Dracula* one-shot and how it plays into "*Curse of the Mutants*"?

VICTOR: *Death of Dracula* is a great one-shot. We went back and forth with a lot of edits and it was worth the work getting it just right. It's not just a good read all on its own, but it sort of reorients us to the new look and feel of vampires in the Marvel U. Once we had our vision clear what vampires were going to be, it became clear that these guys were going to show their fangs in some other books. These vampires are too good and

> ## "Tolkien ... created such a complete, fully realized world for his characters. I sort of feel that X-Men is the comic book version of that."

too cool just to be a sideshow. They're going to turn some heads in the Marvel U.

MARVEL: Your work in comics up until now has revolved around Punisher and Deadpool, neither of whom (despite furious protestations from the 'Pool) would rate as X-Men. Now you're heading into new territory: a mutant team book. What is it about the whole mutant mythos that intrigues you as a writer?

VICTOR: There's just so much history there. One of the things people say they like about reading Tolkien is that he created such a complete, fully realized world for his characters. I sort of feel that X-Men is the comic book version of that.

MARVEL: And about the team book element, you've also been responsible for *Deadpool Corps*, certainly a "team book" in the wild, make-up-new-rules manner in which you wrote it. But this is a book called *X-Men*, so it's go-time for the first classic Victor Gischler/Marvel team book. Was writing a team book something you've had on your "checklist" of comic writing milestones? Or are you approaching this as you would any other comic assignment?

VICTOR: I had no checklist when I came into comic book writing. I've honestly been delighted about every project I've worked on. On the other hand,

SPOILER ALERT! More than one X-Man will bare their fangs during "Curse of the Mutants." Montage by Paco Medina.

m *not* approaching this like any other comic book assignment. When (Editor) Axel Alonso phoned me to talk about X-Men, I could almost feel the phone getting heavy in my hand with the importance of this assignment. I mean, this is the freakin' X-Men, for crying out loud! When I first started writing for Marvel (not really that long ago) it never entered my little brain that I would get within a hundred miles of an X-book. Now here I am. Just shows that if you work hard and drink your milk, anything can happen. As far as it being a "team book," I think writing *Deadpool Corps* has helped. The books are obviously a completely different tone, but having to juggle multiple characters and move them around on a chessboard was good practice. Also, some of my novels have large casts of characters, so that was good practice too albeit in a different format.

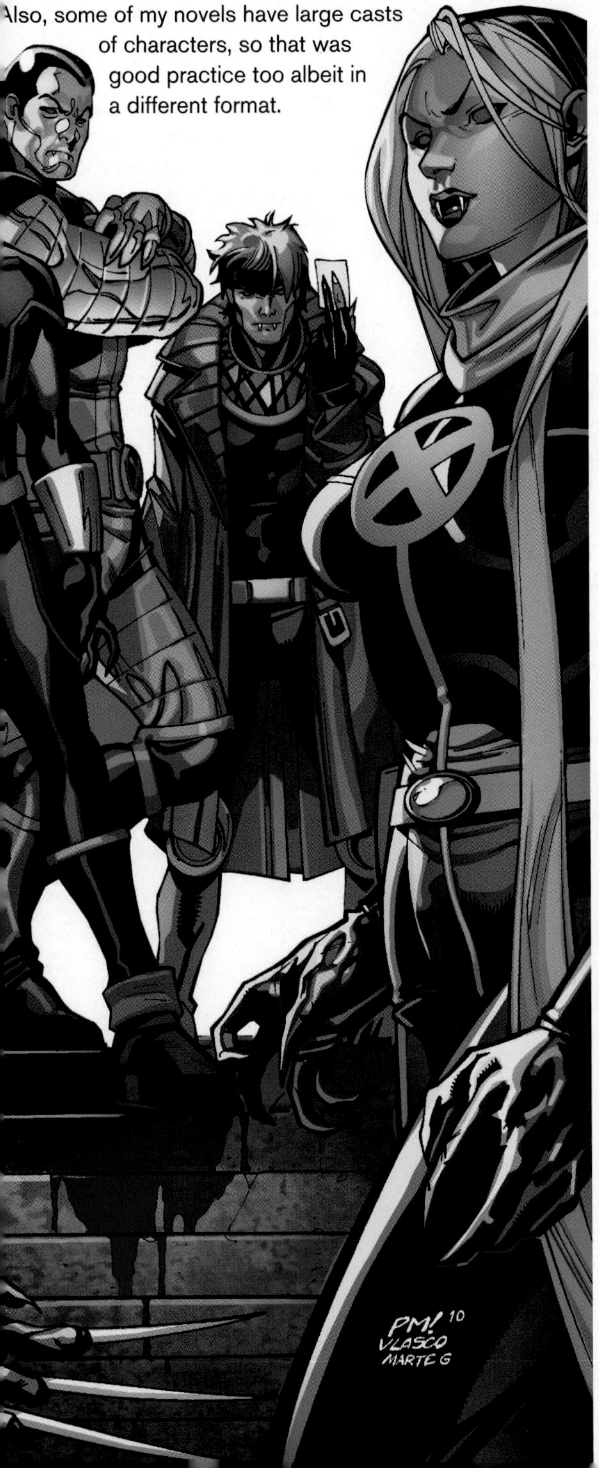
PM! 10
VLASCO
MARTE G

MARVEL: On a similar tangent, what particular elements of writing a team book get you juiced up, and what elements are ones you're going to bypass or play down?

VICTOR: I can't think of anything that I've purposefully played down. But when writing *Deadpool Corps*, I enjoy planning who's going to get the most face time in each issue. The most recent *Deadpool Corps* highlighted Dogpool and the one I'm scripting now is giving the spotlight to Lady Deadpool. Yes, it's a team book, but sometimes one character or another takes the lead for an issue or two. The first arc of *X-Men* is such an event that I'm not thinking that way quite yet ... but I might in future arcs.

MARVEL: You made your name with writing a handful of very well-received hard-boiled crime novels (*Gun Monkeys, Suicide Squeeze*). In fact, your most recently published novel, *The Deputy*, is a return to hard-boiled for you. Is there anything at all about that genre that's going to find its way into your X-Men work? (Or any of your other comics work?)

VICTOR: I think my novel writing style was most useful when I wrote the *Punisher Max: Welcome to the Bayou* arc. That seemed just right for me. I'd love to do more *Punisher Max*, but with Jason Aaron kicking so much butt right now, I know I'm not going to be needed anytime soon.

MARVEL: What dynamics from the craft of writing for novels are best adapted to comics writing, at least as you've come to experience?

VICTOR: Dialogue. When I write a novel, those words are for the reader. When I write a script, those words are *not* for the reader; they're for the artist. The exception is dialogue. Writing good, sharp dialogue is a must-skill for any storyteller.

MARVEL: You've written a couple novels with very campy titles – *Go-Go Girls of the Apocalypse* and *Vampire A Go-Go* (the latter of which seems especially appropriate since we're talking about the X-Men fighting off vampires in your new series). I'm sure your fans in comics who may be unfamiliar with the novels would be interested in a quick rundown on what they'd find if they grabbed a copy.

VICTOR: *Go-Go Girls of the Apocalypse* is a violent satirical novel. The story takes place after the ruin of the world and the only glimmer of organized civilization is clustered around a chain of go-go clubs across Dixie. The novel walks a tightrope between being a legitimate action-adventure story and an over-the-top satire and parody of other post-apocalyptic stories.

The title of *Vampire A Go-Go* makes it sound like a sequel, but it's not. (Don't ask.) We follow hapless grad student Allan Cabbot as he fumbles around

Prague in search of the secret of the Alchemists. Turns out all that lead-into-gold stuff was a cover story. Along the way we get witches, zombies, a vampire, a werewolf...well, the whole horror checklist, although it's more of a parody of a *Da Vinci Code*-type novel than a horror novel. Played for laughs and action.

ALL HANDS ON DECK: Among the mutants in Victor's arsenal are (top row) Jubilee and Cyclops, (bottom row) Pixie and Angel.

MARVEL: You went to University of Southern Mississippi, so presumably you have a deep background in Southern Lit. Which of those authors do you think would translate well to comics? William Faulkner? Flannery O'Connor?

VICTOR: Carson McCullers.

MARVEL: Which, if any, of the X-Men do you think would transfer well to novels and why?

VICTOR: Oh, any of them. A skilled writer could make it happen. Wolverine is an obvious choice. He has lots of backstory and works well as a solo artist as well as part of a team. If you hear they want somebody to do an X-Men novel, feel free to put my name forward.

You'll see Victor's name put forward on the monthly ongoing series X-MEN, the DEATH OF DRACULA one-shot, and plenty more high-profile offerings in the coming year! •

MEET X-MEN WRITER VICTOR GISCHLER

BIO

"Victor Gischler is the author of five hard-boiled crime novels (and two more novels in other genres). His debut novel *Gun Monkeys* was nominated for the Edgar Award, and his novel *Shotgun Opera* was an Anthony Award finalist. His work has been translated into Italian, French, Spanish, German, Czech and Japanese. He earned a Ph.D. in English at the University of Southern Mississippi where they beat him with rolled up newspapers and fed him raw liver. His fifth novel, *Go-Go Girls of the Apocalypse,* was released by the Touchstone/ Fireside imprint of Simon & Schuster and followed by *Vampire A Go-Go.* His new crime novel, *The Deputy,* was just released from Tyrus Books." – From Victor's official website, *victorgischler.blogspot.com*

Victor Gischler

MARVEL CHECKLIST

Deadpool: Merc With a Mouth #1-13

Deadpool Team-Up #900
Deadpool Corps #1-up
Death of Dracula (one-shot)
Prelude to Deadpool Corps #1-5
Punisher: Frank Castle MAX #71-74
Punisher MAX Special: Little Black Book (one-shot)
Wolverine: Revolver (one-shot)
X-Men (2010) #1-up

NOVELS

Gun Monkeys (2001, Uglytown/ Dell Books)
The Pistol Poets (2004, DelacortePress/Dell Books)
Suicide Squeeze (2005, Delacorte Press/DellBooks)
Shotgun Opera (2006, Dell Books)
Go-Go Girls of the Apocalypse (2008, Touchstone Books)
Vampire A Go-Go (2009, Touchstone Books)
The Deputy (2010, Tyrus Books)

X-MEN FACT FILE

FAVORITE X-MAN: Beast
FAVORITE WRITER: Chris Claremont
FAVORITE ARTIST: John Byrne
FAVORITE STORYLINE: *X-Men* #154-167, "The Brood Saga"

WE ARE T

X-Men Editor Nick Lowe Intro

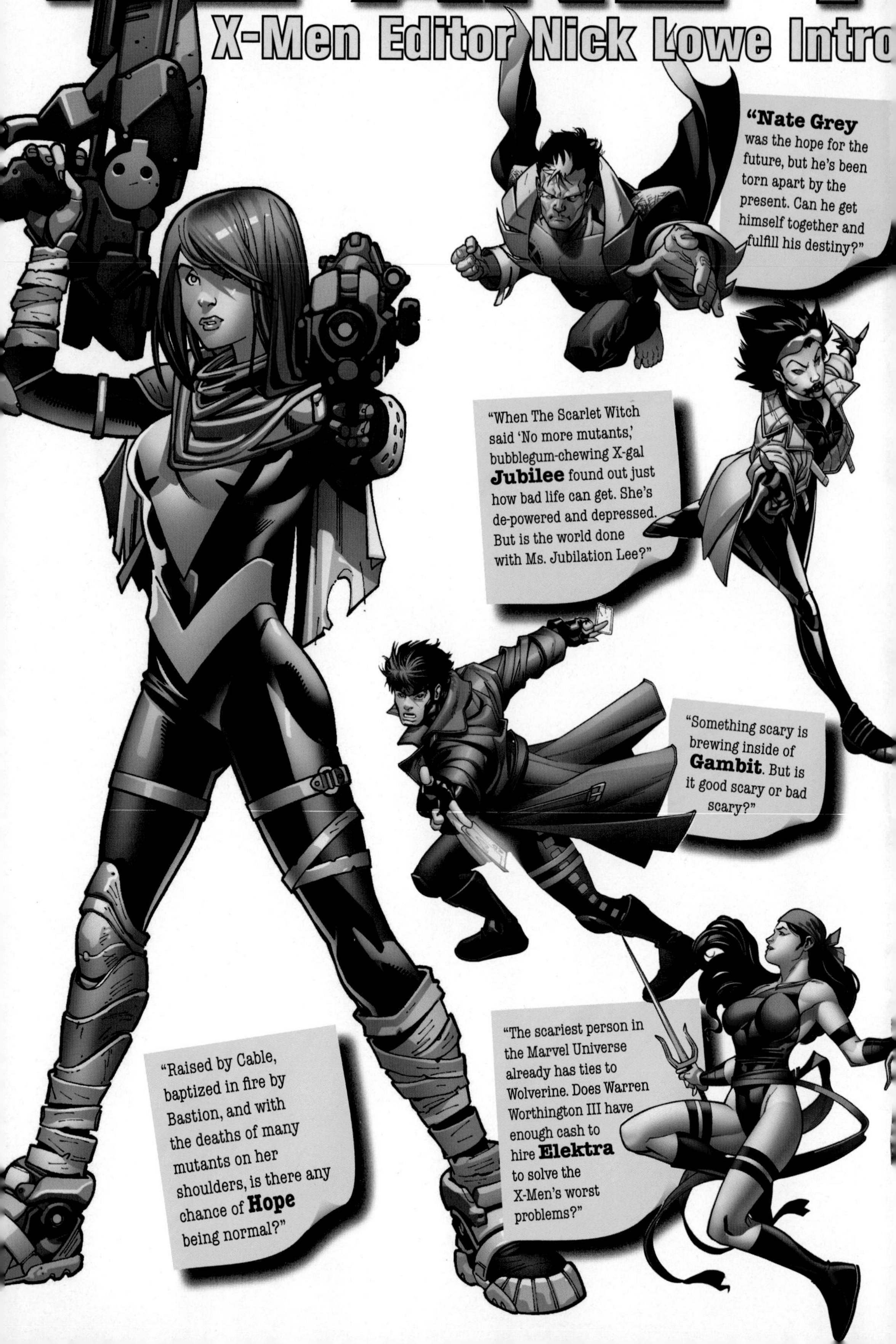

"**Nate Grey** was the hope for the future, but he's been torn apart by the present. Can he get himself together and fulfill his destiny?"

"When The Scarlet Witch said 'No more mutants,' bubblegum-chewing X-gal **Jubilee** found out just how bad life can get. She's de-powered and depressed. But is the world done with Ms. Jubilation Lee?"

"Something scary is brewing inside of **Gambit**. But is it good scary or bad scary?"

"Raised by Cable, baptized in fire by Bastion, and with the deaths of many mutants on her shoulders, is there any chance of **Hope** being normal?"

"The scariest person in the Marvel Universe already has ties to Wolverine. Does Warren Worthington III have enough cash to hire **Elektra** to solve the X-Men's worst problems?"

HE X-MEN!

ces Us to All the Major Players

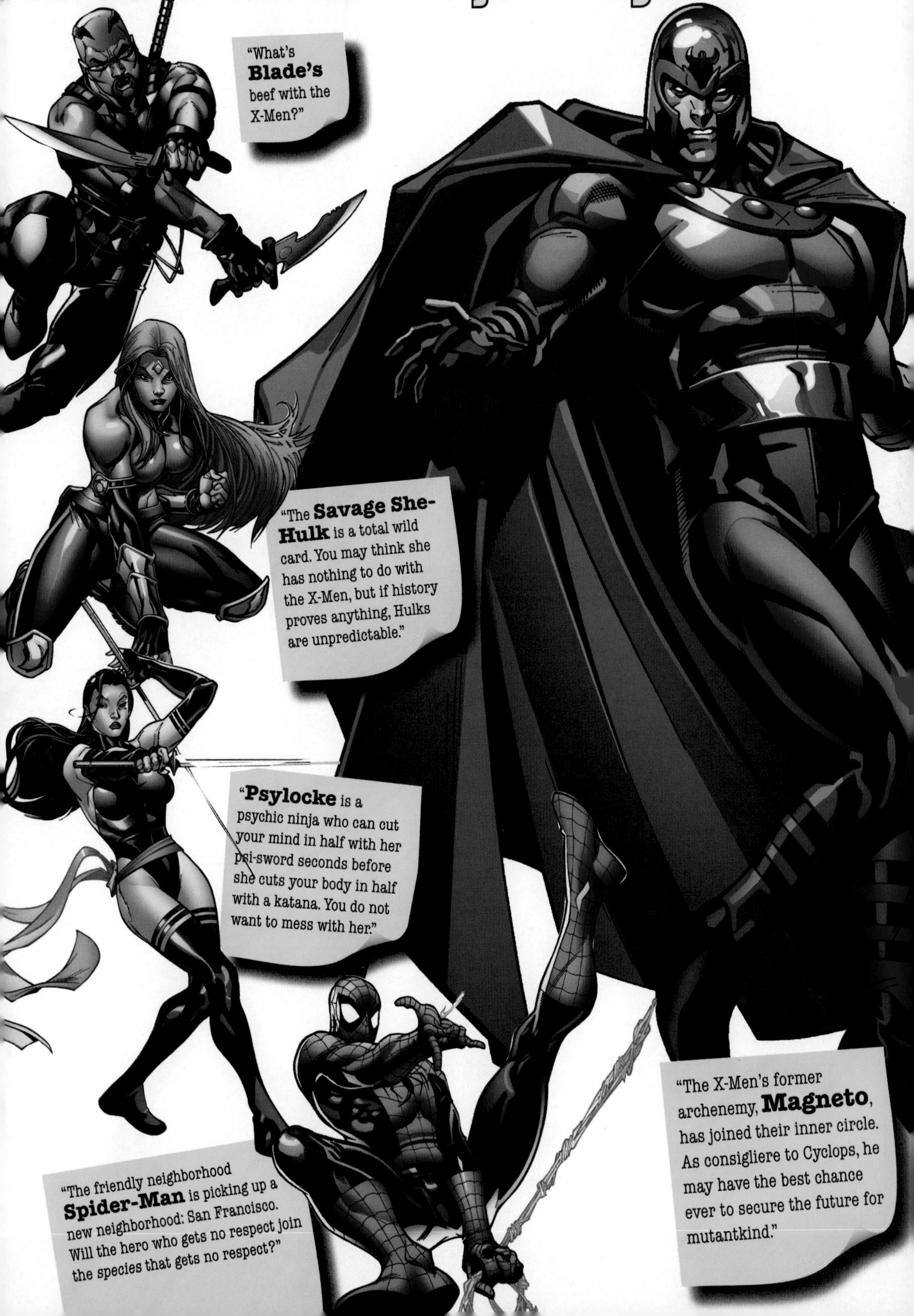

"What's **Blade's** beef with the X-Men?"
"The **Savage She-Hulk** is a total wild card. You may think she has nothing to do with the X-Men, but if history proves anything, Hulks are unpredictable."
"**Psylocke** is a psychic ninja who can cut your mind in half with her psi-sword seconds before she cuts your body in half with a katana. You do not want to mess with her."
"The friendly neighborhood **Spider-Man** is picking up a new neighborhood: San Francisco. Will the hero who gets no respect join the species that gets no respect?"
"The X-Men's former archenemy, **Magneto**, has joined their inner circle. As consigliere to Cyclops, he may have the best chance ever to secure the future for mutantkind."

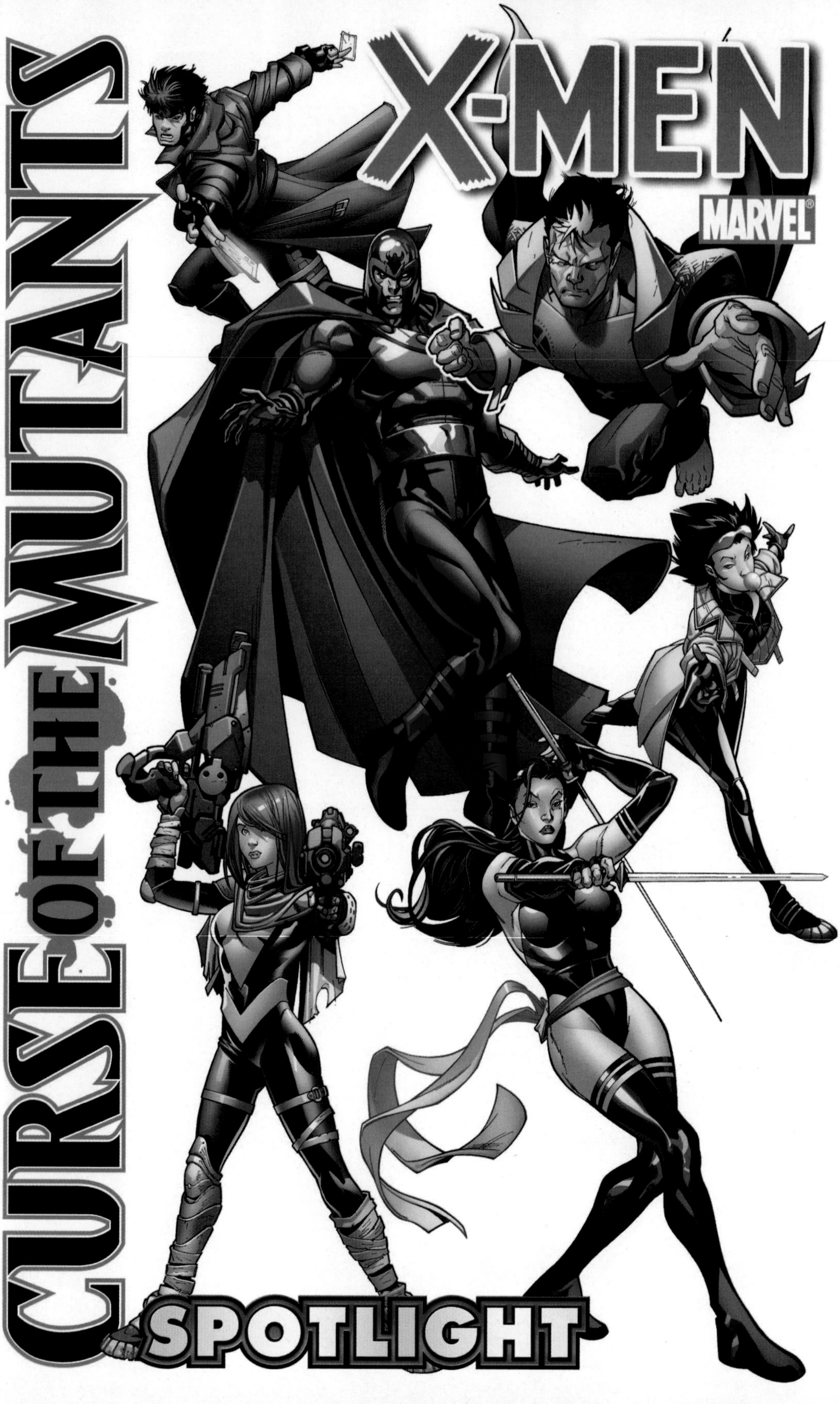

X-MEN
MARVEL
CURSE OF THE MUTANTS
SPOTLIGHT

PLUGGING IN THE SPOTLIGHT!

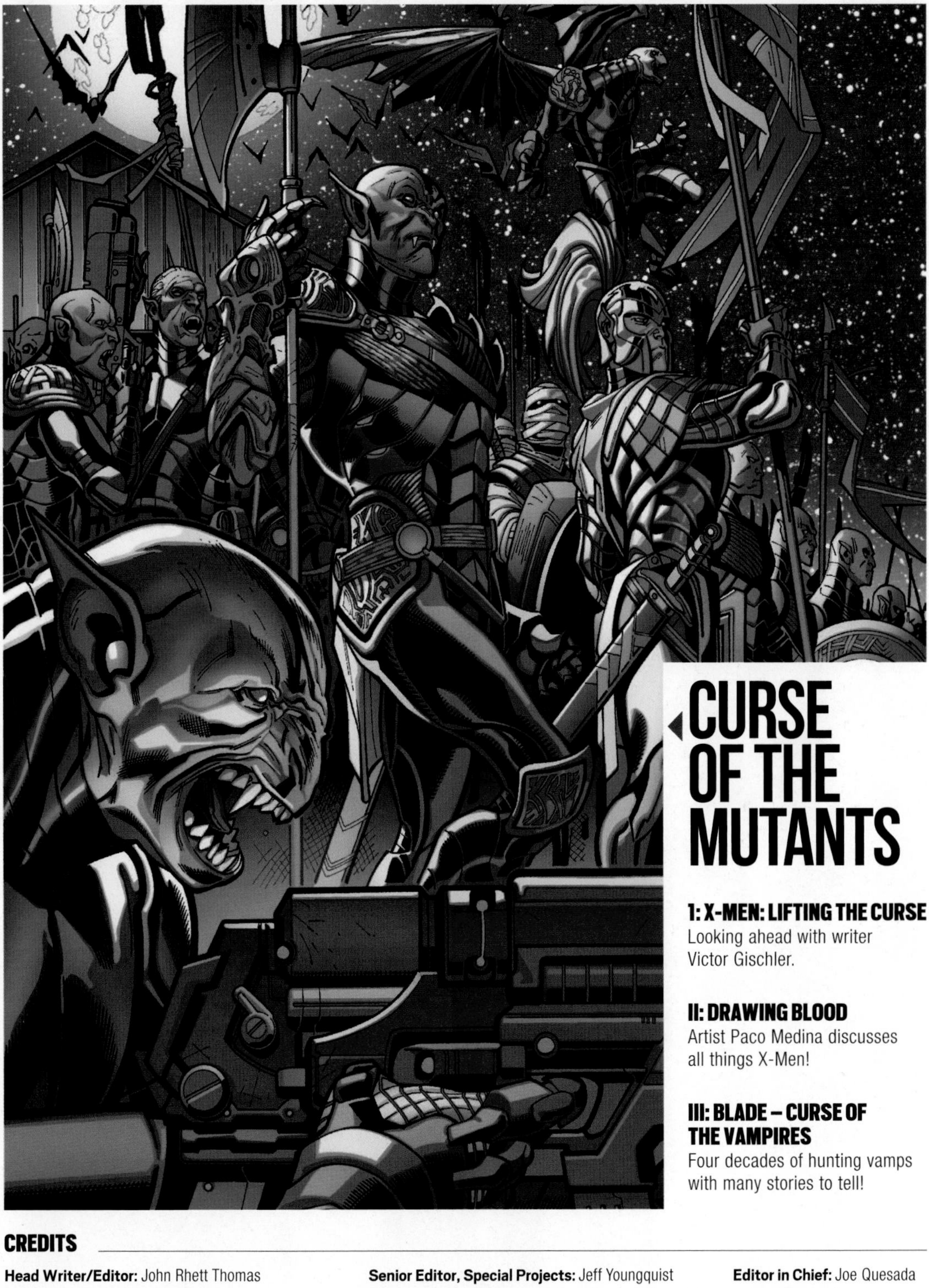

CURSE OF THE MUTANTS

1: X-MEN: LIFTING THE CURSE
Looking ahead with writer Victor Gischler.

II: DRAWING BLOOD
Artist Paco Medina discusses all things X-Men!

III: BLADE – CURSE OF THE VAMPIRES
Four decades of hunting vamps with many stories to tell!

CREDITS

Head Writer/Editor: John Rhett Thomas
Spotlight Bullpen Writer: Chris Arrant
Book Design: BLAMMO! Content & Design, Travis Bonilla, Spring Hoteling & Michael Kronenberg
Senior Editor, Special Projects: Jeff Youngquist
Editorial Assistants: James Emmett & Joe Hochstein
Assistant Editors: Alex Starbuck & Nelson Ribeiro
Editors, Special Projects: Jennifer Grünwald & Mark D. Beazley
Senior Vice President of Sales: David Gabriel
Editor in Chief: Joe Quesada
Publisher: Dan Buckley
Executive Producer: Alan Fine

Special thanks to Anna Ruth.

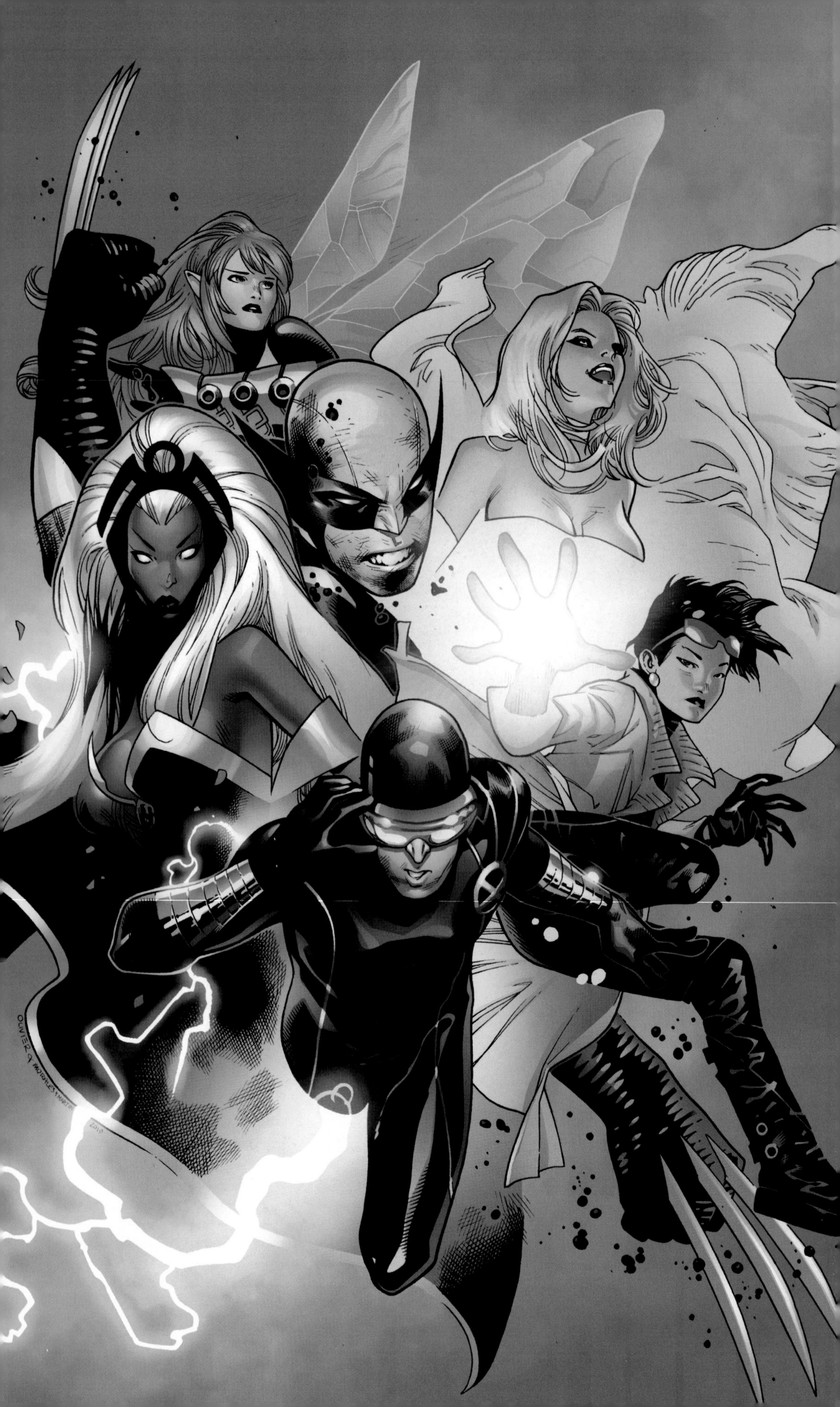

X-MEN: LIFTING THE CURSE

X-Men Writer Victor Gischler Grapples With Mutants And Their Post-Vampire World

BY CHRIS ARRANT

Mutants may be the most misunderstood race in Marvel Comics — but if recent developments are true, vampires are right up there with them.

Kicking off with the world-building one-shot *Death of Dracula*, writer Victor Gischler has expounded on Marvel's long-running race of bloodsuckers with elaborate cultures, twisted allegiances and a hierarchy led by Dracula — that is, until one of his sons takes his place (and his life) in the process. And with a new ruler comes new rules, beginning with turning mutants to their side by transforming them into vampires! In the recently launched series *X-Men*, Gischler kept the vampire torch fired up as the bloodsuckers took on the mutants — and made the fan-favorite Jubilee one of their first converts.

Gischler's been racking up the hits with his escalating comics career at Marvel — going from crime capers in *Punisher MAX* to slapstick in *Deadpool* and onto his biggest book yet, *X-Men*. Gischler has been climbing up the comic charts while also spinning out hard-boiled crime novels — starting with his debut novel *Gun Monkeys*, currently in development as a feature film. Gischler's been the go-to man for vampires in Marvel's "Curse of the Mutants" story arc, and we've cornered the Southern writer for more.

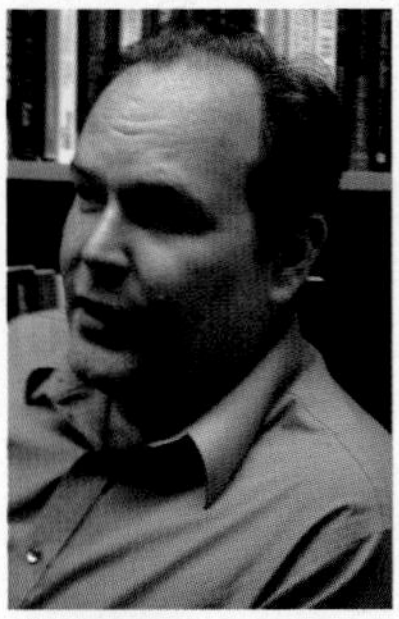

Writer Victor Gischler.

For "Curse of the Mutants," you were tasked with re-inventing the vampires in Marvel from the ground up. Can you tell us how you set out to do it in the beginning?

Actually, we decided to bring vampires into that new *X-Men* book after working hard on the *Death of Dracula* one-shot. We liked what we were doing so much that it just seemed the perfect thing to put our new "re-vamped" vamps up against the X-Men. Although there is much new and cool about Marvel U. vamps, I actually took a good bit of inspiration from research into Marvel U. vampires. There was a lot of good, useful source material.

And now that the story arc is past the halfway point, how did you think your reinvention of the vampire in Marvel comics has turned out?

I just got back from some store signings at Dragon's Lair in Austin and San Antonio and a number of people seem to really dig it. Personally, I'm proud of the work. I think there is still a lot of potential to be mined.

Vampires have a history of coming and going a lot in the Marvel U — but given the fan support for "Curse of the Mutants," I think they'll be around for awhile. Can you speculate on where they might turn up next?

I can't speculate. But Dracula and our new vampire sects are too cool and interesting to let them gather dust, and I wouldn't be surprised to see these characters play key roles in future stories.

> **"I LOVE THAT JUBILEE IS A LITTLE BIT BAD NOW."**
>
> – Writer Victor Gischler

In the *Death of Dracula* one-shot, you laid out a fully formed vampire society. Any chance we'd get a solo book about the vampires?

I think that would kick butt, but you're not talking to the guy with the authority to make that happen. If it did happen, I'd love to write it. If somebody else writes it, I'd love to read it.

(Editor Axel Alonso, are you listening?) When you mention vampires in a Marvel book, Blade can't be that far behind. What do you think he's brought to the X-Men team in this story arc?

He's brought an extra shot of coolness — and naturally, some important vampire expertise and information. Your last question asked about a solo book for vampires. If there ever were such a thing, I don't see how the book could last very long without Blade showing up once in a while. >

Variant cover to *X-Men #1* by Olivier Coipel.

Although Blade's not a mutant, he's part of a misunderstood minority: vampires. Can you compare the two, mutants and vampires?

I think "Curse of the Mutants" touches on that exact theme. Certainly Xarus tries to make that comparison in his pitch to Cyclops.

I've personally really enjoyed your take on Jubilee as a vampire, even though she might be on the side of the bad guys right now. Was she in this idea from the get-go?

I *love* that Jubilee is a little bit bad now. It's cool, and I've never been more of a Jubilee fan than I am right now. Yes, it was very early in the process that we recognized it might be cool to bring in Jubilee. She'd been de-powered, and this was a chance to juice her up a bit.

At New York Comic Con, Marvel announced that the *X-Men* book is going to NYC in a new story arc starting with issue #7. Will vampires still play a role in the book?

No. New and exciting things in #7. Issue #6 will conclude the X-Men's business with vampires — for now…?

We'll be there with what is certain to be an unlucky issue #7 for our adjectiveless X-Men. *Thanks for a great ride, Victor!* ■

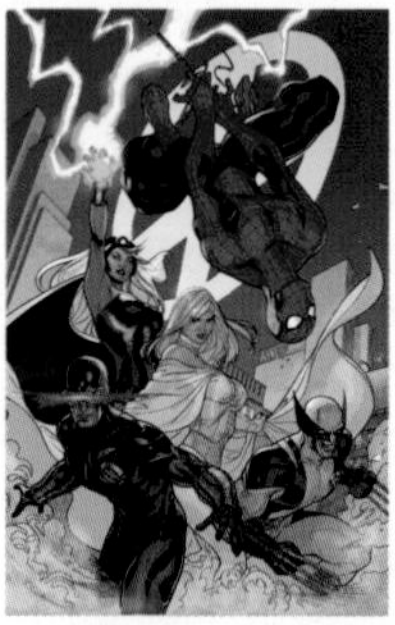

Cover to *X-Men #7* by Terry Dodson

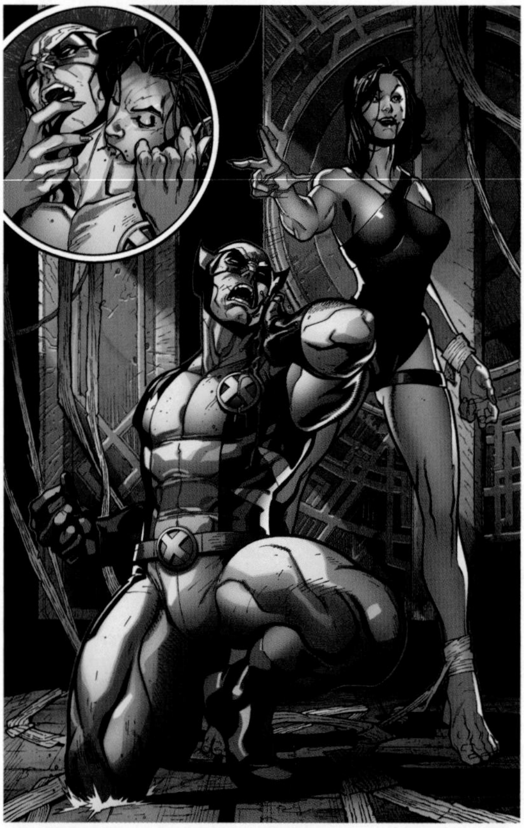

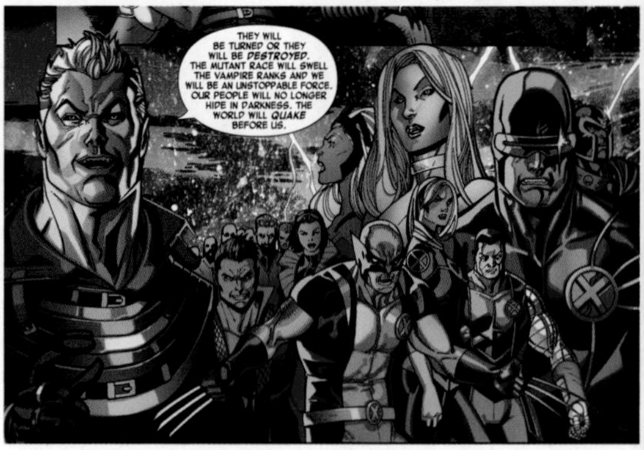
THEY WILL BE TURNED OR THEY WILL BE DESTROYED. THE MUTANT RACE WILL SWELL THE VAMPIRE RANKS AND WE WILL BE AN UNSTOPPABLE FORCE. OUR PEOPLE WILL NO LONGER HIDE IN DARKNESS. THE WORLD WILL QUAKE BEFORE US.

XARUS SPEAKS: The new Lord of the Vampires tells it like it is. (Art from *X-Men #2* by Paco Medina.)

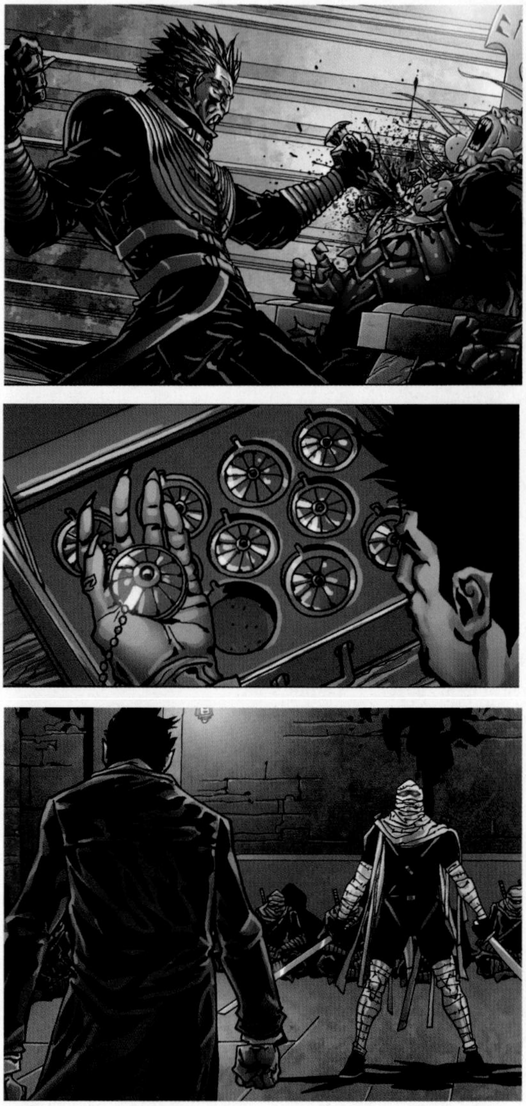

DEATH OF DRACULA: Gischler's exciting prelude to "Curse of the Mutants" featured the stunning death of the Lord of the Vampires (top), technology that allows vampires to walk in the sunlight (center) and the multi-layered societies of Dracula's kingdom (bottom). (Art from *The Death of Dracula* one-shot by Giuseppe Camuncoli.)

BREAKING BAD: Jubilee gives in to vampirism in "Curse of the Mutants." (Art from *X-Men #3* by Medina.)

DRAWING BLOOD

Artist Paco Medina Vamps It Up For *X-Men*!

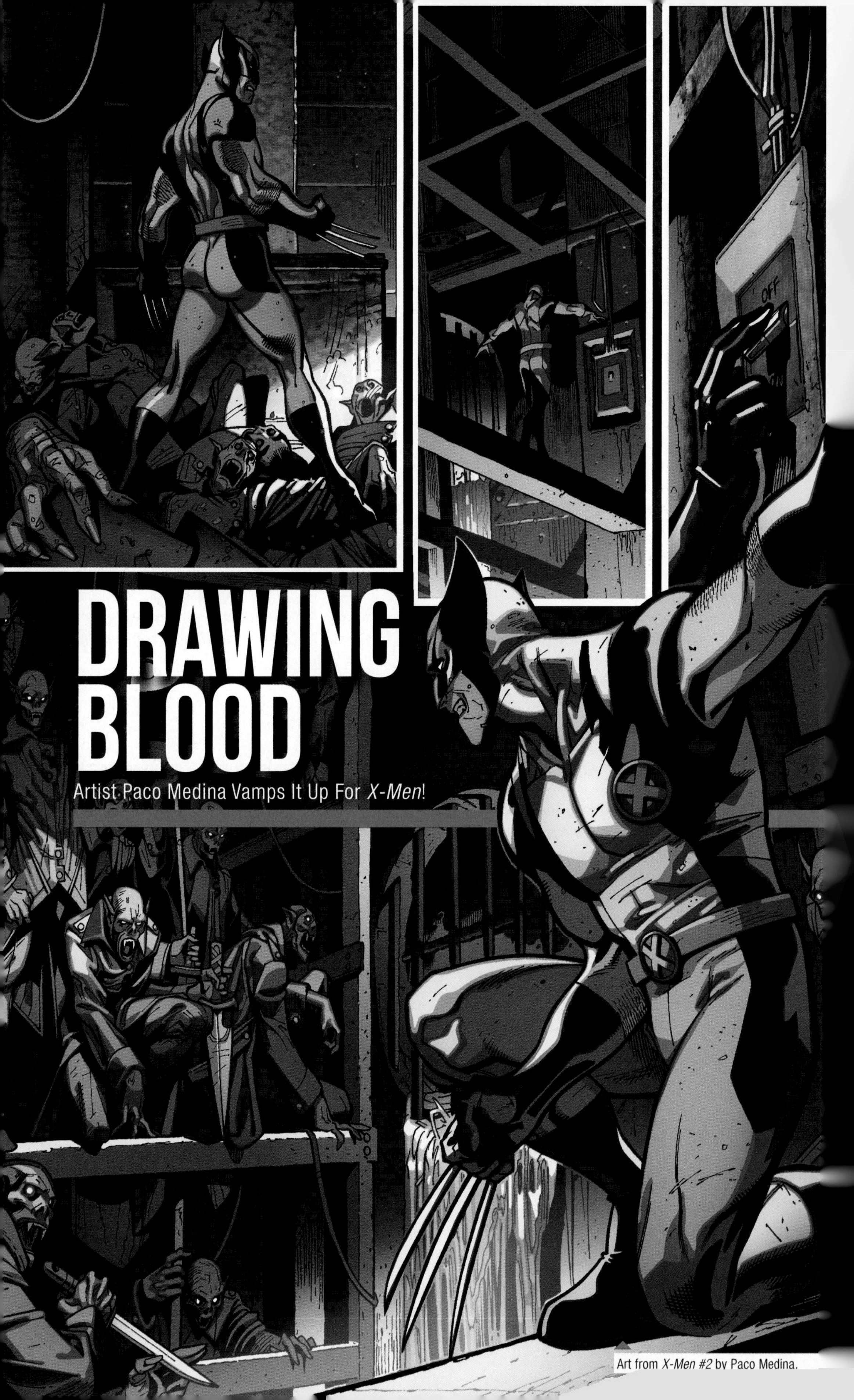
OFF

Art from *X-Men #2* by Paco Medina.

If you've been reading Marvel comics recently, chances are you've seen artist Paco Medina's work.

Medina has risen through the ranks at the House of Ideas from his debut in a 1998 issue of *Thor* to recent runs on *New X-Men, New Warriors* and *Deadpool*. But his current assignment is a culmination of years of work — as an artist, and going farther back as a fan. September's debut of the all-new *X-Men* series saw Medina and writer Victor Gischler take Marvel mutants into the dark world of vampires.

Since the book's launch, *X-Men* has put the mutants on the defensive as a never-before-seen army of vampires rise up against them. Through it all, Medina has drawn scores of X-Men both big and small — figuratively and literally — as well as fleshed out Gischler's complex society of vampires and engineered the resurrection of Dracula himself. For this, Medina has eschewed the absurdist action style of *Deadpool* for the more realistic and stygian world of mutants and vampires with *X-Men*.

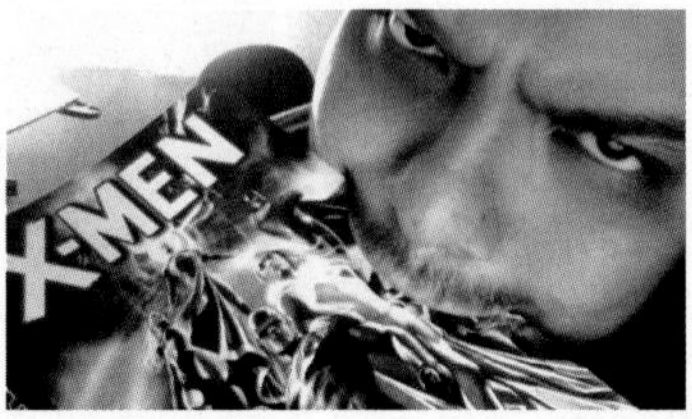
X-MEN

Artist Paco Medina.

It's good to talk to you again, Paco. Last time we talked, you were lighting it up on *Deadpool*; now, you're launching a new *X-Men* series. What's it been like to do this new series?

I think it is a very important and unique moment for me and the team (Juan Vlasco and Marte Gracia). One time, while talking with Juan, we thought about the chance of having such a big assignment — but the day (series editor) Axel Alonso gave us the first script, we fell backwards. We really couldn't believe we were part of this X-Men history. A #1 issue, variant covers — wow! Only until we saw the actual book printed could we believe it.

We are really happy, both as artists and as fans. To have such a big title in your career changes your life forever.

You came off this book from a healthy run on *Deadpool*, one of the last issues in which you drew *Deadpool* joining the X-Men — and now *you* join the X-Men! How'd you wind up on the book with writer Victor Gischler?

Deadpool was pure fun. *X-Men* came while I was working on the last issues of my *Deadpool* run. Axel told me we would be working on a new title. A few days later I was told it would be *X-Men*. So blame Axel for me being in an *X-Men* book. He is the mastermind behind all this. *(Laughs.)*

And well, to team with Victor was of course great news. His strength as a writer is being the novelist he is. We have made a good team, and I think we can mature greatly in our storytelling. Victor is a great guy.

"...THE DARK SIDE (OF X-MEN) HAS BECOME A CHALLENGE. IT HAS DEMANDED ME TO DRAW LESS CARTOONISHLY AND WORK MORE ON MY REALISM."

– Artist Paco Medina

***X-Men* relies less on the slapstick action of *Deadpool* and more on horror-tinged vampires. How did you get in the right mindset to draw this book and the vampires?**

As I said before, *Deadpool* was a party. And the change to the dark side has become a challenge. It has demanded me to draw less cartoonishly and work more on my realism. During these years, I've realized that a comic-book artist must draw everything, and this makes you able to work on a wider range of topics. During my career, I've had my ups and downs — but if I've had something clear in my mind from the beginning, it is that *X-Men* would be something else! In these six issues, I've worked hard to grow as a storyteller and give this title its own personality. There are a lot of vampire stories and versions, but this is our version: Victor and Paco's.

For *X-Men* and "Curse of the Mutants," you're introducing a lot of new villains into the mix. What do you think about vampires and what you've done with this book?

This is a good question. Actually, a lot of these characters were introduced in a previous book. The work of artist Giuseppe Camuncoli on the *Death of Dracula* one-shot was essential for "Curse of the Mutants" because it defined the parameters on all the clans and main characters. I think it was later that I added something to the characters. Actually, this was a peculiar moment to work on vampires. *Twilight* and *True Blood* are fresh in people's minds, but I remember a lot of other examples that, in their moment, were iconic for vampire lore — things like *Interview with a Vampire, The Lost Boys* and *The Hunger* with David Bowie. I think Victor's point of view is interesting. He talks about vampires in his novels — and fortunately, that makes "Curse of the Mutants" a book with a different vision and adds to vampires in the Marvel U.

This *X-Men* series is promised to focus on the mutants' role in the wider Marvel U. — instead of just the X-Men's territory. Any characters you'd like to see drawn into the book in future issues?

Ha! Chris Bachalo is ahead of me in that, as he's drawing the next story arc with Spider-Man! I would have loved to work with Spider-Man. As for who I'd like to draw, I like Iron Man, the Fantastic Four and Thor. Fortunately, I'm a Marvel U. fan, and being part of the Marvel family makes me feel like a lucky guy. Like Forrest Gump, I just run and run.

Be that as it may, you've drawn virtually every active member of the X-Men out there with this inaugural story arc of *X-Men*. The X-Men in this book are more than just a team. They're an entire race of people living on the island of Utopia. How do you keep all the characters and their costumes straight in your head? >

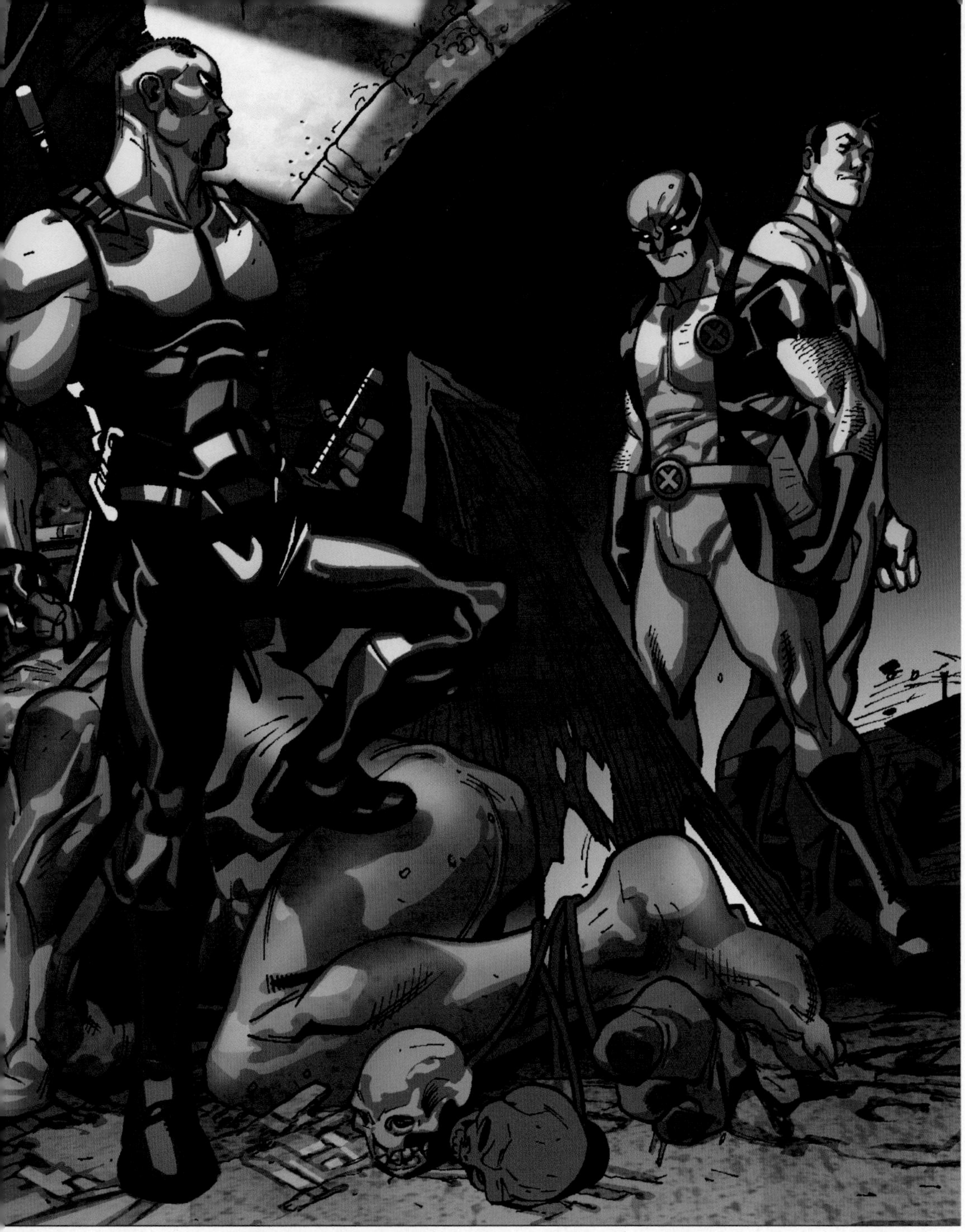

BLADE MEETS THE X-MEN: Blade allies with Colossus and Wolverine in the fight against vampires. (Art from *X-Men #2* by Medina.)

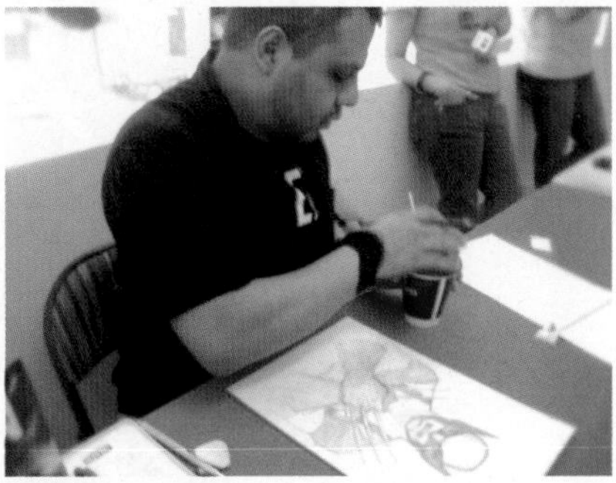

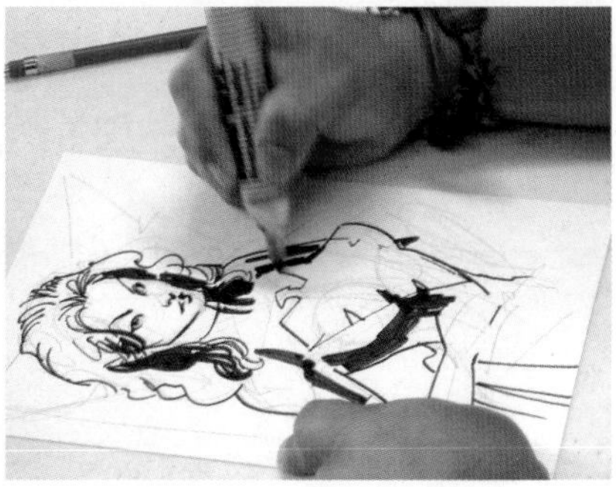

Paco sketches Pheonix and Wolverine for his fans.

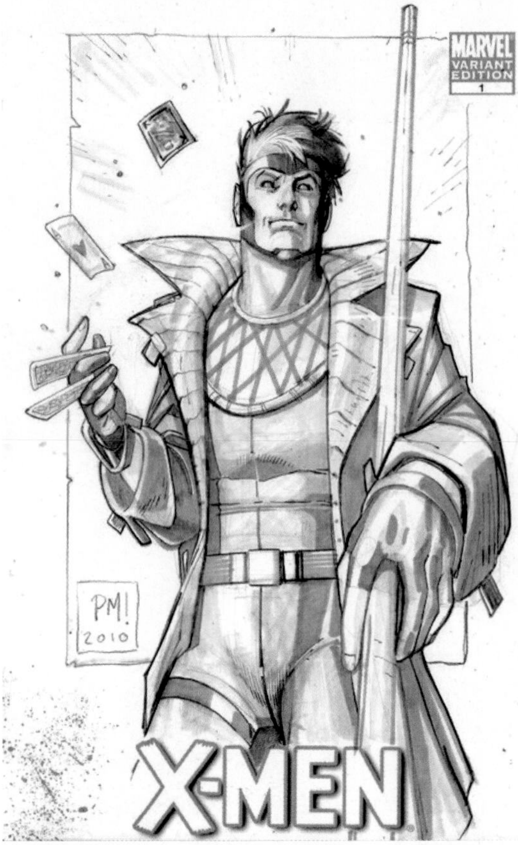
MARVEL
VARIANT EDITION
1
X-MEN
PM!
2010

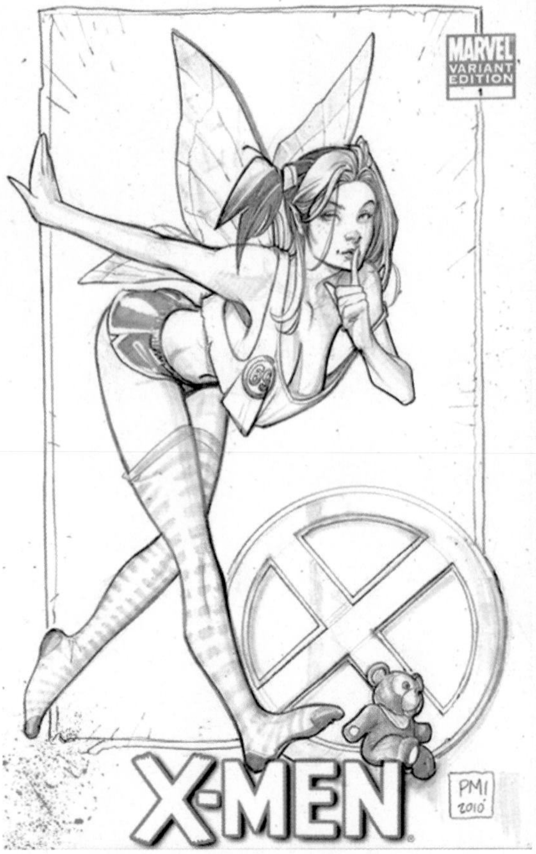
MARVEL
VARIANT EDITION
1
X-MEN
PM!
2010

GAMBIT AND PIXIE: Cover pencils by Paco.

Luckily, I worked with a lot of them before in *New X-Men*, and I became familiar with the mutant family. But now, I have resolved to get myself into each character's personality. Doing that makes the job easier. That happened with *Deadpool*, and I think that now the job will be to know and give life to each character with an "X" on their chest.

Truth to tell, the job of the editor becomes essential in this. Associate Editor Daniel Ketchum helps me all the time with character references, and his help is vital.

Daniel is a great guy and a Facebook friend! Yeah!!

Although he's an old character, you got to take on a new iteration of Dracula as you drew his resurrection in *X-Men*. What was it like to take on this classic character?

It was big. I feel pride for the sequence where the X-Men reanimate Dracula's body. I still have fresh the memory of Gary Oldman's Dracula from the movie *Bram Stoker's Dracula*, and I think that the current Marvel Dracula is closer to the one seen at the beginning of the movie. Dracula with his red armor, bloody. There are a lot of possibilities with a character like that.

Paco wraps up "Curse of the Mutants" with Victor Gischler in the pages of X-Men #6! ■

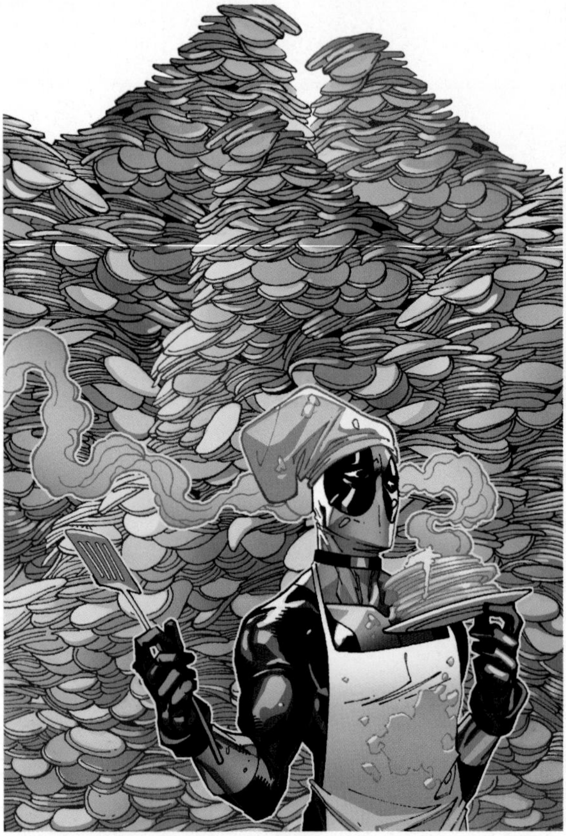

POOLCAKES: Paco Medina's long run on *Deadpool* was full of action and hilarity! (Variant cover to *Deadpool #16* by Medina.)

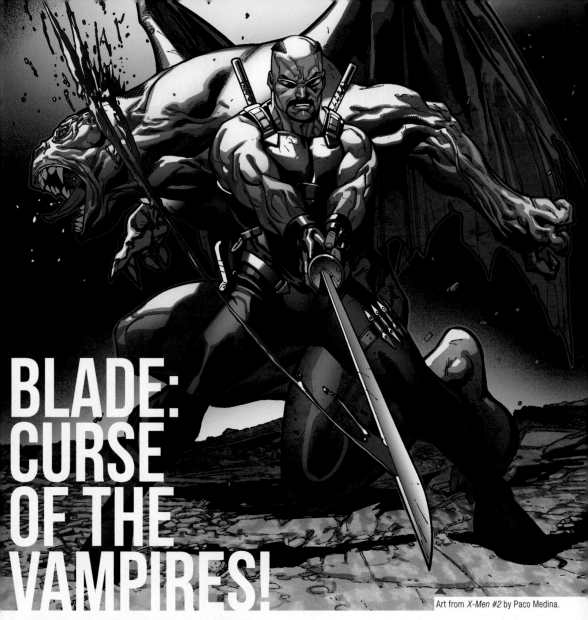

Art from *X-Men #2* by Paco Medina.

BLADE: CURSE OF THE VAMPIRES!

Comics' Legendary Vampire Hunter Sharpens His Knife On The Vampires Of The Marvel Universe!

Since his debut in 1973, the vampiric Blade has cut a large swath across the Marvel Universe. From supernatural tales to face-offs with Doctor Doom and his most recent team-up with the X-Men, Blade has long been Marvel's de-facto face of vampires thanks in no small part to the blockbuster movie franchise fronted by Wesley Snipes.

Legendary comics writer Marv Wolfman joined forces with veteran artist Gene Colan to author Blade's debut in the pages of *Tomb of Dracula #10*, introducing a new kind of vampire and vampire hunter.

"The idea," Wolfman explains, "was to have an action-hero vampire hunter who had vampire blood coursing through him."

Previous to Blade, vampire hunters — such as Van Helsing in Bram Stoker's *Dracula* — were known to be humans hell-bent on vampire destruction. But Blade was different: He was a vampire who hunted vampires.

Readers clamored for more of Blade following his debut in *Tomb of Dracula*, and the character appeared in several subsequent issues. His popularity among fans also spurred solo stories in the anthologies *Vampire Tales* and *Marvel Preview*.

Superstar status aside, it's Blade's animosity toward vampires that drives the character.

"Because of his origin — his mother was bitten by a vampire while giving birth — Blade could never consent to working with vampires," Wolfman explains. "I stretched things myself when he worked with Hannibal King, but King was unique — a vampire with a soul. To me, vampires are like sharks: They are emotionless eating machines who have to keep killing and drinking blood, or they die."

Although Marvel by this point in time had long since cracked the code for creating popular super heroes, handling horror in comics was still a difficult thing to do. Because of the U.S. Congressional Hearings during the 1950s regarding the mature nature of some comic books, the industry had adopted a "Comics Code" to regulate content. This forced publishers to refrain from releasing material deemed too "gruesome" — such as stories featuring vampires, werewolves, ghouls and zombies. **>**

“BLADE’S A GOOD TEAM PLAYER, IN THAT YOU WANT A TEAM MEMBER WHO BRINGS DRAMA AND FUN INTERACTION.”

– Writer Paul Cornell

Wolfman, who was also a respected editor in comics, was always one to push boundaries in the pursuit of a good story.

“We fought with the Comics Code every single month,” he reveals. “After a while, I purposely did something I actually didn’t care about for them to pick on so I could sneak in something else that I really wanted. It was fun.”

Blade continued to pop up across the Marvel spectrum, surging again during the mid-’90s with his own series, *Blade: The Vampire Hunter*, and several one-shots. His popularity hit an all-time high when Wesley Snipes played the vampire hunter in a trilogy of movies beginning in 1998. The character’s most recent comics series was 2006’s *Blade* by writer Marc Guggenheim and legendary artist Howard Chaykin.

“One of the things we tried to do with our *Blade* run,” Guggenheim says, “was to get him out of the ‘horror-genre’ ghetto and have him interact with more of the Marvel Universe. We succeeded for the most part, giving him stories with Spider-Man, Doctor Doom, Union Jack and Wolverine. Would’ve liked to have done more.”

Although that run ended after a dozen issues, Blade’s introduction into the wider Marvel U. continued as he later joined the series *Captain Britain and MI13* — playing upon the character’s forgotten British roots.

“Blade’s key element is that driven quality — not so much seeking revenge as battling a disease, one he’s very familiar with,” says writer Paul Cornell, who scripted that series. “We’d started to show the more vulnerable man underneath. I think he’s got a nice cynical humor to him, too.”

Blade’s cynical humor was on full display in Wesley Snipes’ performances as Blade in the movie trilogy and left an indelible mark on the character in the comics medium. As the third film showed, Blade isn’t averse to working with a team. After all, you need all the help you can get when you’re trying to stamp out vampires.

“Blade’s a good team player, in that you want a team member who brings drama and fun interaction,” Cornell explains. “I think his single-mindedness about his mission can create tensions, which are interesting to explore.”

Blade’s become an unexpectedly vital resource for the Marvel heroes at large, especially in recent months with the “Curse of the Mutants” event which kick-started the new *X-Men* series. Even among some of the most popular characters in comics like Wolverine and Cyclops however, Blade stands apart.

“Blade has a lot of unique and compelling qualities that exist apart from the fact he’s a ‘daywalking’ vampire,” Guggenheim explains. “He’s one of Marvel’s most long-standing heroes of color, and he can go toe to toe — figuratively and literally — with the likes of Wolverine and Frank Castle.”

Check out Blade in the pages of X-Men *and* Curse of the Mutants: Blade #1*!* ■

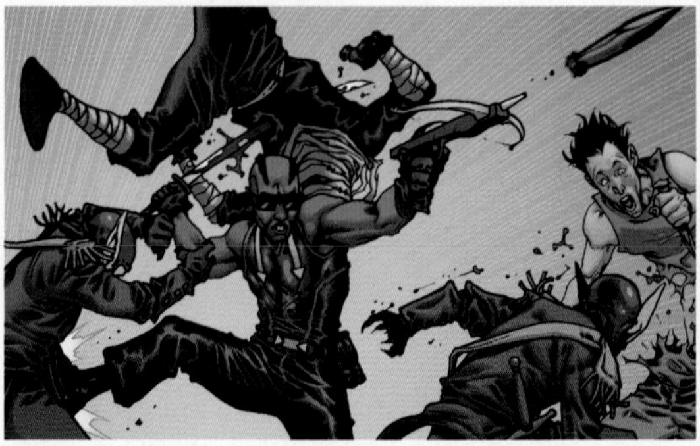

AIMING TO KILL: Blade faces Xarus’ Nosferatu tribe in *Curse of the Mutants: Blade #1*. (Art by Tim Green.)

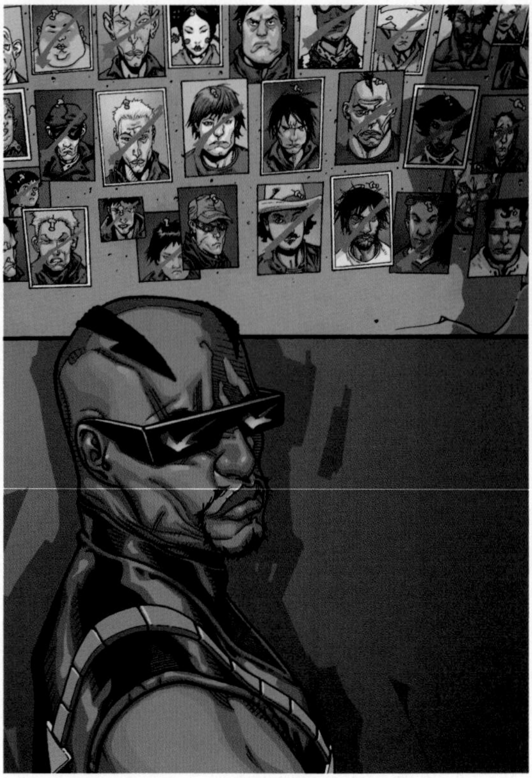

HIT LIST: Blade never stops hunting down his quarry. (Art from *COTM:B #1* by Green.)

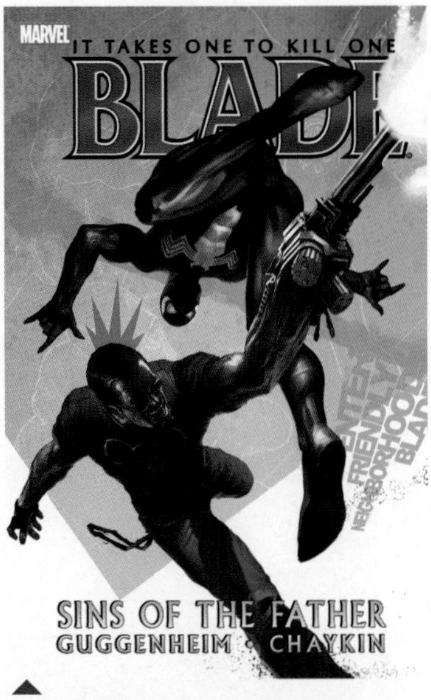
MARVEL
IT TAKES ONE TO KILL ONE
BLADE
SINS OF THE FATHER
GUGGENHEIM CHAYKIN

Cover to *Blade: Sins of the Father TPB*.

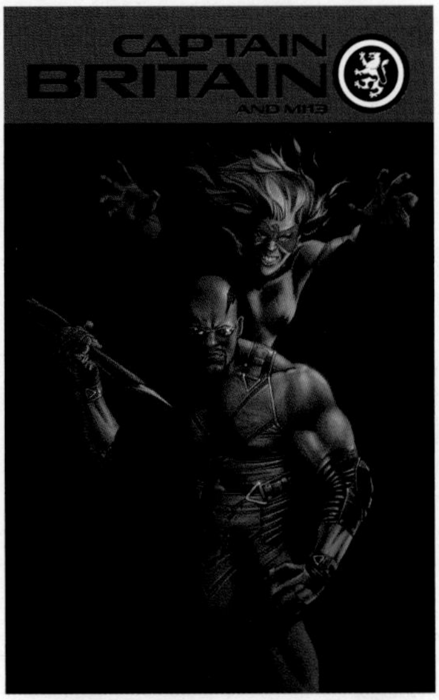
CAPTAIN BRITAIN
AND MI13

Cover to *Captain Britain & MI13 #5*, featuring Blade.

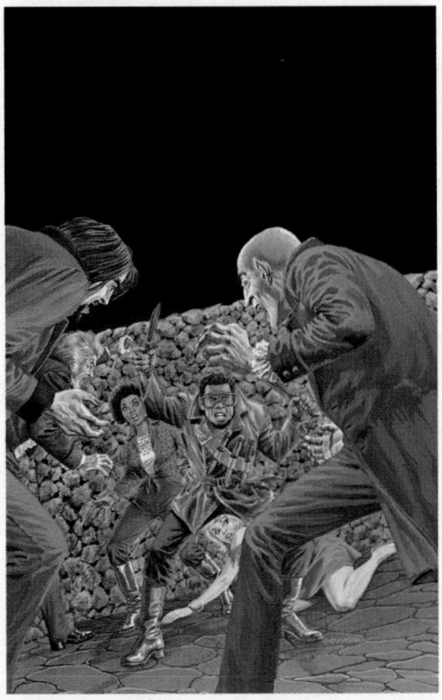

Back-cover art to *Blade: Blade & White TPB*.

BLADE'S CHOICE CUTS

The bloodsucking, vampire-killing, sword-wielding Blade has crisscrossed the Marvel U. for decades, leaving a trail of bodies — and great stories — in his wake. It's the latter we're most interested in right now, so here's a list of Blade's greatest hits for you to track down.

BLADE: SINS OF THE FATHER TPB

Collecting the final six issues of the recent series by Marc Guggenheim and Howard Chaykin, this book shows Blade learning the truth about his father and slicing through some of Marvel's biggest and baddest to get to it. Spider-Man? Yes. Wolverine? Yes! Santa Claus? Heck, yes!

BLADE: BLACK & WHITE TPB

In this titanic trade, Marvel's unearthed some classic Blade stories not reprinted in more than thirty years, including a seminal tale written by X-Men icon Chris Claremont! Required reading for any Blade fan!

CAPTAIN BRITAIN AND MI13: VAMPIRE STATE TPB

Blade returns to his British homeland to stop an invasion led by Dracula and his blood brothers, while also finding time to get closer to classic Marvel heroine Spitfire.

BLADE MAX

In the wake of the movie's success, Marvel took Blade down a dark path with this MAX series that shows off Blade's penchant for gruesome weapons, as well as an undead girlfriend he can't seem to get over. The series builds on the promise of the movies — especially the first — and the art by Steve Pugh is excellent.

BLADE: NIGHTSTALKING

This rare one-shot is only available in the *Blade Trinity Deluxe Edition DVD*, but the cost is worth it for the cover alone. It follows Abigail Whistler, the daughter of Blade's mentor, as she meets her father for the first time. This ain't no *After School Special* approach, as writers Jimmy Palmiotti and Justin Gray show a daughter who is more bloodthirsty than her father would ever allow. Artist Amanda Conner really "vamps up" the Abigail character, played in the film by Jessica Biel.

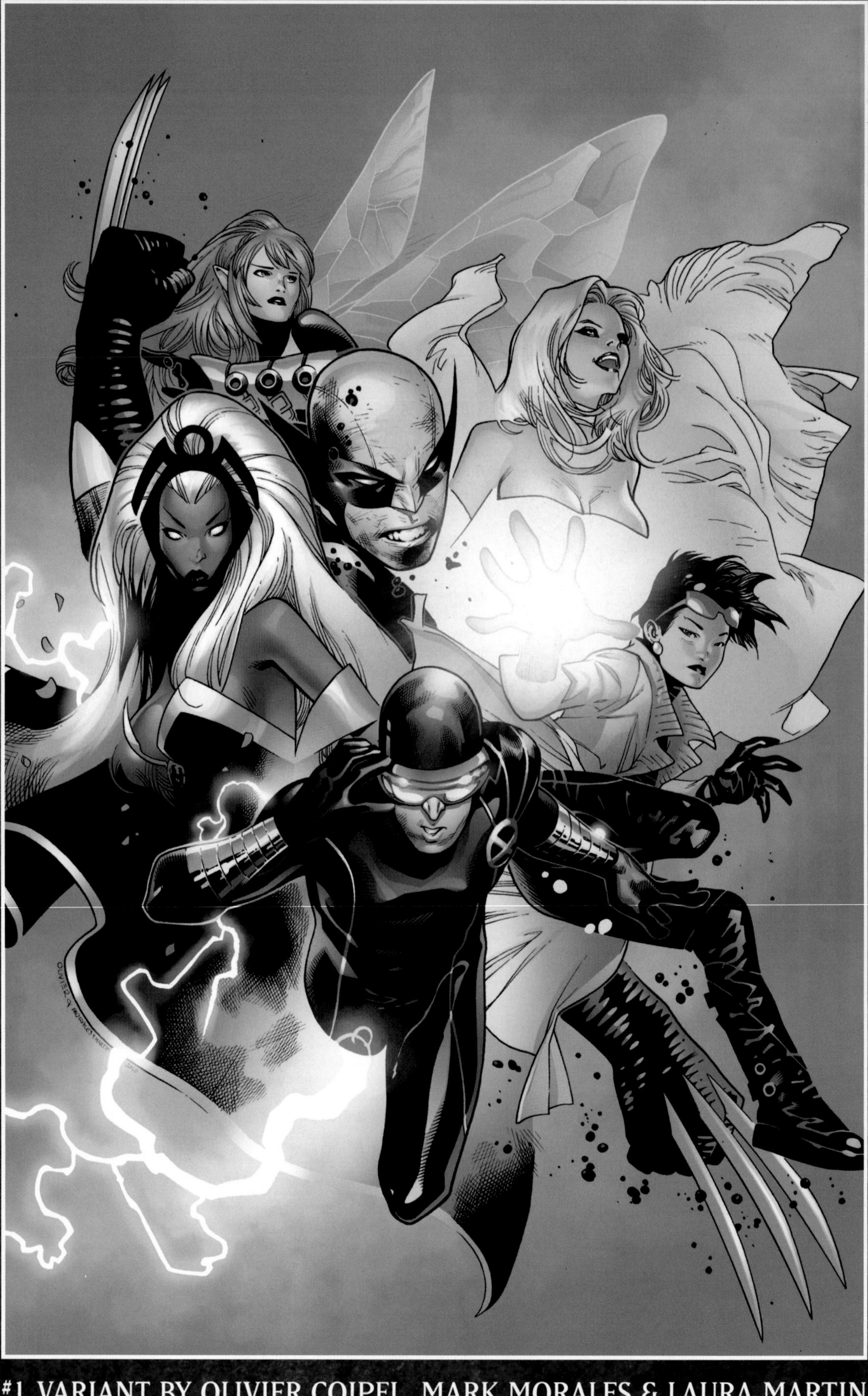

#1 VARIANT BY OLIVIER COIPEL, MARK MORALES & LAURA MARTIN

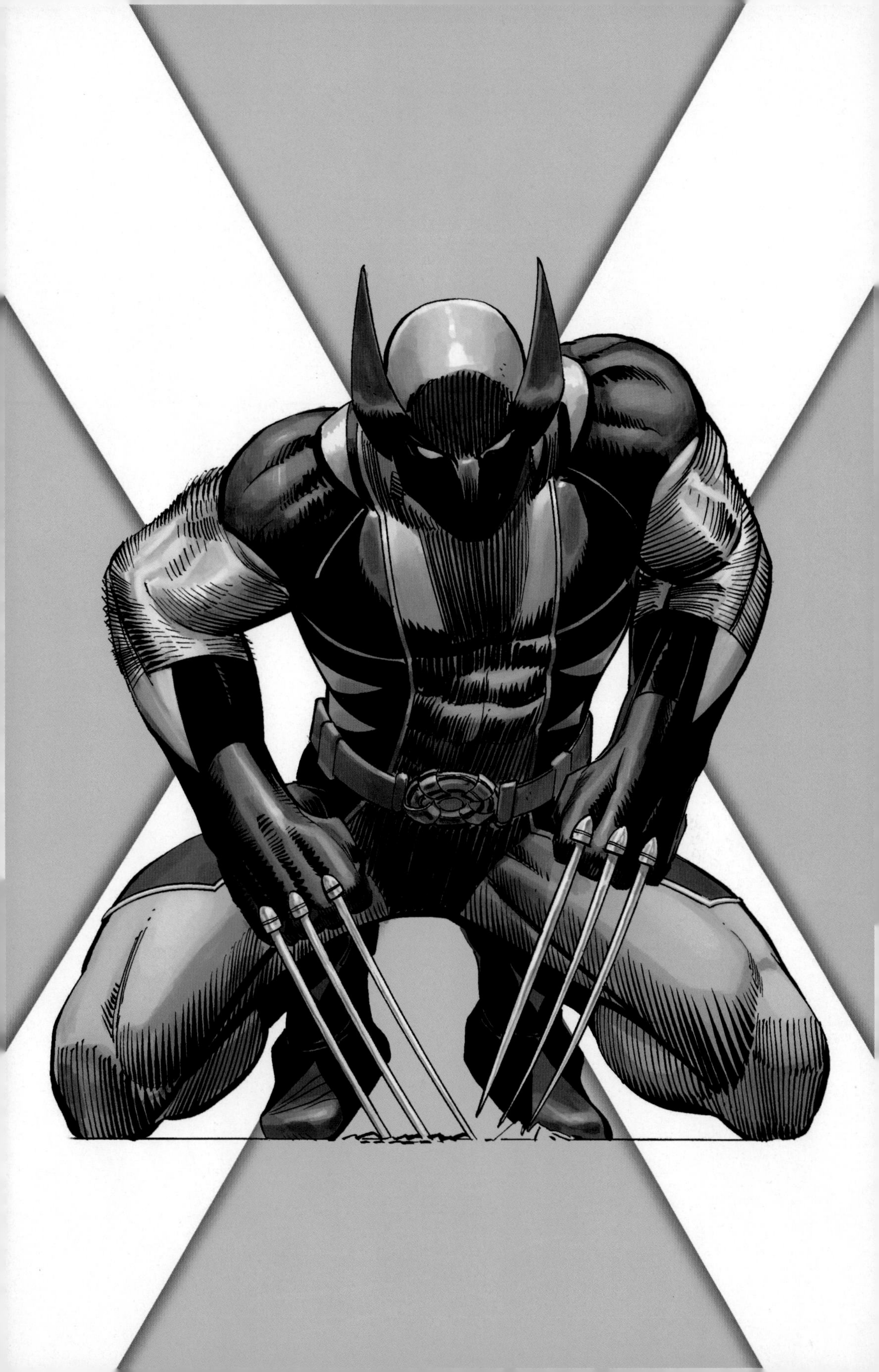

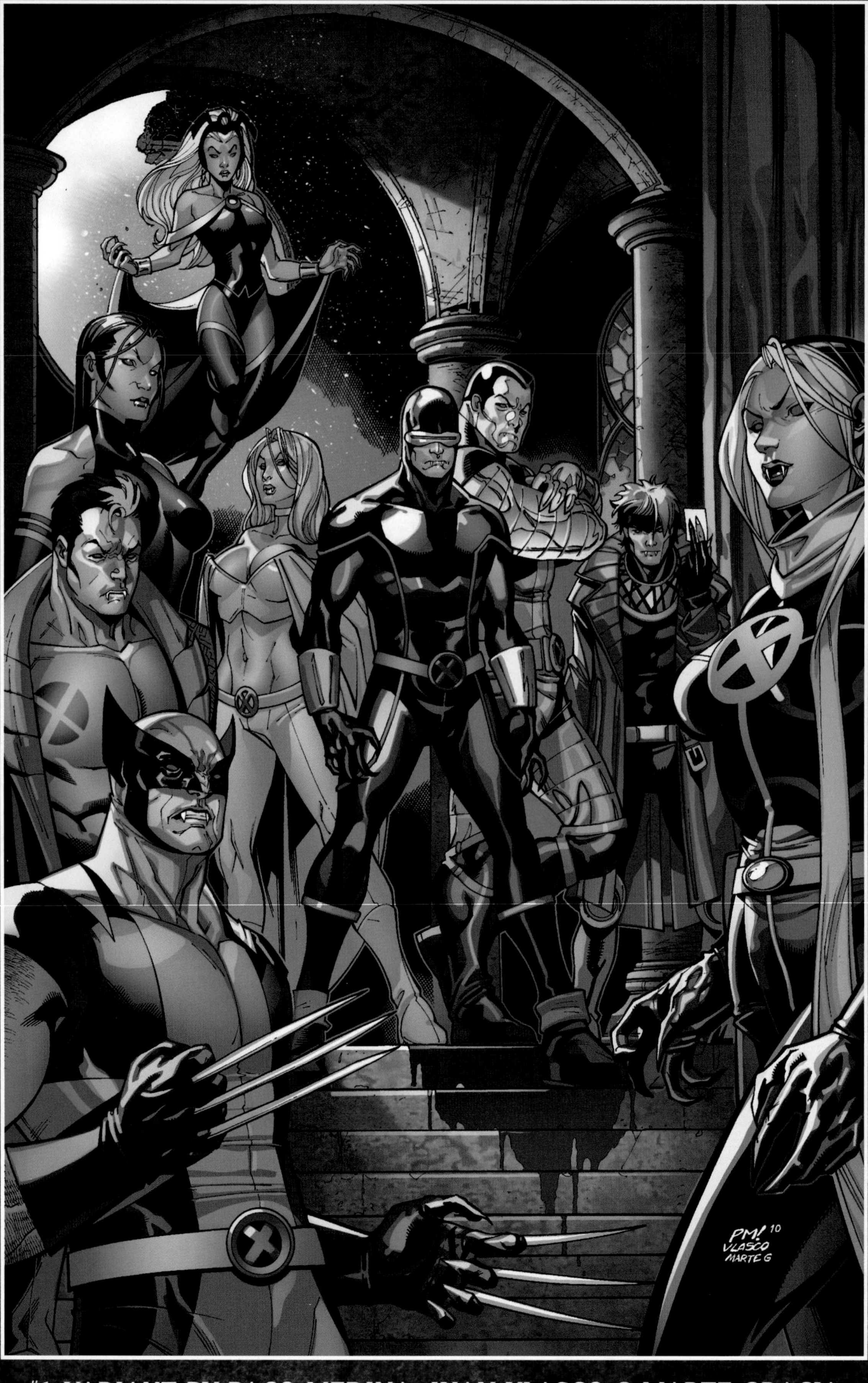
PM! 10
VLASCO
MARTE G

#1 VARIANT BY PACO MEDINA, JUAN VLASCO & MARTE GRACIA

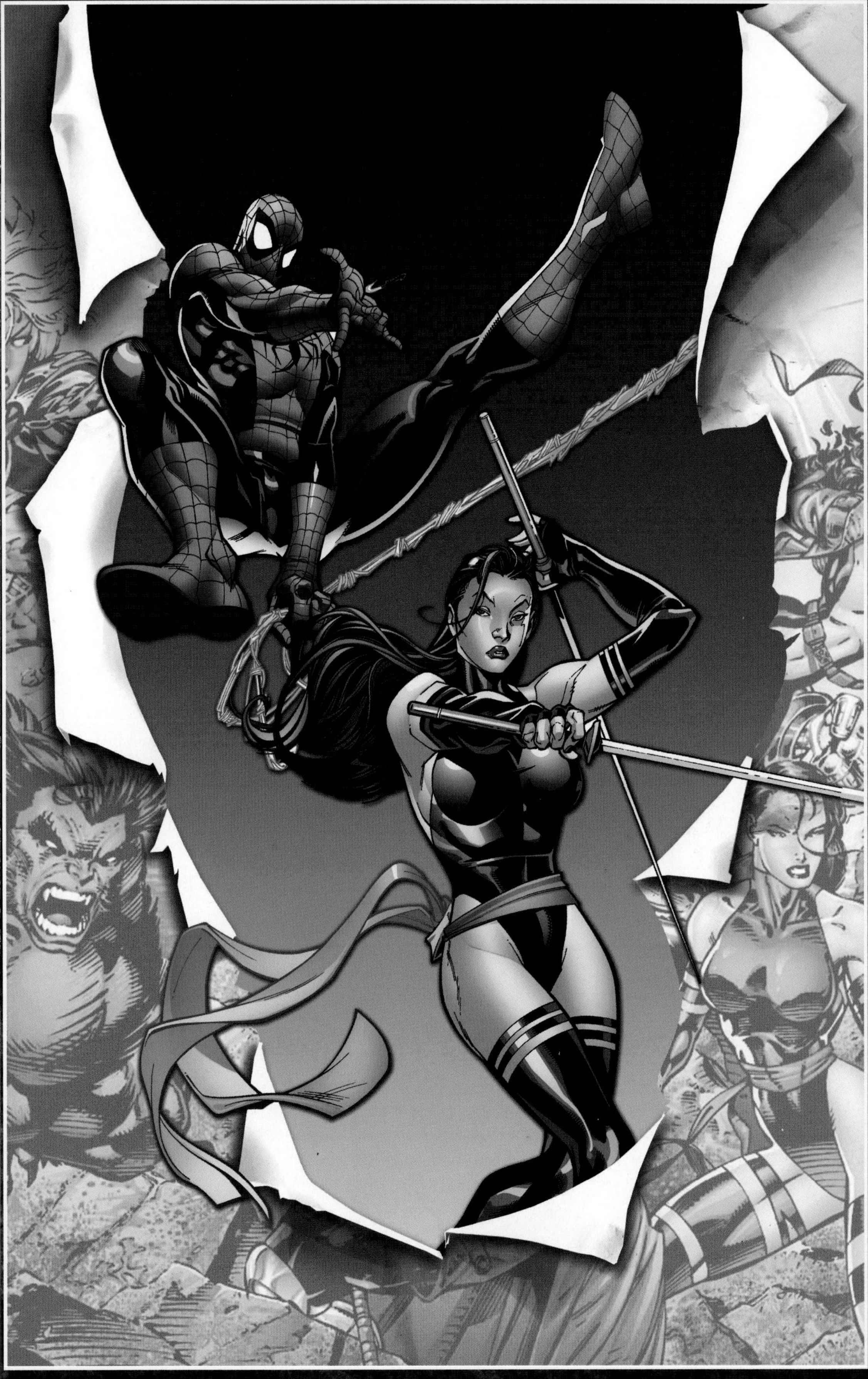

#2 VARIANT BY PACO MEDINA, JUAN VLASCO & MARTE GRACIA

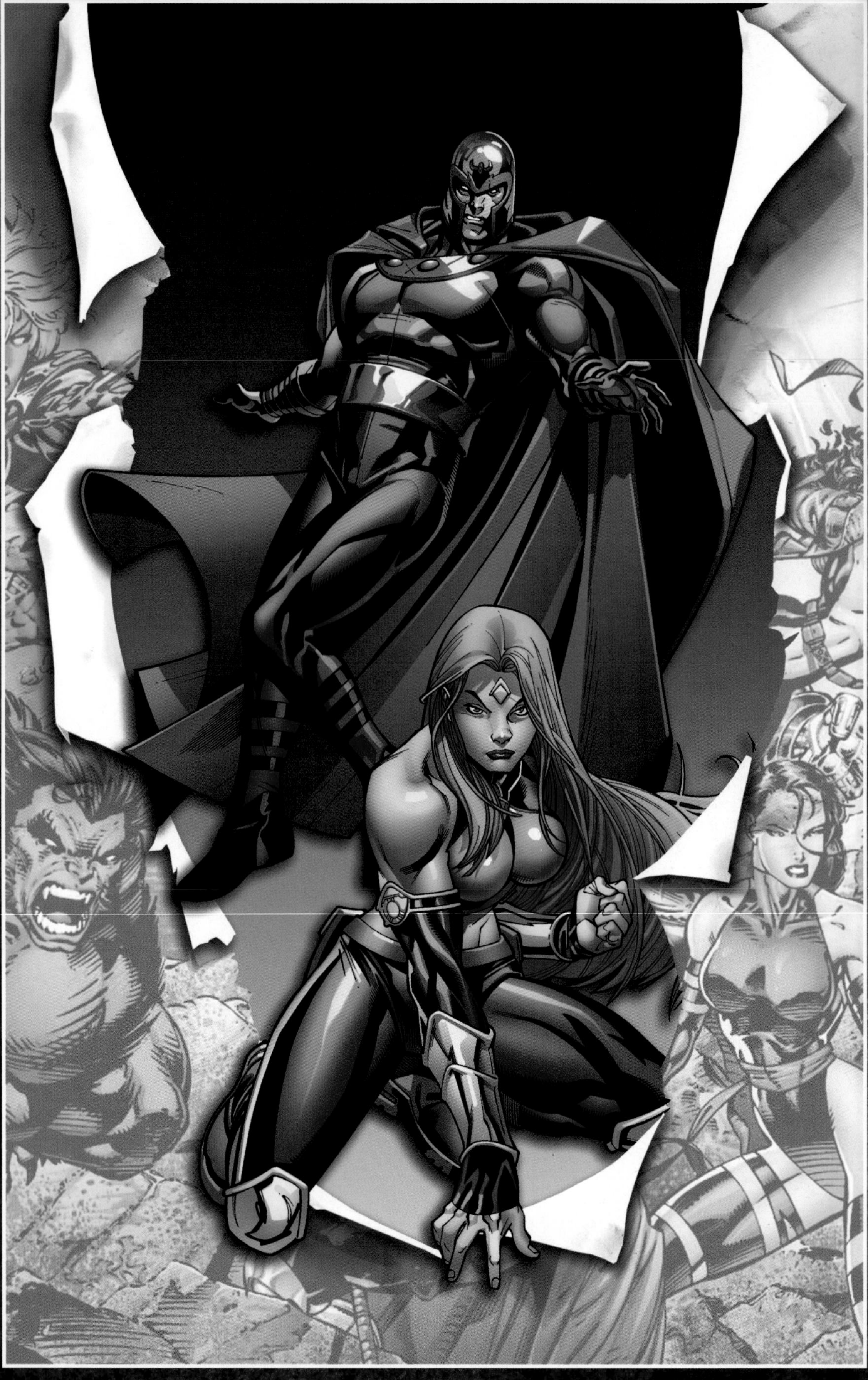

#3 VARIANT BY PACO MEDINA, JUAN VLASCO & MARTE GRACIA

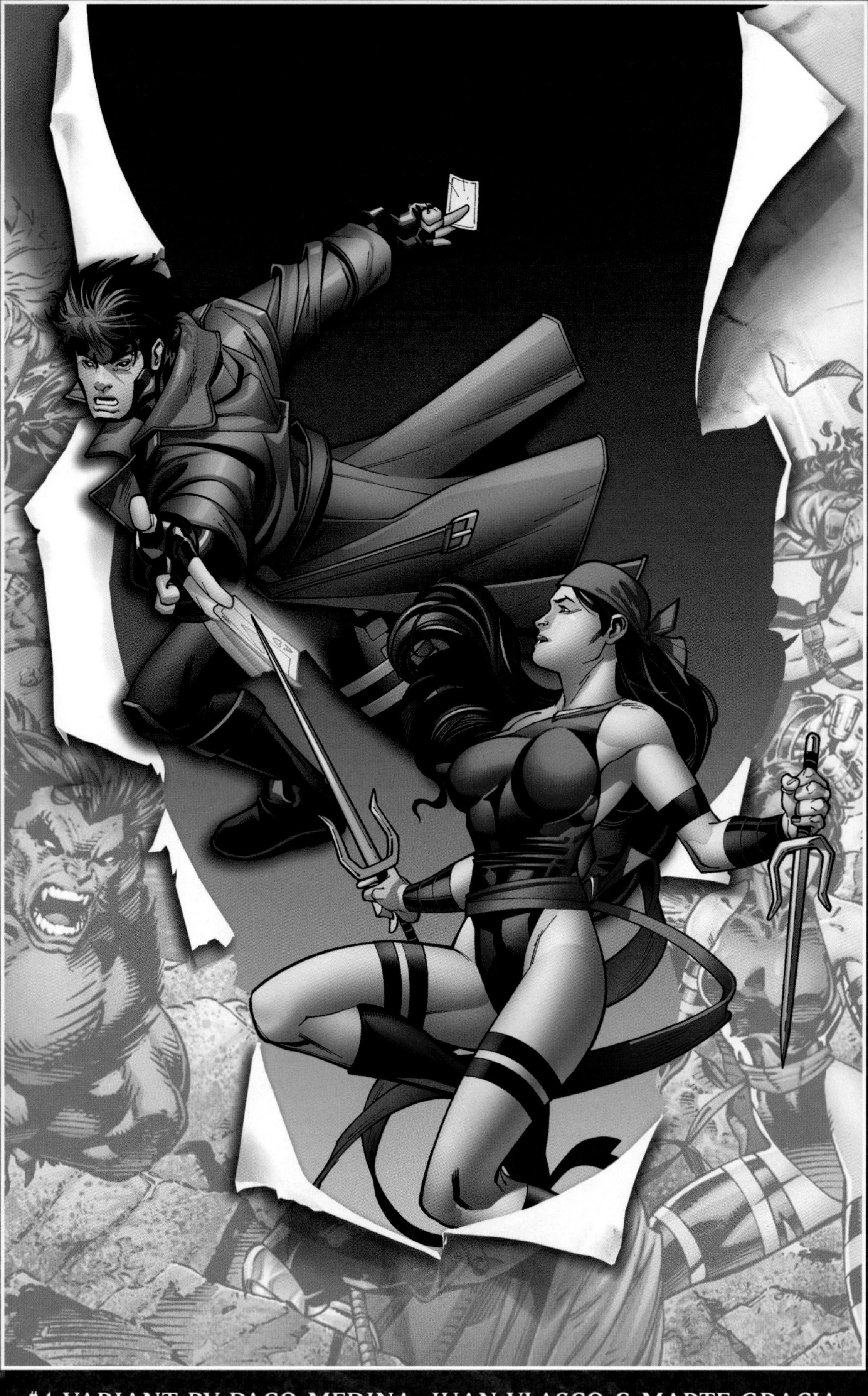

#4 VARIANT BY PACO MEDINA, JUAN VLASCO & MARTE GRACIA

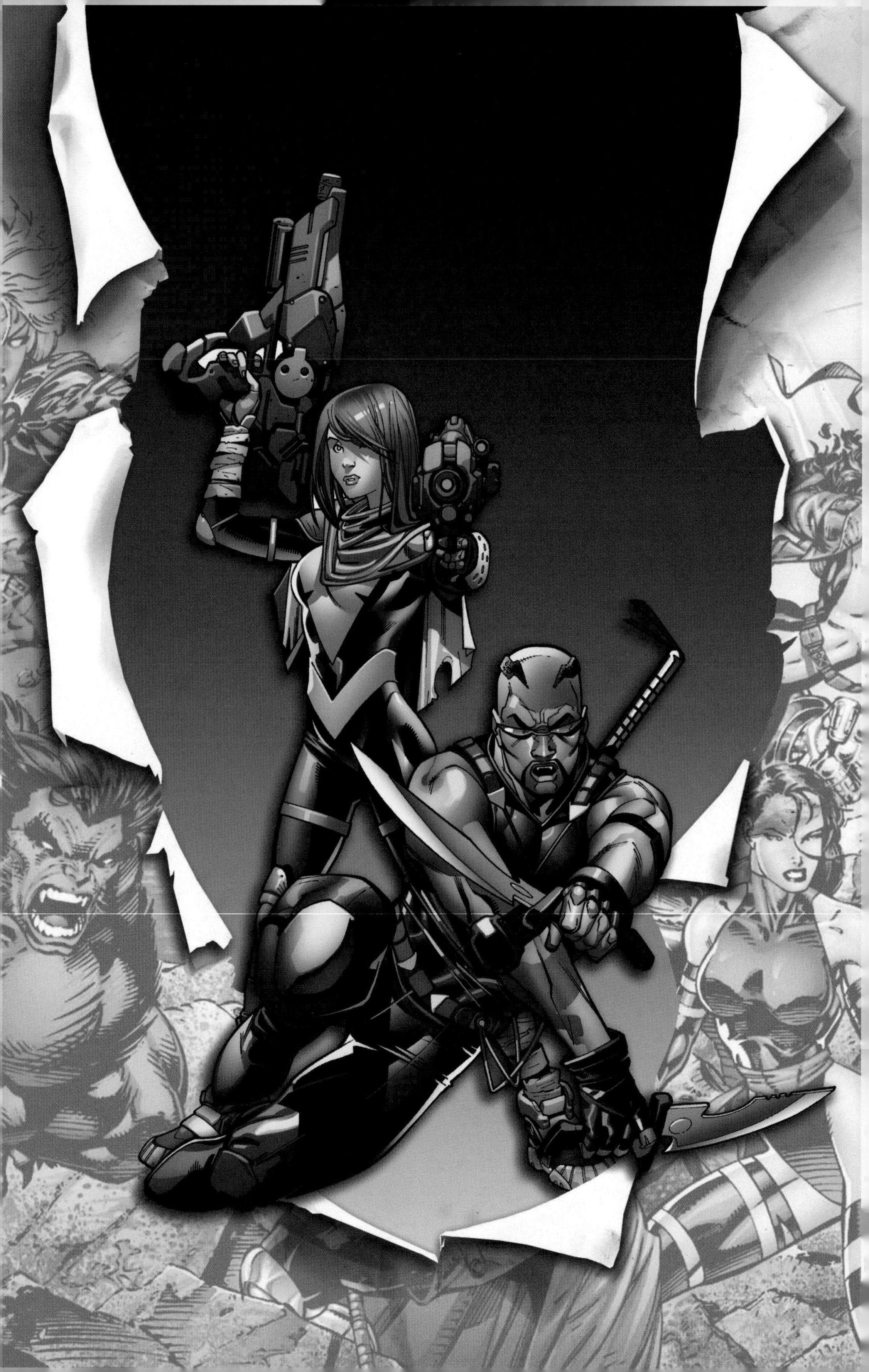

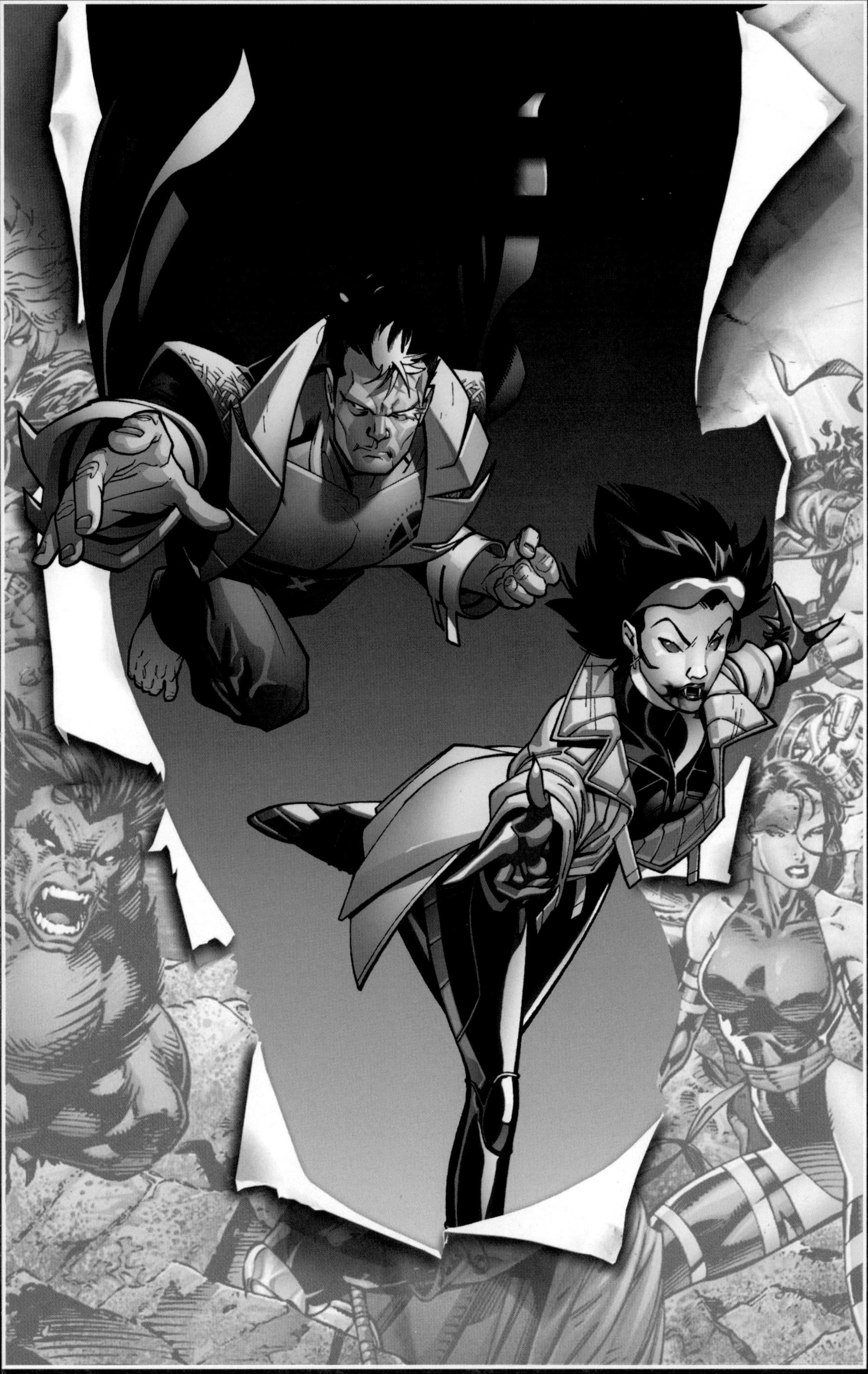

#6 VARIANT BY PACO MEDINA, JUAN VLASCO & MARTE GRACIA

X-FORCE #1, WOLVERINE #1, X-MEN #3, GENERATION HOPE #3,
X-23 #1 & DAKEN: DARK WOLVERINE #1